Shelter from the Storm
By Molly Wens

All rights reserved. No part of this book may be reproduced or transmitted in any form or by any means, electronic or mechanical, including photocopying, recording, or by any information storage and retrieval system, without permission in writing from the publisher.

This book is for sale to ADULT AUDIENCES ONLY. It contains substantial sexually explicit scenes and graphic language which may be considered offensive by some readers.

All sexually active characters in this work are 18 years of age or older.

This is a work of fiction. Names, characters, places and incidents are solely the product of the author's imagination and/or are used fictitiously, though reference may be made to actual historical events or existing locations. Any resemblance to actual persons, living or dead, business establishments, events or locales is entirely coincidental.

Cover Design: Joey Walnuts
Shelter from the Storm © 2008 Molly Wens
eXcessica publishing
All rights reserved

To order additional copies of this book contact:
books@excessica.com

Chapter 1

The frigid air lashed her face. Carissa James glared at the useless cellular phone clutched in her hand. If the damned thing had not cost her so much, she would have smashed it on the asphalt at her feet. There had to be a way to get a signal in this god-forsaken wilderness, she decided as she walked a little farther up the road. The steep incline and the thin air of the lofty altitude had her wheezing in short order as she climbed higher, searching for a spot that would allow the device to find a signal. She reached the top of the crest only to discover that she had wasted her time.

She let out another frustrated growl between panting breaths and staggered back down the sloping highway to her equally useless rental vehicle, a foreign-made four-wheel-drive hunk of junk that refused to crank. The sun was sinking lower. Carissa cursed the day for dwindling and her corporate offices for sending her on this fool's errand. She cursed the rental company for having rented her the defective vehicle and the cellular company for not having a stronger signal. She cursed the mountains for the frigid air that sliced through her thin business jacket and she cursed the garment for not being warmer.

Upon reaching the dead SUV, she wrenched the door open and fairly collapsed onto the seat. Pain wracked her lungs as she struggled to regain her breath. She wondered once again what had made her decide to take this particular assignment. Thoughts of her two small children eating supper, hundreds of miles away, made her homesick. She would have given her right arm to hear their sweet little voices over her phone right then.

As Carissa sat contemplating the calamitous turn her day had taken, it finally dawned on her that she had not seen another car or truck on the narrow highway since her vehicle had sputtered and died nearly two hours earlier. Glancing out at the pavement, it was easy to see that the road had been long-neglected. Her breathing was finally slowing to a more normal pace as she unfolded the map and studied the directions she had acquired at the car rental counter. Trying to make sense of it all was a daunting task in the waning light.

There was nothing on the map that appeared remotely similar to the road that stretched out before her. Visions of Bugs Bunny intoning that he should have taken that left "toin" at "Albuquoique" came to mind, making her snort derisively at her own absurdity. She had known the moment she had boarded that plane in St. Louis that she was making a mistake.

Looking at the hostile terrain around her and the worthless cell phone still clutched in her shivering hand, two questions crossed her mind for the hundredth time since arriving in Wyoming. *Who in their right mind would build a television station here? How could they expect to broadcast?* The car radio would not even pick up static. She shook her head and hunched her shoulders to protect her fading body heat.

She wondered why she was chosen for such a trip. *Surely*, she thought, *there have to be others more qualified to judge whether the station was worth purchasing.* Then, ruefully, the realization dawned on her. She had been the only one stupid enough to accept such an assignment, to give the property a preliminary inspection and report back to the corporate big shots. Now she could not even do that, stranded as she was.

The sky outside the car was turning gray, but not because of the receding sunset – clouds were gathering as the temperature continued to drop. Another pang of homesickness clutched at her chest as the sweet faces of her children flashed into her mind. She missed her babies, missed the flat stretches of her own front lawn, the even planes of the horizontal roads in her home state. She even found that she missed her ex-husband, for all his miserable, moody ways. These treacherous mountains were no place for a flat-lander such as she was.

As the first snowflake fell upon the windshield of the broken-down SUV, panic took hold of her heart. Getting out of the relative shelter of the vehicle would be a foolhardy action. She was not appropriately attired in her business suit and overcoat. Her overnight bag did not hold anything warmer than her flannel nightgown. Staying might prove to be just as dangerous if the road were closed due to snow. She would likely freeze to death long before anyone found her.

The middle of October and already it was snowing in the mountains. Carissa knew that this was not going to be like an early snow back home. An early snow in the mountains meant deadly conditions and treacherous roads. Back home the first snow disappears with the first rays of sun the next day, but here it could become a blizzard that left inhabitants snowbound for weeks. Real fear started to take root as she huddled down farther in the car seat.

Carissa nearly gave in to her despair, almost let the threatening tears spill over. *You are made of sterner stuff than this*, she reminded herself. *If you can survive eight years of marriage to that abusive butthead, you can surely survive this.* Forcing herself to sit up a little taller, watching the unwelcome snow flakes as they fairly coated the windshield in a thin blanket of white, she searched her memories of the lessons her grandmother had taught her about the wilderness and survival in the rocky bluffs of the family farm. But nothing in those memories was going to help her out of this mess.

Turning the key in the ignition to the on position, Carissa hoped there was enough juice left in the battery to keep the windshield clear. She flipped the switch and watched as the wiper blades hesitantly moved upward to form a curving opening to her view. Turning them off again to conserve her limited resources, she kept a vigil on the stretch of abandoned highway in the slim chance that someone might actually come along.

The thought that she needed rescuing was disgusting. Always self-sufficient, Carissa hated timid, weak-minded fools. Being reared by the most stubborn and independent segment of American society – the American farmer – she was loath to admit that she needed help. It went against every fiber of her being.

Within minutes the windshield was covered again. The wipers moved slower this time, a testament to the dwindling power of the battery. Soon she would need to step outside the car to clear the glass. A violent shiver traveled through her at the unpleasant thought. She was going to get very cold.

Before long, having a clear windshield would no longer be an issue, judging by the fading light. Night was descending in rapid order. With the clouds obscuring any possible light from the moon or stars, the darkness was going to be blinding. Again she felt the temptation to desert the useless vehicle and search for any shelter that this backcountry could afford her. She squelched the notion, forcing herself to remain calm.

The front glass was nearly obscured again when a twinkling light caught her attention. At first, she thought it was merely a trick of the graying dusk, playing against the sparkling snowflakes. Then she saw it again, glittering through the layer of frozen slivers of water that clumped together on the windshield. It was growing brighter, reflecting shards of brilliance into her eyes. The wipers, when she turned them on, refused to offer assistance. Opening the door and planting her black pumps on the crunching snow-covered asphalt, she could see a pair of headlights approaching.

Carissa slipped and nearly fell as she stepped out into the road, waving her arms wildly and screaming for the driver to stop. The sluggish vehicle slowed even more as it advanced, coming to a stop just a few feet from where she stood. It was a large van and to her it looked like a golden chariot. The driver's window opened and a man stuck his head through the opening.

"Looks like you could use a little help, missy," the head voiced. "Whatcha doin' out here? Dontcha know there's a blizzard bearin' down on ya?"

"I do now. My car won't run. Can you give me a ride into town?" Carissa was apprehensive, remembering all the horror stories that her mother had fed her about taking rides from strangers. She did not see how she had a choice, however, and hoped the man would help.

"Sure, hop in. I can't leave a woman to freeze to death. Let's get going."

The man seemed pleasant enough, older, estimating from his graying hair and the lines that traveled over his face. Retrieving her purse, briefcase and overnight bag from the rental car, she hurried to find the warmth and relative comfort of the stranger's van. Her feet were freezing in the thin leather of her business shoes, the snow clinging to the tops of her nylon-clad insteps. A shiver ran through her as she rubbed her hands together under the heat vent on the van's dash.

"You ain't from around here." It was a statement more than a question. The man looked at her with watery blue eyes. "A grown woman ought to know better than to climb up into these here mountains without a proper outfit. You'd a-froze to death if I hadn't come along."

"I know. Thank you so much," Carissa responded, eyeing the man carefully.

The man looked at her with what could only be described as irritation. "Whatcha doin' up here, anyway?"

"I'm here on business. I think I took a wrong turn. Then my car stalled out and I was stuck. I tried to call for help but my cell phone wouldn't work."

"Them things'r useless up here," he snorted.

"So I gather. I really appreciate your help. How far is it to the nearest town?"

"'Bout fifty miles, twenty, as the crow flies. Where was you goin' dressed like that?"

Wishing she had brought her map and directions, Carissa tried to think of the name of the town where the television station she was to inspect was located. "I can't remember the name… Jackson, I think. I'm supposed to take a look at the NBC station there, KJWY. Do you know where that is?"

The man snorted again. "Woman, you are hell and gone away from there." He turned to fix her with a calculating expression that had her feeling as if he had just undressed her. "I gotta turn off up here and pick up someone. S'posed to give him a ride down the mountain. It won't take a few minutes."

The mild nervousness that had nagged at her since accepting the assistance of this man suddenly turned to a deep feeling of apprehension. A dark chill began to curl outward from the pit of her belly. That extra sense that everyone has, but so few listen to, was warning her of some unseen danger. That warning grew louder in her head to the point of screaming as the van left the meager blacktop for a narrow strip of gravel that looked to lead nowhere.

Carissa's fingers fussed with the lapel of her coat. Her mind raced, trying to find some way to escape. She was trapped and she knew it. Bailing out of the van would mean frostbite and possible death in this inhospitable environment – staying meant facing the unknown. Sucking in a long, slow, steadying breath, she tried to calm her splintering nerves. Even as her eyes scanned the front of the van for a feasible weapon, her mind tried to tell that inner voice that she was overreacting, that her imagination was getting the better of her.

The van kept on its path, creeping along the winding, skinny trail of snow-covered crushed rock. A small house materialized out of the thickening snow, and the driver slowed to a stop. He turned his head, looking at her with another lewd appraisal. "You stay here, I'll just run in and get 'im."

"Does your friend have a phone I could use?" Carissa had her fingers crossed as she waited for his answer.

A blast of icy wind and swirling snowflakes slapped her face as he opened his door. "Kyle ain't had no use for phones long as I can remember 'im." The man hunched his shoulders against the cold wind, pulling up the hood of his parka and wrapping his muffler up around his face as he stepped out of the vehicle, slamming the door.

The apprehension that had taken hold disappeared, replaced by real fear as she spied a telephone pole just a few yards from the house. Squinting her eyes to see through the driving snow, she could just make out where wires from the pole attached themselves to the side of the old house in the dim light of the outdoor lamp.

A quick glance at the ignition of the van told her the man had taken the key with him. A wave of nausea swept over her. "Fool!" she heard that inner voice scream. The man disappeared inside the house leaving Carissa searching for an avenue of escape.

The thick, whirling snow made seeing anything beyond the old house all but impossible. There was no way of knowing if this Kyle had any neighbors that might be willing to lend a hand. Running blindly into the storm would be foolhardy, at best. With her arms enfolded about her shivering body, she wracked her brain in an attempt to come up with any way out of this mess.

There had to be something in the van, she decided, that she could use as a weapon. Figuring that most men carried tools in their vehicles, it was just a matter of getting out of her seat to have a look around. Quickly moving about the vehicle, it did not take long to realize that this man was not like most guys. No toolbox was to be located. She was dismayed to discover that there was very little of anything in the van, as if it had been swept clean.

As Carissa made her way back to the front of the van, the toe of her soft leather shoe encountered something small and hard, sending it rolling from under the back seat. With a small cry, she seized the object, a screwdriver, and stuffed it into her coat pocket. Her fingers curled spasmodically around the handle as she made her way back to the passenger seat.

Within moments, two men walked out the door of the house. Carissa could barely make out their features through the wet, falling snow. One was the man who had been driving the van; the second was a taller, darker man. He appeared to be younger but harder in appearance, more sinister-looking.

The men moved slowly, inching their way closer to the van, arguing about something. As they drew near, Carissa opened her window just a crack in an attempt to hear what they were saying. With her ear pressed close against the opening, she could just make out most of their conversation in the muting snowfall.

"I still don't get why not here," said the driver.

The dark man looked irritated. "'Cause we don't need witnesses. She might be my sister, but she can still be forced to testify."

The driver shook his head. "You ought to be able to control your women better'n that. We'll go up to Tanner Road, then. We'll use the old shack."

As the men separated, with each heading to opposite sides of the vehicle, Carissa quickly rolled the window up and settled back into the seat, a chill running the length of her spine that had nothing to do with the frigid weather. She said a silent prayer that they had been discussing something other than what their plans were for her. The screwdriver in her pocket gave her some small glimmer of hope as her fingers continued to caress its handle.

The driver's door opened with a cold blast of winter air as the driver pulled himself into his seat, shoving his hood back off his head. Carissa tried not to look at him, afraid that her eyes would betray her fear. A moment later the sliding door behind her opened as the other man entered.

"Girlie," the driver spoke scornfully, "That's Kyle. We'll get you to town now."

Liar, Carissa thought as she turned her body in order to see the dark man in the back seat. The glittering force of his stare drove her backward against the van's door. The smile on his face could best be described as a leer as his chilling gaze swept over as much of her body as he could see. Her stomach roiled and threatened to heave. Every fiber of her being was screaming for her to run, to throw herself out of the vehicle as it backed out of the craggy drive of the decrepit old house.

After a few minutes, they pulled off the narrow gravel road and onto the blacktopped highway again, going back the same direction from which they had just come. This was all the confirmation her suspicions needed. She clutched the screwdriver tighter in her pocket, facing both men as best as she could with her back against the door of the van while the vehicle climbed higher up the mountain.

Carissa steeled herself for what was possibly going to happen next. The anticipation of the unknown danger was the worst of it, she concluded. Finally determining that she could stand no more of Kyle's silent leer, she turned her eyes to the driver.

"Where are you two taking me?" Her voice was calm, belying her inner terror.

"To town," the driver answered disdainfully, drawing a snort from the passenger in the back seat.

"Don't lie to the bitch, Bert," Kyle blurted in amusement. He leaned forward to run a hand down the sleeve of Carissa's coat. "Why don't you tell her what we have planned for her. It'd prob'ly get the whore off."

Carissa's mind raced as revulsion coiled in her belly. Her eyes darted about, hoping to see another vehicle or the lights of a house, as they climbed higher along the road. A glimpse of something caught in the corner of her eye. Turning her head she saw the useless rental car that had stranded her in the middle of this predicament go by in the passenger window. Her right hand began to ache, forcing her to relax her grip on the tool in her pocket.

Bert, the driver, guffawed loudly. "Yeah, remember that last'n? She pissed herself when she found out why her mamma told her she shouldn't hitchhike."

Kyle sniggered as he scraped his knuckle down Carissa's cheek, the sound growing louder as she instinctively jerked away from his touch. "You gonna be a fighter, girlie? I like 'em to scream an' kick."

Her mind would not focus on any one subject, flitting from this horror to that as she wrestled mentally with her situation. There seemed no way out of the mess, her plight was so hopeless: risk certain death in the frozen desolation of this wilderness, or face unknown terror with these two depraved freaks. Again, she felt the icy touch of Kyle's hand on her face, causing her to wrench her head back and her stomach to lurch a little more.

Kyle cackled malignantly. "This'n here is gonna be fun."

Bile, bitter and repugnant, was rising in her throat as the van slowed and turned onto another steep, narrow back road. With each mile, she could feel her freedom, her safety, her very life slipping away. Her eyes darted about, trying to remember every part of the darkened landscape in the falling snow. She had to find a way to escape, and then find her way back out of this place. Her fingers caressed the plastic handle in her pocket, waiting for just the right moment.

"Damn snow's gettin' so thick I can hardly see the road," Bert complained.

"Hurry yer ass up, Bert," Kyle ordered. "I got me a itch that I want this pretty thing to scratch."

As Carissa glanced at the man in the back seat, he ran his hand over the bulging front of his trousers. Again, bile burned her throat and she breathed deeply to dispel the urge to vomit. The van made another turn. The new road was worse than the last, causing the vehicle to lurch and shake over its surface. She wondered how much further it would be before they got to the place where they would abuse, and most likely, kill her. The faces of her children flashed into her mind – her babies that still needed her. She had to survive this, if only for them.

"I'm getting' tired of waitin'," Kyle yelled just before he grabbed Carissa and dragged her kicking form into the back seat, hauling her across his lap. He pulled her hair, yanking her head back and clamping his mouth over hers.

She gasped in horror as she lost her grip on the screwdriver. His breath was foul, the taste of him causing her to nearly lose her tight control over the actions of her stomach.

"Hold your horses, dammit, Kyle. I get some of that too." Bert sounded enraged at not having first dibs, and sped the van up in an effort to reach their destination sooner.

Kyle released her lips and reached his free hand inside her coat to grip her breast. "I'm just gettin'er warmed up, old buddy. She tastes sweet. Can't wait to get my hands on that cunt." He found and pinched her nipple mercilessly.

Carissa let out a cry of pain as she struggled to get loose. This only amused Kyle more, causing him to cackle louder. The pocket of her coat seemed to have taken on the proportions of a black hole as she fished around its confines in search of the screwdriver. Her other hand tried to fend off the loathsome attacker.

Kyle's drooling tongue darted over his lips as he grabbed the front of her blouse and yanked, the delicate fabric offering no resistance and shredding under his grasp.

"Shit!" he yelled, the lust gleaming in his narrow eyes. "Look at them titties, will ya? Big, ripe milkers!"

His cruel fingers clawed their way between the lace of her bra cup and the flesh of her breast. He pulled the flesh out of its confinement with a brutal squeeze.

The pain caused Carissa to scream. She struggled harder, feeling his fingers crushing together over her tender nipple. The center of his lust, hard as granite, was pressing into her back. "Let – me – go!" she screeched at her tormenter.

"Don't be damaging her none, dammit!" Bert was trying to turn in his seat to look at the two in the back as the van careened up another craggy incline.

"Mind the road, Bert. Get us to the shack." Kyle yanked harder on Carissa's hair, snapping her head back as his other hand released her nipple to travel down her nude belly.

Carissa bucked wildly against this new assault, feeling his fingers digging inside her waistband. She clawed at his face with her free hand, trying desperately to stop him.

"Fucking cunt," he bellowed, pulling his hand out of her pants and punching her in the face.

The world exploded into a million shards of colored light as she fell limply against his lap. She tasted blood in her mouth and felt its sticky heat spreading across her face from her nose. Through the haze of semi-conscious shock, she could feel his hand return to her lower abdomen, forcing its way downward inside her trousers and under her panties. He continued to claw his way in and down until his fingers found the slit of her sex. He pinched and pulled on the tender flesh, causing searing pain to rocket through her innards. She heard his breath coming in short gasps, and knew it wouldn't be long before he was on top of her.

She lay, without struggling, attempting to clear her sluggish brain. She heard Bert say that they were almost there, wherever "there" was, at the same time that her fingers finally closed over the handle of the screwdriver.

Kyle pulled his hand out of her pants and lifted her head to his face. "Hear that, girlie? In just a couple of minutes me and Bert are gonna fuck you good."

Just then, seizing the opportunity, Carissa pulled the screwdriver out of her pocket and jammed it into his thigh with all her might, twisting it and pulling down. She knew a momentary victory as the lecherous creep released his hold on her hair. She grabbed the screwdriver again, shoving it in deeper and using it as leverage to bring her legs up and kick Bert in the back of the skull.

Bert fell unconscious while the van veered sharply and slammed into a tree. Carissa pitched forward, her head slamming into the center console between the front seats. Something struck her ribcage nearly knocking the wind from her lungs. She pulled herself upright and bolted for the door, only to have a cursing Kyle snag the back of her coat and drag her backwards. She pulled her arms out of her overcoat, turned and grasped the handle of the screwdriver again, twisting it savagely and causing blood to gush from his wounded thigh and all over her suit jacket. She didn't wait to hear his howl of pain, reaching for the door handle and sending it flying open.

Her feet hit the ground running, heading for the trees of the mountain slope. Her poorly shod feet slipped repeatedly, throwing the unprotected skin of her torso against the snow-covered mountainside.

Between running steps and falls, she managed to button her suit jacket over the tattered remnants of her blouse. It afforded little warmth in the increasing winds and snow of the mounting blizzard. She thought of nothing except escape as she clamored upward along the frozen slope.

Her limbs felt like lead, her lungs burned with the fires of hell as she topped the ridge. She had to stop, if only for a moment, to try to get enough of the thin mountain air. As she gasped, she used her position as a vantage point to survey the snow-covered landscape, glancing fearfully behind her to see if she were being pursued. She saw no one behind her. She could barely see anything at all as the biting wind that sliced through her thin clothing, drove the snowflakes into whirling clouds of white that all but blinded her.

She was lost, cold, bleeding, and worse yet, weakening; her body was shaking uncontrollably in the wintry forest that surrounded her. A voice, soft and sweet, called for its mommy in her mind, forcing her to move, to keep going in hope of finding help or shelter. Her feet felt numb and frozen, she knew that it wouldn't be long before frostbite set in. She had to get them dry and warm. Her hands were not in much better shape as she numbly pulled up the collar of her thin suit jacket. Her face and ears were so cold that they burned in the onslaught of the bitter wind.

Deciding it would be best not to walk along the top of the ridge in the driving gusts, she pointed her icy toes to the other side of the incline and away from the wrecked van and attackers below. Her feet slipped almost immediately, sending her hurtling down the steep mountainside. Sticks, rocks and other debris tore through her clothing, ripping her flesh as she clawed at anything that she could grip in order to stop her downward trajectory. The air left her body in a sharp grunt when a small tree caught her in the midsection, halting her descent.

Carissa lay still, gasping against the pain that wracked her body and the sparse, bitter air that burned her lungs. Every inch of her ached, the throbbing pain nearly causing her to black out. The survivor in her screamed for her to move, to keep moving, to not give in to the exhaustion that was eating her alive. There was a rustle somewhere on the slope above her, bringing the fear back to slash through the pain. She found the strength to lift herself upright, glancing anxiously back up the slope into the blinding snow and darkness.

Panic, something she had always refused to let win, was rooting itself deep in her psyche, and she struggled against its rising tide. She drew panting breaths as she forced her mind to think, to grasp at what the best next move would be. Her body was weakening fast, she knew, as the shivering nearly caused her to drop to her knees against the tree that she used for support. If she moved down the slope again, she figured there was a greater risk of taking another bad tumble, something she wasn't sure she could survive a second time. Climbing back up was nearly impossible, not to mention deadly, since her two attackers were on the other side. She chose to move laterally across the slope using the trees and brush as support to keep her from skidding farther down the grade.

Pulling her jacket tighter around her and blowing on her numb fingers in an effort warm them, she continued on her way. The blood dripping in her eyes from a cut in her scalp that she could not feel was cooling in the wind before she could raise her fingers to wipe it away. The farther she went, the more difficult her movements became. Each step sent jolting spirals of pain up her legs, muting the dull throbbing in her groin and left breast where the cruel hand of the man, Kyle, had brutally assaulted her flesh. The wind was picking up, knifing through her thin clothing. After what seemed like hours, she no longer felt the pain, or anything else. Her steps had become automatic, her eyes unseeing, as she trudged along in the deepening snow. Thoughts of her children kept her going, their joyful, shining faces appeared before her like mirages in the desert, their sweet voices ringing in her ears and drawing her onward.

The world began to spin, and she became vaguely aware that she was falling again. Another tree caught her, causing her to land in a soft bed of pine needles. *"Get up!"* that inner voice screamed and she pulled herself to a sitting position. She tried to clear her befuddled mind as she looked around her, realizing that she was not sitting in snow. The wind was not as sharp here, the ground not as hard. After a few moments, she realized that she was in the shelter of low-hanging pine boughs, their thick needles blocking the snow and wind, and offering a small bit of refuge.

With her numb hands, she dug a small burrow in the thick bed of dry, dead pine needles and settled her bottom into it, pulling the needles up over her legs and feet and leaning her back against the tree trunk for support. She needed rest, that much she knew. She also knew that if she tarried too long she risked falling asleep and freezing to death, and only the scavengers that hunted these woods would find her body. Pulling her collar up higher and hunching her shoulders, she managed to cover most of her face before putting her stiff hands into the pockets of her jacket.

She thought of her babies and what they must be thinking about, dreaming about in their little beds. She thought of her mother, and how proud the woman had been when Carissa had graduated college, started a new career, given her grandchildren. It was the thought of her ex-husband, though, that got her blood pumping again. He would use her absence to attempt to take the children from her mother, to rule over their lives as he had tried to rule over hers. With her father gone now, Carissa wondered if her mother would have the strength to fight the man to save her babies from that fate.

Renewed determination forced its way through the shuddering numbness, bringing her out of her slumped posture, fetching her head up as she blinked back tears. She would not give in to hopelessness; she was made of sterner stuff. Her fists clenched into tight balls at the anger that was taking hold, and she pulled them out of her pockets. She needed to take stock of her injuries, she decided, as she held her hands up to her face in the darkness. Something fell from the grasp of her numb fingers, landing on the pile of needles in her lap.

She groped over the needles in the dark with her numb fingers until they closed around something with a definite shape. Holding the item inches from her vision helped little as she tried to identify it, and her numbed fingers could not feel the texture of it. Finally, she resorted to sniffing it, detecting the slight odor or sulfur. Matches! She had forgotten that she had picked them up at a restaurant in the airport. She was bringing them back to a co-worker who collected matchbooks from all over the world. She hugged the precious item to her throat and said a silent prayer of thanks to whatever power was out there.

Pulling her legs under her, she knelt and bent forward to build a fire. She wasn't sure if her kidnappers were pursuing her, or if the fire would lead them to her, but she had to have warmth. With a pile of needles built up and the rest of the combustible material pulled back, she struck the first match with stiffened fingers. It guttered in the breeze that filtered into her cave of pine branches and went out in a tiny puff of smoke. She tried it again, this time pulling off two matches and cupping her hands around the diminutive flame. Moving slowly, she brought the matches down to the pine needles, chirping in delight as they slowly offered themselves to the growing flame.

Carissa held her hands over the thin flames, occasionally feeding more needles into the fire to keep it from going out until she got some of the feeling back in her fingers. Tingling pain, excruciating in its pleasure, spread up into her forearms. By the light that the fire offered, she dug around in her little shelter to find small twigs and branches and build the burning pile until her face could feel its warmth. Soon she had enough wood to create a semi-heated area within the confines of the pine tree. The falling snow was insulating the branches over and around her, keeping the heat inside, for the most part. As her body warmed, her shivering increased to almost-violent proportions, forcing her to wait until the quivering subsided before she could gain control of her muscles again.

Next, she turned her attention to her feet. There was no feeling left in them as she gently pried her wet leather pumps away from the skin. Not knowing what frostbite looked like, she was unsure if any real damage was done. Her toes did not appear to be frozen, she was able to wiggle them under the sheer knee-high stockings she wore, and the skin was soft. Still, as she held them up to the fire to warm, the burning pain in her awakening feet was nearly unbearable. There was no way that she would be able to continue walking in her flimsy business shoes with their two-inch heels through the thick layer of snow that blanketed the ground.

To take her attention off her aching feet, she moved on to other parts of her body, taking stock of the damage done. Blood that had frozen in her hair was thawing, and coated her hands as she probed her scalp. Her face and head had sustained numerous scrapes and lacerations from the van's collision with the tree and her fall down the rocky, brush-covered slope. There was a large, deep, burning abrasion across her naked chest and several gouges on her bare abdomen, some of them fairly deep.

Removing her jacket and huddling closer to the fire, she discovered bruises and scrapes along her arms, ribs and back. She decided not to bother with her legs upon looking at the tears in her slacks; she could tell they were chewed up pretty badly.

Seeing the torn remains of her blouse, an idea dawned on her. The ruined garment slipped easily from her shoulders. Though the air around her had warmed considerably, the draft of wind seeping through the heavily laden branches felt like ice against her nude flesh. It only took her a moment to slide her wet jacket on over her bra.

Inspecting the white cotton blouse, she could see that nearly the entire front of it, from collar to hemline, had been torn away. What was left was filthy and blood-spattered, but that did not matter for what she had in mind. Digging around in the bed of pine needles, she found a rock that she felt was sharp enough to do the trick. With meticulous care, she removed the sleeves, half-cutting and half-tearing the fabric apart, just below the shoulders. What little remained of the front she cut away and split into several thin strips.

This should do the trick, she thought as she cut one of the strips in half and tied each smaller length of cloth to opposite corners of the back of the blouse. She quickly removed the jacket and slipped the blouse on backwards. She tied it at the small of her back, tucking the tail into her slacks, effectively concealing her front to offer protection where her jacket did not cover. With a shiver, she put her jacket back on and turned up the collar of her blouse, tying another strip of cloth around her neck to secure the collar to her throat.

The sleeves had another purpose. With a feeling akin to glee she heated the cloth over her small fire, touching it from time to time to see if all the dampness had evaporated. When she was satisfied the material was completely dry, she drew one sleeve over each foot, binding each one in place with more cloth strips. When she was done, her feet and legs were covered halfway up her calves.

With a touch of panic, she tossed her last sticks of deadfall onto the fire, causing her to scrounge around in the pine bed searching for more. She found several good-sized chunks of wood on the opposite side of the huge tree-cave with a sigh of relief. The effort of dragging the wood to her little encampment caused her exhausted body to gasp for oxygen. This high elevation, she decided, was no place for a lowlander like her.

She inspected her mangled hands with disgust. The knuckles were scraped raw, her fingers and palms were cracked and bleeding. No matter how expert the manicurist, there was no way to salvage her fingernails, one was torn out of the bed. She had nothing left to use as covering for her hands and wished she could keep them tucked snugly in her pockets for the rest of her journey, wherever it might lead.

Pockets – that was the answer. She reached her hand inside one to gauge the depth of it. Her fingers connected with something hard in the bottom. Pulling the thing out she squealed with delight to find it was a dinner mint. She quickly unwrapped the small, chocolate treat and popped it into her mouth. She savored the sugary taste of it as she dug around to see if she could find another. There were two more and she made short work of them as well, tossing the wrappers on the fire.

Carissa wasted little time in removing the pocket linings from inside her jacket so that she could put it back onto her trembling body. She cut holes along the open edges of each and laced half-strips of cloth around them, successfully creating mitts that would tie at her wrists. The fabric was thin but it would offer some form of protection from the pain of contact with this environment. She had to use her tongue and her teeth to tie the knots that would hold the mitts in place; it was difficult, but she managed it.

She had two lengths of cloth left but nothing was available to cover her ears. She wrapped the remaining ribbons around her precious matchbook and tucked them into her bra for later use.

The wind was howling louder at that point, sending bits of snow through the branches and onto her face. She fed more wood into the meager fire and dug a larger hollow in the bed of needles that surrounded her. There was nothing left to do but wait for daybreak and try to find her way out of the deadly wilderness. To her aching body, the bed she had made was as soft as eiderdown. She lay down, pulling as much of the dry bedding around her as possible.

Chapter 2

Sleep proved to be elusive. Even though her body had been pushed to its limits, the fears that clouded her mind refused to allow her to relax. At any moment her two attackers might come charging in at her, or the fire might go out leaving her to freeze to death in her sleep. Such were the meanderings of her tormented consciousness.

Despite it all, she did manage to doze a few times only awakening at the slightest sound or the dark shadows that loomed in that dream state between awake and asleep. Just as the first gray streaks of the storm-obscured dawn were hitting the world around her, she tossed the last of the wood onto the dying fire. She had no idea what she would find once she hauled herself out of the shelter of the giant pine tree. To make matters worse, she found she really did not care.

The joints of her feet and legs, and the muscles of her back, creaked and groaned in protest as she began to rise from the forest floor. The low-hanging branches above her made it impossible to stand upright, which she so desperately needed to do to relieve some of the stiffness. At least she did not feel the cold anymore. Then it struck her what an odd sensation that was in such a climate as this. It did not take long for her to realize why she felt warm; she was running a fever.

The voice of the survivor screamed at her to move. She had to get out, had to find help, that much was apparent. Reaching for her shoes, she discovered that they had completely dried in front of the fire, a comforting thought as she jammed her cloth-covered feet into them. Crawling to the edge of the tree-cave and pulling on the branches, she discovered that she was nearly snowed-in. Though it appeared that the wind had died back at some point in the night, the amount of snow that had been dumped was unbelievable to her eyes. By clawing and climbing, she finally managed to haul her aching body out and over the snow as clumps of the icy, sticky flakes fell from the branches above, covering her in a frozen mass of stark, white crystals.

After several attempts, she finally managed to stand only to sink nearly to her posterior in the thick, white blanket. Within minutes, she felt soggy as she took the time to look at her surroundings in the drab, overcast morning. Hopelessness nearly swallowed her; it was impossible to get her bearings. Everything was completely hidden under a mantle of endless, pallid snow. As she attempted to move forward on her belly, she realized that she was not going to last long in her present condition in such a treacherous environment.

Deciding it would be best to be at the top of the ridge where the wind might have sheared the snow from the rocky ground, she turned to claw her way up the steep slope. She was less than halfway to her destination when violent chills began to shake her body. Every inch that she moved skyward was hard-won, she had to fight, not only the inhospitable environment, but also her own strengthening urge to give up.

Each time that she wanted to lay her head upon the snow and close her eyes, the tiny faces of her two children would appear to spur her onward. She continued to struggle, kept on fighting her way through the impeding snow. More than once, she fell through a particularly deep drift, the cold flakes sliding under her jacket, hitting her bare flesh like thousands of tiny knives. Her hair was sodden and beginning to freeze in the winter breezes that gusted across the landscape. Her feet, legs and hands had long since lost the ability to feel the cold or anything else. She even considered finding another sheltering tree and using the matches that were tucked inside her bra to light another fire, but she told herself they were probably too wet to be of any use.

The sky was brighter by the time she had managed to climb over the last snowdrift to reach the top. Carissa was elated when she discovered that her estimate had been correct; the snow was much thinner here, and packed hard in most places. There were spots where the ground was bared by the harsh winds that had scoured them through the night.

She chose one of those clear spots, one that was surrounded by sheltering brush, to sit down for a short rest while she cleaned as much snow as possible out of her pant legs and shoes. The shivering that had started halfway up the slope was weakening her already-depleted reserves, and the dark side of her mind tempted her with thoughts of lying down to sleep. Her shoes were soaked through; her saturated makeshift socks clung to her skin. She decided that she would have to try to build another fire and get herself as dry as possible. She wondered if she would be able to get anything to burn up here at the top, even though she was able to find plenty of dried material to use as tinder.

The matchbook was still mostly dry. It took four of the invaluable matches to ignite a diminutive pile of dried grass and twigs. She carefully fed the little flame with shaking hands while hunching over it to block the gusting air until it was as big as the fire she'd had under the shelter of the tree. Up here on the ridge; however, with the wind slashing at her, the heat was inadequate to offer much comfort, so she continued to add enough deadfall until she could feel the fire's warmth. She crawled around gathering as much burnable materials as she could find, and piled it near the fire. She thought that if she was lucky someone might see the fire and send help.

A stab of fright shot through her as she thought of the two monsters from whom she had escaped, but surely they were not still looking for her. Chastising herself for the ridiculous fear, knowing how badly injured at least one of them was, and the storm that had ravaged the mountain, she rationalized that the two must have gone by now. Still, glancing around, she could not shake the fright that was gripping her mind. She reasoned with the irrational fear that tormented her, telling herself that it was the fever causing the frightening thoughts.

Using rocks to anchor a couple of sticks, she hung her soggy shoes over the fire, hoping they would dry quickly. She used another stick to hang the wrappings from her feet and hands over the flames. Sitting Indian-style, she had her icy bare feet tucked in the crook of her knees as she alternated waving the makeshift socks and mitts over the heat, and feeding more wood into the fire. The shivering never ceased, nor did the urge to give up, to lie down, close her burning eyes and never wake again.

As soon as the cloth was dry, she wrapped her feet once more, her hands shaking so badly that she had trouble tying the binding cloth. The shoes were still damp, but she could feel the scant warmth that the flames had given them. With the mitts tied securely in place over her rigid hands again, she forced herself up from the cold ground, knowing that to sit there any longer would be to risk falling under the spell of the illness that robbed her strength. She left the fire burning, not caring if the whole damned forest burnt to the ground, though she knew it would go out without damage in the thin atmosphere of this harsh climate, and the heavy blanket of snow that stretched onward in blinding endlessness.

The wind at the top of the ridge was far more sharp than it had been below. It was not long before she wished she could move back down the slope, to the relative shelter of the snow-covered trees. Then she thought of the road that lay at the bottom of the mountain rise. Surely those vicious men were not still around, but looking down in the direction of the road she could see nothing but a deep crevasse where two ridges joined together at the bottom.

Carissa stopped to take another look around. How far had she gone the night before? Where was that road? She had thought she had a good handle on her whereabouts in conjunction with where she had started this horrible journey. Now she was completely disoriented, the bewildering reality sending a pall of despair washing over her already-flagging spirits. A wave of nausea threatened to take control of her as she let out a piercing shriek of grievous hopelessness. The piercing cry was muted by the endless cushion of white, but still sent birds scrambling from their perches in the trees. For the briefest of moments, she felt herself giving in to the horror and misery of her situation and in to the weakening pain that strained her depleted body.

She clung to the images of her children as they danced in her addled mind, and their voices that echoed within her. Using her hands to cover the deadened skin of her ears in an effort to warm them, she continued on her way, stumbling and catching herself with a grip on a boulder. She moved forward, each step forced and painful.

A thirst, unlike she had ever known, was burning her throat, her tongue feeling as dry as sawdust in her mouth. She suffered the need for water for some time before laughing wretchedly at herself; the harsh sound was that of madness as another flock of birds scattered away from her. There was water all around in the form of frozen crystals, still pristine from the fresh fall. Without stopping her trek, she scooped a handful of the white stuff off a passing boulder, holding the icy flakes in her mouth until they melted before swallowing. The searing pain the cold water caused in her throat nearly dropped her to her knees, but she continued onward.

With no sun peeking through the thick dome of clouds overhead, she had no idea what time of day it was. She knew nothing but the agony of her tortured body and after awhile, that faded as well. She failed to notice that the day was growing darker, or that the clouds above had turned so gray as to be black in the condemning sky. She did not feel the wind as it picked up speed. She just walked, stumbling from time to time, but managing to keep her feet under her.

Tiny, hard flakes began to fall, catching on the wind and whipping about her. It did not matter. She could not feel the cold anymore. There was no sensation left at all, just the need to continue, the need to walk and never stop. She did not even mind that the snow at her feet had grown suddenly deeper or that she was once again climbing upward. The concept never registered as she kept up her steps. A feeling of euphoria enveloped her, leaving her feeling light as air, floating over a vast open space. She almost smiled. The howl of a wolf at that same moment brought her brain out of its fevered sluggishness. She was falling. Not realizing that she had broken through the crust of snow that had hidden a crevice, she was falling.

Her reflexes took over, her hands reaching, clawing, groping for something solid. They found purchase in the tangled roots of the scrub on the ledge above. The sudden stop caused her body to slam against the rock wall in front of her, wrenching a hoarse scream from her raw throat. Her feet kicked about, searching for solid ground and finding a protruding bit of rock. She refused to acknowledge the urge to let go, to fall, to end it all. With all the dwindling strength she could muster, she pushed with her legs and pulled with her arms to the next foothold. There she stopped for a moment, gasping, wanting to vomit.

"Almost there," a voice told her from above. The voice, sweetly feminine and gentle, reached her even through the howling wind. Carissa looked up to see the gorgeous glittering eyes of a wolf some ten feet above. She smiled at the beautiful beast as she hoisted herself up to the next level. "That's it. You can do it, Cari," the wolf told her.

Carissa no longer felt the desolate loneliness in the face of this new friend. "I'm coming," she called up to the glorious white wolf.

"Of course you are, dear. Don't stop now. Just a little farther."

The wolf moved back, allowing her room as she hauled herself up, swinging her leg over the edge of the rim. She pushed, pulled and fought her way to solid ground to lie on her belly, panting and gasping.

"Better get up now. Don't lie in the snow, Cari," the wolf told her.

"How did you know my name?" Carissa asked as if it was the most normal thing in the world to have a conversation with a talking animal.

"I've always known your name. I'm part of you. Come, dear. The storm is worsening and we need to get you to safety," the wolf called over her back as she slowly picked her way over the snowy earth.

Carissa turned to look at the fissure that had nearly swallowed her and beyond. She saw her own footprints on the ground on the other side of the opening and wondered how she had managed to fall so that she had made it across the yawning aperture.

"You must keep moving," the wolf called, dragging Carissa's mind back to the reality of her situation.

She jogged a few steps to catch up, stumbling over something hidden in the snow. She reached out and righted herself against a rock, catching a glimpse of her tattered mitts and the blood that soaked through the fabric. She curled her aching fingers into fists and hugged her arms around the thin jacket that covered her torso, walking forward, following her new guide.

"Wolf, what may I call you?"

"You may call me whatever you like. I *am* your creation."

This seemed like an odd concept to Carissa, to have created an animal out of thin air, but who was she to argue – she was no longer alone. "I think I will call you Alice. That's my mother's name, and you look like an 'Alice.' Mom's the only one who calls me Cari."

The wolf chuckled softly, taking up a position at her side. "Naming me for your mother, now that *is* an honor."

Carissa walked beside her wolf, neither of them speaking for some time as the wind howled and ripped at her ravaged face and body. Finally, Carissa glanced at her companion and said, "I wish I had your fur. I think I have frost bite."

"I know. If I could remove my coat and offer it to you, I would. But, if we hurry, we can find you shelter soon. You must keep moving."

"I'm not going to make it, am I?"

The wolf let go another howl before turning her muzzle to look at Carissa with anger in her black eyes. "You *will* make it. You *will* survive. Banish those negative thoughts. They do not serve you well."

"Yes, Alice. You're right. I *will* make it. I *will* survive."

The snow was getting heavier, coating her head and the wolf's fur before being stripped away by the harsh gusts of wind. They walked for hours, the sky darkening with the approaching night.

"This way," Alice said as she switched directions, heading up another thickly covered slope.

By the time Carissa reached the point where the wolf waited at the top, the world was nearly darkened by the night. What little light remained reflected off the white of the wintry blanket that covered everything, giving her surroundings an eerie twilight glow. She dropped to her knees, gasping for air and grunting against the burning pain in her throat.

"Get on your feet," the wolf growled out harshly.

With the support of an outcropping of rock, Carissa managed to pull herself up, standing on shaking legs, shivering violently. She brushed a strand of blood-crusted hair out of her face with her nearly frozen fingers. Her eyes burned as she tried to focus on the bewildering steep slope below. "You can't mean you want me to climb down that?"

"You must if you wish to survive. There is shelter ahead and warmth. You will find safety there."

Carissa turned to face the white wolf that blended so well with her surroundings. "What shelter? I don't see anything."

"Put your faith in me, Cari. It's there. Now, sit on your bottom and use your feet and hands to keep yourself from moving too fast. Slide down the mountain. It will be as if you were a child again, sledding with your family."

Carissa caught the scent of something on the air, something inviting and warming. She sniffed several more times until she smelled it again. The smoke of a wood fire, sweet and enticing, beckoned to her. She giggled and did as she was told. She let out a squeal as she began her decent, digging her heels in from time to time and clutching at the surrounding brush to control her speed. The snow forced itself up her back and pant legs, stabbing at her burning flesh.

Alice was waiting at the bottom when she finally reached it. Carissa lay with her meager clothing packed full of snow. The world blurred before her, terrible creatures moving in and out of her vision. She shuddered one more time, a reaction to the repulsive fear that was taking hold again. The clawing hands of the creatures reached for her as she tried to focus her burning vision. Their faces turned to those of her attackers, the men who had stranded her in this nightmare. Raising her hands to ward them off, she batted impotently at the empty air and the visions created by delirium. She closed her eyes, exhaustion overtaking her, the vacant void of it swallowing her whole.

"Get up!" the wolf growled, but the woman did not move. "Get – on – your – feet!"

Carissa was no longer able to hear her. Blissful darkness had taken away the pain and the shivering that had plagued her for the duration of her journey. She felt nothing, was nowhere. She gave herself over to the darkness, no longer caring if she lived or died.

The wolf threw back her head and howled into the night. Her mournful cry rang out over the trees and ridges of the cruel mountain. She lamented the life that dwindled before her as the howls continued, seemingly without ending.

Chapter 3

The figure of a man stood, blocking the light of the fireplace through the doorway behind him. The stormy wind whipped at his shaggy hair and the thick flannel shirt that covered his broad torso. His big hand touched the head of the massive dog that danced at his feet, quieting the animal, the fingers of his other hand wrapped around the stock of a shotgun.

"Shh, boy," he said through the thick black beard that covered most of his face, inclining his head toward the animal, but keeping his eyes on the woods surrounding the small, ancient cabin. "It's just a wolf." However, Bryce was not so sure. It was unusual to hear any animal activity in such a storm, and this animal's cry held a quality he had never heard in the howl of a wolf. This howl was more mournful, seemingly full of grief.

He stepped a little farther out onto the planked porch that spanned the front of his rustic home. Slanting his head to put his ear more into the wind he listened, but did not hear the returning cry of the pack, which was also unusual. The wolf's cry reached out again, almost as if the creature was calling to him, its hopeless tone begging for his help.

The low, rumbling growl of the dog he called Skoll brought his attention back from the surrounding woods. He eyed the giant black Mastiff carefully, watching his posture and gauging his intentions. Skoll swaggered back and forth across the deck planking, raising his muzzle to sniff the whirling air. Then he dropped his head again for another soft, low growl.

Bryce Matheney recognized that stance. Skoll employed it only when he smelled blood. He signaled the dog to return to his side, and ran his hand over the thick fur that covered Skoll's neck. Something was definitely out there and it was not just the wolf.

Bryce crouched down, feeling the cold wind that bayoneted through his clothing. He thought of what he'd heard early in the day. A scream, high-pitched and tormented, had rang out over the trees. The sound of it was so distant that he thought he might have imagined it, finally shrugging it off as that of a predatory bird or wildcat. Now he wondered if there was someone out there, floundering in the storm.

He had no use for people – of any kind. He tried to convince himself that, if there was someone out there, it was that person's own fault if he died. Only a fool would venture into the mountains afoot in the middle of a blizzard. As the cold seeped into his bones, he raised up from the crouching position next to the dog and walked back inside, calling Skoll to follow.

The dog hesitated; still growling into the winter wind and glancing pointedly back at Bryce. "Get in here, Skoll," Bryce commanded, bringing the reluctant dog to heel. Firmly shutting the door behind them, the imposing man threw a couple of logs onto the fire to reheat the large room. There was no telling how long this storm would last. Early storms were the most unpredictable; they could last hours, or they could last days. Sometimes the storms would let up only to regroup and attack with an even greater fury than before, such as this winter storm was doing now.

His cabin was a sturdy one, built by his grandfather more than eighty years earlier, and consisting of two rooms. He had made improvements on the structure since taking up residence here more than three years previous, making it more airtight and comfortable, but he had maintained the rustic nature of the building. There was no electricity, and running water came in the form of a hand pump at the old, enameled sink in the kitchen. He had no use for the trappings of the modern world.

"Come away from the door," Bryce told the massive dog. Skoll disobediently continued to whine and dig at the bottom of the frame.

Bryce sat in the huge recliner that faced the fire, one of the few luxuries he allowed himself, and propped his elbows on his knees. He slowly rubbed his hands together as he stared thoughtfully into the flames. A gust of wind dropped bits of snow down the chimney to hiss on the burning embers in the fireplace. It was a bad storm, all right, not fit for man or beast.

"Quiet!" he yelled at the dog, but Skoll was becoming increasingly agitated as he dug around the edges of the door. The animal was determined to get at whatever was out there. The incessant howling of the distant wolf echoed the dog's anxiety. "All right!" Bryce bellowed as he unfolded his long body from its seated position. Walking toward the door, he pulled his parka off the hook on the wall and donned it. Adding a muffler to cover his face and neck and a pair of hunting mittens to protect his hands, he walked back across the room to put another log on the fire, then affixed the screen to the front to keep errant sparks at bay.

The lantern that was blazing on the mantle would be his source of light in the gloom of the stormy night. He lifted it by its handle and took up his shotgun again, hoping he would have no need of it. Signaling for the dog to follow, he left the building and retrieved his snowshoes from the front porch. After laying them flat on the ancient wooden planks, he slipped his fur-lined boots into the clamps and snapped them shut.

Stepping away off the porch in search of whatever was out there; Bryce was hit with the full force of the blizzard, as his eyes watered from the stinging cold. The flakes of snow hit his exposed forehead under the hood of his parka like bulleting shards of glass.

The idea of what the dog was tracking being a fresh kill had crossed his mind but that made little sense. A lone wolf with a fresh kill is not likely to howl and call attention to itself, not to mention that it would be unlikely any animal would be out hunting in this vicious storm.

He followed an anxious Skoll into the stormy forest. The snowshoes made it fairly easy to keep up with the large dog's loping gate as the animal sniffed the ground and the air for whatever he had detected. Nearly thirty minutes later the howling had ceased as the dog became fixed upon a definite goal. He let out a single woof and charged forward, forcing Bryce to pick up the pace in the huge snowshoes.

He lost sight of the dog, but knew there was little out there that the animal could not handle. There was another deep bark from nearby, and as Bryce stepped out of the trees into a small clearing, he saw the dog desperately digging at a small mound in the snow. As he drew closer, he could see a single diminutive hand, wrapped in tattered, blood-soaked cloth, its raw and bloodied fingers peeking from the ragged edges that protruded from the white blanket.

"Jesus!" he hissed into the wind as he dropped to his knees. The snowshoes hampered his movements, forcing him to strip off his mittens, roll onto his back and unsnapped the clamps on his feet to let the shoes fall onto the snow.

Pulling himself back onto his knees, he picked his gun and lamp up from where he had dropped them in the snow. He leaned the shotgun against a nearby boulder and set the lantern on top, before turning his attention back to the person buried in the snow. He carefully lifted the small hand; it looked like that of a child in his own large paw, and felt cold as ice. Probing gently, he searched for a pulse in the delicate wrist, finding no sign of life.

With meticulous care, his bare hands scooped the snow off the body until he found its head and brushed the battered face clean of the last of it. He sucked air through clenched teeth as he gazed at what he assumed was the face of a woman or girl – it was difficult to determine – so extensive was the damage.

Exploring lower he searched for a pulse in her throat and for a brief moment detected a fragile movement, weak and whisper-soft. He moved quickly after that, removing his parka and enfolding her petite body in its warm folds. The huge garment covered nearly all of her, and it seemed to Bryce, that she snuggled deeply as he wrapped it tightly around her. He ignored his own shivering in the biting wind as he bent to reattach the snowshoes before pulling his mittens back onto his chilled hands. He pulled himself upright and bent to pick up the tiny female who lay dying in the snow.

With increasing alarm, he discovered when he closed his fist over the front of his parka to lift her, just how tiny she. There was not much to this bit of female fluff who had mysteriously appeared. It took little effort to hoist her over his shoulder; she weighed hardly anything. He held the frail body, his left hand over her legs; in his right, he grasped the shotgun and the handle of the lantern. "Home, Skoll," he commanded, and followed his trusted companion back to the cabin.

The female on his shoulder never moved except for the limp sway of her lifeless body as he walked the thirty-minute trek back to his cabin. Upon reaching the planks of the front porch, Bryce set the lantern on the railing and laid his gun across the top of the woodpile. It took a deal of coordination to reach down toward the fastenings of his snowshoes, but he managed to remove them without releasing his grasp on the body that he held. Taking his gun and lamp, he kicked the door open and entered the soothing warmth of the cabin.

Setting the lantern on the table near the bed and leaning the gun against the wall, he used his emptied hand to toss a spare blanket over the only bed, which sat opposite the fireplace in the large room. He had to bend low over the bed to lay the person upon the blanket; his hand gently cradled her injured head as he lowered it to the pillow. At that moment, he heard a sound, soft as the beating of butterfly wings. Her swollen, blistered lips whispered a word. It sounded like she had said, "Alice."

Bryce, his face only inches from hers, studied her closely, looking for some sign that she might wake, but she did not stir again. It took only a moment to unwrap his huge parka from about her slight body, noting how she shivered as the cool air hit her damp clothing and seeped through to her skin. From the trunk at the foot of the bed, he grabbed a second blanket to spread over her inanimate form before shutting the door.

Thought of treatment for hypothermia and frostbite flooded his mind. The medical training from his days in the Navy had served him well over the years, and with any luck, would help him to save this woman now. He stripped off his muffler and mittens, flinging them at a chair. He opened the only closet in the cabin and pulled out a large first-aid kit and a box of bandages.

Taking a moment to clear off the bedside table and light two more lamps, Bryce prepared to go to work. He pulled the large, antique, copper tub out from the corner where it was stored near the fireplace and tossed several more pieces of wood on the fire. He filled several tin pails with water at the kitchen pump and set them on the hearth to warm. He also filled the cast iron kettle, setting it directly over the flames to boil. He set the first-aid kit on the table next to the bed and opened it.

He gazed briefly at the filthy, battered face of the woman on the bed. He could not imagine how she must have come to this state of wretchedness. *Damned foolish woman*, he thought. *What was she doing out here?*

He pulled the blanket back just enough to expose one of her arms. Taking the scissors from the kit he began slicing through the sleeve, all the way to the shoulder of what looked like a suit jacket, or what remained of one. The tatters of fabric that covered her hand would have to be soaked from her skin, since it was glued to her by crusted blood. Fear of frostbite demanded that extra caution be taken lest her fragile skin should be further damaged. Ugly bruises and dye from the wet fabric of her jacket discolored her exposed arm. The skin was rigid from dehydration and ravaged by cuts and scratches.

He carefully replaced the blanket and moved on to her other arm. Bending low over the bed to inspect the flesh closely after cutting away the coat sleeve, he found it in the same condition as the other.

He pulled the blanket down to her waist so that he could access her torso. Making short work of the jacket by bisecting it at the shoulders, he carefully peeled the wet fabric away to discover the strange configuration of the shirt she wore. The sleeves were missing, and if he was not mistaken, she was wearing it backwards. He rolled her body slightly away from him to remove the saturated jacket from under her, finding her back completely bare except for the strap of her bra and the scraps of cloth that knotted at the small of her back, holding the shirt in place.

He gently unhooked her bra and snipped the tied cloth with his scissors before rolling her, once again, onto her back, taking note of the damage done to the skin there. His scissors snipped neatly through the tie at her neck, allowing him to remove the filthy rag that covered her front, cutting it free at the shoulders so it would not be necessary to drag it down her injured arms and hands.

He debated whether he should sever the thin straps of her bra but decided against it, pulling each strap down each arm with meticulous care. A small packet, stuck to the flesh of her breast, revealed itself. He removed it, tossing it on the table, then turning to view her unveiled body. Skoll's ears perked up as a low whistle escaped Bryce's mouth. The woman had been through hell, judging by the condition of her.

The fine bones of her ribcage pressed harshly against the strained skin. A huge contusion, purple and black, covered nearly her entire left side. She had painful-looking gouges and abrasions over her entire front torso and something akin to road rash over her soft belly. What stood out the most, however, was what looked to be a large purple handprint on her left breast, the definite shape of fingers easily seen against the creamy skin.

What happened to you? he thought as he continued his examination, lightly skimming his fingers over her ribs to satisfy himself that none were broken. With the tweezers in the medical kit, he removed several good-sized chunks of debris that were imbedded in her flesh. The fine texture of her skin did not escape his notice as he continued to render aid, nor did the heat that radiated from her body. The woman was more than injured; she was ill.

With the last splinter removed, he covered the top half of her feverish body again, removing the blanket from her bottom half. Looking at the flimsy shoes that encased the tiny feet of the injured woman, he felt true disgust for the foolishness that had brought her up here. He pried the sodden leather from her feet and cocked a brow at the clever way her lower extremities were painstakingly wrapped. Not knowing what he would find under the wet fabric that was darkly stained by the leather of her inadequate shoes, he moved slowly, gingerly cutting away at the cloth. At least now he knew why her shirt was in tatters. It was obvious that she had used the sleeves to protect her feet. *Smart girl*, he thought.

As he peeled away the thin material to reveal the first foot, he was surprised at what he found. Although there were minor signs of frostbite, along with some cracking and bleeding of the skin, her foot was in relatively good condition. He surmised that she could not have been out there for very long, but that did not make sense. His home was too far back in the backcountry, at least a four-day hike from the nearest road, even in good weather. There was no way she could have made it, dressed as she was, in the blizzard that now hammered away at his mountain. He shook his head thinking that there was a real mystery at work here.

He unwrapped the other sheathed foot and was pleased to find it in as good a condition as the first. With that done, he worked more quickly as her body began shivering violently. Her fever was climbing, he noted as he cut away at the thin, pinstriped slacks that covered her slim legs. The skin there was chewed up as badly as the rest of her body; raw and marked with deep bruising.

Moving back up to her middle, he snipped away until he cut through the waistband on both sides. He pulled the sodden, tattered fabric from under her and tossed it on the heap near the fire with the rest of her rags. She moaned softly, her teeth chattering in a series of low clicks that were clearly audible. He spread the blanket back over her legs and tucked it loosely around her feet. The fire in her skin was climbing rapidly; he knew he had to bring her temperature down, and also clean her up to prevent infection in her wounds.

He filled the tub from the buckets on the hearth. The temperature was warm without being hot, just right for her fevered body. He gathered soap and a washcloth and filled the buckets again, placing them on the hearth, then tossing several more logs on the crackling fire. Pulling another blanket from the trunk, he carefully spread it over the surface of his recliner. He draped a small towel over the end of the tub, before his attention returned to the frail body on his bed.

He stood over her for a moment looking at her swollen, bloodstained face. He remembered another woman, her face reddened with her own blood, eyes looking into his with such trust. A pang of fierce emotion lunged through him, the pain nearly sucking the air from his lungs. He squelched the thoughts, the pain and the tide of rising emotions to focus on the woman who lay before him.

Slowly, with the utmost care, he pulled the blanket from her body, mindful of any of her wounds that might be sticking to the fabric and fearful of causing more bleeding. She appeared to have lost quite a bit of blood by the pallor of her skin and her emaciated appearance. Once exposed, he was able to see all the damage at one time. She needed a hospital and real doctors. She needed transfusions and medication. All he would be able to do for her was wash her, patch her up as best he could and try to get some food into her system.

He picked up his scissors from the table again, eyeing her panties. Somehow, the thought of removing them seemed like a violation of the defenseless woman. Removing the other articles of her mangled, wet clothing had been more of a mercy than a violation, but the underpants was a different matter. With a deep breath he bent to take hold of them. Looking closer now at the fragile lace, he could see the tears in the delicate fabric. The flesh underneath was inflamed with angry-looking scratches.

He snipped the lace away to look more closely at the injuries. There were several small scratches among the soft hair of her mound and one long gouge punctuated by numerous crescent-shaped marks that could only have been caused by fingernails. Judging by the size of the marks it had been a fairly large hand that had done the damage, probably the same one that had left its print on her breast. His suspicions were confirmed; someone had at least attempted to rape her, leaving her in the wilderness to die of exposure. He felt the heat of rage rising up his neck.

She had to be a hell of a woman to survive what she had been through. Looking at her face again, he felt a grudging respect for her. She must have the spirit of a fighter in her – a good thing. She would need that spirit, that will to live, to survive the battle that was ahead.

He turned back to her marred sex. He wondered if her attacker had been successful. If he had, there was a danger of serious infection, even toxic shock. Moving his hands lightly over her knees with a guilty twinge, he pulled them gently apart. He picked a lamp up from the table, holding it close to the apex between her legs.

The scratches at the top of her mound were raw and inflamed. Infection was already setting in. *The bastard's nails must have been filthy*, he thought. Taking a steadying breath, he reached out a hand to probe the soft flesh between her legs.

The woman's body contorted and her hand grasped his wrist, her jagged claws poking through the shredded covering tied at her wrist and digging into his flesh with surprising strength as she tried to fend him off. Her ragged voice screamed painfully, "NOOO!" The sound died away to a weak moan that bubbled to silence in her throat. A quick glance at her face showed that her eyes were still closed and a fine sheen of perspiration was showing on her forehead and upper lip.

Leaning close to her ear he spoke in soothing tones, trying to calm her and allay her fears. She slowly relaxed her grip on his arm until her hand rested softly against his. He tried to withdraw his hand from the tender, silken flesh only to feel her hand pressing down on his, holding his fingers in place. Another moan elicited from her throat as her hips moved imperceptibly against his fingers. There was a definite reaction in his groin to her actions, punctuated by self-loathing for such a response to the helpless woman. Taking advantage of her stricken form never crossed his mind, knowing that her reaction to his touch was more a need for comfort than desire to appease any carnal appetite. Then she was fighting him again, both arms flailing in the fevered throes of hellish nightmares.

He removed his hand from between her legs and gathered her against him, holding her tightly while he sat on the edge of the bed lest her thrashing cause her body further damage. She quieted almost immediately, curling against him, her head on his chest. For a moment, he held her and nothing more, feeling the soft heat of her nestled tenderly under his chin.

Finally, lifting her slight weight, he carried her to the tub and cautiously lowered her into the tepid water. She groaned as her body began to shiver again, the shaking making the water slosh slightly. He supported her with his left arm behind her shoulders as he smoothed water over her ravaged flesh. Another cry of anguish rang out at the stinging pain that invaded her fevered delirium.

He continued to speak in soft tones as he went about the task of cleaning away the blood and grime that soiled her skin. Removing his arm from round her shoulders, he carefully laid her head against the edge of the tub.

He took each of her hands in turn to gently massage water into the clinging fabric and work those remnants loose from the scabby flesh of her fingers. The skin underneath was cut clean to the bone in some places with blisters caused by frostbite. The fingernails displayed bleeding cracks with one nail completely missing. Again, he wondered at what the woman must have endured to get this far into the wilderness and still be alive.

Clutching the bar of soap, he worked the cloth over it to produce a fine lather. He gently worked the soapy cloth over her face while his other hand spanned the back of her skull, supporting it. He scooped small handfuls of water over her face to rinse away the red-tinged lather, revealing the delicate texture of her skin, marred by injury.

He washed the rest of her body with the same painstaking care, his big hands infinitely gentle. Small sounds, little grunts and soft moans, came from her throat every time the cloth encountered a wound.

When he was satisfied that the rest of her was thoroughly washed, he turned his attention to the hair that was plastered to her head, crusted with blood, dirt and debris. Though the floor was already wet, he decided it would be best to have a pan or a pail to catch the water that would soon be dripping from her tresses.

He fetched a large basin from the cupboard in the kitchen and placed it on the floor at the end of the tub.

Slipping his large hands under her arms, he lifted her along the copper wall of the bathtub until her head lolled back over the edge. He gently lifted the stiff, encrusted hair to dangle over the rim and hang down to the basin.

He held up a lantern to closely inspect what injuries he might find in her scalp. The wounds on her head were numerous. He located three good-sized goose eggs and several lacerations, the one just above the hairline at her forehead being the worst. It needed stitching but with the amount of dirt and debris in the cut he decided that it might be best to leave it open in case of infection.

Wondering if he would be able to get the tangled mess clean, he retrieved a bucket from the hearth and began carefully pouring the warmed water over her head at the hairline. The water that ran through her snarled hair came out at the ends to run into the basin, the color of mud tinted with red.

Starting at the scalp, he worked the soap into her hair, scrubbing gently and trying to avoid aggravating her wounds. He rubbed the bar vigorously over the length, stopping from time to time to remove sticks, leaves and other debris from the tangles. The lather turned a dingy rust color as it did its job of removing the soil. He rinsed the hair by pouring more water over it and squeezing out the excess into the basin. He lathered it again, and for good measure, washed it a third time, emptying the basin into the empty buckets in between washings.

He was finally contented that she was thoroughly clean. The only thing he could not figure out how to do was to stand her up and use fresh water to rinse her entire body, so he had to forego that step. After using a clean towel to absorb the excess moisture in her thick hair, he reached into the cloudy water to lift her out.

The moment that the air of the room hit her wet skin, the shuddering in her muscles started all over again. Quickly, he carried her to the chair and set her upon the soft cotton of the blanket, using the edges to pat her dry. The way the woman's moans increased, he knew that he must have been causing her pain. He stopped what he was doing, deciding it would be better to wrap her damp body in the cotton and let the moisture be absorbed naturally.

He lifted her into his arms again and felt her snuggle against him. Her arm glided slowly from beneath her covering to wind upward around his neck. Once more, he felt a stab of some emotion that he dared not name, as he gazed at her battered face. The force of that sensation dropped him slowly into the recliner where she curled a little deeper into him.

Cradling her frail body in his arms, he could not help the wave of protectiveness he suddenly felt for this pitiful creature. She had suffered appalling atrocities, and courageously fought to survive. There was more to her than just the fragile, damaged body that he held. This was a woman worth saving, and he would do whatever was necessary to see that she recovered.

He raised a hand to her face, and with some relief, found that her temperature was lower now. Waiting for her to relax some, her sleep to normalize a bit, he held her and soothed her with gentle strokes of his hands. How long had it been since he had held a woman in his arms?

His mind wandered back in time to the smiling face of a woman he used to know. Her dancing blue eyes and easy laughter had warmed his heart and given him joy. But another image tainted the memory, the image of that same face, bloodied and mangled, her shattered body hanging limply in his arms. The pain of those memories rocketed through him, as it always did, causing him to clutch more tightly to the fragile creature in his arms. She groaned in protest, and he quickly relaxed his grip, raising a hand to press her head against his chest.

She sighed softly under his touch, a sound that stirred him to his core. Each stroke of her hair against the callused palm of his hand brought him a satisfying warmth. Gazing at her face, he studied every angle and curve. Her ears were nipped by frostbite, leaving them swollen and raw. The delicate skin over her nose, forehead, and cheeks was wind-burned and would soon peel away. Her lips were cracked, blistered and bruised. The swelling of her nose made him wonder if it had been broken. Both eyes were blackened and her right cheek had been scraped raw.

Despite all of this, anyone with eyes could see that she was a beautiful woman. Her heart-shaped face was perfectly proportioned; the bones finely carved as if a great artist had had a hand in her creation. Dark lashes, long and curling, settled against the purple bruises that hid the exquisite texture and pale color of her skin.

Her hair, drying in the warmth of the flames, was becoming a spiraling mass of curls that probably hung halfway down her back. It had a fine texture that felt like silk to his touch. The color was most unusual, now that the tresses were clean. He had thought it would turn out to be black when it was wet, but it was drying to dark brown with deep, dark red highlights that caught the flame in the light of the fire. It gave him the impression of a molten blend of mahogany and copper.

He let his thoughts wander to her body as he had seen it, prostrate and dwarfed by his big bed. She was too thin, but had curves in all the right places. He could feel the softness of her through the cotton of the blanket, a sensation that was anything but unpleasant. She was so small that it would be easy to break her in two. That thought brought back that fierce protectiveness that he had not felt for someone in a long time.

Suddenly aware of the turn his thoughts had taken, he had a surge of anger at himself. She was just another inconvenience to him, a mewling, sick woman who would need constant care, and he would be glad when he was shed of her. Still, when he rose to remove the soiled blankets from the bed, he set her down with gentle care on the chair he had just vacated. He ignored her whimpering protest, removed the wet, dirty blankets and pulled down the warm quilt and sheets that made up his bed.

Skoll had taken advantage of Bryce's brief absence, to investigate the bundled woman. His massive head easily reached over the arm of the big chair to sniff at her face and hair. Moving around to the front of the chair, the animal continued his sniffing inspection. As Bryce turned back to the woman, it seemed to him that she was reacting to the dog's presence, moving imperceptibly toward Skoll as if to touch him. The dog licked her face before Bryce could stop him.

"Back, Skoll. Go lie down," the dog's master commanded. Skoll hesitated, looking longingly at the woman, before settling on his rug in front of the fire. Bryce wondered at the dog's behavior. He usually detested all strangers, snarling and growling at the presence of any human being. If Skoll's intended target did not take immediate heed, Bryce would be hard-pressed to keep the dog from attacking. It was as if the dog had fallen in love with the woman.

Bryce moved to pick her up, carrying her to the bed before unwrapping the blanket that shrouded her naked body and laying her on the clean linen on his mattress. He drew the blanks to her chin and prepared bandages, ointments and antiseptics for dressing her wounds.

He started at her head and worked his way down, exposing each part of her as he worked quickly, before covering it again. He used the antiseptic cautiously to clean her head wounds, the stinging pain of the strong liquid wrenching whimpers and moans from her. With a careful touch, he gently stroked salve onto her wind-burned face, mindful of damaging the irritated epidermis and the bruises that lay beneath.

It was a difficult task to wrap her small, frostbitten fingers and toes individually, his large hands felt clumsy and inadequate attending to the delicate task. With that task completed, he spread antibiotic ointment onto the abraded flesh of her limbs, bandaging the worst of the wounds. He inspected her abdomen again; to be sure he had removed all the debris that had been imbedded in her soft flesh, before dressing the wounds.

The ugly, bruised handprint on her left breast gave him cause for concern. It looked painful, the flesh of it swollen to the point of being hard, and the nipple standing erect, red and inflamed. He knew it must have been causing as much discomfort as any of the other wounds. Withdrawing a bottle of liniment from the medical kit and pouring a small amount onto his fingers, he hesitated as he glanced at her still face. This would not be a good moment for her to finally come round, with his hands on her tit.

Finally, with a resigned sigh, he gently massaged the healing oil into her abused flesh. As he worked, a small, faint moan escaped her lips, her muscles tensing and drawing together under his fingers. He had not seen her move but it seemed that she was pushing her breast into his hands as if she were enjoying his touch. Experiencing some small pleasure himself at the feel of her hot flesh against his own, he hurried to complete the task. He moved to apply liniment to her blackened ribs before wiping his hands on a towel.

Once he had finished, he removed one of his flannel shirts from the bureau near the closet, shaking the shirt free of its folds. Returning to the woman's side, he sat on the edge of the bed to lift her torso and lean her head against his chest. Looking down her back, he saw more scratches, and reached for the ointment.

Applying the greasy medicine with his fingertips, he encountered the definite texture of scar tissue. He stood, leaning forward and bending her lifeless body over his arm to get a better look at the flesh of her back. As he pulled the lamp closer, he could see three slithering marks that spanned her lower back to disappear where her bottom came into contact with the mattress. A fresh onslaught of rage rose in him as he wondered who would whip this tiny, elfin woman to the point of cutting her skin.

That protective spirit was back, causing him to make silent vows once again to the unknown woman whose eyes he had not even seen. She would most likely recoil in horror when she opened them at last to see the monster that he had become. He ran a gentle hand once more over the heat of her graceful back, knowing that it would likely be one of the few chances he would get to touch another human being without the shudder of revulsion that was so common in his experience.

He squeezed his eyes shut, struggling to shut out the grief that he had banished long ago, since coming to this desolate place. He could not allow the presence of this mysterious woman to remind him of all that had been taken from him, all that had made his self-imposed exile necessary. Mustering his anger once again for all things human, he shoved her bandaged arms into the sleeves of the warm flannel, perhaps a bit too roughly, for she moaned pitiably.

With a gentler hand, he lowered her head back down to the pillow and buttoned the shirt closed about her tortured flesh. As soon as he had the garment pulled down over her legs, he could see that it reached just passed her knees. Once again, he was struck by the diminutive size of the tiny woman, and once again he wondered how anyone could hurt someone of such delicate beauty.

Chapter 4

Dawn was approaching by the time he had finished seeing to the wounds of the unknown woman and had her comfortably ensconced in the ancient bed he called his own. Bryce felt the fatigue that was pulling at his body, tempting him to rest, but he had to get something nutritious into her.

Dehydration was a major concern as well. Drawing his hand up to pull at the thick beard that hid most of his face from sight, he tried to decide the best way to get food and liquids down her throat. He opted for soup, deciding to kill two birds with one stone.

Moving to the kitchen, he pulled a can of broth out of his extensive storage pantry. He had just put the soup into a pan on the ancient, pot-bellied, wood-burning stove when he heard screams, grief-stricken and full of horror, coming from the next room.

Setting the pan off the heat, he strode quickly to her side. She had the bedding tangled about her legs, her arms thrashing about, as she fought off the shadowy nightmares of her delirium. Her eyes remained closed as she clawed blindly at the air around her with her bandaged hands. The wound at the top of her head was bleeding again, the sticky crimson soaking through the white gauze that was wrapped over it.

Bryce seized her arms as another scream ripped from her throat. She fought harder, trying to free her legs. Pressing his weight down on her thrashing body, he talked to her softly, attempting to calm her fears and soothe her mind. Within moments, she settled some, mumbling unintelligibly and quivering slightly.

He brushed a stray lock of hair from her flushed face, shaking his head at the rising heat of her skin. Untangling her legs, he tossed the bedding back, away from her shuddering limbs to allow the air to cool her fever. The sounds coming from her throat were hoarse and raw. Mere exhaustion and injury were not the only causes of this fever. There was something else depleting her weakened body, a virus or other infection. She showed all the signs of influenza and he fervently hoped that was not the case.

Bryce returned to his task in the kitchen, but kept an ear to the next room. There were the sounds of rustling cloth and squeaking bedsprings to accompany her soft, whimpering murmurs. Just as the soup had begun to simmer, the room next door fell silent. Dark, chilling fear crawled into his belly, freezing his heart and filling his mind with dread.

He set the soup aside again to walk to the bed, his boots dragging across the stone-tiled floor, fearing the worst. The only sound was the crackle of the burning logs in the fireplace.

As he neared the bed, he saw something that astounded him. Skoll, the enormous Mastiff who hated people worse than his master, was standing beside the bed, his colossal head on the woman's thighs. The white of her bandaged hand lay in stark and miniature contrast upon the jet-black fur of his powerful neck. When Bryce tried to call Skoll away, the dog simply rolled his eyes upward, looking at the man, but not moving from his post.

With a bewildered shake of his head, Bryce returned to the kitchen to pour the broth into a bowl for serving. He found a spoon that he would use to ladle the restorative liquid into her mouth and a towel to spread over the blankets to catch any spills. Returning to her side, he lifted her listless body to slide his bent knee and arm under her for support. It was this way, with her head laying upon his chest just beneath his shoulder, that he was able to use his right hand to pour small amounts of the broth past her swollen lips, while his left hand cradled her head. The dog never moved from his vigilant position by her side.

Bryce was unaccustomed to the responsibility of someone so completely dependent upon him for care. The feeling of protectiveness that was growing toward this unconscious woman was coupled with the fear that his efforts would not be enough to draw her back from the brink of death. The blizzard outside his door howled as its savagery grew. Even if the storm were to dissipate, he would still not be able to carry her out of the wilderness, not in her present condition. She would not last an hour in the frigid temperatures of the early winter in the mountains. All he could do was follow his instincts and training and hope it was enough to sustain her, enough to restore her health.

The first spoonful of broth dribbled off her lips, landing on the towel beneath her chin. He tried to stay his growing alarm as he spoke to her, urging her to swallow. When, on the third bite, her throat contracted and she had consumed most of the warm broth, he nearly let out a whoop of joyous satisfaction. Her face grimaced in pain as the warm liquid flowed down her esophagus; as if the mere act of swallowing were the most painful she had ever endured. After that, he managed to get most of the broth into her belly. She did not once open her eyes or offer any sign of awareness, but instead, remained unconscious in her fevered delirium, responding to very little.

The sun had risen; the only indication of it was the brighter cast to the gray, snow-filled world outside the cabin window. Bryce welcomed the gloominess of the stormy day. He was bone-weary, in need of sleep, and the low light would make that easier.

Taking another quick glance at the woman who slept so quietly under the watchful gaze of Skoll, Bryce turned to clean up the mess he had created. He emptied the ancient copper bathtub, one bucket at a time, and stowed it in the corner near the fireplace. The soiled linens and blankets were draped over an improvised clothesline near the warming flames to dry.

Finally, he gathered the sodden, filthy rags that had been her clothing. As he plucked them from the floor, it occurred to him that, within the articles of clothing, there might be something that would tell him her identity. What was left of the fragmented shirt, he knew, would contain nothing, so it was immediately tossed upon the fire. He found no pockets in the ragged slacks and threw it to the mercy of the flames as well. The jacket, he discovered, had once had a pocket on either side of the front, but the linings were torn out.

He smiled at the sleeping form on the bed. She was a resourceful woman, having harvested even the linings of her pockets to cover her exposed flesh, keeping it protected from the elements. He had little doubt that the fabric he had removed from her mangled hands had been that which was missing from her jacket.

He frowned slightly as he remembered the small packet he had discovered clinging to her damp breast. He had tossed the item aside, more concerned for her immediate needs than what had been wrapped in the raveled cloth. Dropping the ruined jacked in front of the hearth, he returned to the table next to the bed.

Picking up the little item, he turned it over in his palm until he found the end of the cloth where it had been tucked into the layers. He pulled it out, unwrapping first one, and then a second long strip of dirty white cotton. Getting to the core, a small square-shaped object fell into his hand. He held it up to the lamp in the gloom of the dreary afternoon. Turning the small article, a slow, reflective smile stretched the beard that shielded his face, the white patches of hair on his left cheek and jaw dancing in the flame of the lamp.

Held in his fingers was a single matchbook with several of the sulfur-tipped sticks gone. The covering was slightly damp but most of the remaining matches were still in good condition. The woman had, despite being weak and injured, had the presence of mind to keep her one weapon against the cold fury of nature safe and dry. He felt hope for her begin to rise; she was a survivor, and despite her frail appearance, might just be strong enough to recover.

He threw more wood on the fire and pulled the recliner across the irregular floor, positioning it beside the bed. He would sleep in the chair, he decided, next to her in case she began thrashing about on the bed once again. He would keep her safe, make her comfortable and help her get through this ordeal; she had more than earned the right to live.

Watching his human, Skoll refused to be moved, keeping vigil next to the bed. By this time he had one large forepaw on the bedcovers, his head still resting under the swathed hand of the helpless woman. She seemed content with the dog's presence, calm under his touch. It was an enigma to the man; he had never seen the dog behave this way. It was as if Skoll could sense the courageous spirit that she would have to have within her, that will for life giving her a rare quality that bespoke her worth as a person.

Bryce sank slowly into the comfort of his chair and propped his elbows on his knees. He watched the sleeping woman, so pale and vulnerable. He hoped with every fiber of his being that she survived, even knowing the expression on her face when she would finally have a chance to look at him. For a moment, he wondered what it would be like to have her look at him without the usual abhorrence most people gave him. He pondered what it would be to have her smile at him, accept him, touch him.

The thought brought back the feeling of loathing for the species of animal to which he was unfortunate enough to belong. He dug his knuckles into his gritty eyes, wondering why she had to be dropped into his hands. He had moved out here to be alone, so that he would no longer have to see the grimace of revulsion that so readily exhibited itself on the faces of those who saw him.

This cabin, so far removed from civilization, was his escape from the accusing stares and whispering voices that hissed their condemnation behind his back. He had managed, after the years spent here, to find some peace within himself and learn to live with the past. The minute she opened her eyes it would start all over again. He would have to endure from her the fear, the disgust, the compulsion to run away from his presence that he knew too well.

His thoughts continued to trouble him as he rested his head against the back of the chair. He closed his eyes and drifted through a semi-conscious world of darkness, listening to the accusation of the voices from the past. He heard the screams of a woman and saw her crushed body. Her eyes, full of pain and fright, looked at him with absolute trust. Her bloodied lips smiled timorously as he held her lifeless, paralyzed hand.

Bryce was jarred from his dozing state, the shadows of his dreaming visions dissolving in the confusion of waking. A deep gloomy anger darkened his mood as he looked around, trying to remember something.

Then he saw her, the woman on the bed. She was sitting up, clutching the quilt to her flannel-clad breast, her eyes open and staring. She was whimpering in horror, murmuring words that were unintelligible. The dog beside the bed was echoing her voice with soft and cajoling whines of his own.

With a weary sigh he stood, moving away and removing himself from her sight. As he moved he realized that her vision was not following him, but rather, had stayed fixed upon some unseen point in the distance. Cautiously moving closer, he waved a hand in front of her eyes only to see that she took no notice of him or his actions. With some small relief, he saw that the horror in her expression was not directed at him.

The woman was still delirious, trapped in the nightmarish world of demons and specters. He had pity for her and all that which she had fought through to survive this long. With one long stride, he moved closer to the bed and reached out a hand to touch her arm.

With a rasping screech, the woman recoiled in terror, flinching at his touch. Before he could see her move, she had flown from the bed to fling herself into a corner of the room, the flannel shirt riding up her slim legs as she slid her back down the junction of the rough-hewn walls. Her hands, held out in front of her, fended off the unseen incubus of her nightmares, as her ragged voice shrieked, "NO! Let – me – go!"

The terror in her voice, more than anything else, jolted him into action. Crossing the room in quick, cautious steps, he crouched down beside her, careful to keep most of his face turned from her toward the shadows of the corner. She did not seem to see him; her eyes – a shade more green than hazel – were glazed and overly bright.

His hand shook as he slowly reached for her, brushing a curl of silken hair from her face. She blanched, shrinking from his touch against the wall, her diminutive body becoming even smaller as she curled herself into a protective ball. He reached out again, both his hands taking her grappling body into his arms. The woman struggled with enough ferocity to knock him off balance and send them both toppling to the cold, flat stones of the floor.

She continued to fight, screeching without words, as she struggled against someone or something that only she could see. Bryce was on his back, trying to keep her fevered body from the cold floor as he wrapped his legs around her flailing limbs. He clasped both of her dainty wrists in one huge grasp while his other hand pressed her head against his chest and stroked her hair. His concern for the crazed woman was evident in the soothing tones he used to calm her as her body contorted.

Every muscle of the fragile body in his arms flexed and knotted under her skin. She twisted and arched against him, pushing her head into his chest. Her shrieking voice rang out in fright at the unseen foe that tormented her addled mind. She was a difficult handful to hold onto, but he did, trying to sooth her unknown terrors, and his own, with the sound of his voice.

When she finally sagged against his long frame, exhausted and panting, he laid his head against the hard floor and drew a stabilizing breath. He held her gently, stroking a callused hand over the soft flannel that barely covered her slim back, and pulling the shirttail down to conceal her naked thighs.

The searing heat of her illness burned at her flesh as the flames of a fire. Her fever was rising again, causing his brow to furrow with concern. With careful movements while unwrapping his legs from about her scorching body, he drew her limbs up to his middle so that he could slip an arm under them. He rose from the cold hardness of the stone-inlaid floor carrying her with him, clasping her lightly against his chest.

Skoll whimpered and danced about Bryce's legs as the man carried the unconscious woman back to the bed. He tenderly placed her fevered body upon the mattress, stripping back the covers and tossing them over the end of the bed. Without stopping to think, he stalked into the kitchen to get fresh water from the hand pump at the sink. Adding the still-warm water from the kettle on the hearth, he tested the temperature to find it tepid. He needed to cool her, but if the water was too cold, she might go into shock.

With one free hand, he cleared the table near the bed and set the pan of lukewarm water on its worn surface. As he turned to her, his fingers only hesitated for a moment before he unbuttoned the huge shirt that seemed to drown her slender form, and threw both sides open to reveal her ravaged flesh. Her muscles shuddered and twitched in delirium as her voice called out in a series of soft moans and whimpers.

The bruises that marred her pale skin had darkened since he had cleaned her body and dressed her wounds. The ones on her ribs, and left breast looked the most painful and swollen. He pulled two small pieces of sackcloth from the pile he had placed next to the pan of water and wet them, applying the cooling compresses to the vicious-looking injuries.

Dipping in another small cloth and ringing the excess water back into the pan, he surveyed her body. So much of it was damaged that it would be nearly impossible to sponge her down without irritating at least some of the wounds. With a sigh, he set about the task, scrupulously avoiding the worst injuries that had been bandaged. For the better part of an hour, he continued to swab the burning skin of her face, torso and legs, finally removing the shirt from her arms to gain access there.

Running cool fingers over her skin, he could feel that her temperature was lower, could see it in the softened expression on her face. She was sleeping soundly now, her fever and delirium abated. After managing to get a few spoonfuls of cool water down her throat, he settled back into his chair, his watchful eyes never leaving her delicate form.

He searched his memories of the medical training he had taken while a young sailor so many years ago. Questions of whether he was giving the right treatment or had missed something important clouded his mind and threatened his confidence. As he watched, seeing the peaceful slumber that now enveloped her, he had to believe that he was doing everything right, but still there was that nagging doubt.

He wanted, once again, to get her to a hospital, to get her real medical treatment, but the storm outside the walls of the cabin warned him not to even try. The blizzard raged on, dashing snow and ice against the one window that was not shuttered against its fury. He no longer believed that there was a god in heaven but he said a silent, fervent prayer anyway.

He was unsure of when his troubled thoughts had drifted away to be swallowed by the blissful void of restorative sleep, but he was suddenly awake, jolted by some unknown force to alertness. There was the soft, throaty whimpering of the giant dog that told him something was amiss. as he climbed out of the darkness of sleep.

Snapping his head up, his eyes open, he saw the woman staring at him from her position on the bed. Her face held no expression as her hazel green eyes gazed at him from under the fan of those incredibly long, dark lashes. She was sitting in the center of the huge bed, with her legs folded under her, a pillow clutched to her body to hide her nakedness.

Though her eyes were still glassy and too bright from fever, he could tell that she was looking directly at his face, watching and studying him. Time stood still as he waited for her to scream, to turn away in disgust, but she merely watched his eyes. Skoll broke the spell as he nudged Bryce's leg and let out another low whimper.

The eyes of the woman turned to the dog, again with no reaction. Bryce cleared his throat nervously, bringing her unwanted attention back to his face. "It's okay," he said his voice crackling in the tension of the room as he turned away. "You've been ill. How do you feel?"

The woman glanced about the room as if searching for something, before lowering her eyes to her hands clutched about the pillow against her chest. Bryce was on his feet in an instant, snatching the blankets off the floor at the end of the bed. He kept his face averted to hide his left side and offer deference for her modesty. After shaking out the bedding, he offered it blindly to her, feeling it shift from his grasp as she accepted the offering.

Without glancing at her, he strode across the room to remove another of his large shirts from the bureau and tossed the garment on the bed next to her, as he made his way to the kitchen. Once out of sight of the woman, he ran a shaking hand over his shaggy head, berating himself for allowing one single pair of olive-colored eyes to unnerve his mind. He drew a halting breath and forced himself into action, shoving sticks of wood into the old wood stove, stoking the flames to life. There was some tea around, he knew, and she would need its restorative qualities, as well as other nourishment. Bryce opened another can of soup, chicken noodle this time, and put a kettle on to boil.

When he thought he had given her enough time to dress, he returned cautiously to the front room. She had only moved slightly from her former position, having pulled herself into a tight ball and leaning against the headboard with the sheet and blanket clutched to her front. The plaid of the flannel shirt he had tossed to her was still lying, untouched, on top of the blankets as she watched the large dog. Skoll was standing next to the bed, his large jowls resting on the surface of the bedding.

"Skoll," he commanded too harshly. "Out." Bryce lunged for the door, in a hurry to ease what he perceived as her discomfort in the presence of the huge animal.

"I like him," she said in a soft, raspy whisper, bringing Bryce to a halt.

He turned to face the full force of her steady gaze. Feeling uncomfortable under such close scrutiny, he turned his face away, wishing he were anywhere but under her watchful eyes. "He... uh... his name is Skoll. Most people are usually afraid of him," he stated blandly.

He could feel her eyes as if they had a physical touch all their own. The tangible sensation of her heavy gaze was almost more than he could bear. With a voice too gruff from the dread that was threatening to choke him, he spoke again. "Is there something wrong with the shirt?"

Her answering voice was weaker this time, more timid, more fatigued. "I'm sorry. I can't seem to muster the strength" her words trailed off to a gentle sigh.

Bryce felt like an idiot. Of course, she was too weak to retrieve the garment and put it on; she could barely speak. With a sideways glance, he could see the pallid cast to her face and the dark hollows under her tired eyes. He sidestepped, bending to snatch the shirt from the foot of the bed and then carried it to her side, shaking it out and holding it for her.

When she did not move, he stole another glimpse at her from the corner of his eye. She merely gazed at him as she clutched the blankets under her chin.

"Come on, girl," he bit off. "I can't stand here all day."

Still she made no effort to push her arms into the sleeves. He finally had no choice but to turn his face to her, steeling himself for the inevitable. He saw fear in her eyes and in the way she drew back from him. There was no revulsion in her expression but there was alarm.

"I don't bite," he ground out between clenched teeth.

"I... have I done something to offend you?" she asked softly. "Who are you? How did I get here? Why am I naked?" The effort the questions had cost her was evident in the deepening green of her eyes as she watched him.

It occurred to him, as he studied her face, that she was not afraid of the hideousness of his appearance, but rather, the way he was acting. With a sigh he dropped the shirt on the bed, ran a hand through his hair again and turned his face back to the shadows.

"I'm not used to having people around," he offered by way of explanation. "You were out there," he inclined his head toward the door. "I fou... I mean, Skoll found you in a snow bank. You were half frozen. I brought you back here. Your clothes are gone because they were wet and in rags." He sighed before continuing. "You were burning up with fever. I was trying to get your temperature down."

He stood in the uncomfortable silence that followed his account of the events that had put her in his bed. The woman's eyes never left him; he could still feel her heavy gaze, even if he could not see her face from his turned position.

"But who are you?" she asked again.

Her voice was becoming so weak that he had to strain to it. "I'm Bryce Matheney. What's your name?"

"Carissa James. How long have I been here?"

"Since last night."

"Am I hurt bad? There are bandages all over…"

His shoulders tensed as he stopped himself from turning. "They're all mostly superficial, the injuries, I mean. Some minor frostbite and you're banged up some." He busied himself with feeding more wood into the massive grate of the fireplace.

"Is my face bad?"

Bryce froze in his crouched position before the fire. "No, just a few scrapes and bruises," he retorted.

"Then why can't you look at me?"

He dropped his head between his shoulders in defeat at his attempt to delay the inevitable reactions to his appearance. He stood slowly and turned using the mantle for support. The heat of the flames was quickly heating the heavy denim that encased his legs, but he could not make himself step away from the fire.

She looked up at him, worry etched in her wan face. "Do you have a mirror?"

"No," he ground out. "I don't keep any around."

"Just as well. It would only piss me off to see what they did to me." She settled back a little more against the headboard, weakening from the effort of their conversation. The curls that framed her face vibrated as her body shivered under the blankets.

Throwing caution to the wind, Bryce returned to the bed and picked up the shirt. "Let's get this on you," he said, his voice much gentler now. "Then I'll get you something to eat."

He bent his long frame over the bed, holding the shirt out and reaching a hand to her. She lifted her shaking arm, dropping one side of the blanket that had been clutched so tightly under her chin. Hating the desolate emotions that swamped him as one creamy breast was partially revealed to his sight, he averted his gaze, trying only to see the patient, the sick and injured person, and not the woman.

Once her arms had been sheathed in the over-long sleeves of his shirt, he watched her fumble impotently at the buttons with her bandaged hands. His own hands were shaking as he reached out to seize the front of the shirt, buttoning it quickly as his fingers grazed the heat of the flesh underneath.

His eyes snapped to her face, studying her color as he placed a rough hand on her forehead and then the back of her neck. Her fever was climbing again and her eyes were glazing in response. He helped her to slide down the mattress and stretch out under the excess fabric of his shirt, propping the pillows behind her back and head before drawing the sheet up to her waist.

The kettle on the stove screeched out its readiness, calling him back to the kitchen to finish preparing her meal. When he returned, with tray in hand, the woman who called herself Carissa had her eyes closed, her gracefully arched eyebrows drawn together in pain. He should never have allowed her to speak or move about, exhausting her waning strength. He cursed himself for being more concerned about how she would see him than the toll it would take on her health.

Chapter 5

Bryce had only managed to get half a cup of tea and a small amount of soup into her body. Her hand, its bandages blood-soaked from her movements, pushed the spoon away before falling lifelessly upon her belly. She had dropped unconscious again, as her fever continued to climb.

He had spent a great deal of time removing the soiled dressings from her bleeding hands and replacing them with fresh, white gauze, the supply of which would soon be gone. It would not be long before necessity would dictate that he rip his sheets into strips to be used for that purpose. Her wounds would heal, however, as long as he could restore her health.

Now, as he sat watching over her and dabbing at her fevered skin with cool water from time to time, he wondered at the way she had gazed at him so directly. She had not seemed at all disturbed by the disfiguration of his face; she only looked at him as if he were a normal person. This was a puzzling turn of events giving him cause for hope. It had been three years since another human being had occasion to see him, except for old Clancy who, twice a year, brought him the supplies that sustained him. The old man cared little about appearances, only that he was paid.

Hope – a funny emotion for a man such as him. *What exactly do you hope for,* he asked himself. This woman had been thrust into his care by unseen chance. It was not as if she would stay or offer him companionship in his long exile. No, this woman had a home, had a life that did not include a scarred giant of a mountain man who chose to shun society.

Anger began to build within his chest again, anger at himself and anger at this woman whose mere presence had opened old wounds and reminded him just how alone he was. The anger continued to rise, raging in his chest as the blizzard raged outside the door of his sanctuary. Pacing restlessly, he failed to see her skin color deepening with the rosy blush of heat, failed to hear her soft whimper as delirium once again took hold.

Another dawn was approaching, not really seen but felt in the man and his dog. The snowstorms in these mountains could keep man and beast imprisoned for long periods of time, wherein cabin fever could become the enemy. He needed activity, as did Skoll, but because of the weak woman on his bed, he had no choice but to stay put. Casting a glowering stare at her quivering form, and tossing another log on the fire, he wished he could tell her exactly what an inconvenience she had become.

He had done everything he could think to do within the cabin. Dishes were done, the cabin was tidy, and he had even cleaned both his guns at least twice. The firewood boxes were both filled to capacity from the woodpile on the porch. A deck of playing cards was neatly stacked on the table near the fire where he had played solitaire for several hours, until he could stand it no longer. Not even one of the fine volumes from his vast library could hold his attention. Now he stood at the window facing the coming of another day, wondering if *he* was going to survive this ordeal.

A blood-curdling shriek pierced his dark thoughts, bringing him round to face the bed. Carissa held up her hands, clawing at the visions of monsters that plagued her delirium. The sounds of her terrified cries sent his self-indulgent anger back into the recesses of his mind.

He rushed to her side to subdue her flailing limbs before she caused herself harm. Alarm bells clanged abruptly in his head as he made contact with her fevered body, her skin aflame, nearly scorching his. Her temperature was soaring dangerously high; it would not be long, he knew, before she succumbed and died.

Her wails grew louder and her movements more erratic as he wrapped his arms around her thrashing body, bringing her head up to his shoulder, talking to her and calling her by name. Without warning, she fell silent as her body became rigid in convulsive spasms. Her frame contorted, each muscle along its length shuddered as he fought to control the rising tide of panic in his chest.

He had to think, had to decide what to do to assuage her fevered body. Casting his eyes around for something, anything, that would aid this goal; he spied the old copper bathtub in the far corner of the room. Cool water, in great quantities, was needed – and fast, the decision made before he had time to think. Laying her seizing body down upon the mattress, he rolled her to her side, propping pillows and the wadded quilt against her back, hoping that her tongue would not slide into her throat and choke off her supply of oxygen.

Moving swiftly he pulled the tub to the kitchen and slammed a bucket under the pump spout. For the first time since moving to the secluded cabin, he wished for plumbing and electricity to aid in his efforts. He feared the handle of the old pump would snap in two under the ferocity of his grip as he forced water up from the well and into the bucket with increasing speed. With one eye on Carissa and the other on the task at hand, he managed to get the tub half-full in short order with Skoll prancing back and forth, whining.

It was not fast enough to satisfy Bryce's growing panic; however, as he decided not to waste time tempering the frigidity of it with more water from the kettle. He rushed to the bed and fairly tore the shirt from Carissa's body before lifting her, carrying her to the kitchen with a ground-eating stride. Dropping painfully to his knees on the immovable stones of the floor, he slowly lowered her convulsing body into the cool water.

Her heart beat so fast that it seemed the wings of a hummingbird fluttered in her breast. The muscles that stretched under the skin along her spine, her arms and her legs strained tighter as her reflexive response tried to drive her burning flesh away from the shock of cold water. Her head bucked low against his shoulder, her neck muscles contorting and snapping it back.

Bryce kept his grasp on her, his arms snugly about her, as he lowered her seizing form into the water, maintaining his grip even as the water soaked the sleeves of his shirt to the shoulders. The fever's response was almost immediate as her body visibly relaxed in slow degrees; the temperature of the water ascended gradually to match that of the air around them.

As Carissa slowly settled, moaning, into the relief of the cooling liquid, Bryce removed his arm from about her thighs, scooping handfuls of water over her neck and breasts. It was some small relief to feel the fever abate, but fear of other complications arose. The shock to her system could cause all manner of issues, not the least of which was brain damage and pneumonia.

He continued to bathe her with the clear water until he felt the first quiver pass over her pale skin. The diminutive muscles around the tiny hair follicles on her arms drew tightly into little knots of gooseflesh that traveled over her shoulders to spread throughout her body. He placed his hand over her heart, amazed at how his large hand nearly spanned her chest. The beat was steady, slower, a much more normal pace, he decided as he breathed a sigh of relief.

Lifting her body from the water, he could feel the violence of her shivering as he pulled her up against his chest. Belatedly he realized that he would need something to dry her skin. He pulled the now-dry blanket that he had used when he had first bathed her from the low hanging line, using the tips of his fingers from under her dangling legs.

With the toe of his boot, he shoved the recliner around until it faced the fire from across the room, sitting and settling her nude, shivering body in his lap. He unfolded and spread the blanket over her, patting it gently over her limbs and torso. Once the excess moisture had been absorbed, he discarded the damp blanket and leaned forward to pull the quilt from the bed to cover her shuddering form.

It seemed to Bryce that Carissa snuggled closer to him, her head resting low on his shoulder. Stealing glances at her sleeping face, a great relief washed over him at the serene blissfulness of her expression. He had been successful in reducing the fever that ravaged her body, he only hoped that she would not take another turn before she could recover.

He stroked his large hand over the silken locks of her hair, made damp by the cool water of the bath. He knew he should be changing the wet bandages that clung to her body, but could not help indulging himself in holding her tender softness against the hardness of his own long frame. It had been so long since the last time he had felt the warm touch of skin under his hands, against his body.

To his delight, he felt her face nuzzle against the soft flannel of his shirt. He closed his eyes, savoring the moment with a melancholy pang. Violent emotion, a desire for acceptance, for forgiveness, coursed through his chest to his throat to exit as a groan of low despair.

He was disgusted with himself as he gazed at the pixie that snuggled against him. He was a fool if he thought he would ever see her smile, at least at him. He willed that small, wounded part of him that wished he could feel her arms encircle his neck back inside the stony wall of his inner protection.

He set his jaw and rose from the chair, carrying the sleeping woman to the bed. He again inspected and re-bandaged her frostbitten fingers and toes, as well as the various other injuries on her body with bandages made from his extra set of sheets. By the time he was finished, he wished the floor would open and swallow him whole. Though her face exhibited the damage of abuse and exposure to the elements, he could see that her beauty was incredible. He felt like a monstrous freak in her presence, even if she could not see him, but he refused to give in to the dread of it. Instead, he shored up his defenses with the return of his anger.

Without bothering to dress her, he tossed the bed linens back over her naked body. Skoll resumed his vigil at the bedside of the ailing woman, but Bryce sneered in displeasure and stalked away to view the brightening day outside the window. With his hands tucked into his back pockets, he watched as the snow began to let up and the wind to fall away.

Bryce could no longer stand the inactivity of the cabin, and called to his dog as he donned his coat, hat and gloves. The dog refused to budge from his vigil at Carissa's side, causing the man to sneer again. He stalked from the cabin, banging the door shut on his way out.

Once outside, the awesome beauty of the brilliant wilderness in its new array of pristine white snow struck Bryce. The utter stillness was balm to his angry, injured spirit after the onslaught of agonizing emotions he had experienced through the past two days. With a blanket of winter white nearly two feet thick and with more coming down, it was likely that he would be imprisoned with this feeble woman all winter.

The notion of spending the long winter months with the outsider in his midst was too daunting to fathom. The cabin, though always large enough for him and Skoll, suddenly seemed so much smaller now.

Bryce grabbed the scoop off the front porch, using his anger and frustration at the situation to tear into the snow. He dug a path from the front of the cabin to the large shed out back as his thoughts continued their dismal trail through his dark mind. Clearing the doorway to the shed, he wrenched the door open to find his axe. Once he had cleared a work area around the large woodpile near the shed, he took up the tool.

Setting the first log up on the large tree stump that served as his chopping block, he gave a mighty swing, the gleaming metal plunging downward in the muting snow. The timber flew apart in a splintering volley of kindling under his powerful stroke. He took his impotent anger out on the hapless chunks of firewood as his mind continued its furious rant. *How am I going to get through this?* he thought.

He did not think of the unfortunate situation that had forced Carissa James into the wilderness or that none of this was her choice. He only thought of his own inconvenience and the discomfort of a stranger in his home. Was there nowhere to be safe from the people that plagued the world, and more particularly, his life? How far would he have to go to be assured that he would be left alone?

There was the consideration of his food supplies, as well. Would it be enough with the extra mouth to feed? She was small and probably would not eat much, but the idea of her being trapped here with him, should she survive, sharing his things, being underfoot and making a nuisance of herself was an unpleasant thought. He did not even want to think of trying to clothe her; *she did not even have footwear.*

The muscles of his back and shoulders burned in protest as he took another swing with the axe, forcing him to stop and catch his breath. Looking about him, he saw the results of his restless energy in the copious piles of shattered logs that littered the white ground. Notching the axe into the tree stump, he bent to begin the task of stacking the firewood he had accumulated.

He piled the wood brutally, slamming the sticks onto the tidy piles previously constructed before the onset of cold weather. Most of the strewn wood was stacked when he heard the demented screech of the woman in the cabin. The split logs in his arms scattered over the snow-covered ground as he broke into a dead run for the door of the cabin. Visions of her convulsing body clouded his mind as he fought against the rising panic that threatened to suffocate him.

It was a panting Bryce that threw open the door to discover a naked Carissa scampering across the floor, as if trying to escape from something that he could not see. Skoll whined in distress as he paced the room nervously. Bryce hurriedly closed the door and threw off his coat and gloves, turning to her and speaking in soft tones. Pulling the quilt off the bed, he approached her slowly as she shrank against the bottom of the wall.

"Easy, Carissa, it's okay. I'm here to help," he voiced softly. "No one will hurt you."

She saw him, looking up with huge, glassy eyes. Her hands flew up in front of her, intent upon defending herself from the attacker in her delirium. "No, John, don't!" she cried out.

The pain in her expression, the horror in her eyes, was nearly too much for Bryce. This was not the same demon – or demons – that had plagued her earlier nightmares. This one was someone she knew. Thinking once again about the scars that snaked across the small of her back, he wondered if this "John" had been the man who had created them. He knew a sudden burning hatred of the man, whoever he was.

"Carissa, I'm not John," he cajoled. "I'm Bryce, remember?" He watched her eyes as he slowly moved closer, crawling along the floor with the blanket dragging in his hand.

Confusion crossed her face, furrowing her forehead. "B...Bryce?" she stammered in a quivering voice.

"That's right, Cari, you're safe here."

He was close enough to touch her now but held back, afraid that she would begin struggling again. She did not fight but looked at him, her large eyes still showing her fear as she shivered on the cold floor.

"Where's Alice?" she whispered at the sound of her nickname, still recoiled against the wall.

It was Bryce's turn to be confused. "Who's Alice?"

"My friend," she said as she glanced around the cabin. "My wolf."

Bryce was startled at her words, remembering the sound of the animal that had drawn him and his dog into the wilderness the night they had found her. As her shivering became more violent; however, he had to shove the thoughts aside and deal with how to get her off the floor and back to bed.

"I'm going to cover you, Cari. I have to get you off the floor before you catch your death."

The woman showed no sign of resistance as he moved slowly closer and laid the blanket over her shoulders, pulling it closed around her front. Her fathomless eyes watched him as he slowly took her into his arms, lifting her and carrying her back to the bed at the center of the wall.

As Bryce bent to lay her upon the mattress, she clung to the front of his shirt, not willing to let him go. He could feel her warm breath flowing through the soft fabric as she moaned her protest. Straightening, he was dismayed at this sudden turn. The woman actually wanted him near, wanted to be in his arms, needed the comfort that he could offer.

That feeling of protectiveness surged through him again as his arms tightened about the frail body. All thoughts of anger and imposition dissolved at the sensation of her heated body against his with her hands clinging to him so desperately. He savored the sweetness of it, that small bit of acceptance this injured woman offered him.

Walking carefully around the end of the bed, he sat down on his big chair, cradling her against him, caressing her hair and back, and relishing the solace, the warmth that only another body can give. She was still fevered, but not to the point she had been earlier, which was some small relief. He would keep her alive, will her to live; she would survive; that he vowed.

Holding Carissa, with Skoll periodically sniffing at her sleeping form, Bryce felt that he could know happiness if she could see past what made him so repugnant in the eyes of the world... He stopped his train of thought. *How can I expect her to look at me?* he told himself, furious at the notion. To even allow himself to hope was to set himself up for defeat.

Still, he decided, he could enjoy her now, hold her and feel her soft body pressed to his. Somewhere deep inside a throbbing ache started, spreading its painful tendrils throughout his body and centering in his groin. The problem was only made worse when she stirred on his lap, pressing herself closer to the axis of the issue.

Bryce stifled a groan as her head rolled back, her eyes open, drawing him into their immeasurable depths. She seemed to study him for a long while, though he did not know if she were actually seeing him, or if she were lost in the hallucinations of her illness. His discomfort under such close scrutiny was nearly tangible, but he could not bring himself to look away from her intense gaze.

"I'm sorry," she whispered.

He frowned down at her, confused by her words. "Sorry? For what?"

"I think I'm sitting on you. Am I too heavy?"

Bryce, at first taken aback by her words, started laughing, a deep rumble that started low in his chest. It was an unfamiliar sound to his ears, and it filled the room with its resonance. Carissa smiled slightly, lowering her head and closing her eyes. She was once again asleep, cuddling close to the hardness of his body.

The giant of a man could not help the lightness of mood that began to wash over him, as he chanced to hug her closer. That hope that he had been trying to squelch began to swell again, and this time he let it win. It was too much to dare to expect her to find any attraction for him, but just maybe, he might find in her a friend, a companion, to see him through the long winter months ahead.

There was a slight shiver, still, in her body as she dozed on his lap. His concern was eased some, though, by her apparent lucidity. It would be a long road to recovery for her, he knew, but he felt that she had a good chance at this point. Running his knuckles over her cheek, feeling the roughness of the abrasions mix with the silky texture of the fine skin, he found that she seemed cooler than before, another reason to feel relieved.

There was a small movement under his caressing hand. The sound of the woman smacking her lips made him search his memory for the last time he had attempted to get some liquids into her. This, coupled with the sound of his stomach growling, brought him to the realization that he should fix some food.

As he laid her enwrapped body on the bed, tucking a pillow gently under her head, he realized that it had been at least two days since he had eaten anything. Skoll took his food from a self-feeder in the back of the kitchen, but Bryce had neglected his own needs. With a crooked smile at the sleeping woman, he turned to see about finding something for them to eat.

Removing a package of dried beef from the cabinet once he had entered the kitchen, Bryce decided that a big pot of stew was in order, just the thing to help Carissa regain her strength. Skoll sat on his haunches at the kitchen door, thumping his tail in agreement until the man finally tossed a piece of beef into the air. The dog lifted his head and caught the morsel with little effort, then trotted back to the front room of the cabin.

Peering around the corner, the man had to crook a smile at the bewildering dog. Skoll had taken up his post beside the bed again, his boulder of a head resting on the mattress near the frail woman. Shaking his head, Bryce returned to his task in the kitchen. Once the beef was bubbling in the cast iron pot on the wood stove, he returned to the front room to check on his patient.

Carissa moaned softly, her curled body twitched in the world of dreams that held her trapped. Her skin was still hot, causing more concern for Bryce as he straightened the covers on the bed. She continued to languish in the fever that weakened her diminutive body. Sitting on the chair with his elbows on his knees, his fingers steepled at his mouth, he wondered if there was anything else he could do, could try that would break the fever and end the illness.

He could think of nothing but the clouds of fatigue that plagued his tired mind. As he ran a hand through his tangled, dirty hair, he leaned his head back on the chair. Closing his eyes for a moment, he was assailed with images of the face of a broken woman, bloodied and pained, her silent eyes begging him for mercy, for release from the suffering.

Snapping his body upright, fighting back the images from the past, he cast his blood-rimmed eyes at the woman on the bed. This woman would not be dying, he would see to that. A twinge of panic stabbed his heart; however, as her moans grew louder. She had managed to throw the blankets off her fevered body in her struggles against the specters in her mind.

Sitting on the bed, he dragged the wet cloth over her face and neck again, her eyes popping open at the shocking cold. As he continued to sponge her fevered body down, his hands trembled at the touch of her fiery bare skin under his caress. The feel of the creamy, satiny skin made the ache in his chest – and his groin – all the more acute, and he berated himself for it. How could he allow himself to be aroused by this poor creature who had no defense?

Quick to finish his task, Bryce covered the woman and turned away, taking great gulps of air to steady his nerves. He walked to the kitchen, glad of having something to do that could take his mind off the soft sighs of the ailing woman. Working with his hands had always been a balm for him, even in the kitchen. He tried to think of anything except Carissa as he cut up vegetables and added herbs, watching the pot of gravy bubble the food to fully cooked.

He ladled the stew, now finished, into a bowl and accompanied by a cup of tea that he carried to the bed on a tray. Allowing the thick, rich ragout to cool a bit before trying to wake her, he thought of how she felt in his arms: soft and warm and luscious. She had nestled so sweetly against him, nuzzling his chest and sighing, it was bewitching to think about.

When Carissa stirred on the bed, he was pulled from his musings, nearly blushing as if she could read his wayward thoughts. Her long lashes fluttered open to reveal the magnificent eyes that had so captured his imagination. A wisp of a lonely sigh rushed from his lips as he reached to prop the pillows behind her head. A small smile tugged at the corners of her mouth as he drew nearer, causing a faint skip of his heart.

Spreading a towel over her quilt-draped chest, he offered her a sip of tea. She lifted a hand as if to take the cup, only to allow it drop weakly on the bed, casting her eyes to his face in helplessness. He held the cup of now-tepid amber liquid to her lips with a large hand on the back of her head, supporting her as she drank thirstily.

When he gently slid his hand from behind her head, her eyes slipped closed again. The effort of drinking had taken its toll on her flagging strength. "You must eat," he told her as he held a bowl in front of her to catch the drippings of the spoon he held in his other hand. "Please try," he added with concern in his voice.

She opened her feverish eyes and watched his face as he guided the bite to her mouth. The savory stew settled on her tongue as she closed her mouth before she swallowed.

"It's good," she whispered, her voice a husky rasp.

One corner of his mouth twitched as he concentrated on taking the second spoonful to her swollen lips. Her eyes never left his – disconcerting, to his way of thinking – watching him as if to find some hidden truth. By the third bite, however, her eyelids slipped closed as she moved her head to the side.

"No more... I can't," she murmured hoarsely.

Impotent helplessness furrowed his brow as he slid the spoon back into the bowl, watching as her flushed face expressed the pain she was feeling. Tucking the blanket more securely about her curving shoulders, he settled her more comfortably in the bed, watching as she dropped into a fitful sleep. He lifted the tray from the table and carried it to the kitchen, glancing tentatively over his shoulder at the shivering woman.

There had to be something he was missing, some certain task he could perform that would alleviate her illness. He could think of nothing; he had done all that his training and his common sense dictated. As he dipped a serving of stew for himself, he vowed again that she would live, no matter what he had to do.

He ate as he stood at the old sink, pondering the gentle tenderness in the woman's fevered eyes as she had looked up at him. He knew that she must have a great deal of inner strength to survive all that she had endured, but he was starting to doubt that she had enough left to pull her through this malady. He could lower her temperature but it seemed to always return, higher than before. If it climbed dangerously high again, as it had in the pre-dawn hours, he seriously doubted that she would succeed in surviving a second time.

Old wives' tales held that fevers tended to rise in the night. If the old wives were correct, and with the dark of the long nighttime hours upon them, Bryce was sure that they were in for a rough night. He tidied up in the kitchen, putting the leftover stew off the fire to cool, and washed the dishes before putting them away.

Fatigue plagued Bryce; he had not gotten much sleep since Carissa had fallen into his private world. He had just put a pot of coffee on the old stove when he heard the first wails of pain and fear from the front room. Running into the room, he discovered Skoll on the bed, licking the crimson face and neck of the woman as she cried out against whatever she saw in her fevered delirium.

Ordering Skoll off the bed, he returned to the kitchen to draw a fresh bucket of cold well water and carried it to the bedside table. He stripped the coverings from the nude woman and began swabbing her burning skin as she struggled to fend him off. No matter how fast he worked to bring her temperature down it continued to climb through the late hours of the night.

In desperation, Bryce scooped a bucket of snow from outside the door of the cabin. He mixed the snow with the water, feeling his hands ache from the cold as he dipped the cloth in time after time. Her screams and moans grew louder, voice calling out to the names of people that she knew, asking for her mother, calling to her wolf, Alice. She recoiled from the shockingly cold cloth as he ran it over her fevered body.

He was just about to fill the tub with cold water again as Carissa abruptly fell silent, her muscles relaxing, her breathing and heart rate returning to normal. A fine sheen of sweat covered her face and body, Bryce noted, and she was sleeping peacefully. He ran his hand over her face, the back of her neck, her torso, confirming what he hoped to find; her fever had broken.

Chapter 6

The bright sun, its rays filtering through some opening somewhere, was nudging her eyelids open. Something was wrong, she could feel it in the way her body ached and her head throbbed. Carissa was thirsty and hungry, feeling as if she had just crossed some vast desert. She attempted to move, and as she did so, something moved under her, something warm, hard, and alive.

Alarm, shocking her to full awareness, shot through her mind and body, her muscles tensing. Her eyes flew open to find the soft, muted stripes and squares of plaid – flannel plaid – and buttons. To make matters worse, she suddenly realized that she was completely naked, her body pressed to the side of some unknown man, his arm draped casually about her.

With a small cry, she wrenched her body free of his grasp, skittering away across the mattress of a huge bed, a sheet clutched to her breast. A wave of nausea swamped her, the sudden movement causing her head to spin, the room to swing round. Breathing deeply she found that she could not seem to get enough oxygen, the air around her defying her body's needs. Her stomach threatening rebellion, her head dropped forward between her shoulders as she reached down with one hand to steady herself on the mattress.

The man on the bed stirred, disturbed by her sudden movements, bringing her head up again. Raking her frightened eyes from one end of his body to the other, she could see that he was a giant, probably more than six and a half feet tall. His broad chest expanded enormously and fell again as he breathed his waking breaths. His powerful arms rose, reaching upward to his head, the knuckles of his enormous hands gouging into the flesh of his eye sockets.

The stranger raised his head opening his eyes, searching around until he caught sight of her. She moved farther back, drawing her knees up to her chest protectively under the sheet that she gripped more tightly under chin. His head was covered with an uncombed shock of raven-black hair that tumbled over his shoulders, his face hidden by a huge growth of shaggy beard that seemed to have strips of stark white hair in a strange pattern on one side.

As he rose slowly to a sitting position, the full force of his eyes hit her like a powerful fist. They were dark, a smoky gray that smoldered with some secret fire, haunting and foreboding. His left eye was marked by a swath of scar tissue that stretched over the outside corner, down his cheekbone to disappear into a snowy white stripe interlaced with the stark black beard, the contrasting colors of facial hair converging into a mysterious mask. His mouth, what little she could see of it, twisted downward at the corners as an ominous frown crossed his face. Carissa had the impression of a surly grizzly bear, rudely awakened from hibernation.

Bryce looked at the woman, saw the way she studied his face, knew immediately what she was thinking. She was seeing him for the first time, he knew, now that she was free from the delirium of fever that had taken her to the brink of death. It appeared that she did not like what she was seeing by the expression of fear in her lovely eyes.

He felt the sadness that he knew would come from the devastation of the fragile hope he had held in his heart. He waited for the screams, the accusations, the condemnation that he knew would come as soon as she opened her mouth. Anger, blind and forceful, began to rise in his gorge, making him want to punish himself, to walk out the door into the frozen wilderness and never look back.

"Who are you?" she asked accusingly, swallowing hard against a fresh wave of nausea.

He pulled his sock-covered feet toward himself, drawing his knees up slightly and propping his elbows on them to let his long fingers dangle between his bent legs. "You don't remember?"

Bryce watched as Carissa's delicate brows drew together, her eyes rolling downward as she searched her memory. She seemed almost as if the confusion she was feeling was causing her pain. It was easy to see that she was not yet well by the pallor of her face and the harsh darkness of bruises, so evident on her pale skin, that intensified the hallows of her sunken eyes.

Her eyes met his squarely as she answered. "Should I? I…" her voice trailed off as she continued to study his face in confusion and uncertainty.

He was uncomfortable under that steady, green gaze, tempted to turn his face from her, but forcing himself to remain still. If they were to going to be stuck together, she may as well get used to him right from the start.

"I'm Bryce Matheney. I've been taking care of you."

"Taking care of me?" Her bewildered voice had raised an octave. "It looks like you were taking care of me, all right!"

Despite the whole scene, Bryce was elated at the anger that flashed in the olive depths of her eyes. His fingers itched to take hold of her arms, to crush her to him and hug her until she cried out in protest at his tormenting grip. Instead, he clasped his hands together to keep them at bay.

"You've been ill," he said, his voice deep, soft, gentle. "You nearly died from fever. I've been nursing you through it. I'm glad to see your feeling better."

Still unappeased, Carissa's voice proceeded to rise. "That doesn't explain why you are in bed with me!"

His patience running thin, Bryce took a deep breath, trying to calm his rising anger. "I was tired, if you don't mind. I was up for nearly three days straight."

"Did you have to crawl into bed with me? *This* bed?"

The volume of Bryce's voice raised to match hers, his patience gone. He hated the way she stared at him, as if he were a monster. They all looked at him that way. "It's the only bed I have. Did you expect me to sleep on the floor? It's made out of flat rock!"

He watched as the anger passed from her eyes, replaced by fear once again. He had not meant to frighten her but she was testing him and he had not even had a chance to wake up.

"But, I'm naked..." she whispered softly, tentatively, her voice trailing away to silence.

A new dawning of understanding spread through his mind. He suddenly felt like the monster that everyone down in the world believed him to be, insensitive and cruel. Her fear was not directed at him in particular, but the circumstances in which she found herself. Remembering the injuries that told of the attack on her person, he wanted to kick himself.

"I'm sorry, I didn't think," he said, his voice much more gentle now. "I had to cool you down. I used cold compresses and had to get to your skin. I just didn't think. I should have put you in a shirt or something." His explanation seemed to appease her as she relaxed a bit, her face softening. "I'll get you something to put on."

He moved off the bed, nearly tripping over Skoll who still held his position next to the bed. Hearing the woman on the bed gasp, he turned to see her staring at the massive dog. "That's Skoll," he told her. "He never left your side. He's the one who found you."

"Did you do the bandages?" she asked, while patting the mattress beside her. Skoll moved around to the foot of the bed to better reach her sheathed hand.

"Yeah," Bryce answered over his shoulder. "Wasn't anyone else around to do it." He pulled a drawer open in the old bureau and pulled out a clean shirt. "I know it's not exactly your size," he said as he stepped back to the bed. "But, it will cover you and keep you warm."

Looking up from the shirt in his hands, Bryce froze mid-step. His eyes took in the sight of her, her tangled hair flowing down her nude back as she looked at him over her soft shoulder. The sheet was draped down her front, around the small of her silky back with the sun streaming in on her, a tiny hand resting on the dog's massive head. He felt like he was looking at a painting by one of the great masters.

Shaking his befuddled head and clearing his throat, Bryce quickly handed her the shirt and walked to the kitchen. "I'll fix you something to eat. I hope you like salt pork."

"Please don't go to any trouble," she called back as she slipped her arms into the immense garment. She was tired, almost beyond words, as yet another wave of nausea swamped her body. She felt a weakness come over her, something that was completely unlike her. "What happened to me?"

The noises in the kitchen ceased as Bryce stopped what he was doing. He started to return to the front room but thought better of it. "You decent?" he called from around the corner.

"I guess so," she called back as she wrapped the front of the shirt closed. She had a strong urge to lie down but was unsure of herself.

The large man stepped cautiously through the doorway, watching as she held the shirt tightly closed. Suddenly realizing that she could not possibly close the buttons herself he walked slowly to the bed. "Let me help you with that," he offered softly.

"Um, no. Please. D... don't come near me." Carissa tried to move away from him without falling from the bed while still maintaining her painful grip on the shirt, her injured hands aching from the strain.

Bryce froze. He had been waiting for, had been dreading, this moment since he first saw her half-frozen body in the snow. The rage in him was building, a defense to the pain that shot through his heart to remind him of what he was.

"I d... don't... Please... I smell really bad."

As quickly as it had appeared, the rage dissipated, replaced by something completely out of character for him, a giddy emotion that had him grinning foolishly at the embarrassed woman. A soft pink blush crept into her pale face, adding a touch of color that only made his grin spread his beard all the more.

Carissa buried her face in the feathery, makeshift bandages that enwrapped her damaged hands, forgetting about holding the shirt as it fell slightly open to reveal a hint of the creamy swell of her breasts.

"What's so funny?" she mumbled against her palms.

Bryce cleared his throat as he tried to regain control of his twitching lips. How could he tell her that her embarrassment, her reason for pulling away had pleased him? "Nothing, I just... Would you like a hot bath? I imagine you would feel a lot better if you had one." He watched her, waiting for an answer as his eyes wandered downward, taking in the soft billow of milky flesh the open shirt revealed.

Peeking out from behind her hands, she nodded her flushed face, not trusting her voice. Realizing the direction the man's vision had taken, she once again clumsily grasped the flaps of cloth, closing the shirt over her nudity. Her flush deepened as she ducked her head in the uncomfortable silence that followed.

Bryce turned, embarrassed himself for being caught ogling her body. He strode purposefully into the kitchen to start the task of drawing and heating water for her bath, all thoughts of eating gone. He was at a loss with this pixie of a woman who seemed unperturbed by what he was. She had no judgment in her; it appeared, for she treated him as he would imagine any woman would treat any man in similar circumstances.

That tiny strand of hope started to build again, deep inside his heart, a hope for acceptance – at least on some level. His step felt lighter as he filled two pails of water and carried them to the smoldering fire in the front room. It finally dawned on him that the room was far too cool, and a new concern developed as he turned to see Carissa trying to pull the blankets over her half-naked body.

"I'm sorry," he offered quickly. "You must be freezing." He stepped briskly to the bed, taking hold of Carissa's arms before she could protest. He guided her back to the head of the bed before pulling the warm quilt up along her body and tucking it gently around her delicate shoulders.

"What's with the buckets?" she asked.

He threw a couple of logs onto the embers and thin flames in the grate. "I have to heat the water." Once the large kettle was full, he pushed the hanging metal arm that held it suspended over the fire, and turned to look at her. He rubbed his palms nervously down his denim-clad thighs as he added, "It won't take long. I promise."

Carissa had turned onto her side, drawing her knees up and curling her body under the warm bedding, a frown of confusion on her bruised face. "You have to heat it? You don't have a water heater?"

Bryce tossed more wood onto the fire, poking at it with a long stick from the wood box before adding it to the flames, feeling suddenly confounded about how to explain his way of life to her. Finally, he turned to face the full force of her lovely eyes, their steady gaze once again making him want to hide his face.

"No, I don't have a water heater. I don't have electricity, a phone or any of what you would call the 'modern conveniences.' I heat my house with the fire," he gestured toward the massive stone fireplace. "And the wood stove in the kitchen. I cook on the wood stove, too. I don't really have a lot of needs."

Carissa was beginning to feel as if she had fallen through the looking glass into a world long past. She took a closer look at her surroundings, sitting up to better take it all in, feeling another swirl of dizziness swamp her head. Falling back to lean on her elbows and blinking against the surge of nausea, she cast her eyes slowly about the large room.

The walls were made of what appeared to be logs, their long stretches chiseled and rough looking. Two of the walls, at opposite ends of the room, had windows, two on each end – all but one of them were tightly covered with small diamond-shaped openings in each wooden shutter. A broad fireplace spanned the majority of the wall that stood opposite the bed on which she rested.

At the end of the room to her right and along the same wall lay a doorway that she supposed led to the kitchen. On the same wall at the end to her left was another door that was closed. The wall to her left with the one unshuttered window also had a door, which obviously led outside the building.

There were various pieces of furniture, all of which appeared to be antiques. A large recliner sat next to the bed, looking completely out of place. She decided she must be in some hunting lodge somewhere, but for some reason, could not remember how she had gotten here. Looking up at the big man still standing in front of the fire, she felt more confused than when she first woke naked and in his arms.

"Where am I?" she asked as she felt panic beginning to rise. "Is this a hunting lodge? I don't understand what... How did I get here?"

"This is my home. Skoll and I live here," Bryce stated slowly, watching her face closely and wondering how much, if anything, she remembered about how she had gotten to his cabin.

"You live here? Year round, all the time?"

"Yes. My grandfather built this place. It was the honeymoon cabin that he built for my grandmother."

Carissa took a moment to let this sink in before continuing. "How did I get here? Why am I here?"

"I can't tell you why. I rather hoped you could provide that information, but the how is easy enough to explain. Skoll found you out in the blizzard that blew through here. You were unconscious and nearly dead."

"If I was that ill, why didn't you get me to a hospital?" she asked accusingly.

Bryce sighed deeply, suddenly realizing that she may not have any memory of being in the mountains in the first place. "There was no way to get you to a hospital, especially in the middle of a blizzard. I don't think you realize just how dangerous a mountain bliz…"

"Mountain?" she cut him off with her incredulous voice. "This is a mountain?"

Confusion and fear crossed her face again as she fell back against the pillow, causing Bryce to want nothing more than to comfort her, reassure her that she was safe. "How much do you remember?" he finally asked.

"I can't remember what… I don't know. What happened to me?"

Her olive eyes, growing a shade darker in her deepening fear, pleaded with him for answers that he could not give. He felt helpless, wanting to reassure her, wishing he could offer comfort. He turned from her for a moment, facing the fire and trying to calm the dark anger that was once again beginning to swell, knowing that any effort at consolation from him would be met with rejection.

Clasping the rough-hewn mantle above the fire, his fingers encountered the matchbook he had found on her that night. He had carefully re-wrapped it in the same white cotton cloth that she had used to protect it from the elements. He lifted it, holding it in his large hand and studying it. He wondered if it would jog her memory if she saw it.

Turning to face the fear-stricken woman, he held it up between his thumb and forefinger. "I discovered this in your... clothes after I found you. It was the only possession you carried." He walked to her and placed the item in her outstretched hand before walking into the kitchen.

He drew water into the kettle and put it on the stove to heat, adding more wood and stoking the fire. He returned to the main room and retrieved his pails, taking them back to the sink and filling them again. Then he returned to the big room to pull the bathtub out of its corner, glancing briefly to look at Carissa.

What he saw stopped him in his tracks, so pained was her expression. The woman sat upright, the now-unwrapped matchbook lying in the palm of one bandaged hand, the wrappings dangling from the other hand as it covered her mouth. It was her eyes, though, that held his attention so concentrated, the horror of her returned memories evident in their depths as they swam with tears.

Bryce was at her side in a moment, dropping down to sit on the mattress. Before he realized what he was doing, he had taken her quivering body into his arms, cradling her head against his chest with one big hand, his other stroking gently down the soft flannel that covered her back. She did not pull away, but rather, clung to him as the shaking in her body increased.

He knew she was silently crying for he felt her tears soaking through his shirt to the skin beneath. There was a tenderness in his heart for this woman, an emotion to which he was not accustomed and one that he found he relished. He would gladly hold her this way until the world ended, that small hope at his center growing just a little more.

Carissa pulled away, tilting her head back to look at him, her eyes full of pain and tears. "I'm sorry. I didn't mean to fall apart."

She was still so near that he could feel the warmth of her body against his, still had his hands on her arms. His gaze trailed briefly lower to discover that the shirt covering her nakedness had fallen open again, revealing the valley of soft flesh between her satiny breasts. "No need to apologize," he said, his voice low and gruff. "I know you've been through a lot."

He was uncomfortable again under the unwavering scrutiny of her tear-filled eyes. He reluctantly released her, his fingers itching in protest at letting her go. He rubbed his hands together as he walked to the corner to lift the copper bathtub, carrying it to the kitchen. He left her alone with her thoughts as he busied himself with preparing her bath.

Carissa lay back against the pillow, her mind spinning with the memories that had come flooding back. The nausea hit her hard in a fresh wave that had nothing to do with the illness that had weakened her body. The fear, the revulsion of being touched by the man named Kyle came back in torrents that she was hard-pressed to control.

A loud banging noise brought her out of her reverie, causing her to glance in the direction of the kitchen where she saw Bryce, a hammer in his hand pounding nails into the top of the doorframe, a large tarp dangling over the entrance.

"What are you doing?" she asked, her voice small and strained.

Glancing at her with a nail protruding from the hair that surrounded his mouth, he lowered his arms and removed the nail from his lips. "I thought you might like to have some privacy for your bath," he stated simply before returning to his task. Driving in the last nail, he tested the drape of the tarpaulin to make sure it would fully cover the opening. "There you are, all ready for you."

Carissa was embarrassed at all the effort he was making on her behalf. She was weak as a kitten and completely dependent upon his help, a feeling of which she was not fond. Looking at the bandages on her hands, she wondered how she would possibly remove them. Finally, determined not to beg for help like the invalid that she had become, she brought one hand to her mouth to bite at the wrappings.

"Here," he said as he rushed to her side. "Let me."

Bryce took one of her hands in his, smoothing the covered palm gently with one long finger. He lifted a pair of scissors off the table beside the bed, cutting carefully at the white fabric. As the dressings opened, layer by layer, he lifted the cloth away with meticulous care, inspecting each stretch of damaged skin as it was revealed.

Carissa watched his actions, amazed at how gentle his hands were. They were so large and yet so dexterous, so precise in their action, the long, tapered digits graceful and limber. Carissa had the impression of an artist or a musician as she watched him, the sensation of his fingers caressing the flesh of her palm as he finished the first hand sending a tiny shiver up her spine.

"Looks like they're starting to heal," he said off-handedly, as he reached for her other hand.

Once he had finished her hands and had removed the few small bandages from her arms, he pulled the bedding from her legs without warning, causing her to wince in pain as she desperately grabbed at the front of the over-sized shirt, attempting to cover herself. She felt herself blushing again as she realized that she had been completely exposed from the waist down.

Bryce caught a glimpse of soft, dark hair and creamy skin as he pulled the blanket down, the sight at once appealing and devastating for him. Mentally he admonished himself, for he had already seen, and to some extent felt, everything she had to hide. However, it was somehow different now that she was awake and alert. He had seen it, though, just before her swollen fingers showed her humiliation by quickly closing the garment over it, adding a feeling of shame to his already nearly over-whelming mix of emotions. Her nearness was driving him to distraction and making him feel surly.

"All done," he announced, carefully setting the scissors aside after removing the bandage from her head and holding his hands out to her. "It's going to hurt to stand. You really shouldn't try to use your hands or feet for a few more days until they have more of a chance to heal. I'll carry you in so you can take your bath."

This was another humiliation and one she had no intention of being forced to bear. "I'm sure that won't be necessary. If you will just move aside, I'm sure I can manage."

His irritation mounting, he moved away from the bed to allow her to discover for herself just how painful frostbite can be. Immediately after coming to that decision he was sorry; however as she cried out in agony upon putting her slight weight on her feet. The moment she stood, she fell back on the bed, water seeping from the corners of her clenched eyes. The flannel shirt she wore, his shirt, fell open over her thighs, allowing another glimpse of her soft skin.

The titillating sight of her bare thighs, coupled with the concern he felt for the pain that had hit her so hard, galvanized him into action. Ignoring her heated protests, he scooped her into his arms and carried her to the kitchen, setting her on a chair that he had installed next to the tub.

"Now, do you want me to help you get into the tub?" He fairly growled out the question, the frustration in his body starting to show.

"N... no, I think I can manage." She hated the stammer in her voice, showing her nervousness.

"Fine," he replied irritably. "Yell if you need me. I'll be in the next room." He stalked from the room, throwing the tarp closed over the doorway and leaving her to ponder his shift in moods.

"What an asshole," she muttered after him.

Chapter 7

"How's it coming in there," Carissa heard Bryce's impatient voice call. It was all too embarrassing, this helplessness that she felt. She had managed to wash herself with the thick bar of soap he had provided, but it was slow going with hands so stiff and aching. She desperately wanted to wash her hair, but found no shampoo, not to mention that she did not have the strength to lift one of the extra buckets of warm water that stood on the floor nearby.

"I... I'm hurrying as fast as I can," she muttered testily at the tarped doorway that faced the old copper tub. The hot bath felt good now, but at first, the water had burned at the injuries that slashed through her tender skin. She would have loved to soak, to allow the heat of the water to wash away the aches and pains that gripped her body, making the slightest movement difficult. The man in the other room, however, was not going to allow her to relax. She could hear his restless steps on the stones of the floor as he paced back and forth in front of the doorway.

She had to wonder about how he had come to be isolated in this winter-locked cabin without so much as the convenience of electricity or the security of a phone. The scar that she saw near his eye and the strange discoloration of his beard also had her wondering. Had he been in an accident? Was he injured in a fight? Was he scarred fighting in one of the recent wars that continued to trouble the nation?

There was also the matter of his quicksilver change of moods that gave her real cause for worry. Carissa had seen people behave this way before, usually as a symptom of some mental illness such as bipolar disease. A thin shudder ran through her as the thought of being holed up in a secluded cabin with a deranged maniac gave her a stab of fright. What if the man truly was certifiably insane?

So many questions ran through her mind when it came to the man who called himself Bryce Matheney. There was one obvious fact; she was trapped with a stranger, and that was enough to scare her. Being naked and in a tub of water with nothing more than a thin stretch of cloth between them did not help matters either. She felt completely vulnerable to the whims of the giant in the other room, causing her to hurry her movements and become careless.

"Ouch! Dammit!" she cried as she banged her tender knuckles on the side of the tub, dropping the soap with a loud splash into the water.

"What is it? Are you all right?"

Carissa looked up from her now-bleeding hand to see the big man looming over her, dwarfing her as she sat in the murky water. Her hands flew to reflexively cover her breasts, horrified that he was looking at her.

"What are you doing?" she squealed at the sight of him. "Get out!"

Bryce spun round, presenting his back to her and ducking his head. "I thought you'd hurt yourself. I thought you needed help."

"You thought you could just come in here and get an eyeful is what you thought!" She was yelling at him, a reaction to the start his sudden presence had given her. She wanted to take back the words almost immediately as she watched his head come up rigidly and his back stiffen.

"I only came in here to offer my assistance," he ground out.

The dejected sound of his voice touched that part of her that was womanly and soft, a place that held her kindness and compassion. She knew she had hurt his feelings somehow, a thought that gave her little comfort. She fought past her embarrassment to search for some way to soothe his offended sensibilities.

"I... I'm sorry. You startled me is all," she stammered quietly.

"Sorry," he said gloomily. "If you don't need me then..." his voice trailed away as he waited for a response, standing stiffly, his head turned slightly to one side.

"I just...I," she stuttered, searching for the right words.

"What is it?" he demanded his deep voice booming.

"If you will just calm down," she retorted. "I was wondering if you have any shampoo."

His shoulders seemed to relax a little as he sighed deeply. "No. I don't. You will have to use the bar of soap to wash your hair. Sorry, but I'm not set up to accommodate *women*."

Carissa bristled under the way he said the word "women", as if to insult her. "Oh," she said impotently. "It's no big deal. It's just... I can't really..." She felt like a stammering idiot under the cloud of his anger. What had she done to irritate him so?

"What's the problem?" he growled over his shoulder.

"Never mind," she said, trying to sound unconcerned. "I'll figure out a way to rinse the soap out. Don't let me keep you. I'll be fine."

Carissa watched while he rolled his head a little to the side as he brought his shoulders up, heard the way the air hissed trough his teeth as he inhaled sharply. "I didn't even think how you were going to do that. I could help you, if you want. I promise not to look."

"Well, I suppose you've already seen it all, since you're the one who undressed me." She could not help the embarrassed smile that pulled at her lips or the heated blush that crept up her neck.

His voice was much softer when he asked, "All right to turn around now?"

Carissa drew her knees to her chest, wrapping her arms around them and leaning forward, the water sloshing lightly around the edges of the tub. "Yes," she said nervously. "You can turn around now."

Bryce was visibly shaken by the sight of her, with her dark, burnished curls falling down her back, complimenting the soft richness of her creamy skin. She looked up at him slowly, the deep green of her eyes showing brightly in the warm glow of the lamplight as a pink blush suffused her face. Looking at her, he could no longer see the wounds that marred her delicate flesh. He could only see the woman that was splendidly and uniquely her.

"Is anything wrong?" she asked timidly.

Her words, so softly spoken, jerked him from his reverie, reminding him of why he was there looking at her feminine beauty in the first place. The knowledge that he had been ogling her, feasting upon her with his eyes, had him feeling like a lecher. Stepping forward in a lurching motion, he grabbed the first of the two buckets that stood beside the tub.

"Ready?" he asked, his voice husky.

"Let 'er rip," she replied.

As soon as the water hit she let out a shriek. "It's cold!" her startled voice squeaked.

"Oh, sorry," Bryce mumbled as he reached for the kettle on the stove. "Things cool off pretty quick in this weather." He poured some of the hot water into the remaining bucket and the rest into her bath. "That should help." He refilled the kettle at the pump, replacing it on the stove and adding a few more sticks to the fire.

"That feels better. Thanks," she said with a slight chatter to her teeth.

Carissa kept her knees up, tightly shielding her breasts as she fished the cloudy water for the fallen bar of soap. Upon finding it, she tried to gather her hair without exposing too much of her body. She felt his strong fingers take the soap from her as he slowly collected the long tresses. She thought to protest but the touch of his fingertips brushing the skin of her back, sending shivers down her spine, was distracting her thoughts.

She was struck again by the gentle sensuousness of his large hands as they worked the lather into her hair and scalp. Once or twice, his fingers touched places on her head that were sore, but his touch was so light that she felt no pain. She closed her eyes in satisfaction only to be flustered to hear a small moan escape her lips at the pure luxury of having him perform such an intimate service.

Bryce took longer than needed to lather and cleanse her head as he knelt on the floor, so caught up was he in the arousing effects of touching her – and with her full knowledge and consent. More than once his fingers grazed the silken flesh of her graceful neck and soft shoulders. Her body seemed to draw toward his hands as a purring moan escaped her throat, causing a throbbing ache deep in his groin.

He felt decidedly warmer as he lingered over his task, relishing the rich texture of her hair tangled around his fingers. When finally he felt he could not delay any longer, he stood and lifted the second bucket, testing the temperature of the water with the tip of one finger. He watched her for a moment longer, basking in the loveliness of her wet, soapy skin and the graceful curve of her spine as she bent forward.

"Ready for more water?" his shaking voice asked.

"Yes," she whispered softly, still caught up in the sensuality of the moment.

He moved slowly this time, carefully pouring the water in a thin stream over her down-turned head, viewing the movements of her hands as they lifted the tresses into the stream and wishing they were his own. When the pail was empty, he could still see soap bubbles glistening in her hair, and reached for the kettle that was still warming on the stove. He tested the temperature on his open palm before he poured it, straight from the kettle, onto her waiting head.

Carissa pushed the dripping hair back from her face as she tilted back her head to look at him, a lush smile on her lips. "Thank you for your help," she fairly purred.

Bryce was dazed by the dreamy look of her clouded eyes. He wondered if this is what she would look like after making love. Dismayed by the path that his thoughts were taking and frustrated by the reaction of his undisciplined cock, he fairly stumbled backwards, trying to regain control of his body. He felt like a clumsy fool and wanted to get out of there before he made a real ass of himself.

"Do you need anything else?" he asked abruptly. "Can you get out of the tub by yourself?" The olive color of her eyes darkened as the spell of tranquility was broken by his sullen voice, making him curse himself silently.

"No," she answered coldly. "I think I can manage." Her face turned from him in dismissal.

Carissa watched his tense frame as he stalked from the room, leaving the tarp to quiver over the doorway at his departure. The man's sudden changes of humor were starting to get on her nerves.

A few minutes later, as she sat in the kitchen chair with her hair wrapped in a towel, and her body draped once again in the cavernous shirt he had given her to wear, she called out to the other room.

"You can come in now."

She watched as Bryce slowly peeled back the edge of the draping tarp to peer uncertainly into the room. The sight of the big man peeking in as shyly as a little boy amused her. She could not hide the impish smile that curved her mouth or the mocking twinkle in her eyes. If not for the fact that he was a total stranger and they had been thrown together under some very difficult circumstances, she would have laughed outright.

The dark frown that clouded his smoky eyes only served to tickle her further as she drew her bottom lip into her mouth, wincing in pain as she bit down on the tender, cracked flesh in an effort to stem her giggles. She plunged her head forward, unable to look at him without bursting out laughing.

"Has something funny occurred?" he asked in an imperious tone.

The sound of his voice, the tone, and the words he used proved to be her undoing, her body shaking as she tried to keep her laughter silent. She dared not answer him for fear of hurting his feelings once again, but she could not stop the giggles that bubbled up. Bringing one hand to her mouth to silence the peals of laughter, the shirt fell open slightly at the top, revealing the soft flesh that held his fascination.

"Why are you laughing?" he asked, his bewildered voice growing louder.

"I... I'm sorry," returned her wavering voice. She cleared her throat and lifted her gaze to meet his, desperately trying to wipe the smile from her face. He looked like a thundercloud ready to burst, so dark were his eyes. His entire body bristled with indignation, only serving to make the situation more humorous to her, bringing her hand to her mouth again.

"What's so funny?" he demanded.

Carissa let her hand drop as she grinned playfully up at him. "Anyone ever tell you that you're cute when you're angry?"

She watched as the tension left his body in one massive flood, giving him an easy, relaxed posture. The mass of hair that covered his face spread wide, rounding outward at the sides as he grinned back at her. The clouds that had shadowed his gray eyes evaporated, the smoky depths flashing with pure delight. She could swear that she saw him blushing brightly under his beard.

"Well," he started as he shifted his weight from one foot to the other. "I can't say they have."

"You're blushing!" she exclaimed, her mirth rising.

"I am not!" Bryce tried to look stern with his brows drawing together ominously, but the effect was lost to the absurd smirk that still quivered on his mouth. He was charmed beyond words by her playful banter, and that weak hope he nurtured grew a little stronger.

"Oh, stop trying to scare me," she laughed. "I've seen the real you, so knock it off."

He gave in at last, laughing with her and enjoying the sensation of it. The sound of her giggles was like music in the loneliness of his empty life. "You think you're onto my act, huh?"

"Yep," she said, clutching at the gaping shirt again. "You've seen me naked now so I guess there's no use trying to distance yourself with glowering looks." Carissa looked down at the shirt, trying to capture one of the buttons in her sore, inflexible fingers.

Bryce reached forward and nudged her fingers aside, easily slipping the little buttons through the holes. The heat of her skin filtered through the fabric to his hands, tempting him to touch her, feel her warmth against his palms. Her fragrance, tinged with a hint of the woodsy sent of the homemade soap that Clancy brought him in his supply runs, was captivating, as was the way her seductive eyes watched his face while he finished his task.

"So," she said, aiming her olive eyes at him, the smile still on her lips. "When do I get out of here?"

Bryce, realizing she still did not understand the reality of her situation, could not quite meet her eyes. "When the snow thaws."

"So we just have to wait for a warm spell and I can go?"

"Carissa," he finally looked at her squarely. "There are no warm spells up here until spring." He watched as the smile faded from her face and the light faded from the room.

"Spring?" she whispered. "Not until spring?" Her eyes grew wide, haunted, frightened.

"Yes, Cari, spring," he replied softly. "I guess you're not from around these parts. Mountain winters start early and there are no breaks until spring."

"But... but," she stammered, horrified. "I have to get home. I have to get home to my babies!" Her voice rose in volume and pitch as she spoke, panic showing in her bruised eyes. "I have to get home!"

"I'm sorry. There's no way out till the snow melts." That strengthening ribbon of hope began to weaken again, knowing that she wanted out, and apparently with good reason.

The sadness and fear in her eyes turned to anger and then to rage. Bryce watched the change that came over her, waiting for her emotions to turn to hate, wishing he could hear her laugh again.

"You're lying," she accused. "Why are you trying to keep me here?" She was shaking from head to toe, her face growing pale, her lips set in a grim line.

"I'm not trying to keep you here!" he retorted sharply. "If it were up to me you would never have been here in the first place. I liked my life just fine the way it was. Having a sick woman on my hands is the last thing I need."

He'd injured her, he knew it the moment the words left his mouth, and he immediately wanted to take them back. He rushed forward as she painfully pulled herself to her feet, the strain etching white lines around her mouth. As he reached out to support her, she batted him away, straightening her back and refusing any offer he made. Without another glance in his direction she walked slowly from the room, her spine arrow straight, her head held high.

"Dammit!" he swore under his breath after she was gone. For a brief moment he had seen her smile at him, laughing and bringing a warmth to his heart that he had not felt in years. Just like the changing of the winds, that moment was gone and she was angry, had accused him of keeping her prisoner. He sighed heavily as he began to empty the tub, the scent of her still lingering in the air.

* * * *

Carissa had refused to speak to him the remainder of the day, had refused to look at him as he tried to speak to her. The sadness on her face brought darkness to the entire cabin. Even Skoll was inconsolable as he uncharacteristically spent the day lying in front of the fire. Now, as the wind picked up and night brought it's dismal loneliness, Bryce began to wonder if all the long months of the entire winter season would be as dreary as this day had been.

He had tried several times to get her to eat, but she had merely turned away from the proffered food, choosing to lie quietly upon the mattress, staring without seeing anything. Tossing another log on the fire, he decided it would be best if he slept in the recliner that he had returned to its regular position in front of the hearth.

As he tried to make his long frame comfortable in the old chair, his mind clouded with the turn his life had taken since the damnable woman had fallen into his lap. He had been at peace with his solitude, but now he found himself wanting nothing more than to be able to listen to the jingle of her laughter every day for the rest of his life. The sound of it was comforting and joyful, and he wanted it as he had never wanted anything else, a thought that darkened his mood further as he stared into the crackling fire.

The sound of her voice, the horror he had heard in it, when she finally discovered that they would be stuck together until spring, was a cold reminder of why he had become the hermit he now was. People were cruel animals, feeding on the misfortunes and weaknesses of others. They could offer you the world one minute and destroy your hopes the next, and this woman was certainly no exception. She had been nice to him, thinking he would do what she wanted, and then turned against him the minute she found out that he would not be able to get her down the mountain.

Hearing a soft whimper, he glanced back at the woman who was sleeping on his bed. He watched as she tossed lightly before settling, again, pulling herself into the fetal position. She looked damned appealing, dressed only in his shirt after having kicked the blankets from her soft body, the shirttail riding high upon her thighs. Turning back to the fire, he thought back to that morning, seeing her immersed in the old bathtub with her hair flowing about her. He adjusted the crotch of his trousers around the burgeoning stiffness and the ache he felt there. She had been so beautiful, smiling, and later, teasing him.

There was a moan from the bed behind him, causing him to peer behind his chair again. Carissa was on her belly now with one leg bent away from her body; the tail of the shirt had ridden up so far that it barely covered the firmly rounded flesh of her bottom. He groaned out his frustration and rubbed his tired eyes. He was being unfair to her, he knew. None of this was her fault. She was a victim of horrible circumstances that kept her from the people that she loved, and he was not one of them.

Sighing deeply, he stood with Skoll on his heels to draw the sheet and quilt back up her shivering body. Knowing that it was not her fault only served to make the whole situation even more unnerving, knowing that if she had been given a choice she would be anywhere but with him. *But who would choose to be with you?* he asked himself. Returning to his chair by the fire, he knew real self-loathing, wishing he could throw the past away and start again. His chagrin only mounted as he realized that if he had been given the chance, the woman he would choose to start all over with would be this elfin creature that had dazzled his heart.

Bryce dropped into a fitful sleep, images of a tiny woman with a musical laughter dancing in his dreams.

Chapter 8

The next few days were no departure from the angry mood set by her first day back in reality. He was beginning to think he had preferred her in the throes of delirium than the cold, distant, unhappy woman she was now. The tension in the air of his once-peaceful mountain cabin had become nearly unbearable. Even Skoll had responded to it, hiding his big frame in the corner of the main room, or preferring to be outside.

When he had awakened, his body stiff and his muscles cramped in the confines of the old recliner, it was to the soft sounds of her movements in the kitchen. As he sat upright, he noticed that the room was tidy and the bed was stripped bare to the mattress. He could smell the inviting aroma of coffee, and followed the fragrance, intent upon investigating. He found her behind the tarpaulin, at the sink working diligently at washing the laundry that had piled up since her illness. A large wicker basket on the floor held wet sheets, washed to white brilliance, and on the stove was his big wash cauldron, boiling away at the towels and other linens he had used in his care of her.

"What's going on in here," he asked peevishly, dismay written all over his face.

"I'm doing the laundry. If you want me to wash what you're wearing, I suggest you go change."

Her reply had been short and clipped, and Bryce had decided that he was not pleased with the new attitude that had come over her. "That's not necessary. I can manage it." He had spoken more harshly than he had intended, watching as her back stiffened.

She had turned her tired eyes to him, her pale face betraying the weakness of her still-recovering body. "I will cook for you. I will clean for you. This way I can earn my keep, and as soon as humanly possible, you will take me off this god-forsaken mountain. That's the deal and the only one I have to offer. I recommend you take it." Without waiting for a response, she had turned her back on him again to finish off what she had in the sink and deposit the wet towels into the waiting basket.

Moving to the old wood stove, she had opened the oven and removed a pan of what could only be biscuits, perfectly browned and soft. She set the pan on the side table with a bang, returning to the stove to lift the heavy coffeepot. She likewise had slammed the big pot down, causing the table service to clatter against the rough surface loudly. "Sit," she had commanded, gesturing rudely at the table.

Returning to the stove, she had removed the lid from a skillet and had carried it to the table, forking crisp pieces of fried salt pork onto his plate before slamming the skillet back onto the stove. Using a large wooden spoon, she had snagged the linens to remove them from the boiler to the cooler water in the pan set in the sink. She had then vigorously scrubbed the towels over the washboard before depositing them into the rinse water.

"Carissa, you're going to tire yourself out. You'll get sick again," he had hated the tense anger in her posture, and that she felt obligated to do these chores.

She had turned then; her eyes had been green ice as she had glared at him. "You don't have to worry. I'll never be a burden to you again."

For nearly a week since, her attitude had not changed as she had continued to fix all the meals and clean things that did not need cleaning, anything to keep herself busy and away from him. For his part, Bryce, unable to bear the constant angry strain of her silence and busy putterings, had found more and more excuses to be outside and away from the cabin. They had not spoken to each other in days, and Carissa had been taking all her meals separately from him, eating only enough to keep her body alive.

Now, as she slept fitfully in the large recliner, as she had insisted, he was nearly fed up with the cold, stiff silence and the way he was made to feel like a stranger in his own home. He was determined to end it, to have it out with the angry pixie, even if it meant the risk of angering her further.

"Carissa," he said less than gently. "Carissa, wake up."

She stirred sleepily in the chair, slowly uncurling her legs, opening her eyes and gracing him with a groggy expression. "What is it? Do you want me to fix you something to eat?"

"*No!*" he snapped before he could catch himself. He closed his eyes and took a deep breath before looking at her again. "I want to talk to you. We need to get some things straight." He pulled up a rocking chair to sit facing her as he waited for her to fully awaken.

Stifling a yawn, she pulled herself upright in the recliner, an irritated expression on her tired face. Bryce noted that she still looked peaked, her frame far too thin, her skin far too pale. She was working herself to death in her misery and loneliness for her family.

Her surly voice interrupted his thoughts, forcing him to focus on her words. "It's still dark. This couldn't wait till morning?"

"No, it couldn't. This has to stop."

"What?"

"This… thing," he said for lack of a better word. "You and I need to come to an understanding. You don't like me, fine. I can deal with that. Maybe you even hate me. I can deal with that too. What I can't deal with is walking on eggshells in my own house."

"You want me to leave? Great, I'd love to. Tell me how to get off this fucking mountain and I'm gone." She bit every word off, emphasizing the anger flashing in the liquid-fire depths of her olive eyes.

Bryce ran a hand over his forehead, frustration building to the point where he wanted to tear the cabin down around her ears. He was so tired, too tired to keep living in the crackling tension that hissed around them.

"There is no way," he replied more calmly than he felt, "to leave here. The snow is too deep. The landscape under it is treacherous. Another storm could come up without warning, and the nearest road is a four-day walk. That's four days without the snow, much longer with it."

"Bullshit," she spat. "I wasn't out there four days before you found me. I was only out there a couple of days."

He glanced up sharply, looking her squarely in the eye and searching for answers. "That's not possible. The only safe passage takes at least four days."

"All I know is I spent one night out there. The last thing I remember is it was getting dark, and then I woke up here."

"We're getting off the subject," Bryce intoned, trying to still his rising anger. "I want to clear the air here. We have to come to an understanding, because I can't deal with this constant hostility. Winter up here lasts a long time. I don't want that time to be spent at each other's throats."

A cold smile crossed her lips, a smile that did not reach her eyes. "Well, ain't that just too bad. I want to go home."

A white-hot sensation was slithering its way up his spine as a buzzing noise sounded in his ears. "I promise I'll take you to the nearest town as soon as the weather breaks," he growled out. There was just no way of reaching the woman.

Carissa saw the warning light in his eyes, but paid no heed as she charged recklessly onward. "What is your angle? You just keeping me here so you won't get lonely? Is that it? Because, I have to tell you, this is kidnapping just as surely as if you had taken me from my home. It's called unlawful restraint, and it's a felony."

Bryce stood, rising slowly from the rocker, his fists clenching spasmodically at his sides. Taking a step forward, his dark, forbidding face looming over her, he spoke in soft, menacing tones that she had to strain to hear. "Be careful, woman. Don't go too far."

Carissa, looking up at the dark giant with his smoky eyes clouded in anger, felt the cold fist of fear clutching her heart. For a moment, he was no longer the uncivilized mountain man, but the cruel monster of her ex-husband, standing over her, poised to strike, to punish her for whatever wrong she had committed. In her mind, at that moment, she was back in the world of pain and torment, fighting for her life.

Wrapping her arms over her head in a protective stance, she had used too often, her shrill voice cried out, "No! Please don't!"

The horror in her eyes hit Bryce as a blow to the head, staggering him backward away from the tiny, cowering woman. He watched as she clenched her body into a defensive ball, reminding him of a small, wounded animal. The plea in her terrified voice tempered the anger that burned in his mind and deflated the animosity that had been growing.

Remembering the scars that wended across the lower portion of her back, he cursed loudly, unclenching his fists and digging the heels of his hands into his eyes. Taking several deep breaths in an effort to calm himself, he turned to feed more fuel into the fire and collect his thoughts. He desperately wanted to take her into his arms, to comfort her and assure her that she was safe, but he knew that she would never allow it, would fight him and hurl more accusations at his head. He was angry and frustrated with no knowledge of how to reach her, to tell her that he only wanted to see her happy again.

"I would never hit you, Cari," he said softly into the fire, his back still turned to her. "I would never hurt you."

Carissa lowered her arms slowly to glare at him; uncertainty and fear – and the pain of memories – gave her the desire to flee, to be free of him and this place. She knew she should be grateful to him for all he had done, but the visions of her two small children crying for their mother were tearing at her heart, coupled with the fear of what their father would do to them should he get his hands on them. She just could not bring herself to believe that there was no way out, that she would be here, pining for her family, not knowing what was happening, throughout the long winter months.

Seeing Bryce's slumped shoulders and dejected posture, however, made her feel selfish and ungrateful. She had been mean to him, had done everything possible to make his life miserable, and the thought brought guilt crashing in on her.

"I'm sorry, Bryce. I haven't been very nice to you, have I?"

"No." The sound of her soft voice sent a thrill up his spine, ebbing away at the anger.

"And I never thanked you for saving my life."

"No," he answered again, staring into the flames.

"I am grateful, please know that. But I have to get home. My children need me."

He turned then, to see her grief-stricken face, so lovely and forlorn. "I wish I could do something, but you wouldn't survive the first night out there. Another bout with frostbite, and you'd lose parts of your feet and hands. You still haven't recovered, and a few hours of wading through the snow would kill you. Even if you were well enough, I still wouldn't take you out of here, not in winter. The chances of making it alive are pretty slim. One sudden storm and we'd both freeze to death. Don't you get it?"

Anger flashed in her eyes again, just briefly, before her expression changed to one of abject sadness. Finally, she was resigned to her fate as she leaned her head back against the upholstery and sighed. The flames of the fire cast a soft glow on the planes of her face, the effect giving her the appearance of a lost child, scared and alone. He watched as the minutes moved slowly by, waiting for whatever came next and wishing he could see her smile one more time. It was with somber eyes that she turned her attention back to his face.

"So that's it, then. I'm trapped here and there's nothing that I can do about it."

Carissa turned back to the fire before she saw the hurt in his eyes. Bryce turned from her, walking back to the bed and sitting on the edge with his head in his hands. The winter was going to be long indeed, if he had to spend it staring at her mournful face, wishing for something that she would never offer. He lay down with his arm draped over his eyes, thinking about another woman, her bright smile and laughing voice comforting him, telling him of her love.

Bryce awoke with a start. He was covered with a clammy sweat, his body rigid as the images of a foul dream still danced in his head. Something warm rested on his shoulder, a soft caress of kindness. His eyes opened to find Carissa sitting beside him on the bed with concern etched in her tired eyes.

"You were having a bad dream," she said soothingly. "Are you all right?"

Confusion clouded his mind as her words tried to penetrate, their meaning escaping his befuddled thoughts for a moment as he glanced around the cabin. It was daylight and he wondered how long he had slept. Looking back at the woman beside him, he managed to regain his focus as his body became more alert. The scent of her was intoxicating, and her proximity to him on the bed was enough to make his body react. He brought a knee up under the sheet to hide his obvious arousal, feeling like a boy caught in the bathroom with a pornographic magazine. The idea had him smiling sheepishly as he glimpsed the infinite deep green of her eyes.

"I'm fine," he replied as he pushed himself up and back to a sitting position against the headboard. As an after-thought, he brought a pillow around to cover his groin and rested his hands on top of it. "I'm sorry if I woke you."

She cocked an eyebrow at his action but decided not to pursue it. "You didn't. I've been up for hours. I thought you would sleep all day, though."

Glancing out the window, he could see that the sun already sat high in the morning sky. "I don't usually sleep like that."

"You needed the rest. I guess I've been kinda rough on you. I'm sorry, Bryce." She graced him with a sardonic smile. "Mom always told me that I could drive the temperance league to drink. I have a nasty temper."

Scratching his head and grinning foolishly, he decided that he could gaze into her eyes forever and never see all that she was. "That's okay. I have a pretty wicked temper myself."

"So I noticed," she retorted softly, one perfectly arched eyebrow cocking upward. She stood suddenly, patting his arm. "If you feel like hauling that big carcass of yours out of bed, there are some biscuits in the kitchen and I'm cooking lunch."

Still grinning, he tossed the sheet aside and swung his legs off the bed. She turned to look at him from a few feet away; the light of laughter had returned to her eyes giving him a warm feeling in the pit of his belly.

"Nice undies," she laughed.

He looked down at the black long handles that encased his legs, then back up at her smiling face. "At least I don't run around half-naked wearing nothing more than an over-sized shirt."

"Well," she retorted, warming to the teasing tone in his voice. "If someone hadn't cut my slacks up and tossed them on the fire, I might have something else to put on."

"Yeah," he said, standing and stretching his long arms over his head, "But then I wouldn't have the treat of your slim legs flashing around me."

Bryce wanted to kick himself, wishing he could take back the words the minute they were spoken. Ducking his head to hide his embarrassment, he turned and busied himself with making up the bed, waiting for the accusations to fly from her mouth.

She did not hit him with accusations. She did, however, hit him with the wet dishtowel she had been holding – right between the shoulder blades. He heard her indignant gasp just before it hit and her boisterous giggles disappearing into the kitchen after. Bending to retrieve the discarded towel from the floor, he carried it back to her, still grinning foolishly.

Without looking up from the pot she was stirring, she began to speak, "Bryce, I will try to be more pleasant around here. I want you to know that I truly am grateful to you for saving me. It's a debt I'll never be able to repay. The only thing I ask is that you be patient with me. I tend to fly off the handle when I'm pissed, but I don't mean anything by it, okay?"

"I can live with that," he said as he swung his leg over the back of a chair and lowered himself onto the seat. "As long as you make biscuits like this, I can forgive a lot." Snagging a cold biscuit, he clamped his teeth down, savoring the texture of the treat. He looked up to see her staring at him with mock indignation in her fiery eyes, her hands on her hips. "What?" he asked with a full mouth.

"Look at you. I feel like I need to vacuum that bushy beard of yours. You have crumbs all over you. Don't you ever trim that thing?"

He hurriedly brushed at his face, trying to dislodge the crumbling morsels. Swallowing, he looked at her, embarrassment climbing up his neck. "I never saw the need to."

"Well, it needs it, and your hair, too. You look like a grizzly."

He set the biscuit down, uncomfortable under her scrutiny but meeting her gaze directly. "I don't... I'm usually alone up here. I don't usually think about my appearance."

Carissa cocked her head to one side, curiosity written on her face. "How often do you go to town?"

"Never," he stated emphatically as he turned to finish his breakfast.

"Never?" She could not believe that he was so very withdrawn from the world.

"Nope. Never."

"But... how do you get your supplies?" She opened a cupboard, exposing canned goods and sundry items. "How do these things get here?"

With a sigh, he set his second biscuit back on the plate. He turned to face her, spying the disbelief in her lovely eyes. "A man named Clancy comes up here twice a year with a load of goods. I write him a check that he takes back to a bank and cashes. I supplement those supplies with the meat I kill, the fish I catch, and the few things I harvest from the forest." He watched as her eyes brightened slightly and shook his head. "As you can see, the cupboard and the pantry are full. He's already been here this fall, just a few weeks ago. He won't be back till spring."

Slightly crestfallen, Carissa continued with her questions. "How can you stand to live like this, all alone in an empty wilderness? Don't you get lonely?"

Bryce stood, uneasy with the questions and pining for when she was speaking to him. "I'd rather live alone," was all he said before he left the room.

Undaunted, Carissa followed him, dogging his steps with more questions. "Why? Why did you decide to live up here? Are you hiding from something?"

Bryce turned on her, a warning smoldering in the gray wolf-like eyes that glared at her. "Are you always this nosey? Leave it be."

Crossing her arms as he turned away again, she let her curiosity get the better of her. "All right," she said as she watched him pull on his trousers. "If you don't want to tell me your deep, dark secrets, I'll live with it."

"Works for me," he said, pulling a sweatshirt over his shaggy head.

"Who's Anna?"

Carissa watched as Bryce froze while reaching for his boots. She could swear that his hair stood on end like the hackles on a dog's back. He returned slowly to an upright position, his head turning, his eyes fixing her in their hostile depths. He walked to her, each step slow and concise, the dark energy that hovered over the surface of his body crackled in the still air of the room with every movement of his frame. Carissa, like a deer caught, frozen, in the headlight beams of an on-coming vehicle, was held spellbound by the power of his mordant gaze. She stumbled back a step as his hand reached for her, slowly coming up to wrap gently around the flesh of her neck, his callused thumb softly strumming the throbbing pulse along her delicate throat.

Carissa swallowed hard, unable to take her gaze from his dark, blazing eyes, feeling the current of electricity pass from his hand to her skin. In all the years she had been married to the man, John, she had never known the fear that she felt in the presence of this man at this moment. The coldness she saw in his face seeped into her soul, freezing her mind to the point where she could not think, could barely breathe.

His voice, when he spoke, was low and menacing, causing her blood to run cold. "How do you know that name? Have you been going through my things?"

She was imprisoned as much by the grip of his smoldering gaze as she was by the burning touch of his hand on her throat. It took a moment for his quiet words to penetrate the haze of fear that had seized her brain, and another moment to swallow the lump of fright in her gullet. "N-no, I... You-you were having a nightmare, s-s-spoke in your sleep."

The embers of hostility, still smoldering in the deep, gray depths of his eyes, dimmed slightly but his hot fingers continued to stroke ominously against the fine skin of her throat. "Stay out of my business, and never mention her name again, you hear me?"

Carissa could only nod, wishing he would not look at her with such hatred, that she could learn to keep her big mouth shut. It seemed she could breathe again when he suddenly released her and turned. Sitting on the bed without glancing in her direction, he forced his feet into fur-lined boots before standing again. He removed his shotgun from its rack above the mantle along the path he took to the cabin door. Jerking the door open and grabbing his outerwear he started to exit the building.

"Bryce…" Carissa called out tentatively only to see him snap his head around and silence her with a piercing stare just before he walked out, closing the door quietly after him.

Once he was gone, Carissa sank slowly into the rocking chair, her body quivering violently as she drew a deep and shaky breath. Skoll seemed to sense her fear, coming to lick at her face and lay his muzzle on her shoulder, offering comfort. Patting his head with a shaking hand, she tried to breathe through her trembling and regain control of her fear.

"What kind of man is your master?" she asked the massive dog. He licked her face again in answer.

Chapter 9

Several hours later, Bryce had still not returned, and the sun had already dropped behind the tall mountain, plunging the wilderness into total darkness in the moonless night. A cold wind was howling as clouds gathered overhead, blocking the abundant stars from view. Carissa paced the main room of the cabin in the huge, thick socks that Bryce had given her. The tail of his enormous shirt danced about her knees as she moved about with Skoll nervously tagged to her heels. Terrible thoughts crowded her racing mind as the memory of his cruel anger made her shudder.

Perhaps he would never return, preferring to be anywhere but where she was, leaving behind his home and his possessions. She had no idea of how he was fixed financially, but she had to assume he had some form of income if he could afford to pay for his supplies without benefit of a job; maybe he had the means to disappear, to go anywhere he wanted. The thought that he would knowingly leave her all alone in this wintry world did not sound like him, though. For that matter, however, neither did the amount of scarcely controlled rage she had seen in his eyes. If he were capable of such fury, he would certainly be capable of abandoning her to the elements of this wild place.

Her fear of being alone, however, was nothing compared to the pure fright she had experienced when he had looked at her with such hatred. She had been terrified when he had touched her; the heat of his hand had nearly scorched her skin. The terror was compounded when she realized that if he wanted, he would only need to tighten his grip to snap her neck, or choke the life from her body.

Another shudder shook her as she stirred the soup in the pot on the stove, the soup she had made by way of an apology for having upset him, an appeasement for his anger. It was funny to her how old habits were hard to break. She had often done similar things to mollify John's wrath whenever he took umbrage to something she had done, whether real or imagined.

The hour was late, had to be late. The wind howled through the trees as if to tear them out at the roots. Carissa thought of what he had told her about the possibility of freezing to death in the mountain environment. Something might have happened to him, a fall or some other terrible accident, that had him helpless and vulnerable to the winter wind. As she stood before the one unshuttered window and watched the drifting snow that whipped about in the scant light from the lamp on the table, she began to envision the giant of a man with his huge body trapped under a fallen tree, his bearded face contorted in pain. Another scenario of her anxious mind had him falling through the snow into a crevice, such as the one she had encountered while she was lost in the forest.

Suddenly, the thought of his injury, his pain, brought a different sort of panic to her heart, the fear of losing him. It was a terrible, wrenching fear that had her hands clenched in dreadful uncertainty. She did not take time to explore this new feeling; she only knew that something had to be done.

Her decision made, Carissa began scrounging through his bureau looking for clothing to protect herself from the harsh elements. She chose a pair of long underwear that she had to knot at the waist to hold them up and an extra pair of woolen socks. She pulled a sweatshirt over the shirt that she had been wearing as a dress. However, she still needed a pair of boots, a coat and something more on her legs. As she sat to put on the extra pair of socks, she spied the closed door near the bed. She had not looked in there yet; perhaps that was where he kept his dungarees. Tucking her shirttail into the long johns, she walked across the room, and was just reaching for the door handle when the front door of the cabin swung open, letting in a hail of freshly falling snow.

Skoll let loose a loud woof, charging forward as an immense, snow-covered form entered the cabin, blocking the wind from her as it invaded. Carissa whirled round at the intrusion, prepared to do battle if necessary. One massive gloved hand reached up, pushing back the hood that covered the head of the form revealing the dark, bearded face of Bryce.

"What the hell are you doing?" he demanded.

Carissa's hand dropped from the doorknob, knowing he would be angry to find her doing what he would perceive as snooping. That concern quickly diminished, however, at seeing him in one piece, alive and well. She was tossed between throwing her arms around him in joy and slapping him for making her worry.

She chose to yell instead. "Where have you been? I was worried sick!"

Bryce turned to close the door, pushing his big body against it to shut out the freezing wind, before facing her as he set down his gun and removed his gloves.

"You didn't answer me, Carissa. What do you think you're doing?" he asked quietly as he slapped his wet gloves against his thigh. He dropped the gloves on the table under the window and reached up to open his coat, waiting for an answer.

Carissa felt suddenly shy and not a little afraid of facing him again. "I was searching for boots and a coat."

"Were you planning on escaping me in the middle of the night? Am I so abhorrent that you'd rather face death in a blizzard than stay here with me?"

Carissa saw the pain and the anger in his eyes. She felt that she had hurt him again, in some way. "Why would you say that? Have I said anything about your being 'abhorrent'?" Then she thought about everything that had transpired over the past days and knew real shame. "Bryce, I never meant for you to believe… when I said that I want to go home, it had nothing to do with you. I have to get home to my children."

"You don't need to lie to me, Carissa. I know what I am."

Confusion made her step forward, closer to him. She saw more pain in his gray eyes than what her misguided comments of earlier could possibly have caused. She saw the tormented soul of a man who had seen real tragedy beyond her understanding, a comprehension that made her feel more than a little selfish and guilty. She had not taken the time to worry about what her being there was doing to him; she had only been worried about her own needs.

"I know what you are too," she said softly as she reach up to lay a hand on his thick beard. "You're a kind and caring man who went out of his way to save a stranger from certain death. You're a generous man who had to put up with a lot of shit from me."

Bryce froze under her touch, not knowing how he should respond, not knowing what to say to this bewitching creature who was reaching out to him. A game, he decided, it was a new game she played. He could not, however, make himself pull away from her gentle hand had his life depended on it.

"I don't need or want your pity, woman."

"Bryce, I'm not offering pity. I'm trying to tell you I'm sorry and I'm glad you're home safe. I was worried about you." She wanted to throw her arms around him and feel his hard body against hers, know the safety of his embrace. The only thing that held her back was the way he had reacted earlier in the day, frightening her to the point where she thought violence would be imminent.

The contact of her palm against his face thrilled his heart, was more than he could hope for and more than he had known in so very long, but he could not tell if it were genuine. He took her small hand in his own, pulling it from his face but holding it. It was warm in his cold fingers and it was real, the willing touch of another person.

"I can appreciate your concern, Carissa. But that's no reason for you to run off, especially when it's storming out there."

"I wasn't running off!" It was Carissa's turn to be frustrated. "Skoll and I were going out to look for you. You can't imagine what thoughts have been going through my head."

He smiled coldly at her, dropping her hand as he removed his coat and hung it on the hook by the door. "Did you think I abandoned you?"

"No, you idiot! I thought you were hurt! I thought you needed help, maybe you had a tree on you or you fell into a hole. Why are you acting like this?"

"As if you give a shit!" he growled. "You're just like the rest; you can't wait to get shut of me."

Carissa was insulted and angry. Being called a liar, in her mind, was one of the worst affronts a person could use, and he had done it twice now. "Why don't you get your head out of your ass. You know, I'm not buying this "angry man" routine so knock it off. Don't you *ever* call me a liar again. You don't want me to care about you, fine, but don't call me a liar."

He took a menacing step closer to her, hearing Skoll whimper just before scurrying away. "I'd think after this morning you'd watch your mouth around me."

"Yeah? Well, I never was too bright in that department. I survived eight years of hell, married to the worst monster that ever walked the earth. I sure as *hell* can survive you."

The flashing anger in her eyes was incredible, her face, flushed and beautiful. She was a damnably provocative woman, matching his venom unflinchingly, recklessly. "*I'm* the worst monster that ever walked the earth, Carissa. You have no idea what I'm capable of." The harshness of his voice belied his inner turmoil. The mask of anger he wore now was only to hide the reaction he was having to her nearness, the warm scent of her, and the light of life that burned so brightly in her eyes.

"I'm fully aware of what you're capable of doing." Her voice softened as the hurt in his eyes increased. "You're capable of pissing me off. You're capable of acting like a Neanderthal. You also have a capacity for gentleness that most men don't. I see you very clearly, Bryce."

"No, you don't," he rasped out as he shut his eyes.

"What is it with you? Is it the scar on your face? Is that it?" She saw him flinch but he made no other response, compelling her to charge ahead recklessly. "Is it her? Is it this Anna? Does she have something to do…"

Her voice trailed off as his eyes snapped open to reveal that rage she had seen earlier. It burned, yet left her cold as ice, clutching at her heart. Carissa wanted to retreat but forced herself to stand her ground.

"I told you to never mention her again," he said softly. "Why would you bring her up? Are you intentionally trying to goad me?"

Carissa swallowed hard but kept her voice firm. "I'm trying to find out why the hell you hide yourself up here, away from civilization, why you hide your face behind all that hair. I'm trying to figure out why you push people away."

"Drop it," he warned quietly. "Just let it go."

"No, I won't. Who is she?"

Bryce had heard enough, stepping forward to close the gap between them, his movements quick and fluid like that of a predator, and taking some small pleasure in seeing her cringe, if only slightly. "I said drop it! Just shut the fuck up!" his roar overwhelmed the interior of the cabin.

"Holler all you like. You don't scare me," she retorted recklessly.

She was ready to recant those words when, in the next moment, he seized her under the arms, lifting her and pushing her hard against the wall next to the bed. For a full minute, he held her there at eye level, glaring into her face as his breath came in quick, sharp pants. Then he was on her, smashing his mouth against hers as he held her to the wall, crushing his hard frame against her, feeling her small fists pounding against his shoulders.

He came up for air, pulling his fur-shrouded lips from hers, pressing their foreheads together as they both gasped in the thin mountain air.

"Put me down," she said between gasps with more calm than she felt.

He raised his head, pulling back from her and giving her a little shake against the wall. "Don't test me, Carissa."

"You promised not to hurt me, remember? I believed you when you made that promise."

"Maybe that was your mistake," he snarled quietly. She reminded him of a cornered badger – showing no fear and prepared to do battle. Her eyes glittered with a dark green light, and her face was flushed an angry red that all but concealed the fading bruises on her delicate skin. This woman had strength, the kind that is rare and comes from the heart. He had never wanted anyone as badly as he wanted her at this moment.

"No," she hissed. "I didn't make a mistake because you're not the beast you try to make yourself out to be."

Her words hit home and had him lowering her slowly to the floor. He released her, not because he had believed what she said, but because she had. He could see the truth of it in her eyes as she glared unwaveringly at him, letting him see the full force of her ire.

Reaching up to stroke the side of her face with his knuckles, he fixed her with a cold stare, his breathing barely controlled. "Don't push me too far, Carissa. I've been alone up here for a long time. A small woman like you would have no choice if I decided to take what I want."

She swatted his hand back, completely unfazed. "Well, if you plan to rape me then at least do me the favor of getting rid of that nasty beard. It chafes my skin."

He blinked at her words, stunned and falling back a step at her fearless statement, and the way she continued to square off against him, daring him with the green fire of her eyes. She stood, legs and elbows akimbo, glaring at him as if he were a child that had sassed her and needed to be taken to task. He, a man three times her size and nearly a stranger as well, had threatened her with violence, and she was completely undaunted. He could not fathom what had changed since she had cowered before him the night previous, but something was definitely different in her manner.

The whole situation had him bewildered, marveling at all the different facets to the personality of the she-cat that glared at him. He had thought he could intimidate her into silence, but she continued to defy his attempts at control with her fiery temper and tiny bristling body. He was suddenly struck by the humor of the situation, guffawing loudly, his roaring laughter echoing about the cabin.

Carissa watched the play of emotions on his face – from rage to astonishment, and finally, mirth. She could not help but grin in return; it was easy to see that he was a man unused to laughter. Watching his gray eyes light up and the skin around them crinkle with delight held a certain appeal that had her pulse racing.

"Now that we have that out of the way," she directed in a mockingly stern voice, "there's soup on the stove if you're hungry."

As she tried to brush past him on the way to the kitchen, Bryce impulsively grabbed her in a great bear hug, crushing her small form against his, still rocking with laughter. The movement caught Carissa by surprise, had her stiffening against him in defense until his warmth seeped through her body. She found herself snuggling against him, enjoying the affection he was displaying, a benign hug without obligation or lust that was born of the impetus of the moment. He released her as quickly as he had grabbed her, embarrassed at his spontaneity, seeming to search for a place to hide, or a way to draw her attention from the action.

"I knew you were part grizzly," she said with a laugh. "I think you broke a couple of ribs." Cuffing him on the arm, she told him to take off his wet boots and join her in the kitchen, ignoring the blush that crept up her own neck.

"Sorry about that," he mumbled as he bent to do her bidding. The sound of her jangling laughter brought a ludicrous grin to his face, and caused him to feel like a young man again, full of the hope of the moment. "You're looking mighty fetching in my long johns," he called out as she disappeared into the kitchen. Again, he heard the music of her laughter, her only response to his playful words.

Entering the kitchen, he noticed the tarp that had covered the doorway was now gone. He eyed her questioningly as the delicious aroma of the soup she had crafted filled his nostrils. He took the large bowl of the hearty fare that she offered and settled himself in a chair at the table.

"What happened to the tarp?" he asked before taking a bite of the steaming soup. The flavor of it hit his tongue and had him closing his eyes in pure enjoyment. "This is really good. What's in it? Aren't you having any?"

"I already ate. The tarp was blocking the air circulation in the cabin. It got too hot in here so I took it down," she replied without looking up from scrubbing out the sink. "The soup is made with the stuff I found in your cupboards. I threw in a little of this and that, and hoped that it was good. Glad you like it."

She finished her task before removing the boiling water kettle from the stove to pour some into a large pitcher that was half-full of cold water. She turned to look at him then, fixing him with a direct gaze that he found disconcerting. "Let's get something straight, Bryce. I was worried about you today. I didn't know what had happened to you. All I could think about was that you might have been hurt and trapped out there in that storm. Don't do that to me again, okay?"

The spoon that was halfway to his mouth slowly dropped back to the bowl on the table. There was genuine concern and more than a little anger in her fathomless eyes. "Are you trying to tell me you care?"

"Of course I care!" her exasperated voice cried out. "What is it with you? You act like no one in the world ever showed you any kindness." She turned her back on him then, not really expecting a response, as she reached for the pitcher, bending to flip her hair forward into the sink to pour the warm water over her head.

She did not hear him come up behind her, only knew he was there, taking the pitcher from her hand.

"It's been a long time since anyone has shown me any kindness, Cari," he said, setting the pitcher aside and reaching for the bar of homemade soap. Working lather into her silky tresses and taking pleasure in the way the strands curled through his fingers, he felt a deep need to make her understand. This was a new sensation for him, the man who thought he could live without ever encountering another human being. Somewhere in the depths of his soul was a small voice crying out to make her comprehend his loneliness and the reasons for it.

How could he tell her, however, the terrible thing he had done, the reason he had become an outcast from the world down below? It was too much for him to think that this tiny woman who reminded him of a mythical wood sprite would see him in that light. Would her smiling green eyes turn from him in disgust? Would she shudder in horror, demanding that he stay away from him in abject fear?

"That's because you hide yourself up here in this desolate cabin," she replied into the sink, her voice made soft by the sensations of his sensual fingers working on her scalp. "I don't understand why you prefer this but I'm sure you have your reasons, however stupid they may be."

He chuckled softly, a dark sound with little humor in it. "The reasons aren't stupid, Cari. I'm up here because of what I am. The world is better off without me."

"What a ridiculous thing to say! You have no idea how incredible you are. The fact that I'm here standing over this sink having my hair washed should be enough to prove that. I would have died out there if not for you. You saved my life, and more than once. It's not everyone that has the patience and common sense necessary to nurse someone back to health the way you did, and you did it with such compassion and kindness."

He poured the remainder of the water over her head, silencing her voice that was putting tormenting pictures in his head. He imagined what it would be like to spend the rest of his life performing this ritual and others like it every day. Her bottom, nestled so softly against his thigh, had him dreaming of other things as well, as he tried to keep her from feeling the results of his obvious arousal.

"How do you know how much compassion and kindness I used? You were out of your head and delirious." He refilled the pitcher, as she remained hovering over the sink.

"I wasn't out of my head the entire time, Bryce. I remember the gentle voice of a giant who told me that he would make me better, and the way his hands smoothed the pain away. I remember being held and feeling safe. I also remember a big, clumsy oaf, shoving me into a vat of icy water," she said, peeking from beneath her dripping curls, a twinkle in her eye.

The next sound her voice made was a squeal of protest as he decided she could handle the cold water straight from the well, dumping it over her head with a mighty splash. She whipped her hair at him, spraying his laughing face with cold water before grabbing a towel to wrap around her dripping head.

"That was a dirty trick!" she yelled at him, trying not to laugh. "You know, you don't fool me, Bryce. You're just as human as anyone else, even though you want me to believe otherwise, for some reason. In fact, you may be more human than most."

"What's that supposed to mean?" His eyes took in every movement she made, watching her squeeze the towel around her heavy hair before pulling the cloth away to let the curls fall in an unruly veil around her face. Pushing the tresses from her face, she began dragging her fingers through it in an effort to remove the tangles.

"I wish I had a comb," she said into the long snarls before looking up. "It means that you want to be loved, want someone to reach out to you but you've constructed such a wall around your heart that no one can get in."

"Do you always talk to so much?" he asked softly.

"Yep, one of my major failings. I always say what's on my mind."

The gray of his eyes smoldered, growing darker as she spoke, but his face remained expressionless, betraying no emotion as he watched her intently. She wondered if she had angered him again, so motionless he stood while surveying her face. Finally, without a word, he turned on his heel, exiting the room.

With a sigh she returned to trying to de-tangle the mess that was her hair. For a brief moment, she wished for the comfort of her cosmetologist's chair and the wonderful products that would soothe the mass of curls into a manageable style. More than that, she wanted to see the smiling faces of her children and hear their sweet young voices telling her how much they loved her.

She wondered what they were doing at this moment and if they were still safely in the care of her mother. Hopelessness burrowed into her heart, knowing that they would soon be at the mercy of the man who had fathered them, if they were not already living under his roof. She wondered if, when she was finally able to return to them, they would still be the impish, happy little boy and girl she had left behind. Would they still be full of wonder and the joy of life?

Carissa's hands dropped into her lap, her head bent forward in sorrow. The lump in her throat threatened to choke the air from her body, suffocate her with the weight of the sadness in her heart. The storm that howled around the cabin was a grim reminder that she was trapped in the wilderness and there was nothing she could do to help her babies. She said a silent prayer that they would remain safe and the monster would not get his hands on them.

Chapter 10

A few minutes later, Bryce stepped back through the door of the kitchen carrying an ancient wooden box, a gift to make her time spent in his cabin a little more bearable. Despite his current isolation from civilization he did know what a woman's basic needs were; he had not always lived in the wilderness.

Coming to a halt in front of her, he observed everything about her and missed nothing. He saw the way her head was bowed over her slumped shoulders and the way her hands, still red and raw looking from the injuries sustained during her brush with death, clenched together as if trying to restrain them. When she raised her eyes to look at him, he saw the flash of misery that she quickly disguised with a bright smile that did not twinkle in her eyes. He wondered if she were pining for her family, or if she simply wanted to be free of him.

"I... uh..." He cleared his throat. Looking into her eyes could make a man forget where he was, or the thoughts that traveled through his head. "I had this. It belonged to my grandparents. I should've given it to you before, but I guess I wasn't thinking."

Carissa thought his expression was that of a little boy, hopeful that the little girl who took his fancy would appreciated his gift of a dead frog. She glanced at the box in his hand, reaching out to take it, wondering what could be so precious that he would be so nervous presenting her with it.

"Thank you, Bryce," she sweetly replied, determined to love the gift even if a real frog actually jumped out of it.

What she found inside, upon lifting the hinged lid, had her squealing with delight. The items inside were very old, but every one of them was welcome. The box contained a complete toiletry kit. Inside were two polished wooden combs, one silver-handled hairbrush – its bristles still pristine, and another brush with a wooden handle that looked to have seen some use. There was a straight razor with a mother of pearl handle, a cup with lathering brush, a pair of barber's scissors, a tin of talc and a dusting brush, as well as a myriad of other items.

Bryce watched as Carissa ran the tips of her fingers over some of the items in a gentle caress until she touched one of the combs. Carefully picking it up and clutching it to her breast, she gazed up at him with shining eyes. He became caught up in the sweet smile on her delectable lips and the joyous glow to her face, an entrancing sight to behold. Without warning, she launched herself at him, hugging him about the middle tightly; causing his heart to soar as he cautiously wrapped his arms around her shoulders and inhaled her fragrance.

With a giggle of pure delight, she reclaimed her seat, immediately gathering a handful of the dark curls and working at the tenacious knots. "Now, if only I had a mirror so I can see what I'm doing," she voiced hopefully.

"I can't help you with that," he chuckled, watching her struggle. After a few moments, he decided to throw caution to the wind and took the ancient comb from her hand. "Let me see if I can do anything with it."

Bryce, with meticulous care, separated a handful of the unruly curls, gently tugging at the tangled mess with the comb. Her fragrance, soft and womanly, mixed with the clean woodsy scent of the soap, and assailed his senses. He stepped a little farther behind her to hide the burgeoning hardness pressing against the fly of his jeans. Once he had her hair free of tangles, he reached for the silver brush with shaking hands, listening to her breath that sounded like the purr of a cat.

"I think you've done this before," she sighed.

"I have," was all he said as he continued to brush her hair until it glistened.

After realizing that he was not going to stop, Carissa turned and reached for the brush. "Your turn," she said as she pointed at the sink. "Let's wash that mess on your head."

Bryce tried to resist but she would have none of it; giving him no choice but to wash his hair and beard, as she directed. "Hey, I helped you. The least you could do is lend me a hand in return," he grumbled

"I would if you weren't tall as this damned mountain. I can barely reach your shoulders. Now wash," she ordered.

Once he had toweled the wild growth on his head, she attempted to work on the knots in his hair with a comb, finding it necessary to stand on a crate to reach him. "Jesus," she spat. "When was the last time you ran a comb through this? You have mats in the back of your head!"

He shrugged his big shoulders, somewhat embarrassed as he remembered dining in fine restaurants and going to parties dressed in fine suits with a beautiful blond woman on his arm. "Just never seemed to be any reason to," he offered. "I figured that washing regularly was enough."

Hearing the finish on the old comb crackling under the strain and the grumbling complaints of her victim, she realized that there was nothing for it but to take a whack at it with the scissors. Grabbing a clump of matted hair, she reached for the scissors and made the first cut before he had a chance to protest. The more of his hair she cut the louder his objections became, until she cuffed him on the shoulder and told him to be quiet. Standing behind him as she was, she did not see the grin of amusement on his face or the pure enjoyment in his eyes.

When at last she finished, there was more hair on the floor than on his head, but she was satisfied with her handy-work. "You have nice hair," she said appraisingly. "I don't know why you don't take better care of it."

She walked around to his front then and positioned herself between his long legs. With scissors and comb clutched in her left hand, she ran the fingers of her right through his hair, brushing it back from his eyes. It was still long enough to keep his head and neck warm, but it had a style that framed his face, allowing his gray eyes to stand out. It occurred to her that he was truly a handsome man, with the beauty of his unusual eyes, his aquiline nose and the shining black of his hair. She was curious to see what he looked like without the thick growth of fur that hid the rest of his face.

It was almost too much for him to bear, having her so close that he could feel her warmth suffusing the front of his body, hoping she would not notice the way his trousers bulged outward. Seeing the look in her eye and the way she raised the scissors, however, he grabbed her by the waist and set her away from him, a protest on his lips. There was a panic gripping his mind at the thought of her cutting away the beard that hid his face.

"Don't even think about it," he growled sharply.

Carissa's eyebrows shot upward before drawing together is a slight frown. "What are you afraid of?"

He stood abruptly, stepping away from her and the wicked-looking scissors that gleamed in her hand. "The haircut is enough. Thanks, I appreciate it."

Undaunted by the warning that smoldered in his eyes, she tossed the scissors and comb onto the table. "We've already established that you no longer scare me so you may as well get that scowl off your face," she ordered, folding her arms across her chest. They stood, their eyes locked, ready to do battle until her face softened. Reaching out with one hand to touch his arm, she spoke again. "Bryce," her soft voice cajoled. "I know you have scars. We all do. Some of us carry our scars on the inside where no one can see them, but if you look hard enough you can see the damage that's been done. You took care of me when I was sick. You took my clothes off and saw everything I have, including, I'm sure, the scars on my body. I'm not ashamed of them. Why are you ashamed of yours?"

"Drop it, Carissa," his voice growled out in a low, menacing tone, his smoky eyes clouding.

She stepped closer, her body just inches from his, tormenting him with her nearness as she looked up into his face. His head began to swim as he looked into the endless depths of her olive eyes, causing his mouth to go dry and his hands to itch just to touch her. The womanly scent of her was enough to drive him mad as he struggled to control the urge that was so much more than mere lust.

"Don't you know that you're beautiful to me?" she whispered up to him as she touched her fingers to the scar near his eye. "I don't care what's under the beard."

His pulse raced at her touch and her words, nudging him closer to the edge of his ability to restrain himself. The warmth of her fingertips on that scar, that souvenir of a moment in time when he gave his soul over to darkness, spread heat through his body and threatened to undermine his determination. He grasped her fingers in his, an effort to still the throbbing in his groin and the images of her nude body in his mind.

"Then why do you want to cut it off?" he asked, his voice husky with the emotions that set his blood to boiling.

A wicked gleam came to her eyes as a playful grin spread across her face. "In case you decide to make good your threat to rape me, of course."

His free hand came up to stroke her face, his eyes darkening farther, turning almost black. "Careful, Cari. Don't go too far."

"Bryce, why do you constantly try to intimidate me? We both know you won't do anything to hurt me. I know you care about me. It's written all over your face whenever you look at me. I may not be a genius, but I do know when a man looks at me the way you do that he wants me, and not just for sex either. Did you ever stop to think that I might have the same feelings for you? Now, sit down. One way or another, that beard is going to at least get a good trimming."

Stunned, Bryce could only comply, wondering if what she said could be true. Could she actually care about him? Would she still care if she knew the truth? He knew the answer to that as he nervously sat facing her, breath held, waiting for her to start cutting away the safety of his mask.

"You can breathe, you know," she laughed softly. "I won't cut your nose off or anything."

The air left his lungs in a rush, lifting her hair and making her laugh again. The sound of it was musical and soft, and had him wanting to throw her down on the kitchen table and ravish her. "I'm glad I amuse you," he grumped.

"Well, you're a funny guy," she retorted, making the first snip. By the time she was done cutting, he was covered in the thick, coarse hair of his beard.

"All done," she said brightly. "That wasn't so bad, was it?" Standing back to see her handy-work she was struck by the pure manly beauty of him that caused butterflies to stir in her belly.

He watched her face as she appraised him, seeing his own burning hunger reflected in her eyes. Feeling with his fingers, he discovered just how close she had cropped his facial hair. There was not much left. The question of whether she would still find him desirable if she could see the damning scars played over and over in his mind until he found himself handing her the antique razor from the box.

"Finish it," he said, meeting her gaze directly.

She smiled brightly, but the smile soon gave way to a worried frown. "Um, are you sure you want me to do this? I've never wielded one of these things, you know."

"I trust you," he answered, his voice soft and husky.

Digging the strop out of the bottom of the box of toiletries, she hooked it on the back of his chair, dragging the blade of the razor repeatedly along the length of it. Bryce cringed inwardly with each metallic sound of the cutting edge being sharpened. Something akin to an icy fist seemed to be clenching around his heart, tightening with each passing moment.

At long last, Carissa laid the razor on the table in front of him and asked, "What should I use for lather?"

Bryce stood, grabbing the bar of soap off the edge of the sink and breaking off a chunk. He dropped it in the shaving cup and added hot water from the kettle before using the small shaving brush to work up a foamy lather. "I used to watch my grandfather do this when I was a kid. It always used to amaze me. I don't know why."

"Because you were a kid and he was your gramps," she offered.

"That must be it," he said, handing her the cup with a slightly shaky hand.

She took it from him asking, "Am I supposed to wrap your face in a hot towel first?"

"Just get it over with," he grumbled as he closed his eyes.

Letting out a small giggle, she brushed the lather over his beard in increments until all the black hair was covered. Carissa took a deep breath then pushed his face slightly to the side before dragging the blade down his right cheek.

As she moved to wipe the spent shavings onto a towel, he tried to think of something to distract his mind from his ragged nerves. "So, how did you learn to cook so well on a wood burner?" he asked by way of making conversation.

She smiled into his eyes before taking another swipe with the blade. "My grandparents had a farm back in the boonies, my dad's parents. My gram was an incredible person and I loved being in her kitchen, always so warm and smelled so good. It was a huge house. It housed twelve kids. Can you imagine? What a huge family. They had a coal furnace, one bathroom and very basic wiring. When I was little, my aunts and uncles got together and were going to remodel her kitchen. She nearly went through the roof."

Carissa laughed at the memory as she finished the right side of his throat and moved on to his mustache. "She loved to cook on a wood fire. She told them she would take the plumbing and the new refrigerator, though. She told me later that she would have rather had 'one o'dem newfangled clothes washers and a drying machine'. She was a funny woman. She taught me everything about cooking and canning. Her bread and blackberry cobbler were the best in the world."

"You loved her a lot, didn't you?" he mumbled as she finished off his chin.

"Don't talk or you'll end up with a nasty gash," she admonished, stopping to sharpen the blade again. "Yes, she was wonderful. It seemed like she knew everything about the woods. None of my cousins was ever interested but she always took me with her when she went out to gather the wild food. We gathered nuts and picked berries, wild mushrooms and may apples. We also gathered herbs, roots and bark for what she called her 'healin' potions."

"She had all these old glass bottles and jars, all different colors, full of every elixir, tonic and powder you can imagine. People came from all over to get her remedies. She never turned anyone away, whether they could pay or not. They made fun of her, sometimes, because of her moccasins and braids but she didn't care. She would just point out what was funny about their clothes or hair and they would all laugh."

"Are you telling me that you're a half-breed?" he asked with a playful smirk.

"Careful there, Grizzly. You're mighty daring for a man whose throat is at the mercy of my blade," she warned, mockingly brandishing the razor.

He held up his hands in a half-hearted attempt to play the game, but waiting for her to discover what was hidden under the remaining hair on his face was nerve-wracking at best. He had no way of knowing at that point that Carissa had found what she saw so far to be very much to her liking, or that she was daydreaming about being kissed by the sensual lips that were now visible. The only thing he knew was the fear that the destroyed left side of his face would repulse her. He took another deep breath, anticipating the disgust he would see in her eyes, or worse, pity.

"You're going to have to hold very still. This side is a bit rough and I don't want to nick you," she warned softly as she laid the blade to his skin. "Anyway, yes, gram was a Cherokee. Gramps was a bull-headed German, fresh off the boat, when they met. He used to talk about how beautiful she was, and she was gorgeous. They tell me I have her eyes but hers were more brown. My mom is of Irish descent so that makes me a quarter-breed."

Carissa continued in silence until the job was done. Cleaning the remains of the lather away with a damp towel, she stood back to look. What she saw took her breath away and turned her insides gooey. She thought that if she had met this man under different circumstances he would already be parking his boots under her bed.

He had a strong, square jaw and a full sensual mouth that she knew had to have the ability to kiss her witless. A narrow scar ran from the left corner of his mouth up to the hollow of his cheek where it spread out in all directions in a pattern similar to a spider web. Somehow the scar only added to the masculine nature of his face, making him all the more appealing to her eyes. A shudder of pure heat shot through her body, bringing a pink flush to her face, as she stood silently taking in the sight of him.

Bryce caught her shudder, disappointment bringing his hope down as he misinterpreted her reaction. Unable to look at her, unwilling to see the aversion he knew would show on her face, he closed his eyes. This would be the end of it, the hope, the dreams of her in his arms, everything.

"Damn, boy," Carissa fairly purred. "You're a hunk! You've done the women of this world a huge disservice by hiding yourself up here."

When Bryce opened his eyes it was to see the naked desire that burned in the immeasurable depths of her olive-green eyes. He knew instantly that what he saw could not possibly be an act, so raw was the visible emotion. She was so near that he could reach out and seize her, take her into his arms and crush her to his body, all he had to do was reach…

Bryce was on his feet in an instant, grasping her soft arms, pulling her into his embrace, descending upon her mouth in a voracious kiss. His lips worked over hers, feeling her mouth open softly, welcoming him unconditionally. The sound of her impassioned moan set his blood to boiling as his body shook with a need that nearly over-powered them both.

His tongue invaded, seeking and finding hers to entwine in a dance as frenzied as the wind that howled outside. Finally, he was forced to release her lips as the need for oxygen had them both panting. She was clutching his shirt, gasping and leaning heavily into him, her lips trembling as her little pink tongue darted out to taste the essence of the kiss that had so affected them both. He captured her mouth again, sucking on that delicious little morsel, unable to get his fill.

He came up for air a second time, struggling to regain control of his unruly need. "Cari," he rasped against her forehead. "If you want me to stop, tell me now. I don't think I can control myself much longer."

Carissa tilted her head back, reaching up, pulling his face down to hers. "Control is over-rated. I want you, Bryce. Make love to me." Her voice, throaty and soft, was a plea, begging him to take her, to make her his. "If you stop now, I may never recover."

His lips sought hers again, crushing her soft body to his, dragging her feet from the ground. His frame shook as he carried her to the big bed in the main room and laid her upon the mattress. His lips left hers to forge a path along her jaw to her throat as his hands fumbled with her clothing.

"You picked a hell of a time to get fully dressed," he growled in frustration.

Carissa chortled as she wiggled under him, helping him remove the layers of clothing that restricted his movements, his need to get to her skin. When she finally lay nude upon the mattress, a naked feast for his eyes, his mouth fell upon her, devouring her flesh as his hands roamed the heated length of her.

Her hands pulled at his shirt, desperate to feel his skin against hers as he moved down her body, worshiping every inch of her with his mouth. He broke away only long enough to pull the layers of his shirts off and fight his way out of his slacks, socks and long underwear, until he was naked and pressing against her in moaning pleasure. His hard center pushed against her smooth flesh as his mouth consumed hers.

The creamy satin of her inner thigh caressed his hip as she curled her leg around his waist, propelling him beyond the edge of his tenuous control. He drilled into her body, penetrating her soft, drenched flesh with the hard power of his shaft, wrenching a cry of shocked bliss from her throat. All rational thought burned away over the flames of the pure primitive drive, their combined primal urgency joining them as one.

Carissa's body bucked wildly as Bryce reared up on his arms, throwing his head back, pummeling her softness with his steely force, moaning in guttural torment. Her fingers raked his chest, clutching at him as she cried his name in a shuddering scream. Her body seemed to crash inward on itself, the shards of it exploding outward in shattering release, nearly drowning her in darkness. Bryce soon followed, slamming into her as his own snarling howl tore from his chest and splintered the air of the cabin before he collapsed on top of her, drained and sated.

Carissa brought her hands up to caress his hair, holding his panting body to her own, shivering frame. A single tear escaped the corner of her eye and slipped into her hair as she fought to regain her breath. As Bryce rose to his elbows to see her face, she saw the concern in his eyes and the depth of emotion that had driven his passion for her.

"I'm sorry," he whispered as he brushed away the tear from her face with his fingertips. "I didn't mean to hurt you."

"You didn't, Bryce," she murmured around the lump that had formed in her throat. "You just taught me what I've been faking all these years."

Chapter 11

The touch of Carissa's hand on his scarred face brought Bryce out of the dream-state that had him floating in the afterglow of their passionate coupling. He quickly captured her hand, shifting his weight off her and rolling to his side. A groan of protest tumbled off her lips as he pulled himself out of her body and gathered her into his arms.

"I think we scared poor Skoll," she told him with a laugh.

Bryce raised his head to spy the dog whimpering in the far corner, and laughed. "This was definitely something he's never seen or heard," he laughed in return.

"He's very bonded to you, Bryce. Where did you get him?"

"Just before I came up here I saw a man beating the hell out of him. Had him on a short chain in a mud hole with dirty water and no food. The poor animal was half-starved and hardly able to stand. So I threw the guy in the mud and took the dog. He's been with me every since."

"He's a good dog," she said as she watched the mammoth animal thump his tail against the floor, as if to acknowledge that he knew he was the topic of their conversation.

"Yeah, he is but he doesn't trust people anymore than I do."

She looked into his eyes, seeing the deep pain hidden in their depths. "Why don't you? What happened?"

He kissed her soundly to silence her questions, fearing the truth and what it would do to the light in her beloved eyes. Rolling onto his back and taking her with him, his hands stroked the length of her silky spine, hardly believing that he was holding her. Carissa filled his senses with her womanly body, her every movement fueling his desire. Her questions forgotten, she returned his kiss, moving her small body over his, her hands roaming the planes of his hard muscles.

More than five years of celibacy, the three years he spent in seclusion and the two years before – after that terrible day – were left behind as he reveled in the pleasure of this enchanting wood sprite who had taken hold of his heart. He growled in response to her warm breath on his skin, her gentle touch and her fiery eyes. Digging his fingers into her hips, he guided her over his hard center, lowering her soft, wet flesh onto his powerful core, impaling and imprisoning her.

"Bryce," he heard her say in a soft moan, as she slid down the length of him. To him her voice was a tender caress, a sensation for which he had longed since first he had laid eyes upon her delicate face. He pulled her body down for another kiss, invading her mouth with his tongue, as he began to move slowly under her. With each slow thrust, her voice emitted another tiny cry, her body moving in time with his.

"Carissa, you're like a dream," he whispered as she rose upward to ride his hard body.

Her fingers dragged down the powerful muscles of his hard chest, grazing over the ragged scars that marred his skin, to the ripples of his belly. Every thick inch of his rigid cock evoked pleasures she never thought imaginable as he moved slowly in and out of her flesh. His hands on her hips drove her onward, lifting and pulling her back down in heated torment.

He watched her face, softened in pleasure with lips slightly parted, as each torturous stroke brought them closer to that moment of infinite ecstasy. His hands moved upward, skimming the silky curves of her waist, over the gentle ridges of her ribs and finally to the rounded globes of her breasts. His fingers found her nipples, teasing the hardened pink jewels, rolling them until she was writhing on top of him, her breath coming in panting moans.

Releasing one breast, he trailed his fingers down her breastbone and over her belly to splay his fingers across her mound. He slipped his thumb between their fevered bodies, hooking it under her pelvis to find the hard little clitoris that was the nerve center of her pleasure. He stroked his thumb across the wet knot, delighting in her reaction as she cried out and bucked wildly.

"Oh, Jesus, Bryce!" she whimpered.

"Yes, baby, tell me."

"I... I'm gonna come!"

Her screaming voice was like music in his ears as he pounded up into her, driving her to the edge and beyond. Savoring every sensation, he felt her muscles clench around his shaft as her body shuddered, convulsing over him until she fell forward in a panting heap on top of him. He wrapped his arms tightly around her, feeling her inner muscles gripping and quivering around his cock in an incredible embrace until he could stand no more.

He slowly rolled over on top of her, trying to keep his movements slow within her but the way her legs wrapped around him with her knees clenching his ribs was more than he could bear. Within moments, his shaft was pounding into her again, thrashing her body with his strength. The world seemed to shake violently as he grew closer and closer to the edge with her voluptuous frame and stroking hands driving him onward. Finally, with a feral growl he exploded within her, spraying his seed into her belly, and for the briefest of moments, he was sure he had died in the rapture of their coupling.

At last the clouds began to clear from his vision and his mind until he became aware that the tiny woman under him was laughing softly against his neck. Still struggling to control his breathing, he raised his head and looked into her eyes. "What's so funny?" he asked softly.

"You fuck like a wild man," she said sweetly.

Raising himself onto his elbows so that he could better see her beautiful eyes, he grinned sheepishly and said gallantly, "I was quite swept away by your charms."

She exploded in peals of laughter at his mocking statement, tangling her fingers in his hair. "You're a wonderful lover, Bryce," she murmured around a yawn.

Bryce chuckled and gently shifted his weight off her diminutive frame. "That's because you're easy to love," he mumbled in return as they both drifted off into an exhausted slumber, wrapped in each other's arms.

It was some hours later when Bryce awoke to find he was alone. At first, he thought it had all been a dream until he rolled onto his side, catching the scent of her on the bed linens. He came upright in bed, looking about the darkened room and not seeing

Carissa anywhere. Then he caught sight of the soft glow of lamplight coming from the kitchen, and heard the muted sounds of her movement within, drawing him from the bed. The cabin had grown cold, as the fire had died away to glowing embers in the hearth.

Carissa turned away from the stove to see Bryce crouched down in front of the fireplace, her mind still reeling from their steamy sexual encounter. Her breath caught in her throat at the glowing image of his sculpted frame in the scant light of the flames he was stoking to life. Fresh heat raced through her veins as she remembered what it was like to be held in his strong arms and loved by his muscular body.

She returned to the task of loading more wood into the old pot-bellied stove, her hands working around the blanket that she had wrapped around her naked body to ward off the chill of the mountain winter. She straightened to pull the pot of leftover soup onto the hot burner plate, and added another can of broth to the contents of the vessel. A contented smile played at her lips as her new lover moved up behind her, encircling her with his arms and reaching inside the blanket to cup her breasts.

Sighing softly, she melted back into him, resting her head on his shoulder. His hand came up to her face, gently turning her head to accept his kiss. She turned in his arms, raising her hands to his face as the blanket dropped to pool about their feet. The kiss penetrated her mind and heart, causing the very air around them to become warm.

Releasing her lips, he buried his face into the unruly curls that danced over the curve of her neck, pressing her heated skin against his own. "The bed was cold and lonely without you," he breathed against her throat.

"I'm sorry," she murmured in response. "I didn't mean to wake you."

"It was the empty bed that woke me." He lifted his head to look at her lovely face. "What are you doing?"

She grinned openly. "I got hungry. You wore me out and worked up my appetite."

He chuckled and lifted the long fingers of one big hand to smooth an errant curl from her eyes. "I'm hungry, too," he whispered, a wicked gleam in his eyes. "I think I'd like to have a bite of you." He lowered his mouth again, capturing her tremulous lips in another rousing kiss before trailing downward to her throat, nibbling at the skin that covered her pulsing artery.

She moaned softly as she pushed at his chest saying, "I have to eat, my stomach is growling. I'll die after another round with you if I don't."

"Well, we can't have that," he laughed as he reluctantly released her. As she turned back to the stove, his arms came around her again. "I can't get enough of you," he whispered, his hot lips against the shell of her ear.

"You want some soup?" she asked, with a quiver of pure pleasure.

"Yes, I think we both need to keep our strength up. I plan to spend the rest of the winter in bed with you."

She giggled enthusiastically, as she reached for the ladle to dip into the rich soup of beef and vegetables. After pouring two bowls, she handed them to Bryce who carried them to the table while she dug a couple of spoons out of the utensil drawer. He grabbed the blanket off the floor and wrapped it around himself, sitting in a chair and pulling her down upon his lap. Her hip settled over his groin as he engulfed her in his arms to warm her body with the folds of the soft blanket and another ardent kiss.

"Eat," she said on a panting breath as their lips parted.

He took the spoon with a reluctant sigh. "Anyone ever tell you that you're bossy?"

She giggled as she picked up her bowl and stirred the contents, steam rising to entice her with the rich fragrance. "All the time," she laughed. "By the way, I cleaned up your mess on the floor over there." She pointed to an area on the floor of the kitchen where she had swept up the hair clippings from earlier.

"My mess? Just who was doing the shearing?" he asked, adoring the sound as she laughed at his indignant tone, running her knuckles down his shaven cheek.

"If I'd known that all I had to do to get you in bed was shave, I would've done it the moment I found you in the snow," he said amorously. He was rewarded with her sharp little elbow stabbing him in the ribs, causing him to grunt loudly and her to giggle wickedly.

They ate in silence for a few moments, looking longingly into each other's eyes as Skoll begged silently from his spot on the floor. "If we were at my house, we would be eating some fresh-baked bread with this," Carissa sighed wistfully.

"There's a jar of yeast in the pantry if you want to make some bread," he told her. "I don't know if it's any good. It's been in there for awhile. I tried to make some once but it didn't turn out so well. I dropped it and the floor broke. See?" He pointed to a cracked flat rock in the stone floor.

She laughed at his little joke before snuggling against him. She set her bowl on the table and turned to nibble along the stretch of muscle that spread out from his collarbone. It was all the prompting he needed to reach over her and sweep his arm across the table; clearing the surface in a loud clatter of wooden bowls and metal spoons hitting the stone surface of the floor. Skoll's patience had paid off as he busily cleaned the floor with his huge tongue while Bryce lifted Carissa's giggling body up and onto the table.

Bryce bent over Carissa, laying her on her back, trailing kisses and the tips of his fingers down the silken skin of her torso. She writhed and moaned in heated pleasure against the rough surface of the wooden table, her hands tangling in the thick, black locks of his hair. She let out a little cry as his mouth captured one of her nipples, suckling the knotted bud; while his other hand kneaded the rounded flesh of her other breast. Neither of them noticed as Skoll let out an indignant groan and quickly exited the room.

His mouth abandoned her right breast as he moved to her left one, capturing the neglected left nipple gently between his teeth. Her back arched, pushing her flesh against his mouth as she whimpered at the sensations he created in her body. His right hand moved lower, skimming over the soft down of her sex before his fingers worked tenderly to open the flower of her lips and stroke the wet flesh within.

With a moan, he released her nipple and worked his way lower over the soft silken flesh of her belly, and lower still, to brush his lips against bony protrusions of her pelvis at her hips and the satiny skin of her inner thighs as they dangled over the edge of the table. Her sweet moans enticed him, urging him to taste the wetness at her center, his tongue laving her swollen lips in slow, teasing circles. When the realization that he had stopped his tantalizingly slow torment of her body finally penetrated the haze of carnal pleasure that clouded her mind, she opened her eyes to find him standing over her, grinning wickedly, a mischievous gleam in his eyes.

"Why are you looking at me like that?" she asked suspiciously.

"I'm thinking that I need vengeance for what you did to me earlier," he intoned with mock maliciousness.

"For what? What did I do?" She was suddenly wary, wondering what she had done wrong.

"You shaved off a mountain man's beard, evil wench." He laughed at her startled expression.

"It needed shaving…" she began, only to see him move suddenly away, out of her limited range of vision.

When Bryce returned to stand between her legs again, he held up the gleaming scissors, laying the closed straight razor on her belly with his other hand, grinning in lustful glee.

"Exactly what are you planning?" she demanded as she rose up on her elbows.

Bryce pushed her back down saying, "You better hold still. You don't want to get nicked."

He bent to take a few locks of her feathery pubic hair in his hand and snip it off with the scissors. She let out a squeal of indignation, drawing a soft chuckle from his throat. He snipped another handful of hair as she tried to wriggle from under his grasping hands.

"Don't make me spank you," he said with mock sternness.

She laughed aloud. "You're evil!" she exclaimed.

"And you love it," he returned.

He set the scissors on the table to take hold of her feet and prop them on the table's edge, pushing her knees far apart and leaving her wide open. "Keep your legs like that," he ordered.

He returned to the pleasurable task of closely cropping her pubic curls and tossing the spent hair on the floor. When he finished that task, he ran his hand over the stubbly surface, finding just how arousing the experience was for her in how wet her flesh had become. Carissa moaned and moved her hips up against his hand without realizing it.

Bryce stepped out of her view again, returning with the old shaving cup and brush in one hand and a wet towel, heated with the water from the kettle in the other. He was rewarded with another squeal as he laid the hot towel over her sex while he worked the lather in the cup. Again, he grinned at her with a licentious spark in his eyes. Setting the foam-filled cup aside, he removed the cooling towel from her skin, taking just a moment to drag the cloth down the swollen cleft, drawing a loud moan from her mouth.

He tossed the towel aside, taking up the cup and using the brush to slowly spread the lather over the entire area of her sex, teasing her with the feathery bristles. Looking decidedly evil, he held up the razor, opening it and dangling it before her eyes. She moaned out a nervous laugh, trying to bring her knees together before he could start the final step.

"I'll punish you," he warned as he arched a brow at her.

She let her knees drop apart again, not at all perturbed, but very electrified by his expression. Her entire body had come alive under his play, strangely stimulated by the eroticism of his actions. Bryce brought the razor down, sliding the blade gently over the top of her mound and downward and wiping the blade clean on the discarded towel. He made a second swipe and then a third. With each strip of skin he bared, the sensation of cool air brought her a strange new stimulation, causing soft moans and a fresh flood of wet excitement to gush from her insides.

He took his time, enjoying the power to explore and tease her body that she was allowing him. If she had shown any true objection to his plan, he would have quickly dispensed with it, not wanting to do anything that would upset her, but to be able to take such liberties with this delectable creature had his own body aroused to the point of rock-hardness. He was relishing every sensation that her prone body was evoking in him, every sound that her throat emitted as his hands worked.

"Now, hold very still," he warned. "This area here is a little tricky."

She moaned again as he took one of her swollen lips between his fingers, stretching it while he dragged the blade over it. He repeated the action on the other side, his hard cock throbbing in anticipation as he removed the last of her intimate hair. Once she had been completely denuded, he stepped away to return with another warm towel and cleaned the remains of the soap from her skin. This simple action drew another low moan from her lips as she once again began to writhe under his touch.

"Now I dine," he said with a chuckle as he pulled up his chair and sat down.

Carissa cried out as his mouth descended upon her flesh, now overly sensitized by the erotic shave he had just given her. His tongue came into contact with her clitoris, sending a jolt of electricity through her body. He reached up with his left hand to tease one nipple while simultaneously caressing her drenched pussy with his right. Slipping a finger into her, he timed his strokes with the flicks of his tongue across her clit until her entire body clenched, raising her hips off the table. Her inner muscles clamped around his thrusting finger as she screamed and shuddered in the throes of a sublime orgasm.

He slowed his movements for a moment, giving her a chance to calm herself, before increasing the intensity of his assault on her flesh once again. It was not long before she was bucking against his mouth again, crying out and clutching at his hair. He pushed her to a third climax before the demands of his own rigid arousal could no longer be denied.

He stood abruptly, kicking the chair aside and lifting her legs up nestling her thighs against her upper body. His cock seemed to know where to go without any direction from him as he plunged deeply into her, holding there, enjoying the hot velvet of her canal. He could not remain still for long, his need driving him beyond reason, his hips pulling back slowly and plunging forth again. Somewhere in the rapturous fog that had enveloped him, he heard her cry his name as he continued to lunge in and out of her body.

He could feel her muscles tightening around him as her own pleasure was driving her again to the pinnacle of ecstasy when, pulling her legs down to wrap around his waist, he lifted her against his body. Holding her upright he pounded into her, feeling the intensity of her small body as she bucked wildly against him, throwing her head back and voicing her climax in small, sobbing cries. At the same moment, he launched his seed into her womb in a guttural cry of pure euphoria, stumbling back under the force of his climax and falling against the wall for support.

Holding her shuddering body tightly, still hard inside her, he carried her from the kitchen into the main room and laid her on the bed. He shifted his panting body off her, pulling her up against him as they lay on their sides, gazing at one another.

"I think I have a splinter in my butt," she said.

Bryce guffawed loudly and reached down to cup her offended body part. "I'll suck it out later. Right now I'm exhausted. You wore me out."

She snuggled up against him, enjoying the feel of his hand massaging her derriere. "Has your need for vengeance been slaked?"

"For the moment, love," he laughed, reaching for the rumpled bedding to cover their shaken bodies. "No woman has ever affected me like you," he added with a touch of sadness in his voice.

Carissa wondered at that note of melancholy, making a mental note to ask him about it later. For the moment, however, she could not keep her eyes open, and gave in to the drowsy after-effects of their primal sexual encounters. She dropped off to sleep wrapped in the warmth and comfort of his body, and dreamed of waking to make love all over again.

Chapter 12

The days tumbled by into weeks with the bliss that only two lovers could find when exploring one another's bodies and minds. They opened to each other, talking of their pasts, their dreams and their disappointments. They made love passionately in the dark of cold night and the light of new day, some days barely venturing from the huge bed that became the center of their world. Skoll would prance endlessly until Bryce would be forced to leave the warmth of Carissa's body to take his stalwart companion out for some exercise and to hunt for fresh meat, protein to keep up the strength of the ardent lovers.

Bryce had killed a turkey one day in late November; his pride in this rare accomplishment evident when he carried the bird into the cabin, declaring that Thanksgiving must be near. He was crestfallen, however when he had seen the sadness that clouded her eyes for a moment before she had hidden it behind a sunny smile. He knew that she pined for her children, her loneliness for them sometimes evident in the way she would cry in her sleep, calling their names and moaning. Each time that she spoke of her family, he was reminded that one day she would be leaving him, to return to her children and take up her life where she had left off, and he would again be alone.

Bryce had told Carissa of his time as an investment advisor back east, and his childhood in the mountainous climes of Wyoming. He talked of his father, who still lived in Casper, Wyoming and his mother who had died while he was away at college. He had done his graduate studies at Yale, his grandfather's alma mater. He talked of his beloved grandfather, who had built the cabin, and that man's great love for the woman who had died before Bryce was born. The man never remarried, spending the rest of his life mourning his great love.

Bryce talked of all these things but still refused to tell her how he had acquired the scars that marred his face and covered much of his chest. Pressing him on the question would often lead to his sullen dark moods, but Carissa refused to give up. Something was eating away at his soul, no matter the small happiness they had found together, and she knew that unless he let go of that pain, he would never truly be free of the nightmares that haunted him.

As they sat, naked and wrapped in the old quilt from the bed in Bryce's recliner, on one of the long nights that marked early December, Carissa felt his fingers tracing one of the faint, snake-like scars that curled over her lower back. The sensation was just as arousing as any other he had given her body over the past weeks, causing her to sigh contentedly as she snuggled against his warm, hard body. Her hand, which had been enjoying the rough texture of the two-day growth of beard on his jaw, gently tugged his face around to look away from the blazing fire and at her face.

"My ex-husband did that to me," she murmured. "It's what happens when you serve him with divorce papers. He tore the electrical cord out of my toaster, held me down and beat me with it."

Bryce could not help the rage that burned in his eyes at her admission. "If I ever see the son-of-a-bitch, I'll kill him," he growled earnestly.

She shook her head against his chest. "No, Bryce. He was paid back. I stopped him myself, and when the ambulance came that day it was to take him to the hospital, not me. I'm not a woman to give in to such mistreatment." She sighed as she looked at the flames on the grate.

"He wasn't always like that, you know."

"They never are," he retorted.

"No, you don't understand. He was a good man and a good husband, until the accident. He worked in the manufacturing business. He was one of the managers at a plant, and was well liked and respected. We were really happy together." She stopped and sighed again. "Then, at one of the loading bays, an over-head door malfunctioned and dropped on his head. There was spinal damage. He had a severe concussion. He was in a coma for nearly four weeks. When he came around, he wasn't the same. The nerve damage in his neck caused chronic pain and there were other issues. I can't remember the big words the doctors used but the personality centers in his brain were affected.

"After that he became withdrawn and hateful. He would lie around the house for days, and then suddenly go nuts, lashing out at everyone and everything. Before the accident he was so thrilled to find out I was pregnant. Afterwards he hated me for adding another burden to his life. He became so unpredictable that I was walking on eggshells all the time. He had never hit me, but I was scared just the same. When Jon-Jon was born, he swore that he would do better. He went to see a specialist and was diagnosed with bipolar disease, brought on by the brain damage from the accident. He was put on medication and for a while it looked like everything was going to be all right.

"Shortly after I discovered I was pregnant again, he decided to stop taking the medication. Things got bad then. I was in my eighth month with Alicia when he hit me the first time. He knocked me across the room. He was insane at that moment, and I managed to get out of the house to the neighbor's. He was locked up in the psych ward. I gave birth while he was in the hospital, and he didn't even get to see his new daughter until she was two weeks old. When he came home, I told him that if he ever went off his meds again he would be out of my life forever. He cried and promised to take care of the kids and me, and spend the rest of his life making it up to me.

"There were times when he'd just seem to give up. He'd stay in bed for weeks at a time, and have nothing to do with any of us. Then the doctors would change his medication again and everything would get better again. One day I came home from work early to find the house in a shambles with him on the floor in the kitchen ranting about something. He looked insane, clutching a huge knife, and when he saw me, I swear I saw murder in his eyes. I ran out of there fast.

"He was taken back to the hospital and I packed up my kids and moved away. I couldn't take anymore. Every day I'd wonder if that would be the day I would wake up to find my children slaughtered and my own throat cut. When my attorney served him with the papers a few months later, he came to my mother's house and started beating me. Mom tried to stop him but he hit her, too. While his back was turned, attacking Mom, I broke a vase over his head. The worst of it was that my kids saw it happen and Mom got hurt.

"I got full custody of the kids. He wasn't even allowed supervised visits. But before I left on my business trip, he was petitioning the court, saying that he was under a doctor's supervision and his condition had been stabilized. I'm so worried that he will get his hands on them. I'm scared of what he'll do."

Bryce's arms tightened around her little body as if to shield and protect her. He had no words that would offer comfort, only the anger he felt toward the man who had caused so much pain in Carissa's life, and the sadness of knowing she would have to leave him at the end of the winter. He did not want to think of the loneliness or the emptiness of his mountain cabin after she was gone. She had become everything to him, his world and his reason for living.

"Bryce," she said softly, looking into his eyes. "I told you mine, now it's your turn."

"Drop it, Carissa," he told her for the hundredth time. How could he tell her what had happened and what he'd done? How could he bear to watch that light of love go out in her fathomless green eyes?

She sat up and pulled slightly away from him. "I won't drop it, Bryce," she said softly, gravely. "Something is eating you alive. I can feel it and I can see it. I know that something truly horrible happened. If you tell me what it is, maybe I can help you through it."

He lifted her off his lap, standing and depositing her nude form back onto the chair. "Leave it be. Leave me be!" he yelled.

Carissa sat in stunned silence, staring up at his face and the anger that smoldered in his gray eyes. She watched as he turned on his heel, pulling clothing out and dressing in fluid movements. He looked like a predator, quick and graceful and out for blood, his eyes dark and foreboding. As he pulled his boots on, Carissa decided that enough was enough and stood to face him boldly.

"That's enough!" she yelled. "Where the hell are you going in the middle of the night?"

He merely glared up at her from his position on the edge of the bed. *My God*, he thought, *but she's beautiful.* He did not stop what he was doing, however, as he stood to walk around her. He had to get away from her before he did something stupid, such as unburden his heavy soul.

She blocked his path, putting all her diminutive weight and strength into shoving him back. "You don't get to walk away from this. Why are you so scared to open up to me? Don't you trust me by now?" Her voice had dropped to a soft plea.

Bryce hated the pain he saw in her eyes and knew that she was feeling betrayed. He grasped her arms, giving her a little shake before drawing her into his embrace. She was shivering, as much from emotion as from the cold, he knew. He hugged her tightly, burying his face in the fragrant locks of her hair and inhaling her essence as if for the last time. She had hit the point dead-on when she had asked if he trusted her. He did not know if he could trust her with this terrible secret, if he could trust her to still care about him, to not fear him as all the others had.

He scooped her body up into his arms, and turning, laid her down on the bed, settling her against the pillows. After retrieving and tucking the quilt around her, he sat on the edge of the bed and turned his face away from her, slumped forward with his elbows on his knees. They sat silently for long moments before Bryce finally spoke.

"I want to trust you, Carissa, but I'm not... I did something bad, really bad. I have no right to expect anyone to care about me, especially someone as special as you." His voice trailed off into the torment that was consuming his soul.

Carissa sat up and drew her knees to her body, leaning forward and wanting to touch him. She pulled her hand back, deciding to let him talk in his own time and to listen quietly. Her heart was breaking at the pain she heard in his voice, a pain born of self-loathing and self-recrimination.

He pushed his hand through his hair, the length of it falling about his shoulders in a cloud of black. Keeping his back to her, he searched for the words to tell her what he had done. "I was married," he said at long last. "I don't think I told you that. She was beautiful and I loved her. She had a way of smiling at me that made everything disappear except for her smiling face. She wanted lots of kids and a house in the country – and she wanted me." He stopped again, bowing his head and rubbing his palms together between his legs.

Taking a deep, shaky breath, he continued. "Her family was in Washington State. We had decided to come out west to visit both our families. We took an extended vacation and drove across country, sight-seeing and..." He stopped as if the pain of memory was too much for him, his voice dying away on a quiver.

He cleared his throat and started again. "We'd already spent a few days at my dad's and we went up to Yellowstone. We were on route fourteen, heading north. It was getting dark. There wasn't much traffic, still early in the season. We wanted to camp near Indian Creek, maybe do some fishing in the morning, or just go hiking."

He fell silent. Memories came flooding back, terrible memories of his wife's horrified voice screaming, memories of her bloodied face begging him to help her. He struggled to get control of the pain that threatened to choke the life out of his body. "We were laughing at some stupid joke. I turned to look at her, she was so beautiful and so happy. Then her expression changed to horror and I turned to see but it was too late. There was a truck, a fucking drunk driver, they told me later. It was coming at us. I tried to get out of the way but it was just too late. I heard her scream and then everything went black. I guess I was knocked unconscious."

His next words were spoken, haltingly, in hushed tones, the pain in his voice, unbearable to hear. "When I woke up, my legs were pinned. Everything was dark except for a beam of light from somewhere above us. It took me a minute to figure out that the roof of the car was gone and that a truck was sitting on top of us, one of its headlights was dangling and still lit. I heard a sound like the gurgling of water and turned to see Anna. She was pinned and covered in blood. Blood was coming out of her mouth and nose. Her eyes were staring straight up, she wasn't moving."

He ground the heels of his hands into his eye sockets, as if to drive out the images that clouded his vision. The memories sat like a weight on his chest, pushing the air from his lungs, crushing his heart in its grip and robbing him of his strength. There was no way to shut out the sound of the appalling scream that played over and over in his mind like a broken record. The sensation of the crimson stickiness of blood on his hands was so real he had to look at them, try to wipe them clean on his jeans. The smell of pain and fear hung in the air of the cabin as it had permeated the air that night. Above all, the vision of her eyes, their light dwindling in his sight, hovered in front of him, haunting him to his core.

"I pulled myself up as much as I could and leaned over to look at her. She looked at me. She was terrified and in so much pain. I could see the chassis of the truck was crushing her. She was cut nearly in two above her waist. Each breath she took was more pain than she could stand. She put her lips together, said one word, 'Please' and it sounded like death in my ears."

Bryce stopped again, his body rigid as the torment of that moment ripped through his soul. The memory of that sputtered word, the blood that splattered on her scant breath was fresh in his mind, as he relived the anguishing devastation of that night. A sound akin to that of a wounded bear rumbled in his chest as he fought his way through the pain.

He could not explain the horror of seeing her like that, the look in her eyes as pain, unbearable and anguishing, grilled into her. How could he tell Cari the way Anna gasped for every breath or how she had looked at him when he had tried to tell her she would be okay, that she just had to hang on? They both knew she was dying, no one could survive the injuries that she had sustained. Every word of comfort fell inadequately from his lips.

"A park ranger was there, told me to hang on, he was going to call for help, but Anna was pleading. She needed me to help her." He clenched his eyes closed, lost in horror. The truck had shifted; the soundless scream that had come from Anna's mouth was all it took. He could not let the pain continue, the begging in her eyes, the need for release was all it took. "I put one hand over her eyes. I couldn't stand to watch them anymore. She was hurting so... I... couldn't.... I put the other hand over her mouth and nose... suffocated her... choked the life... I killed her. I had to."

His words died away to a rattling, painful snarl in his throat. He took several shaking breaths before continuing. "The ranger saw what I was doing and tried to stop me. It was too late; she was gone. I killed my wife. They called me a murderer. I killed her to stop her pain. I had to. She couldn't stand it." A sob tore from his throat as he felt Carissa's warm body pressing against his back, her arms wrapping around his shoulders and pulling him back into her. "I loved her and I killed her."

"You didn't kill her, Bryce. A drunk did. You only eased her pain." Carissa crooned behind him, against his ear.

He reached around and pulled her into his arms, burying his face against her neck. His body shook violently as she ran her hands over his head and shoulders, trying to soothe away the guilt and pain that had been consuming him for years. "I love you, Bryce," she whispered.

He pulled his head up to look into her eyes. He was searching for the loathing that he expected to see, still believing that she would turn from him now that his ugly secret was out. What he saw became his saving grace, for what he saw was the truth of her words. That light had not gone out, but was burning more brightly than the sun, and brought warmth to the cold, dead recesses of his damaged soul. He found redemption in those eyes, atonement in the way she welcomed him into her heart, unconditionally and without reservation. She was his salvation.

Burrowing his face in her hair, he hugged her tightly, nearly crushing her in his fierce embrace. When her ribs began to throb under his grip, she began to work his arms loose, pushing him gently back on the bed. She helped him to remove his clothing, then slid under the blankets with him to press the heat of her body against his still-shaking frame. Murmuring soft words against his skin, she held him until he dropped off into a deep, dreamless sleep. Carissa had reached him at last, broken through that wall that he had erected around his pain, and helped him to let go. She closed her eyes and drifted off, listening to the steady rhythm of his heart under her ear.

A clear sky and bright sunshine streamed through the windows of the cabin, setting the room ablaze with unfamiliar brilliance, as Bryce slowly climbed out of the deep sleep that had subdued him in the night. Heat suffused his muscles, along with a sensual pleasure that robbed him of his ability to focus his mind. Something small and alive was nestled between his legs; warm breath and wet heat surrounded the area of his groin. A moan escaped his lips as he tossed the blankets back to discover Carissa's burning green eyes smiling up at him from her position below his waist.

"About time," she said as she slowly stroked her small hand down the length of his shaft. "Your dick and I have been up for hours, just wondering when you'd get in on the act."

A deep, throaty chuckle rumbled in his chest and rasped into a growling moan as she lowered her sweet mouth over half the length of him. "Dear God, woman," he groaned as his hips rose of their own volition. "You must be a witch."

His hand reached out, boring his long fingers into the tangles of her hair. The moist inferno of her mouth drove his need to a fevered pitch, relentlessly caressing and teasing him. He warned her of the impending explosion building in his center, but she pursued that release, quickening her pace as she moved over his throbbing cock. With one mighty thrust, he drove into her throat, detonating in streams of heated liquid and ragged growls.

His sated body sagged onto the mattress, shuddering as she slowly caressed his throbbing member with her tongue, drawing the pleasure out as long as possible. Finally releasing her feast, she slid her body up along his until she lay upon his chest, ruffling his hair lightly with her delicate hand. She smiled impishly into his eyes, causing his heart to skip a beat.

"What a way to wake up," he grinned back at her.

"I tried everything else. You were sleeping like a log."

Bryce stroked his hands down the silken curve of her slender back and over the rounded firmness of her bottom. "You've been wearing me out, sweetness," he said as he squeezed the tantalizing flesh under his fingers. He worked his hands lower, between her thighs to the wet silkiness of her sex, his fingers dancing slowly along the length of her slit.

Her impassioned moan was all the incentive he needed to roll her onto her back and return the favor. His movements were slow, almost lazy, as he explored her body with his mouth and his hands. He kissed her lips languorously, his tongue teasing its way past her small, white teeth to the sweet nook of her mouth where it waltzed gently with the pink flesh of her tongue. Drawing the kiss out, he kept his hands in play, lightly sweeping her arms with his fingertips and tangling softly in her hair.

Ending the kiss, he rolled onto his side and propped his head up on his hand to better view the expressions on her lovely face as he pursued her pleasure at a leisurely pace. The faint scars on her face from her misadventures in the wilderness were fading slowly away, he noted with no small amount of joy. She would not be marked for everyone in the world to see, as he was, something he would not wish on anyone.

As he trailed his fingers over the rest of her curved body he inspected each of her injuries with care, each of them having healed completely. Though one or two of the scars looked as if they would be permanent, he felt that the rest would disappear with time. Her hands, he noticed as he laced his fingers through hers, were still rough, dry and red but they would heal soon and the fingernails were growing back nicely. He kissed her fingertips, drawing each into his mouth to suckle individually, drawing sweet sighs from her lips.

He returned to lightly stroking the skin of her torso, starting with the delicate, tender flesh at the base of her throat, trailing along her collarbones and down her arms, one at a time. To him, the experience was similar to caressing the fine petals of a spring rose. His fingers moved on, light as a feather, to the straight line of her breastbone, lingering in the valley between her firm, plump breasts as she arched her back and caught the tempting treat of her lower lip in her sharp, little teeth.

"You're driving me crazy," she moaned up into his smoldering eyes.

A deep, husky chuckle rumbled in his chest as she squirmed urgently under his touch. "Good, then we're even," he grinned in return.

Circling a finger around the globe of her left breast, he moved round and round the quivering flesh in ever decreasing circles until he came in contact with the straining peak of her dark pink nipple. Her voice whimpered at him, her back arching against his hand as he twirled the hardened knot between his fingers, pulling gently to heighten her pleasure. When he had teased the bit of flesh into a tortuous welt, he moved on to the right one, treating it with the same tormenting thoroughness.

By the time he slid his open palm over the gentle slope of her belly, Carissa was writhing in pleasurable agony and moaning her urgency. Bryce slipped his frame down the bed, keeping his eyes at the same level of her body as his hand, watching how her skin tightened under the touch of his hand. Her body was mesmerizing to him, an obsessive delight to see, hear, taste and smell. He took in every nuance down to her insistent whimper as he tickled her navel.

He moved his body down farther, sitting to take her slender leg into his hands and caress the entire length. He enjoyed the way her bottom lifted as his fingers moved near the apex between her thighs, and the moan of protest as he released that limb to take hold of the other. Finally, he spread her knees widely, seating himself between them as his hands skimmed up the silken flesh of her inner thighs.

Carissa let her eyes travel the length of her body to where he was kneeling, gazing at her with a burning passion that only fueled her own flames. His hands were driving her to the edge of her endurance, and if that were not enough, she could feel on her skin everywhere that his eyes touched, a blazing path over her flesh that heightened the color in her cheeks. His thorough inspection had her wanting to cover herself or throw him down and have her way with him; she could not seem to make up her mind.

Bryce traced his fingers over the top of her mound, around the closely cropped hair that was slowly growing back, and down the junction of her legs. He loved the way her hips gyrated and squirmed in an effort to direct his fingers to the place of her desire. His amusement increased with each pleading whimper and deranged moan that tumbled from her mouth as he mercilessly teased her senses.

A small squeal of fevered delight erupted from her mouth the minute his fingers at last came into contact with her most intimate flesh. He gently pried open the swollen, aching lips of her sex to see what secrets they concealed. Therein he found enough to have his pulse racing and his cock pulsating with an almost electrical shock. The rosy color of the inner flesh and the amount of liquid heat glistening within the folds fascinated him. The hard kernel of her clitoris peeked out at him from under its hood, begging to be coddled by his tongue.

He had to have a taste of her, had to feel her dripping warmth in his mouth and her body shuddering under him. Without further prelude, his mouth claimed that prize wrenching a sob from the throat of his victim as his long, tapered finger slowly slithered into her body. He hooked the tip of his finger upward, finding that mysterious section of succulent flesh that, when stimulated, would send her into mindless spasms of pleasure.

He flicked his tongue over the rigid gem of her clit in time to the movements of his finger, rewarded within moments by her shuddering screams while the muscles inside her body clamped around his digit, and she bucked wildly against his face. They seemed to go on forever, those waves of ecstasy that had seized her body, his mouth driving her harder and higher. Finally, her convulsing body crashed against the mattress, quivering, panting, moaning in sobs.

Bryce was shaking when his mouth released her; the pulsating hardness of his cock would no longer be denied. Rising up on his knees, he grasped her hips and pulled her bottom over his thighs, impaling her almost brutally on his shaft. He pummeled her small body in a frenzied siege of carnal force, pushing her to another shattering climax before he exploded in a river of seminal fluid.

Absolutely slaked, his exhausted body fell forward on his hands, his arms straddling her shoulders as he locked eyes with her. "I love you," he breathed out. "You're my whole world."

Chapter 13

Carissa awoke with a gnawing in her belly and a tight soreness between her legs. Still there was a contented smile on her lips when she rolled over to touch Bryce, but the smile faded when she discovered him gone. The late afternoon sun streaming through the windows, which she had opened earlier to the light, was casting long shadows across the stone floor.

Her brows drew together, her full lower lip protruding in a slight pout, as disappointment offered the only cloud in this otherwise beautiful day. Her smile soon returned however, as she allowed herself a long and luxurious stretch under the blankets. It felt wonderful to be alive.

Sitting up, she found the cabin to be warm with a roaring fire on the hearth and the delicious aroma of something wonderful bubbling on the stove. She wasted little time in hauling herself out of bed, laughing about how strange it felt to be on her feet – she so seldom was anymore. Bryce's discarded shirt still held his scent as she slipped her arms into the sleeves and held the soft flannel collar to her nose. It was a wonderful fragrance that brought that soft, moist heat flooding between her thighs again.

The huge shirt flowed loosely about her slender body as she padded across the cold stones of the floor with bare feet. Upon entering the kitchen, she was disappointed again that Bryce was nowhere to be found, but the old bathtub sat on the floor, hot vapor rising to mingle with the steam of the stew that simmered on the stovetop. A soft smile curved her generous lips upward at the thoughtfulness of the man who now owned her heart. For a giant growling bear, he definitely had a sweet side that endeared him to her, something that only made her want to love him more.

She paid a quick visit to the chilly privy through the pantry, an ingenious little room that Bryce had said his grandfather had built because his grandmother had refused to use an outhouse. It was reminiscent of the old-fashioned "water closet" of by-gone days. After using the commode, one had only to pull a chain to release the water stored in a tank high up on the wall to flush the waste away, the water carrying it through nearly fifty yards of pipes to an ancient septic system down hill below the cabin. It amazed Carissa how the water tank refilled from a large reservoir mounted on a sturdy log shelf, a float valve terminating the flow of water once it hit the right level. Bryce had to fill the holding tank with buckets when it became too low, using a set of steps that had been built for that purpose.

Returning to the kitchen and its inviting warmth, Carissa let the shirt slither to the floor as she stepped into the tub, her body slipping down into the water to immerse as deeply as the little reservoir would allow. It was difficult to imagine ever being anywhere as heavenly as this cabin in the middle of nowhere with this man who made her shiver and moan.

The only thing that could possibly make it better would be to have her children with them. The contented smile faded at that thought, her mind turning to the tiny faces of those most dear in her life. It had been so long since she had seen them, so long since she had been able to wrap her arms around their small, wriggling bodies and hold them the way only a mother knows how to do. She wondered if they were eating right, if they were well, how much they had grown.

Tears threatened to spill at the worry that their father might be in control of them at this very moment, might be frightening them. She would not allow herself to think that he might be physically hurting them; it was too painful for her mind to grasp.

Unbidden reminiscences of holidays shared came from the reaches of her memory with bright shining eyes and childish giggles as laden stockings were ransacked and gift-wrapping was torn asunder. Impish squeals of delight echoed within her homesick mind, bringing the tears that she tried to hold in check. That chamber of the heart that her children occupied ached fervently as her desire to be home nearly overwhelmed the happiness of being with the man she loved.

Carissa heard the cabin door open, felt the cool draft wend its way into the kitchen and across her wet skin. She quickly stanched to flow of tears, scrubbing her face quickly with the woodsy-scented soap. If Bryce were to see that she had been crying, there would be concern in his eyes and she only wanted to see his joy, to feel his happiness.

Bryce entered the room, a gorgeous smile on his dark face and in his hands, a wreath of pine boughs interwoven with blue Juniper and bright orange Bittersweet berries. Skoll accompanied him, trotting into the room and pausing his dancing gait to lick at Carissa's face. The broad, boyish grin, so wonderful to see on Bryce's face, turned to a worried frown when he looked at her wet face. She knew she could not hide the redness of her eyes and nose, or the tears that still glistened in her eyes.

"What is it?" he asked as he shooed the dog away.

"You made me a wreath? It's beautiful. Thank you," she said as she smiled up at him.

"You've been crying," his deep voice stated abruptly. "What's wrong?" He tossed the wreath onto the table and knelt beside the tub.

Another tear slipped down her cheek as still more danced in her eyes. "Don't mind me. I'm just feeling emotional. What do you expect after what you did to my body this morning?" She made a little laugh but it sounded more like a sob.

He was not buying the explanation for a minute, could see the sadness in her eyes. He knew what was going through her mind and it only served to remind him that he would have to give her up one day, a thought that tore at his own heart. A strange impotent anger filled his chest; he was helpless in the face of his future loss and the unhappiness on Carissa's face, even if she was trying to hide it.

"Are you sure that's all?" His gruff question came out more harshly than he had intended.

She merely nodded, her smile tremulous as she laid her head against the back of the tub and closed her eyes. She had to get hold of herself, was determined to keep him happy within the seclusion of this wilderness. A sigh escaped her lips as his fingers smoothed back a curl that clung to her damp cheek. His touch, his smile, his smoldering gray eyes were the only joy she knew at present, and her soul needed him.

His lips brushed her forehead in an achingly tender kiss that threatened to have her weeping again. To distract her mind, she sat up and handed him the bar of soap still clutched in her fingers, a soft smile on her lips.

"Wash my back?" she asked sweetly as she gathered her dark, burnished curls and pulled them over her alabaster shoulder.

Bryce was motionless for long moments studying the contours of her face and the emotion in her eyes before taking hold of the soap. He ignored the proffered washcloth, preferring to massage the suds over her silky skin with his bare hands. She was intoxicating to him, a drug to which he had become irreversibly addicted. How was he going to live without her sweet smile, her warm body next to his, or the way his heart raced every time he looked at her beautiful face?

Cupping his hands, he dipped into the water to pour over her back, rinsing away the lather before smoothing his palms over the wet skin. He told her to lift her chin so that he could pour fresh warm water over her head and wash her hair. It was a task that he had come to enjoy; an act of tender care that stimulated his desire for Carissa. Not just sexually, but for her entire being; mind, body, heart and soul.

His hands shook as he rinsed the last of the soap bubbles from her hair, his mood growing considerably darker. He held a towel for her as she stepped from the tub onto the cold floor. Her body shivered slightly as it left the warm water of the tub, her nipples drawing taut, begging to be touched and teased. He turned from her, walking to the main room of the cabin struggling to keep his own emotions in check.

Carissa, confused by his sudden abrupt departure, bent to retrieve her discarded shirt, pulling it over her still-damp skin. Using the towel to dry her tangled locks of hair and hanging his sweet gift of the wreath on her arm, she left the kitchen in his wake, wondering if he were feeling all right. She found him standing in front of a window, his hands on his hips, his back rigid as he stared out into the waning afternoon sunlight.

"Bryce?" she called out softly when she saw him.

He did not turn, only stared silently, seeing nothing. He was angry, almost as angry as he had been the day she had told him the story of how she came to be lost in the wilderness. He had wanted to kill the bastards who had dared to lay a hand on her, and he had wanted to do it with his bare hands. He knew their names well: Kyle Pritchert and Bert Adams. There was no one that he could direct this new anger at, however. All he could do was turn it inward, try to contain it and keep it from her as he struggled to get past it.

Carissa's shoulders rose in a sigh as she watched him, wondering what he was thinking, but not daring to ask. There was a sudden gaping distance between them, something that she did not like, but she did not know what to do about it. Her head shook in dismay at his lightning quick moods, wishing she could bridge the gap between them.

She spied something on the rumpled bed, a fairly large package wrapped in cloth and tied with twine. There was a small bouquet of Juniper and Bittersweet sprigs, tied within the bow that held the edges of the cloth closed. "What's this?" she asked, her voice betraying the delight she felt in her heart.

Bryce turned to see her, the shirt that covered her was open down the front, exposing the tantalizing line of her breastbone that led to her navel, and then to her sex. Her slim legs peered out from the folds of the over-sized garment, begging to be caressed, stroked with the flat of his hand. What captured his heart most, though, was the infinite green light in her eyes that drew him like a moth to a flame.

"I know it's still early for Christmas but," he said with a slight dejected note to his voice, "I thought you could use it now."

He thought she looked sweet and innocent like a girl when she dropped the wreath and took hold of his gift. She had a delighted smile that he found infectious as she carefully pulled the string from the package and removed the cloth. Her face was frozen in wondrous surprise for just a moment at what she found inside, her eyes rising to meet his, a squeal emitting from those succulent lips. She tossed the wrapping aside as she bounded to him, his gift still clutched in her delicate fingers, her arms wrapping around his neck in joy.

"Did you make these?" she asked, her voice astonished.

"Yes," he answered with much less enthusiasm. "When I was a kid I learned by helping a couple of Indian friends of my grandfather's. They made and sold them at a little stand they had."

"They're wonderful!" she twittered as she ran to the bed, hopping onto its massive mattress. "I can't believe you made me moccasins! You're so wonderful. I can't wait to try them on." Within moments, her feet and calves were laced into the warm, soft confines of velvety rabbit fur, her breath exiting her body on a soft sigh. "I feel so bad," she said, distending her lower lip in a mock pout. "I didn't get you anything."

Bryce watched as she sat on the bed, leaning forward over her knees, admiring his handiwork that now warmed her little feet. Her fingers caressed the luxurious fur in enticing strokes that had his mouth watering. A smile broke across his lips as he slowly joined her, sitting on the edge of the bed. "You like?"

"Oh, yes. Thank you so much. You're the sweetest man for doing this. I don't think I've ever known anyone as thoughtful as you. You take such good care of me." She reached out a hand to touch the side of his face.

"I just thought you might like to get outside for awhile," he said as he captured her little hand in his own large paw. "You've been cooped up in here for too long."

"I don't know about that," she said, a bawdy gleam in her eyes. "You've kept me too busy to think about it." She was rewarded with his rich chuckle as he leaned back on his elbow in front of her.

He ran his free hand over her knee and down the front of her fur-encased leg. The sound of a soft sniffle brought his sharp attention back to her face. "What is it?" he asked as she tried to smile over the tears that were welling once again in her olive eyes.

"Oh, nothing. Just being emotional again. You're so good to me," her voice wavered and cracked before the first sob broke.

Bryce gathered her fiercely into his arms, holding her diminutive frame as it shook miserably. Each choking sob tore at his heart until her sadness became his own, clawing at his insides. He held her until the wracking sobs had subsided to hiccupping gasps and his clothing was soaked with her tears.

Finally exhausted, Carissa pushed back from Bryce, gazing into his face, seeing the sorrow in his eyes. "I'm sorry," she hiccupped. "I don't know what's come over me."

"You're homesick," he said simply.

"Bryce," she said timidly, her eyes pleading. "I want you to come home with me."

He felt his heart race and break at the same time. To think that she would want him with her and with her family was so much more than anything for which he could have hoped, a blessing straight from her heart. However, that would mean leaving the sanctity of his mountain world, something he had vowed he would never again do. Life within the society that had shunned him, had castigated him for what he had done, was not for him. He would never be accepted again, a truth with which he was well acquainted. No, he would never leave; it just was not possible. Her plea tore at his heart bringing a pain in the center of his chest around which he was hard-pressed to breathe.

He grazed her cherished face with the tips of his fingers, wishing things could be different. "No, baby," he replied on a ragged breath. "I belong here. I'll never leave this place."

Fresh tears stabbed the backs of her eyes as she tried to swallow around the new lump forming in her throat. Her voice was small, broken, when she tried again. "Please, Bryce. I don't want to be without you. Please won't you come with me? I need you and I know you need me."

He drew her to him again, holding her as if it would be the last time. "I'm not welcome down there. I belong here." Through the nearly intolerable anguish, a thought struck him. It was a chance, small and hardly possible but he had to try. "Why don't you get your kids and bring them here? We can be together always, up here. What do you say?"

She pulled back wondering if she had heard him correctly. Had he really asked her to live with him? Did he intend to spend the rest of his life with her, being a father to her children, in this remote wilderness? The thrill that tickled her spine at his words soon diminished as thoughts of her children living on this mountain brought reality slamming down upon her. "Bryce, we can't. What about school and medical care? What about my mother? We're all she has now. I can't take the kids and abandon her like that. This is no place to raise two small children."

He knew she was right, knew the truth of it before he had spoken the words. He could see the heartache in her eyes, knew that she was feeling what he was, just before he saw the flash of anger. Her fine-boned hands pushed against his chest, shoving him away as she swung her legs off the bed and stalked away. As she neared the door she stopped and turned to face him, her face flushed, unspent tears still shimmering in her eyes. She gave no heed to the shirt that remained unbuttoned or the alluring picture she made, framed in the last rays of the dying day.

"You are so full of shit!" she yelled. "Why won't you go down there? What are you so afraid of?"

"I'm not afraid of anything," he declared calmly. "I just have no business down there. This is my home. This is where I belong."

"That is such fucking bullshit and you know it. Just exactly what is there up here for you? An empty cabin and a lot of trees, and you ain't exactly the tree-hugger type. I should have known you were lying to me."

Bryce struggled to keep his temper under control, knowing that she was lashing out because she was hurt. "What are you talking about? I never lied to you."

"Yes, you did. You told me this morning that you love me. That was a lie," she spat. "If you were really in love with me, you would come with me."

Bryce was on his feet, his own fury bubbling to the surface when she threw his own words back in his face. "And if you loved me you would stay." His voice remained calm, far calmer than he felt at this moment. He knew he was being unfair but he was fighting his own battle against the pain in his heart.

"How can I do that? Huh? Tell me what happens in the dead of winter and one of my children gets sick. Do we wait for him or her to die? Do we pack the kid on our shoulders and carry him out? There are no schools up here. How are they supposed to get an education? Or were you just planning on keeping them ignorant? You know I have no business bringing them here." Her voice had grown shrill but she was past caring.

Yes, he knew, but that did not make it any less painful to see her, hold her, and know that she would be leaving him far too soon. "So, you're just gonna run off."

"You know, I think you want me to leave you all alone up here! That way you can worship Anna in peace. You don't love me. You'd rather wallow in your own self-indulgent crap than face the responsibility of life with another human being."

"Careful, Carissa," he said, his voice low and menacing. His eyes held a warning light meant to turn her blood to ice. "You are stepping way over the line."

She ignored the warning in his eyes, or being more honest, she intentionally threw more fuel on the fire. She was hurt and angry and wanted to make sure that he was hurt too. "No. I don't think I've gone nearly far enough. It's her you love, a dead woman. You don't love me. You don't want me, not really. I was just a sexual substitute for a dead woman."

He stepped closer to her, close enough to grab her and shake her until her teeth rattled, but he did not touch her. He was afraid to, afraid that he would tear her head off. Instead, he kept his voice low, striving for calm as the heat continued to rise in his neck. He stressed each word as he spoke in a voice so low she had to strain to hear it. "Never mention her to me again."

"Or what?" she asked, glaring up at him. "Are we back to making threats then? You feel the need to brutalize me now? I can't believe that I was willing to…" her shaking voice broke off, the growing pain in her chest choking her lungs.

Bryce forced himself to take a step backwards, to put distance between him and the angry hellcat that goaded him. He wavered between the urge to grab her tiny body and wring the life from her, and the desire to take her into his arms and soothe away the hurt he had caused.

"You don't have any idea what you're talking about," his voice climbed. "I won't go back to that life. I lost everything – wife, family, friends. Everyone I knew turned on me. These scars that you seem to like so much are just a reminder that I am a killer, and no one down there is about to let me forget it!"

"Oh, I get it now," she retorted softly. "You're just a coward."

Her words struck hard, wounded him deeply, but only because she was right. He was afraid and he knew it, afraid of what he would find when he reached civilization, afraid of doing that which he knew he was capable, and afraid of proving that he was exactly what everyone believed he was. The knowledge of it, the truth of fear brought the anger to the surface, burning like molten lava.

"That's enough!" his voice roared through the cabin, filling it with his rage. Skoll whimpered softly and slunk away to his corner. "You don't have a fucking clue what the hell you're talking about so just shut your mouth!"

Carissa watched as his fists clenched at his sides, his body crackled with the effort to control himself. She cared little, only cared that she was losing him. While they fought, he was slipping away. The pain in her chest burned as her heart was being ripped in two, and she lashed out at him one more time.

"Go ahead then," she said in a voice so broken it was barely audible. "Stay up here and rot. Live alone with your memories and your guilt; choke yourself on them. Spring won't come fast enough to suit me, and when I'm gone you can remember what you threw away. I put my heart right in your hand, offered you all the love a person has to give and you tossed it back in my face. I hope you live to be a very old man and I hope those memories torment you the rest of your miserable life."

Carissa turned away from him then, her shoulders slumped, her head bowed. He had seen the pain in her eyes, a hurt so near the pain he last saw in Anna's eyes. Her words had stung, driving home the truth of his bleak and empty future. How had he let this tiny creature become so dear to him that to let her go would tear him apart so badly? How had she managed to find her way in, past the walls that he had so carefully built to protect himself from emotional entanglements?

She looked so small, so helpless, as her body quivered in defeat. Only hours earlier they had been happy, joining bodies, clinging to one another in blissful love. Now they were miles apart, a chasm opening between them that seemed impossible to bridge. He wanted to reach out, take her in his arms and make her believe that everything would work out, and put that light back in her eyes. He could not do that, however, could not give her that false hope that would make their parting all the more painful. As he watched her rigid form, a plan started to take root in his mind, a plan that might restore her joy and help her forget about him.

Chapter 14

"Mommy!"

Carissa heard the cry, so small and weak. She wanted to go to it, follow the sound of that frightened little voice, but she could not move. She was struggling against pain, against the hands that held her. The man was all around her, pinching, grabbing, hurting her body, and he would not let her go. Breath, foul and sickening, was exhaled upon her face, her stomach curdling as the stench assaulted her nostrils.

The child's voice cried out again, smaller this time, weaker than before and so full of fear. She heard John's maniacal laughter whirling about her as if caught in the bitter wind. Her claws scored a hit, striking the face that loomed above her, his lecherous sneer turning to rage as the blood beaded on his skin.

"Mommy, please don't go," another sweet voice begged. The world was growing dark, the pain in her body fading. Then she was running, slipping, falling, cold snow was against her skin and the biting wind lashed at her. Hot breath burned her neck, panic and fear pushed her onward.

"I'm coming, babies," she told the faceless voices that called to her. "Mommy's coming."

"Cari," a soft feminine voice said, so near to her that it could be heard above the wind. "Cari, look at me."

She turned, panting, desperate for life-giving oxygen, as she looked at who had spoken her name. It was a wolf, so white that she blended with the surrounding snowy landscape, her eyes a gray so dark as to be black. She knew this wolf, this friend.

"Alice?" Carissa asked.

"Yes, Cari. You must hurry. Your children need you. They are so young and so lost without you. You must hurry." The wolf's dark eyes glittered in warning, a message hidden in their depths.

"But, I'm trapped. I'm lost. I can't find my way home!" Carissa cried.

"Cari."

"Alice! Where are you?" The wolf was gone and everything turned black. "John's here, isn't he? Alice, please!" Carissa was alone.

The hard warm arms of a man closed around her, shutting out the cold, easing the pain. She was safe again. Where was Alice? Her children, what had happened to them? She pushed against the protective warmth of the body that held her so tenderly.

"Cari."

"Nooooo," Carissa moaned. "Alice! No, don't go."

"Carissa!" someone called desperately.

Carissa struggled to free herself, fighting against her own need to stay within the circle of those wonderful arms. Her voice moaned out again as tears spilled from her eyes, slipping down her cheeks. The hands connected to the arms grasped her roughly, shook her body.

"Cari, wake up. You're having a nightmare. Wake up."

Carissa's tear-soaked eyes flew open to see the owner of those arms. "Bryce?"

"Yes, baby. It's me. That was some dream. Are you all right?"

Bryce's eyes, a smoldering gray that reminded her so much of the wolf, were darkened with concern, watching her face intently. She felt the touch of his fingertips as he brushed the tumbling curls away from her face, the caress making her want to melt into him. The memory of their bitter fight flooded her mind at that point, causing her to draw back away from him.

"I'm fine," she informed him frigidly. She looked about her, seeing the gray, pre-dawn sky in the windows and groaning as her stiffened neck throbbed in protest of her movements. She was sleeping in the recliner again, having refused to share the bed with Bryce anymore.

Bryce felt her body turn rigid and released her, knowing that she was still angry with him. The pain he had caused her was now perfectly masked behind a veneer of cold animosity. She was worried; he could see it in her eyes and wondered if she was thinking again of her children. He pulled himself up from the spot where he had been kneeling beside the chair, his mind still working at the plan he had been formulating the night before.

A wolf howled somewhere outside the cabin, drawing a low warning growl from Skoll as he bolted toward the door. Carissa leapt to her feet, dashing to the window to glance at the dawning wilderness. The wolf cried out again, this time farther away and Carissa threw the door open. Skoll loped outside, his hackles raised; ready to run into the forest until Bryce halted him with a sharp command. Carissa laid her hand on the dog's head, glancing about for the creature that had been trying to tell her something.

"Carissa, get back in here before you freeze to death," Bryce sighed in exasperation.

She reluctantly stepped back over the threshold, Skoll by her side as she closed the door. "Something's wrong," her voice wavered as she gazed at Bryce with pleading eyes, her anger apparently forgotten.

"What are you talking about?" Bryce inquired as he studied her face sharply.

"Bryce, I have to get home. Something's wrong, I know it."

"Just because a wolf howled at dawn? Carissa, you're not making sense. I'm sure everything's fine." He hated the way her eyes implored him, hated the worry she was feeling.

Carissa's anger came flooding back, stiffening her spine. "Don't patronize me, you ass."

He smiled ruefully, knowing that she was not likely to ever forgive him. She was right, however; she needed to leave this mountain sanctuary, needed to be free of him. "As you wish," he fairly growled as he turned to dress. "I think you and I could stand a little time apart, don't you? We also need fresh meat. I'm going hunting for a few days." He pulled a thermal shirt over his head. "I'll leave Skoll here with you. Don't leave the cabin. You never know when a grizzly might wake up looking for a snack," he added knowing that the only bears in the state lived in the national parks. "We already know there's a wolf out there."

"So, you're just leaving?" She wanted to slap him for looking so good, pulling on his clothing. "How long will you be gone?"

"I don't know," he said as he finished lacing his hunting boots. "Four or five days, probably."

"What if you get caught in a storm? What if you get hurt and can't make it back?" He was being a complete idiot, in her estimation, and she was suddenly afraid for him.

"Are you genuinely concerned for me?" he asked with a sarcastic gleam in his eyes. "Or are you worried that you'll be left all alone to fend for yourself? Don't worry, if you ration everything properly, I'm sure you'll have enough food to last the winter."

Carissa crossed the room with lightning speed, the flat of her hand connecting sharply with the side of his face. "You son of a bitch!" she screamed at him. "Go on then, get out. Run away and hide. That's all you're good for anyway!"

He seized her arms, lifting her from the floor, her bare feet flailing wildly as he threw her at the bed. She landed hard on the cold mattress, the air leaving her lungs in a less-than-feminine grunt. She no sooner got her bearings than he was upon her, pinning her small frame to the rumpled sheets. He caught her tiny wrists in his great hands, clasping them above her head as he sat with one knee on either side of her ribcage. Her startled eyes stared at the rage on his face, the hatred that froze her aching heart.

"You don't know when to shut up, do you?" he ground out between clenched teeth, seeing her flinch at the wrath in his voice. "I warned you not to push me too far."

Bryce brought his mouth down hard on hers, grinding her lips into her sharp little teeth. He felt her recoil under the sheer brutal force of the kiss, heard her moan of startled pain. He broke the kiss and trailed his lips across her cheek to the pink shell of her ear. "What are you going to do now?" he whispered softly. "Do you have anymore scathing words to hurl at me?"

His mouth worked lower, nipping at the fine line of her jaw before returning to her lips for another unmerciful kiss. When her struggling body went limp under him his kiss softened, his tongue teasing her mouth open and entering to explore. He heard a soft moan and raised his head to see the tears that rolled freely from her eyes. The rage inside him dwindled quickly away at the heartbreaking sorrow he saw in her.

Releasing her hands, he slowly took her face in his hands to dry her face with his thumbs. "Cari, I'm sorry," he rasped as emotion threatened to choke him. Her face had turned ashen, making the angry, red swelling of her soft lips more pronounced. She was blankly staring at him, swallowing hard. He could feel her chest expanding under his heavy body as she tried to breathe.

Bryce hauled himself off her and turned to sit on the edge of the bed. His voice let go an anguished growl as he dropped his head into his hands, searching for something to say or do that would reverse the damage he had done. There was nothing, he knew, that make her forgive him. Nothing would bring back her trusting smile or that cherished light in her eyes. He could not fix this.

Without looking at her silent form again, he shrugged into his parka and gathered his things. Skoll, nervous and whimpering, tried to follow him as he reached for the doorknob, but Bryce ordered him back. Before leaving, he turned and gazed at her expressionless face. "For what it's worth, Carissa, I do love you. I always will," he said quietly. With those words, he turned and walked out the door of the cabin, a determined set to his jaw.

Carissa lay still for a few moments longer, trying to regain control of her body. Her stomach was in complete rebellion after he had inflicted her belly with his weight. The room swam around her, threatening to toss her off the bed. She continued to swallow hard against the waves of nausea and the bile that kept rising in her throat. Bryce had frightened her so badly that she had nearly fainted. He had been so angry, so full of malevolence that it had been apparent she had pushed him too far. The tears continued to flow unabated, soaking her hair and the bedding under her.

Skoll whimpered softly, drawing her attention away from the closed door. She tried to sit up, only to have the room dance dangerously around her. Another vicious surge of nausea hit her and had her running for the privy. She barely got the lid up in time before the meager contents of her stomach heaved forth. She retched uncontrollably for several minutes, even after her belly was empty. Finally, her drained body crumpled to the icy stones of the floor, shivering and weakened.

Carissa's addled thoughts turned to Bryce and what he had said before he left for his hunting trip, or more precisely, the way he said it. His voice had sounded so final, as if he had been saying a last good-bye. She was suddenly worried that he would not return, would leave her there to sit out the winter alone. Fresh tears welled in her eyes and spilled onto the floor as she thought of life without him, and the hard words they had said to each other.

She swiped at the salty drops impatiently. *What's wrong with me?* she wondered. Crying was not something she normally allowed; she abhorred weak, weeping women and now she was becoming one. Her stomach gave another pitch, the nausea returning as she tried to sit up. She staggered to her feet, grabbing at the short staircase to her left for support as the floor tilted, threatening to drag her back down.

Each unsteady step she took brought her closer to the kitchen, to a chair where she could try to collect herself. Bryce had left a fresh pot of coffee on the stove; the smell of it nearly caused her to vomit again. She could not remember the last time she felt this way; even her teeth hurt, she realized as she put her head on the table.

Her heart skipped a beat as she tried to remember if she had ever had these symptoms before this. How long had she been trapped in this wilderness - six weeks? Had it been eight? Sitting up, her mind racing, how could she have been so stupid? It was true that her body had never had a regular monthly cycle but she had never gone six weeks without her period. Her last one had just ended before she had gotten on that plane that had left her in the middle of nowhere.

Well, this certainly adds a new wrinkle, she thought as a slow smile crept along her face. A baby – she was going to have a baby. Her hand instinctively went to her belly, an age-old protective gesture for the new life growing under her heart. The smile disappeared, replaced by a worried frown as she wondered what Bryce would say or do when he found out.

Skoll laid a large paw in her lap, seeming to sense her need for support. She reached over to scratch his ear, saying, "What do you think the big man will do, Baby? Do you think he could be happy about this? Maybe this will be the fire under his butt that'll get him out of here." She wrapped her arms around the dog's neck, tears flowing freely again. "I don't want to leave here without him. Why can't he see that the rest of the world can be damned? We could have each other." The dog only whimpered softly in reply.

Another thought dawned on her, causing a heart-rending fearful sadness. What if he did not return? What if he really meant to leave her alone all winter? The way he had sounded just before he had walked out the door... She refused to let that notion continue. Positive thought was what was needed to keep the new life within her healthy and happy. Oh, Bryce had been carried away this morning, but she knew he would never hurt her, he was just trying to scare her, to get her to stop...

"I'm a horrible person, Skoll. I said terrible things to him," Carissa told the confused dog as she pulled herself to her feet on the rocking floor. "I hope he forgives me. He just has to."

Carissa pulled a tin out of the cupboard and found one stale biscuit inside, nibbling at it as she made her way back to the main room. So many fears crawled through her dizzy mind. She needed prenatal care but none was to be had in the wilderness. Things had to be patched up with Bryce, but she wondered if he would even give a damn after how she had behaved. Would she be able to convince him to leave here and be a father to his child? There were so many questions and so few answers.

The hours ticked slowly by into days of pacing and restlessness. It seemed she was constantly on the verge of tears or struggling against the same nausea that had accompanied her first two pregnancies. She had slept on the big bed, warmed by Bryce's scent that still clung to the sheets. She had cleaned the cabin and read from his library of books – leaving untouched on the bedside table the book that Bryce had been reading – to keep occupied, but the boredom and anticipation of his return were eating away at her mind. Still, she had what she hoped would be a wonderful surprise when he returned. She held onto that one slim chance that he would make the choice to leave with her, giving her the calm to while away the empty time.

On the afternoon of the third day, she heard a strange noise outside the cabin. She had just had her second round of morning sickness when she saw Skoll clawing at the bottom of the door, growling low in his throat. "What is it, boy?" she asked as she peered out the window. "It sounds like an engine. I think someone's out there."

The noise drew closer, a flash of bright sunshine on metal twinkled through the trees, such a strange sight after so long seeing only that which the vast wilderness offered. Carissa's pulse picked up speed as the flashes of reflected light slowly took shape, winding in and out of the shadows of the forest. She could not imagine who this stranger could be but images of the two evil men who had kidnapped her speared her mind. Could they have been searching for her, finding her at last while she was alone and vulnerable? Skoll seemed to echo her thoughts with the escalating agitation she could hear in his constant growls.

Carissa bolted the door and shuttered the windows before reaching for the shotgun that adorned the wall above the mantle. She briskly loaded the gun, laid it carefully on the bed, and rummaged through the old chest-of-drawers for more suitable clothing than the over-sized shirt she wore. She dressed hurriedly in a pair of long johns, sweatshirt, socks and the soft, warm moccasins that Bryce had made for her. Taking up the gun again and watching through the diamond-shaped opening in the shutters, she waited for the vehicle to pull up in front of the cabin.

It was a snowmobile with a single rider – a man – on it. The man was dressed in what appeared to be a heavy black parka and snow pants with a day-glow orange vest over the parka. He shut off the vehicle and dismounted, looking around almost warily. The man seemed to have an unmistakable air of authority in the way he carried himself. She saw something shiny on the left front of his vest as he walked up the shoveled pathway that led to the porch steps. The object could only be described as a badge of some sort, a realization that helped calm her a little. She still did not move to open the shutters or the door, waiting, instead, to see what would happen next. As he came more fully into view, she could see the unmistakable handgun strapped into a holster on his hip.

"Carissa James!" the voice of the man yelled. "Are you in there? U.S. Park Service, ma'am. I'm here to get you out."

She remained where she was, her hand still clutching the shotgun. Skoll's growls turned to deadly snarls as the man stepped up onto the wood planks of the porch.

"Ms. James, U.S. Park Service. I know you're in there. It's okay. You're perfectly safe now. Just open the door."

"How did you find me?" she yelled back.

"We got the call from Lewis McAlester up near Mount Hunt. Said that Bryce Matheney was holed up with a missing woman. Now, why don't you open the door so we don't have to shout?"

Unsure of herself, Carissa waited for a moment before ordering Skoll silent. She maintained her grip on the gun as she slid the door's bolt open and stepped back. "Come in," she told the man.

The ranger opened the door cautiously, pushing against the rough wood until it swung fully open to reveal a disheveled woman leveling a large shotgun on his midsection. He froze his steps and slowly raised his hands. "Now, Carissa, you just put that gun down. You're safe. I'm not going to hurt you. See my badge? I'm Ranger Doug Smith and I'm here to help."

She studied his face for a moment, seeing the calm of a man who was trained to handle such situations and take control of them. Turning the gun away without relinquishing it, she took another step back, shushing the dog again when she heard his low warning growl. She motioned him inside out of the winter chill and told to close the door.

"You are Carissa James, are you not?" he asked quietly.

She nodded before she spoke. "How did you find out about me, again?"

"We got a radio communiqué from Lewis McAlester. He said that Matheney had a kidnapped woman up here."

"I don't know McAlester and Bryce didn't kidnap me. He saved my life."

"You're fortunate, Ms. James. Matheney is a dangerous man. We've been looking for you for some time. We'd given you up for dead after your car was found buried in the snow. Look, there's a US Park Police helicopter waiting for you. It gets dark up here fast so we better get going."

Carissa knew a small amount of panic. How could she leave right now? How could she not leave and miss the opportunity to get back home to her children?

"I can't leave just yet. I need to wait for Bryce. He should be back by tomorrow or the next day."

"Ma'am, it was Matheney who had McAlester radio in. He knows that we are coming to get you. McAlester's place is a long way from here and I doubt that Matheney will make it back any time soon. We really have to get going."

Stunned, Carissa sank into the old rocker, the loaded gun nearly slipping from her fingers. Her body trembled as the implication of the ranger's words hit home. Bryce no longer wanted her in his home or his life, had risked much and traveled far just to be rid of her. She looked up as Smith carefully took the weapon from her hands and unloaded it.

"I guess," she uttered shakily, "I can be ready in just a moment."

"I'll wait while you gather your things," he said kindly.

"That's okay. I...nothing here belongs to me. I don't even have anything to wear." The pain of hot, bitter tears pricked behind her eyes but she refused to let them loose. Bryce had left her, abandoned her to return to her own life without him. She wanted to be angry, to hate him for what his actions were saying but her heart was broken and there was only room for the anguish.

"We were told you would need appropriate clothing. I have a snowsuit for you outside. I'll be right back." The ranger walked back outside leaving Carissa alone with her sorrow.

She walked through the cabin, touching various items in the dim room, the sound of his voice playing those words endlessly in her brain: "I love you. You are my whole world." How could he have said that, felt that way, then just leave her without a word? Her hand fell upon the novel he had been reading that was still sitting by the bed. She picked it up, clutching it to her breast while she fought back the tears that now filled her eyes.

There was a knock at the door, pulling her out of her reverie. Skoll lowered his head, growling at the intruding ranger as the man opened the door.

"Skoll, quiet," Carissa said softly, bringing the dog to silence. She looked up at the ranger. "What about the dog? I can't just leave him with no one to look out for him."

"Ms. James, that dog is as tough as this wilderness. He'll be just fine until his owner gets back. Here's the snowsuit. We better get moving." Smith laid the warm suit on the bed and stepped back. "If you want me to wait outside while you get dressed…"

"No, that's okay," she answered as she stared at the book in her hands. "Hang on a minute; I need to leave a note. Let me find something to write with." She disappeared into the kitchen, taking the book and the suit with her. When she returned, she was fully clothed, still holding the book. After making up the bed, she placed the book on the pillow where Bryce normally laid his head. She banked the fire on the hearth and closed the screen, careful that no errant embers had escaped. With one last glance around the cozy, rustic cabin where she had found a brief moment of happiness, she turned to the ranger and said, "Let's go."

The ranger opened the door and was nearly knocked to the floor as Skoll bounded out of the cabin at a dead run. Carissa ran out onto the porch calling after the dog, but he disappeared into the trees. She could hear his excited woofs from a distance, echoing back up to her through the clear mountain air.

"I can't just leave him out there," Carissa told Smith.

"Ms. James, that dog will do just fine. It's getting late. We really have to go." Ranger Smith mounted the waiting snowmobile and fired up the motor.

With one last glance in the direction the dog had taken Carissa closed the cabin door and joined the ranger, straddling the seat behind him. She buried her face in the back of the man's parka, squeezing her eyes shut against the urge to turn around one last time. With each passing minute and each mile that took her farther from Bryce's home, the pain in her chest grew until it threatened to choke the life out of her.

The snowmobile came to a halt in a large clearing as the sun was dropping low in the sky. Smith pulled a radio mic out of his parka and spoke quickly, presumably calling the afore-mentioned helicopter, but Carissa, lost in her own misery, paid little attention. Soon there was the unmistakable air-chopping noise of her new mode of transportation, which landed some yards from them, kicking up snow all around. Carissa was all but thrown into a seat, strapped down and then lifted into the air and off the mountain that had been her prison and her home these many weeks. The rest of her trip was a blur, lost in the pain of her broken heart and the loneliness that had come to envelop her soul, but she was finally going home.

Chapter 15

"More tea, Ms. James?"

Carissa was staring out the window at the striated cloudbank below, lost in her own inner world, and did not hear the woman. When the question was repeated, Carissa's misty eyes turned away from the window in confusion. She glanced up to see the flight attendant with her drink cart smiling at her expectantly, awaiting an answer.

"Hmm? Oh, no, thank you," she told the attendant before turning back to the window to further contemplate all that had happened to her life in the past two months. She was thinking of Bryce, wondering if he had made it home safely. Had he found her note? Did he care? She watched the mountains that were still visible through the breaks in the clouds. She had been in the air only a short time, but felt as though it had been forever. Another wave of sadness washed over her and exited her body in the form of a plaintive sigh.

"Okay," a masculine voice said. "That's your tenth sigh since we left the ground. Are you all right, miss?"

Carissa turned again to see the man sitting next to her. He was young and handsome with dark hair, blue eyes and an impish grin. It was easy to see that he probably had young women falling at his feet wherever he went, but Carissa was completely unaffected by his charm. A giant with smoldering gray eyes and a damaged soul had stolen her heart.

"I'm sorry," she smiled politely at him. "I didn't mean to disturb you."

"You didn't. I was just wondering if there was anything I could do to help," he said hopefully. "I hate to see a beautiful woman in distress."

He was flirting with her; she could see that, though she wondered how anyone could find her attractive enough to bother with. The ill-fitting clothing she was wearing had been donated to her by the wife of the sheriff of Teton County, Wyoming. Her dry, frizzy hair was begging for a trip to the beautician and her pale face had not seen makeup or moisturizer in nearly two months. On top of it, she was feeling ill and the bucking of the small Embraer commuter aircraft on the air currents was not helping at all.

She smiled at the sincerity that she saw in his face. "I'm all right, really. Just feeling a bit airsick."

"Is this your first time in a plane?"

The question reminded her of the last time she had flown – the trip that had forever changed her life. "No," she said as she turned back to the window. "I flew to Wyoming two months ago on business. Now I'm going home, finally. I can't wait to get there."

"You don't look like you're anxious to get home. You look more like you wish you didn't have to leave."

"You're wrong," she stated softly, adamantly, without turning to face him again. "I'm glad to be seeing the back side of this place. If I never see another mountain as long as I live it will be too soon."

The man returned to his newspaper, glancing at the pictures and the words and wondering if he had offended the pretty woman next to the window. A headline caught his attention, causing him to address her again. "The stewardess called you, Ms. James. Are you Carissa James, the one who was missing in the Tetons?"

Carissa sighed again, wishing the damned media people had just left her alone, instead of shoving their cameras in her face and chasing her around the little community of Jackson, Wyoming. "Yes, that's me." Did the whole world need to know what had happened to her?

"Wow," he said with a low whistle. "You're a lucky woman. That Bryce Matheney is a dangerous man. He killed his own wife, you know. He got off on some technicality, but he shoulda got the death penalty. I grew up in these parts and I remember when that happened. He's one evil bastard."

Carissa was furious with the irritating man and his vicious comments. "You don't know what the fuck you're talking about," she ground out through clenched teeth, turning to fix him with a near-lethal glare. "He risked his life to save me and get me home. Does that sound like the actions of a killer? It's no wonder he doesn't want anything to do with you pious assholes." She turned back to the window, completely ignoring the young man and the startled look on his handsome face.

Everywhere she had been in the days following her extrication from the Teton Mountains, it had been the same story. People had marveled at her ability to survive with such a horrible beast as Bryce Matheney. He had been called a murderer, a blight on society who had killed his own wife in cold blood. Some even said that he had caused the accident in a murder/suicide scheme because he thought she was having an affair. They said that the scars on his face had been put there by the Almighty, as a fitting punishment, branding him a killer for all to see.

A very select few people had actually been sympathetic to the man, claiming to have known his family and him since he was a child. None of those people, however, was willing to stand up for him against the popular opinion that he was a monster that needed to die a horrible death.

Carissa had cried when alone, wanting to turn to him, to tell him that it would be all right, that she would make it all right for him, but he was not there. She had failed to convince him that what they felt for one another was strong enough to defeat the stigma that had been attached to his name and his life. Not even the note she had left him had been enough to bring him down out of his refuge and back to her.

Now, sitting in the cramped plane that was taking her from his world, bitter tears flowed freely, silently sliding down her face and falling on the second-hand sweater she wore. Another piece of her heart broke off, amplifying the pain in her chest and the impotent anger she felt toward the people of Jackson Hole, Grand Teton National Park and anyplace else where they sat in judgment of the man she loved. She wordlessly cursed them all to the same hell to which they had all wished to condemn him.

She thought again about the whirlwind of questions and shutter clicks that had swamped her when the helicopter had landed at Jackson Hole Airport near the little town that was Jackson, Wyoming. The name of it barely registered in her memory as the place where she had been headed at the start of that fateful business trip. She had been hustled from the aircraft and into a police car that took her to the sheriff's office. Reporters and camera crews followed, just a small group that only proved to be the start of a major media feeding frenzy.

Even the tabloids had gotten in on the story, the fact that she was holed up with a dark giant of a man with a reputation for violence had only added fuel to the fire of their need for more scandalous stories.

Mike Claire, the CEO himself, of Claire-Smith Broadcasting, Incorporated had heard the story on CNN and had contacted her at the Teton County Sheriff's office. He had expressed his "heart-felt joy" at finding out that one of their "most valued employees" had been located, stating that the company had spared no expense in trying to find her after her disappearance. Carissa had her own ideas on what they had actually done to locate her, but had kept her mouth shut and thanked the man politely. He had told her that she would be fully compensated for the incident. The company would take good care of her and see to it that her family would have everything they needed to help in her return home.

Yeah, right, she thought. *He just doesn't want his precious company sued for having put her in that dangerous situation.* She also wondered how they could think that they could possibly compensate her for the time lost with her children and the hell they must have been through without their mother.

She fully intended to take him up on his offer, however, if she needed to hire legal representation to fight her ex-husband. Her numerous conversations over the phone with her mother had confirmed her fears that John was trying to take her children. She would fight him tooth and nail to keep that from happening, no matter the cost.

The sounds of the voices of her children were almost enough to push her over the edge when she was finally able to speak to them. She had been enraged, however, when a camera crew from her own TV station had ambushed her family, putting footage of her children on national television for all the world to see. Her poor babies had looked so frightened when she saw the news segment on her hotel room set, and she had wanted to wrap herself around them, shielding them from the traumatic event. She had decided that the first free minute she got, once back home, she would let news director Christopher Davidson have it with both barrels.

The law-enforcement officials of Jackson Hole had to be dealt with first, however. They had interrogated her for several hours that first night, until she finally begged to be allowed to rest. That was when the sheriff's wife had intervened on her behalf, demanding that a doctor have a look at her, and saw to it that she had been given a comfortable room in one of the luxury hotels in town. The doctor had been concerned that she was under weight but pleased with her condition otherwise. She had decided not to tell him she was expecting, determining that it would be better to keep that tidbit to herself, and not have the world find out about it. She would wait until she got home to see her own doctor for pre-natal care.

It was not until the next morning that she was informed of the fate of her two kidnappers. She had asked the sheriff what action was being taken against the two men and he finally told her that action would not be necessary, that the men were dead. "Their deaths were pretty gruesome," Sheriff Tomlinson had said with a bleak expression. "At least one wild animal, if not more, had a pretty good meal. Evidence inside the van suggested that the culprit was a wolf, but no one has seen a wolf in these parts for a lot of years."

Tomlinson then handed her a large box that contained the personal effects that she had left behind when she had been forced to flee the van. "What evidence?" Carissa had asked as she slowly removed various items from the box, one at a time, to look them over carefully. She found a small tuft of white fur stuck to the inside of her over-coat, clinging to the dried blood that stained the lining. She immediately tossed the coat into the trash with a shudder of revulsion as he answered.

"There were several bloody paw prints inside the van which could only have been made by a wolf. Looked to be a white one, too, from all the hairs found on the scene. That would be a rare animal for sure. What that animal did to those two men is the stuff of nightmares." He had stopped for a moment, seemingly in need of mustering his self-control to stop himself from gagging before continuing. "According to the M.E., those boys were still alive when that animal was eating them."

Carissa had been surprised that hearing the gory details of their deaths did not cause even the least bit of queasiness in her stomach. "How could the coroner tell?" she had asked.

"Well," the man had said slowly, blanching further, "the amount of blood in the van, for one. The wounds had continued to bleed after being inflicted. There was blood splatter patterns on the roof and walls of the van that suggest blood spurting from arterial wounds – the hearts of the vics were still beating. There were quite a few defensive wounds on their hands and forearms, and a fair amount of their own gore under their nails. Both men had lost their livers and had continued to bleed from those wounds. Kyle Pritchert was found outside the vehicle, with a blood trail under the snow where he had tried to crawl away. Quite a bit of his entrails was found under the snow, too. Must've fallen out as he dragged his body." The man had shuddered at that, and turned to questioning her again, about how she had managed to escape the kidnappers.

A woman had burst into the sheriff's private office at one point, screaming at Carissa, calling her a murderer, accusing her of being responsible for her brother's death. Carissa was later told that the woman was Kyle Pritchert's half-mad sister, a woman who had been completely dependent upon Pritchert. Though she had pity for the woman, Carissa simply could not bring herself to feel sorry that her tormentors were dead, or about how they had died. She shuddered again when memories of how she had been viciously attacked came from the corners of her memory, plaguing her already-troubled mind. They had been truly evil men.

She thought of the wolf in her dreams, Alice, the white wolf who had helped her and had warned her. She had quickly dismissed that thought with a shake of her head, however. Alice was a figment of her imagination; something conjured in her addled mind during her horrendous experience while lost in the Teton wilderness. Her lips curled in a sinister smile at the thought that some force out there had gotten vengeance on her behalf, however, no matter how fanciful that idea was.

The flight attendant's voice over the loudspeaker, telling them to fasten their seatbelts for their landing approach brought her thoughts back to the present. The shuttle flight would be landing at Salt Lake City where she was to make a connection with the Claire-

Smith company jet that Mr. Claire had insisted she take. After the comments of the young man in the seat next to her, she would be glad of the privacy. She just did not think she was capable of dealing with any more idiots at this point.

Before retiring to her own seat, the flight attendant bent over to speak to Carissa, telling her that someone would meet her at the terminal to take her to the private flight that would carry her home. Despite the misery in her tired soul, she felt a certain thrill of anticipation, an impatient restlessness that had her arms itching to hold her children and hug her mother. She was going home at last.

As she listened to the plane's landing gear whirring into place, she thought again of Bryce. How could he have just turned his back, sent her away without a word? She knew a certain betrayal at his actions and a desire to erase him from her memory, to forget the man had ever existed, no matter how impossible a task that was. Tears welled again, threatening to spill over as she blinked impatiently, forcing them back. He was an asshole of the highest caliber and she hoped he was miserable in the empty solitude of his damned mountain.

What Carissa did not know was that her wishes had come true. High up on that mountain, a giant of a man had been reduced to a broken, vacant shell, giving in to the despair that had taken hold of his life, despondent and lost in his dismal loneliness. He had not eaten or slept in days as he sat alone in his chair in front of a cold hearth clutching the discarded shirt that she had once worn. Not even Skoll, desperate to be let out of the anguished atmosphere of the cabin, could get the man's attention, and was forced to eliminate his bodily waste on the cold stone floor.

Bryce's last vision of Carissa replayed constantly in his mind. She had been looking around, searching the trees, and even at a distance, he could see the sadness in her eyes. He knew that he had wounded her deeply, knew that she would never forgive him but it was for the best. There was no way he would be able to leave his home or live among those sainted members of society who had condemned him to this exile. He was where he belonged, alone on his mountain with no one around to judge him for what he had done.

Carissa, he reminded himself, had never judged him. She had offered him only love and understanding and he had tossed her away as if she had meant nothing. The woman had taught him to love again, to open his heart and feel and had given so freely of herself. He had rewarded her by sending her away, broken-hearted and with his betrayal in her eyes.

He had hiked – even run at times – through the snow and ice without stopping, for the whole of the dark night and into the day, just to catch that last glimpse of her before she was gone from his life forever. His muscles had burned and his lungs had ached but he had made it in time to see her leave with the park ranger who had come to retrieve her. When Skoll had come running out of the cabin, barking and happy to see him, he had thought that he would be seen. He knew that if Carissa had seen him, had come to him in the shadows of the trees, he would never have been able to let her go.

It was for the best, he told himself time and again. She would have a better life without him, a better future without the disgrace of his past to drag her down. Coward is what she had called him and he knew she was right. He was afraid of the world below, afraid that he would never be more than what society had named him – a monster. Carissa was an angel compared to his devil, and deserved better than what he was and would always be.

But the pain ate away at him, the loss of her love and her strength was enough to drive him mad. The peace he once had in his soul, hard-won after his retreat to this secluded place, was gone forever in the flash of deep green eyes and the tinkling music of her laughter. Peace – that was not really the word for what he had found up here on his own. It was more of an acceptance of what the future was for him, of the reality of spending the rest of his days alone. That reality, after knowing the kind of love that Carissa had so willingly granted him, was too much to bear now, too much for him to carry on in this empty existence.

This cabin had been a happy place once, a very long time ago, and in the recent past. It had been the honeymoon cabin of his grandparents and a place of wonder in his childhood. He had known true joy making love to the elfin woman that had captured his heart and taken it with her when she left. As he sat with his head in his hands, clutching at the dirty hair that tumbled over his face, he knew that he could no longer soil that spirit of love that had once been such an important part of this place.

He stood and walked to the door on shaky legs, pulling his coat off the peg as he stepped into the sharp December wind without bothering to close the door. There was no sense in continuing like this, no need for it when he could simply walk away. There was a place where he could go, a place that would take him with mercy and blissful darkness. He would go there and leave the memories of the cabin behind forever.

Another storm was brewing, but he paid it little heed as he walked out into the forest. He found the place at the bottom of a steep incline where he had found the nearly-frozen body of Carissa. His breath caught in his throat as he remembered how close to death she had been and what it was like to feel her tiny, fevered body curled up on his lap in front of the fire. He forced himself to turn away, not to stare at that frozen spot on the ground any longer.

He climbed that steep slope down which she must have tumbled that night, his bare hands clawing through the thick blanket of icy snow. This would be the way to his salvation, the place that would take away all the pain. Skoll, oblivious of where his master was going, sniffed along happily beside Bryce, glad to be out of the cabin.

Over the top of the ridge, Bryce climbed, slipping his way down the other side, to walk along the edge of another ridge. He had taken this path so many times in the summer months, hunting and hiking and exercising with Skoll. Rarely in the winter months had he been here, the environment looked almost foreign. He continued onward for several hours, ignoring the biting wind and the flakes of snow that stabbed through the short growth of beard on his face. There was only one thought on his mind – getting to his destination.

Finally, he came upon the place he had been seeking. The huge crevasse yawned before him, beckoning his broken spirit and offering eternal solace. His grandfather had called the place Suicide Gorge, a seemingly bottomless crack in the mountain that could swallow a man whole. A small, tortured smile played at Bryce's lips as he thought how this hole in the ground was finally going to live up to its name. He stood for a moment on the brink of the precipice, thoughts of the dark loneliness of his life pounding at his brain. Skoll whimpered softly and Bryce knew a moment of regret for the poor animal that would be left to fend for himself.

"I'm sorry, boy," he told the dog and prepared to take that next step. Just then, a thing below him caught his attention. It was small and flashed only briefly but he knew he had seen something. He kept his eyes focused, hoping to see it again without really knowing what it was. Another gust of wind kicked by and the thing flashed on the current. It was something caught in the tangle of roots below, beneath the rocky ledge.

Without thinking, he dropped to his belly, reaching his half-frozen fingers downward, clutching blindly at the thing. On the tail of another blast of icy wind, he felt something soft touch his skin and he closed his fingers around it. Pulling himself up to his feet with the item grasped in the palm of his hand, he leaned against a tree to discover what he had found. It was a scrap of cloth only a couple of inches long, once white but now stained brown with what looked to be blood.

Bryce examined the cloth, felt the texture of its tatters against his palms. It was thin and delicate and something he had seen before. With a startled gasp, he looked again at the yawning hole in front of him, knowing now the path that had brought Carissa to his cabin. There had been something inherently magical about the woman; in the manner in which she had stolen her way into his heart. Had that magic been what brought her to his door? Had it been fate that the two of them were brought together, to give the other what they both needed most in life? How had she managed to cross that crevasse without plummeting to her death?

Bryce was shaking from head to toe, clutching the scrap of material in his hand. He had been about to kill himself, end it all so that he would not have to face the remainder of his years alone, but Carissa had still managed to touch him, to steer him away from those thoughts. She had reached out with that tiny piece of cloth to remind him there was someone who would always love him. He suddenly realized that he had let her down enough, that dying in this fashion would be just one more betrayal that would again break her heart.

He turned away from the gorge and pointed himself back to his home, calling Skoll to join him. Survival, at this point, was the most important thing he had to offer. If he never saw the beautiful woman again at least he would die with the knowledge that he had not given up, had not thrown away his own life. He would go on living, and that life would be the only monument to their love that he had to offer.

The trail back to the cabin was difficult; the exposed skin of his face and hands began to burn as the growing storm picked up speed. Darkness had fallen by the time he and his shivering dog found their way through the forest to see the old cabin standing like a beacon in the shadows of the night. The interior was cold and dark with tendrils of airy snow swirling across the floor through the open door. There was a definite aroma of feces and Bryce shot the dog a scathing look but held his tongue knowing the animal could not help himself.

Once inside Bryce set about lighting a fire and bringing in wood to see him through the long night ahead. Once the wood box was full and a fire blazed on the hearth, he lit the lamps that would chase the dark shadows back into the corners of the room. Then, with a disgusted grunt, he cleaned up the mess the dog had made, scrubbing the stones of the floor with strong disinfectant.

"Jesus Christ, Skoll," he exaggerated. "I need a crane to move this shit." He glared at the dog as Skoll cocked his head and wagged his tail joyfully.

With that distasteful task completed, Bryce stowed the scrub bucket and returned to the main room of the cabin. Everywhere he looked he saw reminders of Carissa, items she had used or touched that brought her face to mind. He did not know how he would do it but he was determined to survive, to live for her even if they never saw each other again.

With the business of living in mind, he decided to find someway to distract himself from thoughts of her. He spied his book, a copy of *The Sound and the Fury* by William Faulkner, nestled on the pillow of his bed, laid there by Carissa's own hand, that he might find it with little effort. Even in her sadness, she had been taking care of him, a thought that both warmed and grieved him at the same time.

Picking up the book, he decided it was too dark, the theme too emotional for him this night, and carried it to the bookshelf that lined the wall next to the closet door. He needed something lighter, a hunting story or mystery novel, to draw his attention away from the oppressive sorrow that surrounded him. He set the book on the shelf and reached for another without paying much attention to how he had placed the novel. It teetered and landed with a loud thump against the hard floor, falling open.

Looking down he saw handwritten words on the front inside cover of the old leather-bound volume, words that he did not remember having been there before now. He bent to retrieve the book, walking to the table beside the bed and holding the book up to the lamp that burned there. His heart caught in his throat, his hands shaking and his pulse racing as he read the signature: "Cari". Reading the note and reading it again, his emotions began to take hold of him, a snarled mixture of rage, elation, guilt and anguish.

His knees felt weak causing him to sink to the mattress and struggle to bring his breathing and his heart rate under control. Skoll sensed his state of mind, touching him with his nose, nudging to get some response out of the man. Bryce glared at the dog, silently willing him to sit, to be still so that he could think.

"How can she do this to me?" he asked the dog, anger and grief evident in his voice. He dropped the book to the floor, pressing his face into his hands, growling his frustration and rage into the chilly air.

Chapter 16

Dear Bryce,

A man is here to take me away. He says that you sent him. I'm sorry that my presence has brought you such discomfort or that you felt the need to send me away. I thank you for saving my life and for the brief happiness that I knew with you.

I had wanted to tell you this in person and not in a note that you will read later, but you took the easy way out, not even bothering to say good-bye. I'm going to have your baby and I just thought you should know.

I don't intend to raise this child alone. All of my children need a father, a decent man that can be counted on to be there for them. I had hoped that you wanted the job, but I know now that you are too selfish to give a damn. I will never love anyone the way I love you, but I need someone with me, a companion to grow old with, who will share in my dreams and offer me his. You don't need to worry, your son or daughter will have a family and will be well-provided for. I only hope that it doesn't upset you too much to know that another man will be rearing your child.

Despite everything, I want you to know that my only wish for you is that you find happiness in your solitude, though I know your heart and know that you will be miserable. I will mourn for you and I will always love you, even if you don't care what happens to me or our child. You are a fool, Bryce, to throw away what we have, and I'm a fool for letting you get by with it. Take care of yourself and think of us from time to time.

All my love,

Cari

Bryce read her words again; he had lost count of how many times. The fire in the grate was dying, dwindling away in the passage of time while he digested her words over and over. He was going to be a father; the idea was trying to sink in, to be recognized for its reality. He was going to be a father. He had impregnated Carissa and she was gone. She was gone and someone else would be father to his child.

He knew her well enough to know that she meant what she had written. She would find somebody else to be a father to his child, someone who would be there no matter what life threw his way. Some other person would know the beauty of waking next to her every morning; feel her warmth and her strength. Another man would make her eyes sparkle and smile while he rotted in his mountain banishment.

Anna popped into his mind, reminding him of the dreams that he had once shared with her, dreams of their future and the family they had planned to create. He had believed that he would never again have the opportunity to know that hope or that joy, and now the chance of a new future had been dropped in his lap. He had tossed it away with both hands, but he told himself it was for the best. His child would have better prospects, a better likelihood of a good life without him as a father. If the child was a son, that boy did not need to have his father's name to drag him down, to make him a subject of ridicule. If the child was a daughter, a girl with her mother's green eyes and dancing curls...

Bryce had always wanted kids, had always wanted the chance to give his children the same happy childhood that he had known – a son to whom he could teach the ways of the mountains, a daughter to cherish and spoil and whose boyfriends he could frighten. Someone else would benefit from the life he had created with Carissa, someone else would teach these things to his child.

The child was his, though. How could anyone else know what his child would need to be healthy and happy? How could Cari assume that some other man would be good enough to raise his son or his daughter? Did she honestly expect him to just sit back and allow it to happen, forget his responsibilities to his own baby?

Anger began to build from deep within toward the beauty who had taken his heart – and his baby – to live without him, to bear his child and give it someone else's name. He would see her in hell first, he decided, as he tossed the book back to the floor. *The bitch had better be prepared*, he thought, *because I'm going to claim what's mine.*

Skoll yelped and ran for cover as Bryce vaulted from the edge of the bed, stalked to the closet and jerked the door open. He rifled through the contents, searching for the extra equipment he would need to make the arduous climb down the mountain through the storm that still raged along the rocky slopes. Any article that was unfortunate enough to get in his way suffered a vicious pitch out into the middle of the room.

His bedroll was still by the front door where he had dropped it after his return – when he had watched Carissa disappear with her arms wrapped around the park ranger's middle. He would need to carry shelter in the form of a small tent, food with extra rations for Skoll and a small lantern so that he could travel at night. He intended to get to her as fast as he could, to set her straight and make her understand that *he* would be keeping *his* child and she could be damned.

He gathered his equipment and supplies and crammed everything haphazardly into his backpack, removed it all and packed it again, this time taking care to do it correctly. He struggled to get hold of his emotions, the fury in him raged like the howling wind outside. He had no plan, only knew that he had to get to her, stop her from giving his child to another man. Logic dictated that it would be impossible for her to find someone so soon but that did not matter. He was furious and he wanted to confront her now.

* * * *

The day was waning as the Claire-Smith company jet touched down at Abraham Lincoln Capital Airport in Springfield, Illinois. Carissa's heart had skipped a beat when she had seen the skyline of her hometown, her impatience to see her family causing her to wish she could jump out of the damned plane and land in her own yard. It seemed strange to look at the bare ground and not see a ceaseless blanket of snow covering everything.

She pulled her second-hand jacket on over her arms, wishing that she could greet her family wearing something a little more appealing. Most of her things that were found in that evil van had been ruined, so she was forced to make do with the castoffs that had been donated after her rescue. She had her seatbelt off before the craft had stopped rolling along the tarmac, and was fidgeting at the door before the co-pilot could get it open. The man was hard-pressed to restrain her as he lowered the door, dropping the steps into place.

A long, black limousine pulled close to the aircraft, stopping a few yards away. "Oh, hurry up," Carissa hissed as the small staircase was locked in place. The back door of the limo opened and the first person that exited it was her mother, Alice, the older woman's face glowing radiantly as she smiled. Then both children burst from the vehicle, an explosion of exuberance and youthful enthusiasm. They were screaming excitedly, as only small children can do, with their cheeks glowing and their hair dancing on the December breeze.

Carissa shoved the co-pilot out of her way and nearly sprouted wings on the way down the stairs. Both children hit her at once, knocking her to the ground as she bent to scoop them into her arms. All the hurt, all the sadness disappeared in the warm glow of being smothered with their hugs. Little Zane was trying to choke her with his arms from behind as baby Sheanna clutched the front of her sweater. Both crooned, "Mommy, mommy," endlessly as Carissa's joyful tears fell.

"Mommy's home," she told them. "Mommy's home."

"My baby's home," a voice said from above her. Carissa looked up to see Alice, tears streaming down her face, smiling broadly at her.

"Mom!" Carissa cried as she struggled to her feet while still clutching Sheanna and with Zane still holding fast around her neck. She shifted her diminutive daughter to one arm while circling her other around her mother's shoulders, sniffling softly, her entire body shaking. "I'm so sorry, Mama. You must've been worried sick. I'm sorry," she sobbed into her mother's collar.

"Shh, Baby. Don't you worry about a thing. You have nothing to be sorry for. You're back safe now," Alice murmured, hugging her only child in return as she struggled against her own tears.

Carissa pulled back to have another look at her mother's face and the two children that wriggled against her body. It was easy to see that the past two months had aged Alice – her tired face was pale and drawn, her hair was more gray than it had been. The two kids still clinging to Carissa appeared to have grown, but their faces had not changed, were still the cherub-like visages that she had held so desperately in her mind and heart.

A sudden flurry of movement to the left drew her thoughts away from her family as she turned her head to see who was now exiting the long, black car. Her mouth clamped shut in disgust when she saw the two men, both of whom she had been planning to admonish for what her little family had been through. She watched as they approached, scathing words forming in her brain to be held in check as she decided which one to start on first. Her mother whispered urgently that they had insisted upon coming along, that she had wanted only family to greet her daughter. Carissa wondered how they could dare to invade her privacy and the homecoming she had so anxiously anticipated.

Christopher Davidson was the first to reach her, his face beaming, his hand out when he got within range. "Carissa, damn, it's good to see you. I hope your trip home wasn't too…"

"Who the hell do you think you are?" her demanding voice cut him off. She set Sheanna down and reached up to take Zane's arms from round her neck, lowering him to the pavement. "Mom, take the kids back to the car, please." She waited a moment for her mother to do as she asked before turning to the two men beside her. She looked at Davidson, a man she had always considered a friend, her anger toward him visibly crackling over the surface of her skin.

"Chris, I cannot believe that even you would stoop so low as to put the faces of my two children on national television. Have you lost your fucking mind? How many times did you ambush my mother and my babies after I disappeared? Do you have any idea how many freaks out there would use the kind of information you made so public to harm my kids? I could tear your goddamn head off, you stupid son of a bitch!"

"Whoa, there. Slow down just a minute," the other man said.

Carissa turned from Davidson's startled face to look at his companion, a man she truly despised and the station manager, Tom Mavis. He had been hired by the corporate office only weeks before she had taken that trip to Wyoming but he had shown himself to be an unpleasant, uncaring person with no concept of how human beings should treat each other. The arrogant bastard glared at her, seemingly perturbed that she would have any opinion about how the station used her family to garner ratings. He stepped up to her, ready to do battle, his beady eyes sweeping her from head to toe.

"I'm the one who told Chris to cover the story. Corporate wanted it for the news wire, and as our employee, we expect you to comply. It's only because Chris insisted upon giving you and yours a little privacy right now that there isn't a crew here to cover your homecoming. We're going to have a camera crew at your house tonight to interview you and your family for the Early News, we'd like you to be sitting down to dinner so we can get a good shot of the family together."

Carissa was astounded, looking at each of their faces in turn. Davidson appeared embarrassed, if not a touch angry while Mavis was all but rubbing his hands together in avaricious glee. The look in the latter's eyes told her she would do as she was told if she knew what was good for her.

"Chris," she said, her voice tightly controlled. "You and I have been friends for a long time. I have always valued that friendship and respected your ability as a newsman. I was angry with you before because you always put the news first and friendship second, but I could understand that, it's the business you chose. But, know this; if you allowed this arrogant, greedy, slimy piece of shit to dictate what you put on as news, then you have lost my respect."

Mavis, incensed at her insult, had just opened his mouth to offer a scathing retort when Carissa turned on him. She directed her next words at him, daring him to take offense.

"If I didn't know any better, I would say that you engineered this whole fiasco just for the exclusive the station could get on the story, but that would require more cunning than you possess," she sneered. "Don't even think for one minute that I'm going to allow you to disrupt my life and my privacy – and further endanger my kids or cause them one more moment of grief – because you are sadly mistaken. I will meet the fucking crew at the door with my father's shotgun. I will destroy the camera and fill their asses with buckshot if they come knocking, and then I'll take that gun to you. You want to fire me? Go right ahead.

"I have enough on you and the entire Claire-Smith Corporation to sue you into the ground. And don't think I won't do it, either. I've had enough, *do you hear me*? My family has suffered enough because of you people."

Carissa had begun to advance, each step toward him causing him to retreat slowly. She was daring him to take action, hoping that he would so she could really let him have it. "I'm spoiling for a fight, you asshole, so bring it on! I was sent off on a wild goose chase, kidnapped, viciously attacked, injured, scarred for life, nearly killed by the environment and disease, and trapped in a wilderness a million miles from nowhere for seven weeks.

"My mother spent those weeks' worried sick, not knowing if her only daughter was alive or dead. My children woke up screaming with nightmares every night. I suffered for not being able to let them know I was alive or hold them and tuck them in at night. To top it all off, my ex-husband is using my absence – that you caused – to try to take my kids away from me and abuse them. So don't even *dare* try to make me comply with your sick fantasy of having my family's misfortune boost your ratings. In short, *Mr. Mavis*, you can go straight to hell."

Carissa charged between the two men just as her tirade ended, marching to the limousine and yanking the door open. She tossed her meager bag of belongings onto the seat before climbing in and slamming the door. Pressing the automatic door lock switch, she yelled to the driver to take them home, leaving the two men to stand on the tarmac in the tiny airport.

Carissa's departure and arrival times had been kept strictly secret because of the media frenzy surrounding her rescue. Apparently, the word had gotten out, though, because several reporters stood on Carissa's lawn as the limo turned down her street. Most of them milled about aimlessly until they saw the sleek black car turn the corner, headed their way. Suddenly they banded together as a small group, ready to pounce on the occupants of the vehicle as soon as they pulled up.

"Jesus," Carissa hissed when she saw the throng.

"Carissa Jane!" her mother admonished. "Mind your language."

"Sorry, mother," she replied dourly. "Driver, don't stop. Get us out of here."

"Where to, ma'am?" the man behind the wheel asked.

"Nowhere. Just drive and give me a chance to think."

Carissa was livid, wondering why people would not just let her family be. Closing the partition between the driver and the passenger compartment and fixing her mother with a glum expression, she held out her hand.

"Mom, do you have your cell phone? I got mine back but I think being exposed to the elements probably destroyed it."

"Mommy, what's wrong?" Zane asked.

Little Sheanna burrowed against her mother's side, whimpering softly, uncertainty evident in her enormous eyes. Carissa wrapped an arm around her, hugging her tightly before punching the digits on the keypad of the small phone.

"Nothing, baby," she told her son. "Just a change in plans, sweetie."

"Cari, who are you calling?"

"You remember my friend Melissa that used to be a reporter at the station?"

"Yes, of course. The two of you have been friends for years. We talked on the phone several times since that awful day. She'll be tickled to hear your voice. Didn't she take a job in the governor's office?"

"Yep. She's his PR person. I'm going to ask her to do me a fav..." Carissa stopped short as someone on the other end of the call answered. "Melissa? Thank you. It's good to hear your voice too... Yes, I'm thrilled but I haven't been able to go home just yet... Yeah, reporters, trampling my lawn. Can you help? I can't take the kids through that mess..." Carissa fell silent as she listened to her friend until a bright, devious smile spread across her face. "Yes, a black stretch job, like we hired for Amelia's bachelorette party... You're an evil saint, Melissa!" Carissa laughed. "That's perfect. I knew you would come up with something. Did this number show on your caller ID? Okay, I'll wait for your call. Thank you so much... You too. Take care."

Carissa disconnected and handed the telephone back to Alice. She sat grinning at her mother, a wicked gleam in her green eyes. She hugged each of her children, tickling them until they giggled merrily.

"Well?" demanded Alice. "What did you two hatch?"

"Misdirection," Carissa snickered. "The same type she uses whenever her boss wants a little private time away from the public eye," she opened the partition and called out to the chauffeur. "Driver – I hate calling you that. What's your name?"

"Greg Lyman, ma'am."

"Greg, I'm Carissa, as I'm sure you know, and my mom's name is Alice. I have a big favor to ask of you. Would you mind taking us for a nice drive in the country for about an hour?"

"Not at all, as long as the station people don't mind the extra charge."

"Trust me, Greg; they'll pay if they know what's good for them. Here's the deal: my friend is sending out about a dozen cars just like this to distract the media. One will try to pull in the drive, then leave and try to get the reporters to follow. They'll be chasing phantoms all over town. Melissa is going to go wait at the house and give us the all-clear as soon as they're gone, so we probably don't want to go too far out."

Greg chuckled as he answered, "I'll take you out to the lake and give the kids a chance to stretch their legs a bit. How does that sound?"

"Perfect," both women called in unison. Once they were at a small lakeside playground they all got out to allow the children to play on the swing set in the chilly twilight. Greg leaned against the vehicle and lit a cigarette while mother and daughter sat on a nearby picnic table to watch the kids. Alice took Carissa's hand and squeezed it affectionately.

"I'm so happy to have you home, dear. I don't mind telling you that I was scared to death, not knowing where you were, but I knew you were alive. I have you right here." Alice balled her free hand into a fist and pressed it to her breast, covering her heart. "I never gave up hope for even one minute."

"That was one of the worst things about it, Mom, knowing that you would be so worried. I saw you and the kids in my dreams every night. I missed you all so much I felt like I was coming apart."

"I know, baby. It was the same for me. Then when I found out that you had been holed up with a murderer…" Alice gave a little gasp. "It liked to scared the daylights out of me."

"Mom, he's not a murderer. He's not a bad man, just a jackass."

"The news reports said that he had killed his wife because she was about to leave him and he wanted her money. Did they get it wrong?"

Carissa snorted. "He didn't murder anyone. She wasn't leaving him. They were planning a family, for crying out loud. It was an accident, Mom. He said that she was nearly cut in half. He was badly hurt, too."

"So you're saying he didn't kill her?"

Carissa stared across the gently rippling water, a sigh slipping from her lips. "You remember when grandma was so sick? When the cancer had nearly eaten her alive and the pain was so terrible?"

"Yes, but what's that got to do with it?"

"You said that you wished you had the courage to give her something to make her sleep and never wake up, to end her pain, remember?"

Alice's eyes misted over for a moment as she remembered how terrible those last days of her mother's life had been. "Yes, I remember. I can't believe you brought that up."

"I'm sorry, Mom. I didn't mean to upset you. Bryce did have the courage. His wife was in horrible pain. There was no way she was going to survive her injuries. She could barely speak but she begged him to make the pain go away. He did what he had to do to release her from it. It haunts him. He has terrible nightmares about it."

Alice leaned away from her daughter, eyeing her as if trying to see into her mind. "You're in love with him!" she exclaimed.

Tears welled and Carissa struggled to fight them back. "Am I that transparent?"

"Well? Where is he?" Alice said, ignoring the younger woman's question. "Shouldn't he be here with you?" She was silent for a moment before continuing. "Or doesn't he feel the same about you?"

"I don't know, Mom," she answered, misery evident in the catch in her voice. "I think he cares, just not enough to get him off that damned mountain. I think, after the accident, people treated him so badly that he just ran away from it all, took up residence in the middle of nowhere and refuses to come back down. He wanted me to stay."

"That's just ridiculous! Is he nuts? What did he expect you to do, just forget your kids and your life here? I don't think I like him and I haven't even met the idiot. If he was willing to just let you go then he's not worth his salt."

Carissa opened her mouth to respond but Alice's cell phone chirped loudly, signaling Melissa's call. Carissa took it from her mother's hand, spoke briefly and then called her children to her. "Time to go home. Everyone into the car, let's go. We have to hurry."

Greg opened the door for the little group, telling Carissa that he would take the back way to her home so that no one would see them. The two women thanked him, riding to the house in silence. As they pulled up they saw Melissa waiting impatiently by the front door, fairly dancing in place when she saw the car. Before the vehicle had stopped, Carissa's friend was jerking on the door handle trying to get the limo open.

Melissa hugged each of them as they stepped from the vehicle, wrapping her arms around Carissa a second time before she was done. "I was so thrilled when I heard you were all right and on your way home. We thought we'd lost you."

Carissa presented her friend with a teary smile. "It was a long haul but it feels good to be home."

"Let's get inside, girls, before those reporter-fools come back," Alice instructed. She turned to the driver and handed him two twenty-dollar bills. "Greg, you've been wonderful. Thank you so much for all your help."

The driver thanked her, adding, "Any time you ladies need another run around town you just give me a call." He tossed an informal salute at Carissa before getting back behind the wheel.

Alice hustled the little party into the house, instructing the children to take their coats to their bedrooms. "I'm glad I got the chance to move in here before you got home, Carissa. Two month's worth of dust had collected on everything. I got all the bed linens changed and did the little bit of laundry that was left from when you…" her voice trailed off as if just mentioning the incident that took her child away would bring bad fortune.

"Oh, Mom, you shouldn't have. No wonder you look so tired. You shouldn't have worn yourself out that way." Carissa was touched by her mother's efforts and hugged her again.

"Nonsense," Alice retorted. "I needed to keep busy. Besides I made your aunts come help me."

Carissa giggled at the thought of her many aunts bossing and tripping over each other as they took over her home. She inhaled deeply of the familiar fragrance of the house, noting the added aromas of flowers and scented candles. It only took a moment for her to jog out of the foyer and into her living room, gasping at the abundance of floral arrangements and other gifts that were placed throughout the homey room.

"My God!" she exclaimed. "What a welcome. Where did all these come from?"

"It seems, my girl," Alice answered with a chuckle, "that you have a great many friends and admirers. Some of the things are from the family but the rest started to arrive within hours after your rescue hit the news. There were quite a few balloon bouquets as well, but the kids had a good time with them."

"Oh, I'm home!" Carissa squealed as she hugged her mother. "I want a hot bath, my couch and some cocoa, in that order."

"Do you want my bubbly stuff?" Carissa's four-year old daughter asked as she tugged on her mommy's sweater. "I gots lots."

The women laughed together as Carissa bent to pick Sheanna up and fell to the floor when her son tackled her. Melissa stepped away from the joyous roughhousing to close the curtains and blinds throughout the house – just in case, as she put it.

"I'll put some cocoa on," Alice said merrily.

"I want cocoa," six-year old Zane cheeped as he ran after his grandmother.

"Carissa, I'm gonna get going," Melissa smiled. "How about if I give you a call tomorrow? Maybe we can get together for lunch if everything settles down next week."

"You don't need to rush off, Miss. I just got home," Carissa said as she hugged her daughter on the floor.

"Exactly. You need time with your family. But as soon as you get settled in I want to hear all about this dangerous, dark man that you've been stranded with," Melissa said with a wink. "He sounds like a dream." She walked back out the door with a knowing smirk on her face, reminding Carissa to lock up.

Alice walked into the living room to see Carissa flop down on the couch. "Go get your bath," she said to her daughter. "Then we'll sit down and have a nice long talk while the roast heats in the oven. I think you have a lot to tell me."

Carissa felt uncomfortable under her mother's appraising gaze. It was as if she had just been transported back to her childhood, her mother eyeing her, knowing that she had gotten into the cookie jar.

"Yes, Mom," she said as she slumped off to the bathroom.

Once alone behind the closed door of the little room, Carissa felt a sudden melancholy as she remembered bathing in the old copper tub before the pot-bellied stove in Bryce's cabin, his hands tangled gently in her soapy hair. She turned on the water with a sigh, wondering how he was doing and if he thought of her. Depression seemed to seep into her very bones, causing an ache that would remain with her for some time to come.

* * * *

Bryce was out of the cabin before the black night sky had lightened to a stormy gray. He had secured the rifle in the ancient safe at the back of the closet, taking the shotgun with him. He had bolted all the shutters and affixed the steel-barred grating over the outside door, not knowing how long he would be gone and not wanting anyone or anything to gain entrance to his home. Satisfied that the structure had been safeguarded against intrusion, he started out on his journey, a dark scowl on his bearded face and Skoll in tow.

The wind whipped at him, causing him to cover the exposed areas of his skin more firmly. Each stinging crystal of ice that found its way through the protective covering only reminded him that he was determined to brave the very fires of hell, if need be, to find Carissa and confront her for what she was trying to do to him. She would pay, he decided, as he staggered through the raging storm; he would see to it.

Chapter 17

It did not put out the same amount of warmth as the fire on the hearth in Bryce's cabin, but Carissa decided that her little fireplace, blazing happily in her spacious living room, was more than adequate. She lounged on her soft couch, a cup of morning tea in her hand, listening to the argument in the next room. Her cat, Blondie, had decided to curl up on the cushion next to her – as happy as the rest of the family to have her home. He had slept curled up next to her head all night, claiming that spot on her pillow since the children had claimed the positions at her sides. They had slept as one happy family on the same bed, crowded together and wonderfully at peace.

She burst into peals of laughter as a naked little girl streaked through the room with Alice in hot pursuit, demanding that the child stop. Sheanna squealed, her childish giggle drifting as music to Carissa's ears from where Alice had her cornered in the kitchen.

"Zane, you better hurry up, young man. The bus will be here soon," Alice called down the hall to the boy just as the girl escaped again.

Carissa listened to the tune of the morning without lifting a finger to help – as Alice had insisted. Her mother had heard her earlier, in the bathroom, vomiting pitifully, and had sentenced her to a morning on the couch after her first night home. The younger woman smiled again as she took another sip of tea and pulled the cotton throw a little higher up her body, enjoying the luxury of the moment.

She snuggled deeper into her warm robe, feeling privileged to be back in her own clothing. Her smile faded, however, as she caught the delicate fragrance of the aromatic sachet that perfumed the contents of her closet. The garment held none of the woodsy aroma of the mountain cabin, none of redolence of Bryce, or his musky scent that clung to the clothing she had worn there. She pushed the collar away from her nose and focused on the squeals and giggles of her two children.

Alice continued to bark orders at the two excited, happy children as she tried to coerce them into getting ready for the school bus that would carry them out of their little subdivision. Zane was in first grade, a little demon with letters and numbers and excelling in the social skills that would serve him well in his bright future. Sheanna was in pre-kindergarten, a creative child being prepared for the years of school that were ahead. It was wonderful to be home again to see the joy sparkling in their bright eyes as they made ready to face the new day. The children were wrestled into clothing, fed and sent out the door as the bus pulled to a stop in front of the house.

Exhausted by the ordeal, Alice flopped down into the easy chair next to the sofa. "Those kids wear me out," she laughed. "I don't remember you being that rambunctious when you were little."

"Sure, I was, Mom. It's just been a few years." Carissa grinned at her mother as the older woman bristled at the reminder of her age.

"Are you telling me that I'm old?"

Carissa refused to answer, grinning into her mug of tea, pretending she had not heard. They sat in silence, tension building in the air of the still room as both thought about the talk that was ahead. She had managed to hold her mother off the night before, stating that she was too tired from her trip to focus properly, but she knew that Alice would not be diverted much longer. Still, she nearly choked on her tea when her mother finally spoke.

"It will be nice to have another grandchild," Alice simply stated.

Sputtering on the sip she had just taken, Carissa managed to swallow before turning to face her mother. "How did you know?" she demanded. She had not told anyone except for Bryce, but that had been in a note high up on a mountain along with the man for whom it had been left.

"It's as plain as the nose on your face. Anyone with a brain can see you're pregnant. I assume that it was Bryce and not those two horrible…"

Carissa cut her off before she could finish the nasty thought. "It's Bryce's! Those two assholes didn't get that far before I got away."

"Well, that's a relief. So, what now? What was his excuse for not facing his responsibility?"

"He didn't give me one," Carissa sighed, reaching out to set her teacup down. "I didn't exactly get a chance to tell him. By the time I figured it out, he was gone. Told me he was going hunting, the big liar. The next thing I know, Dudley Do-Right shows up to whisk me away."

"You mean to tell me, Carissa Jane, that he doesn't know he's about to become a father?" The expression on Alice's face reminded her daughter of the one time she was caught in a lie and punished for her transgression as a child.

"I wouldn't exactly say that, Mom. I left him a note. It was all I could do."

"Good Lord! That poor man! To find out in a note…"

"What would you have me do, Mother? It's not like the FTD guy makes house calls up there. He's the one who left without so much as a 'kiss-my-ass'. There's no mail, no phone – hell, there isn't even electricity."

"Just what kind of place is it?" Alice's bewilderment was evident in the squeak of her voice.

"It's a frozen step back in time. He cooks on a wood-burner, heats with a fireplace and reads by oil lamp. He eats what he kills and gets supplies twice a year from some old codger, and that old codger is the only one who ever sees him. He hides up there like the world is out to get him."

"Well, maybe you're just better off without him then. You don't need a man who isn't even strong enough to face his responsibilities. What you need is a man that will take care of you."

Alice's words hit Carissa hard, wrenching a sob from her throat. "I love him, Mom! What am I going to do?" She covered her face with her hands, the tears flowing between her fingers to fall on her robe. "He's a good man," she sobbed. "I know, I felt it." She was not sure if she was defending him to her mother, or to herself.

Alice watched her daughter's heart breaking and wanted to twist the life out of the man who had caused such pain. That any man, no matter what his circumstances, would shirk his responsibilities was bad enough, but to cause *her* daughter such injury was going too far. If she ever got her hands on Bryce Matheney, whoever he was, she was going to tear him limb from limb. For now, all she could do was wrap her arms around her aching child and pray that the girl found some way to get past the loss she had suffered.

She had to shore up her daughter's spine, help her find her strength again.

"You're not Luke Skywalker trying to pull Darth Vader back from the dark side of the force, Carissa. Some people just can't be saved, and all you can do is try to go on."

"I thought that once he read the note he would come to me, get off that damned mountain. Even if he didn't want me anymore, I thought he would want his baby, but he didn't," Carissa sniffed loudly. "He doesn't want me. He doesn't want the baby. He told me he loved me and I believed him. It was all a lie. He's just like all the other men I've ever met. He loves me as long as I give him what he wants and do things his way. What's wrong with me?"

"There's nothing wrong with you!" Alice took her daughter's weepy face between her hands. "I never want to hear such talk again. Now you go in the bathroom and wash your face and we'll see if we can come up with some sort of plan to get your life back on track." When Carissa hesitated, Alice took on the bossy tone that only a mother can achieve. "Get moving, young lady. March!"

Carissa had to smile despite herself; no matter what, her mother would be her mother – something in which she could find comfort. She did as she was told, walked into the bathroom, switching on the light to stare at the reflection that gazed back at her in the mirror above the sink. Thoughts of Bryce, his hands on her body, his lips touching hers, filled her aching mind. Shutting her eyes tightly against the vicious pang of loneliness that swamped her, she held her breath, waiting for it to pass.

When next she opened her eyes, her heart nearly froze. Standing behind her, in the mirror, was Bryce, his dark eyes glittering hotly as he gazed back at her, his face once again wreathed in a shaggy beard. She blinked several times before whirling round to throw her arms about him, only to discover he was not there. His presence had been an illusion, a trick her lonesome mind had played upon her raw heart. There was nothing left but to hang her head and cry again, the desolate sobs drawing the strength from her limbs until she slumped to the floor to vent her anguish.

* * * *

The man stepped off the road into the thick layer of dingy slush that covered the shoulder. It was a reaction to the raucous blasting of an SUV's horn as the vehicle flew by, spewing salty muck over the weary traveler and his four-legged companion. He was well aware of the spectacle he created: a giant of a man, shaggy and unkempt, in full pack gear, carrying a weapon, with a giant of a dog, sauntering along beside him. His only hope was that no one would recognize him; no one would approach him as he made his way along the last leg of his journey back to civilization. Keeping his hood pulled up around his face, he avoided eye contact with any passers-by.

Bryce walked with a grave determination, his eyes glittering like black star sapphires in the pale gray daylight. He dreaded the thought of how people would perceive him if he should happen to meet anyone before he reached his destination. He dreaded it as he would a trip to hell, though that was where he'd been since he started this trip back to civilization. It seemed like a lifetime had passed since he had been around the mechanized world of humans, and he wasn't enjoying the view.

Skoll pranced nervously alongside, looking to his master for reassurance in this unfamiliar environment, but Bryce had little to offer. The man's steely resolve kept him from turning back around, to return to his home and never look back. He hated the sounds and the smells, hated the dread that hovered over him, a noxious vapor that cast an invisible pall over his thoughts. He had been a fool to pull the half-dead woman out of that snowdrift, a fool to let her slither into his heart the way she had. He was a bigger fool for letting her walk out of his life – for sending her away to have his baby on her own.

How could you know? he asked himself. The answer was that he should have known; it was the natural order of things. Having sex, unprotected, with the enthusiasm and frequency of teenagers, for as many weeks as they had, should have been a clue. However, he had not been thinking with his brain during that time, and now he was faced with the reality of the situation. He was going to be a father and *no one* was going to raise his kid but him. Carissa could be damned to hell, for all he cared, if she thought that he would just stand back and let her do what she had said in her note.

Thoughts of the bewitching woman waylaid him as he slogged along through the wet snow of the mountain highway. His steps began to slow as he remembered that last time he held her flushed body in his arms. The way her hands felt on his skin and the sound of her moaning cries filled his mind, causing an ache in his groin. He heard a sound that caused the dog's ears to perk up and realized it was his own pained growl.

Even now, as angry as he was, he wanted her as he had wanted no other.

Refocusing his thoughts, shoving her burning eyes and beautiful face to the back of his mind, Bryce took the turn that he recognized. The strip of snow-covered gravel would lead him to the house of the only person aside from Carissa and the man, Lewis McAlester, who had seen him in the past three years. He hoped Clancy was in good humor or there would be a gun battle. The old fool was as cantankerous and mean, as Bryce was himself.

After another hour or so of walking, Bryce saw the dilapidated old house that served as Clancy's home. The sun was setting, casting long, eerie shadows across the littered yard. The last time he had been here was the last day he had spent in the world of civilization, when he had stopped to set up an account with the old curmudgeon. He stopped about thirty yards from the structure, surveying the area carefully, before calling out.

"Bill Clancy, you in there?" Bryce yelled, pulling back his hood.

"Stay where ya are!" came the answer from behind the front door. "I got a gun pointed at your guts and I'll kill ya where ya stand!" The old man's voice sounded like rusty hinges, as if it had not been used for some time.

Bryce swore under his breath as he lifted his hands slowly out away from his body, the fingers of his left still clenched around the stock of his shotgun. "I'm not here to rob you, you old fool!" Skoll had taken a defensive stance, a low growl rumbling in his throat.

"Matheney? That you?"

"Yeah. Open the damned door."

The door to the house creaked open to reveal a bent old man, his round belly protruding from between heavy suspenders. "Hell, boy, if I hadn't recognized that big dog of yours, I mighta blowed your head off. Still might, if ya ain't careful." The old man was grinning but still had the muzzle of his gun leveled on Bryce.

"Old man, if you shoot me, you'll just piss me off."

Clancy's malevolent smile faded as he lowered his weapon. "Yeah, I guess you'd just up and shoot me back. Well, get in here. I ain't gonna heat the whole outdoors."

Bryce lowered his hands to cradle his own gun in the crook of his arm as he stepped forward. He walked slowly, never taking his eyes off the old man that held the door for him. With a low whistle he called Skoll, the dog falling into careful step beside him.

"I don't want that dog in here. Chain him out back," Clancy ordered.

"Nope, the dog stays with me." Bryce nearly smiled as the dog emitted another warning growl.

One look at the determination in Bryce's face and the old man stepped aside to let them pass, giving the wary animal a wide berth. "What the hell ya doing down here in the Hole? Get too cold for ya up there?"

"I need to use your phone, Clancy. You still have one?" Bryce said by way of an answer.

"You came all the way down here to make a phone call? She musta been a hell of a woman." Clancy cackled.

"Woman?" Bryce's eyes narrowed, his dark glare having its desired effect on the old man who twitched nervously.

"Yeah, that TV executive that ya shacked up with ya. It was in all the papers and the news on the box. They made you out to be some kinda kidnapper or something," Clancy muttered as he looked anywhere but at the giant that glowered at him.

"Jesus!" Bryce hissed. "I should've known. I need your phone." He walked toward the back of the house.

"Now hold on there," Clancy chased after him. "Is this gonna be a local call?"

"Nope, long distance," Bryce returned as he snagged the extension off the kitchen wall.

"I ain't paying for no long-distance calls."

"You'll be compensated," Bryce said as he wracked his brain for the right number.

"It'll cost ya twenty dollars," the old man's demeanor changed as he started to haggle the price of the call.

"Fine, you'll get paid." Bryce answered off-handedly.

"I'll get paid now," Clancy held out his gnarled hand.

Bryce sighed as he replaced the receiver in the cradle. "Where the hell am I going to get cash money?" he asked as he turned to face the old-timer. "You know I don't carry it. After I make the call you can run me up to the bank and I'll get your money."

"All right, then. Make it short."

Bryce grabbed the receiver once again, struggling to remember the right combination of numbers, dialing them on the old rotary phone. By the fourth ring, he had almost convinced himself that he had the wrong number until a familiar voice answered the call.

"Matheney here," the voice said.

Bryce nearly smiled; his father had been answering the phone that same way as far back as he could remember. "Hello, Pop."

There was silence on the other end, the strain of it stretching out for what seemed several minutes, when, in reality, it had only been seconds. "Bryce? Son, is that you?"

"Yes, Pop. It's me."

"My boy! How are you, son? I've been hearing about you on the news. I was worried about you."

"I'm good, Dad. Listen, can you come to Jackson and get me?"

"Hell, boy, I'll leave right now! It will be good to have you home for Christmas. My boy is coming home."

"Whoa, Pop. Take it easy. I doubt I'll be home for Christmas. I just need a ride."

Disappointment was evident in the elder Matheney's voice. "Well, sure, whatever you need, son. If I leave right now I can be in Jackson by midnight."

"No, I don't want you driving at night. Morning's fine. I really appreciate it, Dad."

"All right, I'll be there before noon. It sure is good to hear your voice, Bryce. I can't tell you how much I've missed you."

"Same here, I'll see you tomorrow, Dad. You can pick me up at Clancy's place."

"Is that old fart still kicking around? I'll be damned. He was ancient when I was a kid. Watch yourself around that one. I'll see you in the morning, son. I'll get there as early as I can."

"Thanks, Pop. I'll see ya." Bryce settled the receiver back on the hook, a sad smile tugging at his lips. He had thought of his father often, but had refused to acknowledge what his absence had cost the man. He quashed the guilt that was snaking in the pit of his belly, turning to fix Bill Clancy with a chilling glare. "Mind if I use your couch for the night?"

"I ain't running a motel here, Matheney," the old man sneered.

"You'll be compensated for that, as well. Will another twenty do you?"

"Thirty," Clancy countered.

"Done. Take me to the bank."

Bryce walked out the back door without another word, Skoll hot on his heels. Clancy had no choice but to follow, directing the towering man to a decrepit old Jeep that sat in the carport next to the house. He didn't trust the big man, never did, but he trusted money – something that had his heart.

Not until they got to The Jackson State Bank on Center Street did Bryce chance to glance about him, seeing the many people that hurried, heading home at the end of the business day. Christmas garland and wreaths marked the season, decking the streets with a festive air that Bryce did not feel. He had forgotten the time of year in his haste to get to his final destination. It had been a lifetime since his last Christmas, one filled with joy and laughter. He and his wife had spent it in New York, his father as their guest.

He thought of that day now, the expensive fake tree in the corner of their penthouse living room, Johnny Mathis crooning carols on the stereo. His father had laughed and offered a toast at dinner, winking at Anna. But when Bryce tried to fix his mind on the laughing face of his wife, all he saw was Carissa's shining green eyes and beautiful smile. Stifling a groan, he hauled himself out of the Jeep, leaving his gun and his dog to keep Clancy company.

He recognized the teller at the counter, and, from the look on her face, she recognized him too. He refused to acknowledge her identity as he filled out a withdrawal slip, knowing that the old biddy would proclaim his presence to the entire town once he turned his back. In a hurry to conclude his business and get out of town, Bryce handed her the slip, drumming his fingers impatiently while he waited. The nervous woman counted out two thousand in twenty-dollar bills, not daring to look him in the eye. As he left the building, Bryce could feel the eyes of every person in there. He wondered if it would always be this way for him, to be an object of ridicule and gossip wherever he ventured.

Once back at Clancy's ramshackle house, Bryce found a chair in which to rest his tired frame, Skoll hunkering down at his feet. It had been a real ordeal, climbing out of those mountains. The way had been tough for the first four days as the blizzard dumped plenty of fresh snow on him and his dog. They had been forced to dig in on several occasions, when the wind and flying snow had become too harsh to continue. What was normally a four-day hike had turned into nearly a weeklong struggle, and Bryce was bone-weary.

He declined a simple meal of ham and beans, offered by his reluctant host, too exhausted to find an appetite. He took the ham bone for Skoll, however, and listened as the dog chomped noisily on his prize.

Bryce leaned his head back on the dusty upholstery of the old chair and closed his eyes against the fatigue that plagued him. He was shocked to find, when he opened his eyes again, that morning had already arrived. He stood immediately, ignoring the stiff ache of his reluctant muscles as he stretched to bring back his circulation. One glance out the window told him it was just past dawn, and it looked to be a bright, sunny day. Bending low to retrieve his gun from the floor next to his chair, he opened it and checked the load. He did not trust old Clancy anymore than the old fool trusted him. It would have been just like the old man to unload his weapon and try something stupid.

Skoll was on his feet almost as soon as Bryce, following him to the door and out into the early sunshine. If the dog was dismayed by his new surroundings, he showed no sign as he sniffed around, exploring the junk-filled yard. Bryce propped his gun against the rickety porch rail, shrugged into his coat to ward off the early morning chill. He desperately wanted a cup of coffee but was leery of anything that came from Clancy's filthy kitchen, and he certainly did not want to go to town now that everyone was sure to know of his return. He rubbed his eyes, breathing deeply of the morning air, hoping its brisk nip would revive him.

Despite the circumstances, he was looking forward to seeing his father again and hoped the man was still in good health. Donnan Matheney was a robust, hulking man, much like Bryce. Though his father was approaching his seventieth year, he had always taken pride in his physique and his strength. Like Bryce, the man was well-educated and well read, and though he had spent his professional life in a suit and tie, he had spent his free time in the physical pursuits of outdoor life. Bryce's childhood had been full of camping trips, hunting, fishing and football games. He wondered if he would be afforded the chance to show his own child those carefree activities and show him, or her, about life in the mountains.

His mind turned once again to the elfin woman that now carried his offspring. Was she still thinking of him, as he thought of her? Did she feel the same loneliness that now ate at his soul? Closing his eyes, he could almost smell her soft, womanly fragrance; hear her sighing breath as he nuzzled against her throat. The taste of her succulent lips was still fresh in his memory, as was the feel of her soft body pressed against his. He groaned aloud, the constant ache in his groin throbbing cruelly, as her laughing eyes flashed into his brain.

Growling at his unruly thoughts and the subsequent stiffening behind the zipper of his trousers, Bryce snatched up his gun again, stalking off the wobbly back porch of the old house. He went in search of physical activity, anything that would distract his mind – and his body – from the beautiful woman that haunted his every moment. He found what he was looking for in the woodpile near a ruined shed. Snatching the rusty, weathered axe from the chopping block, he tore into the unbroken logs, sending them flying in a hail of wooden splinters and shattering bark. Skoll paid his human no mind as he continued to explore his surroundings, knowing instinctively that the man needed to work this out on his own.

Three hours had passed before Bryce finally stopped, exhausted and covered in sweat and wood chips. He notched the old axe into the block and retrieved his coat from the fence post over which he had tossed it. Running a blistered hand through his hair to dislodge the debris, he grabbed his gun and walked to the house to see Clancy watching him amusedly. The old man was leaning against the porch rail, a cup in his hand and a leering grin on his weathered face.

"Yep, she musta been one hell of a woman," the old man chortled. "And if ya think I'm gonna pay ya for doing my chores, you're wrong."

Bryce refused to look at him, instead choosing to go inside, hoping to find a way to wash up without getting any of the man's filth on himself in the process. "Christ, Clancy," he yelled. "You live like a goat. This place is a pigsty."

"Hey, ya don't like it, ya don't hafta stay," the old man yelled back as he followed Bryce inside. "This is my home and I live how I see fit."

"The *good people* of Jackson ought to condemn this place. It's disgusting." Bryce slammed the bathroom door, causing the dilapidated house to shake, as he set about in an attempt to clean himself up.

"There's a car pulling up," Clancy called out just as Bryce was looking for a clean towel on which to dry his face and neck.

Giving up on his search, Bryce Matheney walked out of the bathroom with water dripping from his beard onto his shirt. He moved to the back door where Clancy was glaring out the window, a rifle clutched in the old man's fingers.

"Put that thing away," Bryce ordered as he jerked the door open. A wide grin split the black fur of his face as he crossed the yard in a ground-eating stride. He reached out a hand, saying, "Pop! Damn, it's good to see you."

Donnan Matheney grabbed his son's hand and pulled him into a great bear hug. "Son," he replied. "You're a sight for these old eyes."

Pulling back, his hands still on his father's arms, Bryce took a long look at the man. "You must have been flying. It can't be ten yet."

"I couldn't sleep after I talked to you last night," the elder Matheney laughed. "I left home before five this morning. I couldn't wait to get here. How you been, boy?"

"I'm just fine, Dad. You're looking good. Retirement has been good to you." Bryce studied his father's face, which was as his own had once been, and the startling blue eyes with which his mother had fallen in love. He noted that Donnan's chestnut hair was now sprinkled with silver strands that sparkled in the morning sunshine.

"I do all right," Donnan said as he leaned back against his vehicle. "What's all this about a woman that was kidnapped?"

Bryce ran a hand over his damp beard, puffing a breath out through tight lips. "I'll tell you all about it on the way. Just let me get my things and my dog and we can get on our way." Bryce turned back to the house without waiting for his father's response.

"Hey," Donnan called out. "Where we going?"

"Illinois," Bryce tossed over his shoulder. He hurried into the house, brushing past a curious Clancy, retrieving his pack from the corner in the kitchen where he had dropped it the night before. As an afterthought, just before walking out the door, he turned back to the grizzled old man. "Thanks, Clancy," he said.

The old man actually blushed and gave his shoulder a shove. "Go on. I'll be glad to be shed of ya. Let me know if ya still want your supplies in the spring."

Bryce gave him a curt nod, exiting without another word. He joined Donnan at the car, letting go a shrill whistle that brought Skoll on the run.

"What the hell is that?" a startled Donnan barked when he saw the Mastiff. "A horse?"

Bryce grinned at his father. "That's my dog, Skoll. Mind your fingers around him."

"He looks dangerous," the elder Matheney said askance.

"He is. Like I said, mind your fingers," Bryce returned, his smile dropping away as he folded his long frame into the gleaming Cadillac. "Let's get going, Dad. I want to get this over with."

"Get what over with, son?" Donnan asked as he slid behind the wheel. "Just what are you up to?"

"I'm going to get my kid."

The startling revelation caught Donnan off-guard, freezing his hands on the steering wheel. *"You're what?"* he yelled.

"Start the car, Pop. I'll tell you on the way," Bryce said with a sigh. Then he added, as an afterthought, "I guess I should ask if you mind driving me across country."

Something akin to anger glittered in the older man's eyes. "I wouldn't miss this for the world." He fired up the engine. "Are you telling me that I'm a grandfather and no one saw fit to let me know?" Donnan pulled the car out of the drive and pointed it east.

"Well, technically, no. The baby isn't born yet."

"Huh? Would you mind explaining yourself, boy?"

"Yeah, sure," Bryce smiled ruefully. "I suppose you heard all the news reports about the TV exec that got herself lost in the mountains?" When his father nodded, the younger man continued. "Well, I found her – half-frozen and nearly dead – just down from my cabin…"

Donnan Matheney listened as his son told him about the woman who was trapped with him in the winter-locked cabin, the men who had kidnapped her and the ordeal of nursing her back to health. While the miles sped by Bryce explained the situation and the temptation that had gotten the better of him, and of finding out about the baby in a note. The one thing that Donnan noticed missing from the story was his son's feelings about the woman. He could tell that the younger man was purposefully avoiding the subject, giving only the facts about the situation that he felt Donnan needed to know.

The car pulled to a stop, prompting Bryce to look at his surroundings. "What are we doing here?" he asked.

"This is my home, son. You remember 'home', don't you?" Donnan bit off sarcastically.

"Yes, I remember, Dad. I just was wondering why we stopped. There's a long way to go before we get to Illinois."

"We stopped because you need a shower and a fresh change of clothing. You reek. You could stand a trip to the barber too. You can't mean to go claim your woman looking and smelling like something the cat dragged in."

"Sorry, Dad," Bryce said with a sheepish grin. "I guess I could wash if I'm going to force you to share a car with me. But, just so you understand, I'm not going there to 'claim my woman', as you say."

"Uh-huh," Donnan intoned knowingly. "Is it safe for him to be in my house?" he asked, inclining his head in the direction of the mammoth dog on the back seat.

"Yeah, he'll mind his manners." Bryce exited the car, opening the back door to let Skoll out.

"Great. After you clean up we'll continue this little talk and get something to eat. You must be starving. We'll start out in the morning. I don't want to hear any arguments. I'm going to have my boy under my roof for at least one night out of this."

"All right, Pop. Anything you say," Bryce said. It would be good to get some food and sleep in a bed before heading out. He followed his father into the house where he had grown up, dark thoughts clouding his mind as he thought of Carissa and the time they had shared. He was beginning to feel that he was making a mistake and wondered how she would react when he confronted her at last.

Chapter 18

Donnan Matheney looked with pride and affection at his tall son, now clean-shaven, dressed in the khaki Dockers and button-down, blue cotton shirt he had loaned the boy. "You smell a heap better than you did earlier. I was going to cook some stew, but I figured you would rather have something that you likely haven't seen in awhile."

The elder Matheney set a steaming plate of spaghetti and meat sauce on the kitchen table, motioning for Bryce to sit down. With mouth and eyes watering, Bryce looked at the huge pile of pasta and red sauce. He could not remember the last time he had eaten anything that did not either come from the mountain wilderness, or was not freeze-dried or canned. "Is the sauce homemade?" he asked hopefully.

"Yeah... well, sort of. The tomatoes came from a can but I don't think even your mom could top it. Wine?" Donnan held up a couple of glasses and a bottle of Merlot. "I know it's a bit early yet, but the sun will set soon enough." He poured the rich ruby liquid into his late wife's prized crystal, handing his son a glass.

Bryce took a sip, held it in his mouth to savor the taste that he had been denied for so long. "Damn," he declared after swallowing. "That's good. I can't remember the last time I took a drink."

"It's good to have you home, son. I don't mind telling you that it's been damned lonely around here. I hope you're not planning to go back up there anytime soon. It would be a crying shame to lose you so soon."

Donnan set his own glass down and dished up another lavish helping of pasta. He set the plate on the table, took a seat opposite his only son.

"I don't know, Pop. I want my kid," Bryce said, staring into his glass. "It's going to be a hell of a fight. Carissa is one hell of a woman."

"You can't really mean to try to take her baby. I don't believe you would even think of such a thing."

Bryce shot his father a withering glance, setting his glass on the table. "She means to have someone else be father to *my* kid – said so in her note. I'll see her in hell first."

"Bryce, are you listening to yourself? Do you hear what you're saying? Why are you so angry with her? Just exactly what did she do besides give herself to you?" Donnan reached a hand out to his son.

"She left me, Dad!"

"What the hell did you expect? You sent her away."

"If she really cared, she would've stayed," Bryce said bitterly. "She just got on that damned snowmobile and didn't even bother to look back."

"Dammit, boy," Donnan yelled at his son. "You sound like a spoiled kid! You could've gone with her. You knew she couldn't stay. She had a family to get back to. If you had one-tenth the brain I thought you had, you'd be with her now, starting your life together. You love her, don't you, son?"

Bryce dropped his head into his hands, dragging shaking fingers through his hair. He could no longer look at his father.

"Yeah, I love her. I can't stand being without her. Dad, it's tearing me apart, but you know I can't live down here. I'm afraid I'll end up killing someone one of these days, every time they start in on me about… Anna." He snatched up his glass, drained it and set it down.

"I should've wrung her father's neck for starting that business."

"Dad, he lost his daughter."

"Yeah, and so did I! I loved that girl like she was my own. And you lost your wife. She was a wonderful woman. But losing her didn't give him the right to lie, telling everyone you murdered her to get to her trust fund… it was just plain wrong!" Donnan leaned forward with his elbows on either side of his plate, his ice-blue eyes penetrating Bryce's deep gray ones. "It's time someone took a hand in it."

"And do what, Dad?" Bryce ran his hand down his face, grazing the craggy scar that skittered across his left cheek and down his jaw, a reminder of his reality.

"Sue the bastard. Take him to court and make him answer for his slander. He's made a wreck of your life, Bryce, and you just sat by and let him." The elder Matheney refilled both glasses, pushed the plate of cooling food toward his son.

"Dad, you know I won't do that. The man has a right to hold a grudge. What I did was unforgivable. I killed his daughter, for God's sake."

Donnan felt the real physical pain he glimpsed his only son's eyes. He wanted so much to take that pain away, to give back the love of life with which his boy had once been blessed. He suspected that there was only one person who could do that, one person who had managed, even briefly, to break through the boy's defenses. All Donnan had to do was get Bryce pointed in the right direction. "You didn't kill her, boy. A drunk did. You just eased her pain."

Bryce froze just as he was about to take another drink, his glass hovering halfway between the table and his mouth. A spark of shock shone in his eyes briefly before a slow, crooked smile spread across his face. "That's what Carissa said – nearly her exact words, if I'm not mistaken."

"She sounds like a smart girl, though I have my doubts seeing as she hooked up with you. Get your head out of your ass, Bryce. Go after her – and not because of the baby, either. Go after her because you love her and win her back. You need her."

"After what I did to her," the younger Matheney said, the smile falling away from his face. "I doubt if she'll want anything to do with me. I wouldn't blame her if she slams the door in my face."

"I wouldn't blame her either, but you owe her the opportunity to do just that," Donnan admonished. "Now, eat your supper. It's getting cold. In the morning we'll start sorting it all out."

Nearly eleven hundred miles away a woman stood in her kitchen, staring blankly at the cookie dough she had been stirring. She had wanted to do all the things that she would normally do to make Christmas happy for the children but her mind kept drifting to a lone cabin, nestled in the Wyoming wilderness. Tossing back her long, burnished curls, she wondered if Bryce was well, if he was taking care of himself. She wondered, also, if he had given her another thought since sending her away so unceremoniously.

Carissa's tears had long since dried up, cried out in the long, empty hours of the nights that had passed without his comforting warmth and heated caresses. In her heart, she knew she would never see him again, that he had retreated again into his lonely existence, content in his solitude. The ache in her soul was slowly giving way to bitterness, an ugly emotion that was turning her hostile.

"Cari," her mother cajoled, "You've been staring at that mixing bowl for half an hour. Hadn't we better get those cookies in the oven?"

Snapping out of her reverie, Carissa shoved the ceramic bowl aside. "Have at it," she muttered as she stalked from the room. Alice had insisted upon staying through the holidays, not giving her daughter even a moment alone. She loved her mother but Carissa wished with all her being that the woman would just go. What she was feeling was not fair to the older woman but she simply could not help it.

Since her second day home, Carissa had been lashing out at everyone around her, even refusing to take calls from family and friends who only wanted to welcome her back. When her doctor had asked for a medical history of the unborn baby's father, she had nearly slapped the woman.

The doctor, the same woman who had seen her through her first two pregnancies, had smiled knowingly, saying that Carissa was merely feeling the effects of the hormones that were changing because of her very healthy pregnancy. Though the good Dr. Monroe was concerned about her patient being underweight, she was confident that all was progressing as it should. Carissa found some comfort in that, knowing that she could at least have this small part of the man for whom she pined.

To make matters worse, she could not even return to work. The corporate Vice-President of Human Resources had decided that she should take a full month, with pay, to recuperate before returning to the station. In the mean time, she was twiddling her thumbs at home, wishing she could find a way to take her mind off the man that had sent her away. Her emotions alternated between wanting to hire a guide to take her back up on that mountain – just to tell Bryce where to stick it – and wishing the ground would swallow her.

She no longer felt like herself, a thought that troubled her to no end. It was impossible to take pleasure in all the things that she used to enjoy, or even in her children, it seemed. In a conversation between her two kids, she had heard Zane tell Sheanna that "mommy's sad." They were well-tuned to her emotions and missed nothing about her demeanor. She wanted to pull herself out of this black hole that was swallowing her, but she was afraid her inner strength had failed her at last.

Now, with Christmas only a week away, she was hard-pressed to put on a happy face, to make-believe that all was well, if only for the sake of her small children. Carissa went through the motions of decorating, baking and shopping for gifts but her heart was still in that mountain wilderness. She felt as if she was torn in two – between two worlds – with neither half being able to function without the other. Her existence had become hollow, emptied of all the joy life had once held.

"Damn him!" she yelled in the still air of her bedroom, tossing a shoe at the far wall. *How could he have just dumped me like that?* she asked herself for the millionth time. The ice that was forming around her heart was growing thicker, shutting out all emotion except for the festering anger toward Bryce.

"Carissa Jane," came Alice's sharp voice from the doorway. "I want to talk to you."

"Not now, Mother. I ain't in the mood," Carissa responded without turning.

"That's exactly what I want to talk to you about," Alice declared, entering the room and shutting the door. "You have two small children out there who almost lost their mother. They are wondering where she is, even now. You have *got* to pull yourself out of this funk."

Sighing deeply, Carissa flopped down on the bed, sprawling backward with her arms stretched over her head. "I know it, Mom. I just can't seem to help it."

"You're so angry, Cari. And don't tell me it's pregnancy hormones. We both know better. Honey, you have to get past this. You simply have to."

"Don't you think I know that? Dammit, Mom! It hasn't even been two weeks. I keep thinking that if I could just go back and tell that son-of-a-bitch off I could get on with my life. I really hate him."

"Hate? Sweetheart, that's not hate, it's 'hurt.' He hurt you and you want closure. It's understandable but there's not much you can do about it. It's time to buck up and get on with your life. Those kids need you."

Carissa growled as she pulled herself upright. "What am I going to do, Mom? I can't eat, I can't sleep. I can't even smile anymore. I want to tear his heart out. I'm sorry I've been such a bitch. I really am."

"Oh, Cari," Alice crooned as she took a seat next to her daughter. She took Carissa's hand in her own. "Trust me, honey. You don't want to tear his heart out anymore than I do. No mother wants to see her child suffer, but there's nothing we can do about it. We have to carry on."

"I'll try harder, Mom. I will. I promise."

"Why don't you take a nap? I'll take the little ones shopping and give you some time alone, okay?" She waited for her daughter to nod. "I never told you this, but your daddy and I had two wedding dates. We had a terrible fight before the first one and I cancelled it. He got bent out of shape and left, went to work on high-rises, moved to New York. It liked to have broken me in half, knowing I would never see him again."

Carissa stared at her mother, dumfounded. "He left you?" she squeaked.

Alice nodded, a mysterious smile on her face as she patted her daughter's hand. "He was gone for almost a year. One day I opened the door to find him standing on the stoop, a foreboding grimace on his face. Well, I was so happy to see him that I almost threw my arms around him, until my pride got the better of me. I held my head up and asked what he thought he was doing there, standing on my mother's front stoop."

Alice stopped, her eyes taking on a far-away glaze as she lost herself in her memories. Her face had softened, a faint blush creeping along her neck and face, fanning out to her gray-streaked auburn hair. She sighed deeply, wistfully, before continuing.

"Well, he just growled at me – you know how your father could do that when he was irritated. He told me that he hadn't wanted to be there anymore than I wanted him there but he had no choice. When I asked him what he meant, he told me that he had been forced there, sent home by something that was stronger than he was.

"I just scoffed at him. Then he told me that his spirit animal had made him come, would not let him sleep. Of course, I was young and foolish and told him I didn't believe any of his Indian ways." Alice's smile grew. It seemed she had forgotten that her daughter was sitting next to her as she continued her story.

"He grabbed me by the arms and said, 'When White Wolf tells me to do something, I do it.' Then he kissed me. Oh, I struggled and pretended that I wanted him to let me go, but I decided right then that I loved that damned wolf, whether it was real or not. We were married three months later and had a very happy life together.

"The point I'm trying to make here is that, if it's meant to be, it will be. If you're supposed to be together…" Alice stopped when she glanced at her daughter's pale face. Carissa's eyes had grown huge; her free hand was at her throat.

"Cari," Alice said in alarm. "What's wrong?"

"W-white wolf? Daddy was brought home by a white wolf?"

"Or so he said. Are you all right?"

Carissa jumped to her feet, pacing the room in short, quick strides. Her pallor of earlier was being quickly replaced by a rosy flush that colored her heart-shaped face. She started to giggle, causing her mother to believe her young daughter had lost her mind.

"Carissa, answer me. What's wrong with you?"

Her daughter stopped in mid-stride, whirling around to look at her mother. "Bryce is coming. He's coming here, probably on his way right now."

"Excuse me?" It was Alice's turn to be shocked. "Where did you come up with that notion?"

"Mom, I saw the wolf, too," Carissa said breathlessly. "She helped me find his cabin that night in the snow. And he heard her. It was her howling that brought him out to find me. I see her sometimes in my dreams. I don't know if I believe in Gram's mysticism but she always told me that there are forces at work that we cannot understand, that would help us in our lives. Don't you see?"

"No," Alice replied softly. "I don't see. Maybe we should call your doctor or something."

Carissa laughed again. "Mama, I'm not losing my mind – or maybe I am, I don't know. From the moment I met him, it seemed that we were supposed to be together. He's an idiot sometimes but he has to know it, too. That night the wolf told me that she was part of me. If that's true, then that force – or whatever it is – is part of me, too. If it was me that brought him out of the cabin that night, if that part of me touched him, then it only stands to reason that we must be connected somehow."

"Are you talking about those fanciful tales your grandmother used to tell about 'the two halves'? I swear, Carissa, the ideas you get in your head. Do you honestly feel that everyone only has half a soul and is in search of their other half?"

"You found yours with Daddy," Carissa rudely reminded her mother.

"Okay, I give up. If that's what you want to believe, if that will help you get through all of this, then go ahead. But, I just want you to know, I think you're setting yourself up for a big disappointment."

Carissa grabbed her mother in a sudden, fierce bear hug. "Don't worry, Mama. He'll be here, you'll see."

* * * *

The sun sent flames of pink and orange over the sky as it peeked over the horizon, casting a cheery glow over the earth. Donnan Matheney studied the sunrise before turning to his son. "Looks like snow before nightfall," he said.

"Yeah, let's get moving. I want to get out of state before it hits."

Donnan grinned at his son. "Been a long time since you and I had a road trip. Seems like we should be throwing in the camping gear and fishing poles."

Bryce answered him with his own strained smile. "Yeah. A fishing trip might be a better idea."

Donnan shook his head as he slid behind the wheel of his Cadillac. "Son, you're going to worry yourself half to death over all of this. We ought to be taking a plane. It would get you there quicker."

"Nope," returned Bryce. "Couldn't put Skoll in the cargo hold of a plane."

"You could put him in a kennel," his father suggested.

"And come back to find that my Mastiff had eaten someone's prize poodle, or worse yet, one of the keepers? No, thank you. Safer to keep him with me."

The elder Matheney chortled softly as the dog was loaded into the back seat of the car. "Will he eat my car when we stop at a hotel? You know there's no way they're going to let that Goliath stay in the rooms."

"He'll be all right, Dad. Besides, he'll guard the car against thieves," he said with a malicious grin.

"Well, there is that, I guess." Donnan turned the ignition, listening with satisfaction as his engine purred to life.

"Listen, Dad, you don't have to come. It's pretty unfair of me to coerce you into this. I think my driver's license is still good. I could just rent a car and go by myself."

"Are you crazy, boy?" Donnan retorted, insulted, as he put the car in gear and pulled onto the street. "I wouldn't miss this for the world. It's not every day that a man gets to meet his future daughter-in-law and mother of his grandchild. Besides, I'm looking forward to her taking you down a peg or two. You've had it coming for a long time."

"Yeah, I know," Bryce responded sheepishly. "I haven't been much of a son these past years." He shook his head ruefully at himself. "I wouldn't say Carissa is your future daughter-in-law. I don't want to disappoint you again, Pop, but she may want nothing to do with me. Most people don't, you know."

"That's because you spend most of your time pushing them away. If everyone knew you the way I do, they would see a good man," Donnan told him earnestly. Then, as an after thought, he added, "Even if you do act stupid sometimes."

"I guess I had that coming," Bryce said. Skoll moaned in the backseat, in apparent agreement.

The two men traveled in silence for some time until the elder switched on the car radio. The announcer was giving the tally of the previous night's college basketball scores, stating that the University of Colorado had suffered another loss, by a mere six points, bringing the total for the season thus far to three wins and five losses.

"What the hell?" groused Bryce. "What happened to the Buffaloes? Last I remember they had a pretty tough team."

"You been away for awhile," Donnan replied, warming to their mutual love for sports. "They're off to a rough start but they'll come back round. You have a lot of catching up to do, Bryce. You been gone three years and weren't really here the two years before that. But you're back now, that's what's important. I'm going to give that woman a great big thank you for getting you off that mountain."

"Yeah, she did do that," the younger Matheney stated dourly. "I wonder what kind of trouble I'm getting myself into here."

"Seems to me you're already waist-deep in it, son."

"She's going to make it rough on me."

"And so she should."

"She's a hard-headed woman."

"So was your mom."

Bryce smiled at that, remembering all the times that his mother had laid into his father, causing the man to give up whatever argument they were having. "How's old Ray Hill? He still practicing?" Bryce decided to change topics.

"Yeah, but he spends most of his time flying around to all the golf courses. Has both his kids working in the firm now." Donnan switched on the windshield wipers. "Looks like that storm's starting earlier than I thought. It could get right nasty out here."

He settled back, falling silent, watching the heavy snow descend from the heavens, until he realized what direction the conversation had taken. "Say – what are you thinking? You're not planning to go in there, threatening her with a troop of lawyers, are you? Because, if you are, you can count me out. I'll turn around right now."

"But what if she decides that she doesn't want me to have anything to do with her *or* our baby?"

"Then it's no more than you deserve, abandoning her the way you did," retorted Donnan.

"I didn't abandon her. She wanted to leave so I got her out," Bryce shot back.

"Yeah, by sneaky, under-handed... You took the coward's way out, boy, and I raised you better than that. I swear, I think living up there like an animal has turned your brain to mush."

"That's enough, Dad."

Donnan chanced a glimpse at the pain in his son's eyes. "I'm sorry, son, but you have to know how I worried about you. I never knew if you were alive or dead, healthy or sick. All I ever got were the two letters a year that you had that old fool, Clancy, send me. I just never knew what was going on.

"Many's the time I wanted to make the trip up there, check on you, spend some time, but you made it pretty clear that you didn't want anyone around. So, if I get on you, know I have that right for the hell you put me through."

Bryce turned to face his father. "You're right, Dad. I'm sorry. I am. I just couldn't deal with all those people, the way they were. Everywhere I went; they pointed and called me murderer. Hell, one look at my face and kids would run, screaming. People looked at me like I was some kind of monster and I just couldn't take it. I know what I did and I didn't need them reminding me of it every day of my life."

"Bryce, you didn't do anything wrong. You keep punishing yourself for something that any man would have done. Hell, I would have done it for your mother under the same circumstances. It's too much to ask a man to watch his wife struggle in that kind of pain, knowing that there's no hope. You did the right thing."

Bryce was just opening his mouth to respond when he saw his father's hands clench on the steering wheel, the man's face contorting in sudden alarm. The next moment both men were hurled against each other and the dashboard as the Cadillac landed in a ditch, narrowly missing a semi that had lost control on the slick highway. The big truck careened dangerously before righting itself and continuing on its way.

"You okay, Dad?" Bryce asked carefully, doing his own mental check of his body parts. He reached in the back seat to check on his whining dog. Skoll was scared but looked unharmed.

"Yeah, I think so," he said as he gingerly fingered the growing bump on his forehead. "How about you?"

"I'm all right. I wonder how bad the car is."

Both men climbed out, Donnan forced to shoulder his way through a door that was jammed in a pile of snow formed by previous visits of the road plows. It was plain to see that the vehicle was damaged and would need repairs before they could continue their trip. Bryce's head dropped forward as he contemplated his rotten luck, though grateful that his father was all right.

"Well," Donnan said as he reached in his pocket, pulled out his cell phone, "Looks like we spend at least one night in Cheyenne."

Chapter 19

"Well," Donnan said as he slipped the cell phone back into his shirt pocket, "They can have the suspension parts by morning, providing the shipment can get through the weather. The fellow at the garage says he thinks he can have us under way by early afternoon tomorrow."

Bryce swallowed the bite of shrimp he had been chewing, savoring the garlic flavor of the sauce. "Sounds good. Are you sure your head is all right?"

"I'm too hard-headed for a little bump like this to cause any trouble," his father responded, slicing off another thick bite of succulent steak. "I'm kind of glad we're getting this chance to spend a little more time together."

Bryce smiled around the food in his own mouth. "All things considered," he said after swallowing. "I am too. Damn, this is good. If I stay down here very long I'm going to get fat."

"Nah," his father laughed. "You're too mean. All that orneriness just burns it off."

"We better hurry, Pop. I don't want to leave Skoll alone too long in the room. If he starts barking, our secret will be out and the management will call animal control." Bryce grinned at the image of the scrawny, bespectacled man opening the door to discover the behemoth of a dog snarling at him.

"Son, just where the hell did you get that beast? I don't think I've ever seen an animal that big that wasn't wearing a saddle."

Bryce laid down his fork, taking up his bottle of beer and washing down the scampi that he was thoroughly enjoying. "A few days before I headed up to the cabin I found him. He was emaciated and bloody and beat half to death. A guy had him chained in a mud hole. Heard him yelping when I walked by, saw his owner whipping him with a broom handle."

"Uh-oh," grimaced Donnan, knowing his son's dislike of abusive people.

"Yep. So, I took the dog, found a vet. She thought he was probably six or eight months old but it was hard to tell because he was so under-weight, said the animal wouldn't survive a week. I set out to prove her wrong. In truth, I didn't think the poor thing would make it to the cabin but he refused to give up. I think I even carried him part of the way. He's been with me since, even saved my neck once when I crossed the path of a hungry bear, just out of hibernation. We got used to each other, you could say."

"What are you going to do with him now that you're back in the world of the living? He's not exactly the most people-friendly animal."

"Dad, I've been trying to tell you that I'm not staying. I can't live down here and you know it." Bryce set his beer down and leaned back in his chair. "Look at the way everyone is staring at me. I'm a freak here."

Donnan set his own beer down with a loud clunk. "Dammit, boy! If the scars bother you that much, then get the surgery. I don't understand why you refused it, anyway. You carry those scars like a shrine to the sacrifice you made of your life, so what do you expect?"

The smoldering gray of Bryce's eyes darkened to glittering black onyx, a muscle ticking in his scarred jaw. "I don't expect you to understand, Dad."

Donnan, not deterred by his son's harsh expression, affected one of his own. "Oh, I understand, all right. I understand that you spent the last five years feeling sorry for yourself. I understand that you spent the last three hiding from the world, refusing to defend yourself because you think you deserve what Sam Cannon has done to you. You think Anna would've wanted you to forfeit your future, *you life*, for her memory? You think she'd be happy at what her father did? You did what she wanted, what she needed – nothing more. If she knew what her own father'd done, she'd let the SOB have it, and you know it."

"Drop it, Dad." Bryce ignored the people that now stared at the heated argument. His jaw clenched tighter as he fought to control the ire that threatened to take over.

"No, son. No, I won't. This foolishness has gone on long enough. You're a grown man and I can't tell you what to do with your life, but dammit, I can have my say. It would've broken your mom's heart – and Anna's – to see what you've done to yourself. You have a chance for a new start and you're too blamed stupid to see it. I don't even know this woman, this Carissa, but already I like her – and I pity her. She's obviously a strong woman, a survivor, and she deserves better than what you're giving her."

Unbidden, a vision of fathomless green eyes flashed into Bryce's mind. He saw them as he most wanted to remember them: full of laughter and sparkling with love and passion. His fists clenched against the need to touch her, hold her again, as he had during those short, happy weeks in his cabin. His anger somewhat deflated, he sighed, leaning on the table and staring at the now-cold lunch that sat before him.

"You're right, Dad," he said. "She deserves better, but she got me."

"So what are you going to do about it?" the elder Matheney asked pointedly. "How are you going to fix this mess you made?"

With a remorseful half-smile, Bryce answered, "I don't have a fucking clue."

* * * *

Alice Albrecht watched in amazement at the sudden flurry of activity over the past three days. Her daughter's house was nearly turned upside down, as Carissa cleaned, decorated, baked, shopped and wrapped – all to create a wondrously festive atmosphere. The children were genuinely thrilled to have their real mother back at last, to bring out the joy of the season. Twinkling lights hung on the outside of the house and the trees in the yard sparkled with the tiny bulbs that lit up the night.

Carissa was brought to tears the day that she took the kids to the mall to visit with Santa and ride the North Pole Express, the little kiddy train that traveled center court. When Santa asked what little Sheanna wanted for Christmas, the child kissed him on the cheek and thanked him because he had already given her mommy back to her. When it got to be Zane's turn, all the boy wanted was to know that his daddy would not take him away from his mom.

Wednesday, just four days before Christmas, was to be the day of what Carissa hoped would be the last court date concerning John's efforts to take their children. The hearing had been continued just after she had returned home; the children's attorney asserting that, since their mother had just been through a harrowing ordeal – not of her own making – and had not had time to prepare or retain her own counsel, the extra time would be needed. John's lawyer had fought the request but the judge had found a compromise in allowing Carissa a scant two weeks in which to make herself ready for the fight ahead, and she was not looking forward to it. She had her mother to lean on for support, but still wished that she had someone else to be there for her, someone who was willing to be a father-figure for her children, someone whose name is Bryce.

As she stood over her washer, adding detergent to the soiled clothes and water in the tub, Carissa felt a stab of anger at the man. With each passing day, her faith that he would return to her was shaken, dwindling slowly. Still she had to put on a brave face and hope for the best. It was all she had to go on as the long winter nights held her prisoner with lonely thoughts of his sheltering arms and ardent kisses. There were moments when she would have offered the sacrifice of her own right arm just to see his wolf-gray eyes again, full of passion and fire.

Slamming the lid of the washer down, she grabbed up her basket of towels and shoved those thoughts aside. He will be here, she told herself time and again, but she would make him wait, make him say what she needed to hear before she rushed back into his embrace. He would have to make her believe that he would never leave her again, that he would never again hide from life in that wilderness cabin.

"Your attorney called while you were shopping," Alice told her, a cryptic note in her voice. "He says that he wants you to call him right away. I'll fold those. You go call."

Carissa handed off the basket, walking to her office in the back of the house with a faint sense of foreboding hanging over her. As far as she knew, everything was in place for the hearing that was just a day away. Picking up the phone, she wondered if something had happened that would cause the venerable Mr. Goldman, attorney-at-law, to call so urgently.

Ten minutes later, a distraught Carissa returned to find her mother finishing with the folding. One look at her daughter's ashen face told Alice that something had gone terribly wrong.

"Cari?" Alice ventured softly as Carissa sank into a chair across the room. "What's wrong, honey?"

"John found out I'm pregnant," Carissa whispered without looking at her mother.

"Oh, no. How?" Alice dropped the last towel at her feet in front of the couch.

"I don't know but he's planning on telling the court that I was away for so long because I was shacked up with my lover while my kids were going without, as if… He's going to say that I chose to be up there, instead of with my kids – that I planned the whole thing – and make me look like a whore in front of the whole world." Carissa lowered her head, visibly shaken by the conversation she had just had with her lawyer.

"Who did you tell?" Alice moved, dropped to her knees in front of her stricken daughter.

"No one. You and Dr. Monroe are the only ones who know. I didn't tell anyone else. Did you?" Carissa asked, already knowing the answer.

"No, Cari. You know better than that." She took her daughter's icy hand.

"Mom," Carissa's shaky voice was barely audible. "If the media gets hold of this – and they will – there's no way that judge is going to rule in my favor. Especially since John has the whole world convinced that he's all but cured of his disease. It's going to be another feeding frenzy. I can see the headlines now: Kidnapping victim in love-nest scandal with wife-killer. What am I going to do?"

"Don't think like that. We'll get through this, honey, I promise you." But Alice wasn't so sure. Her daughter had been through a lot, this just might be enough to send her over the edge.

* * * *

"We're making pretty good time, son," Donnan Matheney told his passenger. "Why don't we stop for the night and start again early in the morning?"

"I was hoping to at least make Lincoln tonight," Bryce answered. The cold Nebraska sun was still well above the horizon. "How 'bout stopping in Kearney for early supper and then I'll take over the driving. There's not much traffic out here. We should be able to hit Lincoln before it gets too late."

"Yeah, hardly any cars at all. You suppose everyone else knows something that we don't?" his father asked. "I could use some coffee. Supper sounds good. Breakfast was a long time ago."

Another gust of wind drove the fresh, powdery snow across their path in swirling clouds of white. For the most part, the wind had been at their backs all day, but it looked now as if it was changing directions – all the more reason to get as close to the state line as possible, to Bryce's way of thinking. He didn't want to get caught in any more bad weather before he got to his destination.

His destination, he thought, as the car pulled onto Exit 272, heading into Kearney. He wondered again just what he was going to do when he finally reached Springfield, Illinois. More importantly, what would Carissa do? Would she send him packing, slamming the door in his face? *Pop is right,* he thought. *She has that right and I owe her that opportunity.*

Kearney, a relatively small town, boasted several eating establishments. The Matheney's selected the Cellar Bar and Grill on Second Street. Bryce had a hard time making up his mind between the southern friend catfish and the halibut steak, finally choosing the latter, while Donnan ordered the smoked pork chop. They both topped it off with a fat slice of apple pie and steaming coffee for desert.

Donnan leaned back in his chair, patting his belly. "You sure you still want to continue on? After a meal like that all I can think of is finding a bed," he laughed.

Bryce was already tipping the waitress, however, and shoving his chair back to rise. "Yeah, Dad. You can snooze in the car," he paused as he accepted a small parcel from his server. "I'll give this bone to Skoll when we find a place to bed down. Let's get going."

"You sure are in a hurry," Donnan complained as he tossed his napkin onto his plate. Shoving back his chair, he muttered, "She must be a hell of a woman."

"She is, Pop," Bryce supplied with a rare smile, before leading the way back to the car.

The day was fading fast and he wanted to get as far down the road as possible before dark. He stopped at the driver's door of his father's Cadillac, glancing at the man over the roof. "What am I going to do, Pop, if she turns on me?"

The older man, anxious to see his son settled and happy again offered a suggestion. "Work your damned ass off to win her back. Son, if she's half the woman that you described, you'd be a fool to let her go a second time." He pulled the door open, entering the passenger side and reaching behind him to give the big dog a pat. "Hadn't you better give the big guy a stretch? I'd hate for him to urinate on my leather seats."

"Yeah," Bryce begrudgingly agreed before grabbing the leash off the seat.

Though Skoll did not look happy about being on a chain, he seemed more than satisfied at being out of the car. After drinking from the water bowl brought for the trip, the dog set out to examine the parking lot and surrounding lawn. Bryce, for all his size and strength, was again amazed at how difficult it was to keep the animal under control as it darted between the parked cars, exploring the terrain.

Donnan followed along, silently amused at Bryce's struggles with the big animal. "Appears to me that dog could use some training," he suggested.

Bryce offered a sheepish grin. "He's not used to being corralled. He's had free run of the mountainside since he was a pup."

"Which just illustrates my point: what're you going to do with such an animal in a city?"

"I have no idea but I'll bet it'll be fun finding out."

"There may be hope for you yet, my boy," the elder Matheney said with a smile. "At least this time you didn't insist you'll be heading straight back to the mountains."

Bryce nearly lost his hold on the big dog's leash at the shock of realization. Donnan was right; he was coming to accept the reality that he might not be going back. To his further surprise, the thought did not trouble him much; but the thought of Carissa's possible reaction to seeing him again did.

"She may send me packing back to the mountains, though, Dad."

Donnan Matheney chuckled while shaking his head. "I don't know this woman, and I don't pretend to know what passed between you two up there, Bryce, but I don't think she'll send you away."

"Why's that?" Bryce asked as he struggled to get Skoll back to the car.

"Because," his father began as he leaned against the car, watching the dog make another bid for sweet freedom. "She loved you enough to let you give her a baby, that's why. I'm not talking about the mistakes made by teenagers here. The two of you are too old for that. I'm talking about a grown woman who gave herself completely to you. There has to be a lot of love in a woman to do that, and that kind of love doesn't die just because you got pig-headed and acted the fool."

"So you think there's hope, eh?" Bryce inquired optimistically.

Donnan grinned at his son, anticipating the moment when he got to see Bryce's eyes light up with joy once more. "Oh, I think she's going to make you pay, make you suffer for it. If she's worth her salt, she'll make you wish you were dead by the time she's done with you, but in the end, I'm sure she'll come around."

Bryce cast his father a dismal glance as the dog finally decided to cooperate, jumping into the back seat and shaking wet snow all over the interior. "Get in the car, Dad," he groused as he opened the driver's door.

They rode in silence for a time after that, except for the errant chuckles of the elder Matheney, who was obviously enjoying what was happening to his son. The sun was setting, casting pale, hazy yellow and lavender across the snowy, windswept landscape. The wind was picking up speed, the drifts growing in ever-larger waves along the roadside of the uneventful countryside.

"No matter how many times you go through Nebraska, nothing ever changes," Bryce observed testily. "Everything looks the same."

"Yep. Nebraska is...," Donnan fell speechless as a gust of wind drove another whorl of powdery snow across the highway.

Bryce took his foot off the accelerator as the cloud of snow swirled gently some yards ahead, growing larger, seeming to stall in its spot on the road. The cloud swelled, separating, forming and taking shape. It took on an almost canine appearance, its legs lifting as if to take flight across the plowed asphalt. Then its head turned toward the car, the yellow glow of an animal's eye glinting so briefly that both men wondered if they had actually seen it. Then the cloud dissipated, the snow swirling again, skating off into the vast empty field on the other side.

Skoll gave a decided whine from the back seat as the car slowed almost to a stop. "White wolf," Bryce whispered to himself.

"What the hell was that?" Donnan demanded, rubbing his eyes. "Boy, I think we better call it a night. I'm seeing things."

Bryce immediately crushed his foot down upon the accelerator, the tires spinning slightly on the thin sheen of frost and ice on the pavement. A sudden desperation came over him, a need to get to her, the woman whose voice called to him in his mind. Something was wrong, she was in trouble and he had to get to her.

"Jesus, Bryce!" Donnan hissed. "Take it easy. You trying to get us killed?"

"We have to hurry, Dad. I have to get there."

"Why? What's the problem?"

How could Bryce explain to his father something that he, himself, did not fully understand? He only knew that he had to get to Carissa, had to help her. He had no way of knowing what the problem was, but he knew she needed him.

"I don't know, Dad. I just know I have to get there."

"This is nuts. Slow down, Bryce, you're topping ninety."

Bryce eased his foot back but kept moving along at a steady speed that his father still considered unsafe for the conditions of the winter highway, but he refused to say another word about it after seeing his son's set jaw and the determined gleam in the younger man's eyes.

After a time, Donnan finally spoke up, "Uh, son, you just passed the last exit to Lincoln."

"I know, Dad."

"I thought we were going to stop there for the night?"

"We're still making pretty good time. I think we can make St. Jo before too late. That way we might be able to miss the next front that's trying to come through."

"If you think so, but I still say we should've stopped. I'm going to close my eyes for a bit. Looking at the road in Nebraska always makes me sleepy."

Bryce smiled, switching on the radio to find an oldies station playing an old Brenda Lee song. "There you go, Dad, something from your generation."

"Watch it, pup," Donnan said with mock sternness, one eye cocked open.

Bryce answered with a chuckle, feeling good about the camaraderie he had missed in the years of his isolation. It felt good to be behind the wheel again, as well, with the hum of an engine vibrating around him. He was enjoying the trip far more than he cared to admit, all things taken into consideration.

Bryce chuckled at the sounds coming from his father as the miles passed. The man sounded like a buzz saw, so loud were his snores. Skoll whined in irritation on the back seat, his movements becoming more restless until Donnan awoke with a snort.

"We should be getting to St. Jo pretty quick, shouldn't we, Bryce?" the older man asked.

Bryce offered a crooked grin. "We passed St. Jo a few hours back. You snored right through it."

"What time is it? Where are we?" Donnan asked, his voice demanding.

"It's around one in the morning and we'll be coming up on Hannibal soon. I thought we could stop there for the night, if you want," Bryce answered.

"So much for a leisurely trip across country with my only son...," his father muttered dourly.

"I'm sorry, Pop. I didn't realize that's what you had in mind."

"Would it've made any difference if you had?"

"Probably not," Bryce returned, his jaw set like granite.

"All I can say is, she better be worth all this fuss."

"She's worth that and more. I can't shake this feeling that something's wrong, that she needs me. I'm worried sick."

"I can see that, son. I'm sure everything's going to be fine. Just stay positive," Donnan offered with a yawn. "Either get me some coffee or get me to a hotel. I'm beat."

"The exit's coming up. The sign says there's an Econo Lodge up ahead, at Route 61. That sound all right?"

"Works for me. Hope they let the horse in," Donnan said, indicating the dog behind them.

"I'm more concerned about whether he can hold his water a few more minutes. I should have stopped an hour ago to let him out." Bryce laughed at his father's concerned expression, the dog whining to let them know he was aware he was being discussed.

After walking the dog, the men quietly smuggled him into their room. Bryce fed the road-weary animal before collapsing on one of the beds, while Donnan took the other. It seemed like they had just closed their eyes when daylight peeked through the hotel room window, bringing them all awake.

Bryce, ever in a hurry, was quick to dress and walk his dog, getting back to the room to discover his father in the shower. While he waited, he switched on the television, absently flipping through the cable-fed channels until an image on the screen made his heart jump.

He quickly adjusted the volume to hear the story on one of the cable news channels. A picture of Carissa, her face a study of anger and humiliation as she desperately tried to evade ravenous reporters and photographers, was displayed in the corner of the screen while the anchor read the story. Shock hit him hard, causing his blood to run cold, as the sober woman's voice spilled from the television speaker.

"...ex-husband, alleging that her disappearance was contrived, while the Claire-Smith Broadcast Executive was secretly meeting with her lover in his mountain retreat. Due to scheduling conflicts, the hearing in family court scheduled for tomorrow, has been postponed until the day after Christmas. This also leaves Ms. James at risk for charges stemming from the deaths of the two men alleged to have abducted her, as well as filing a false report with the Teton County Sheriff in Wyoming. Ms. James was not available for comment.

"In other news..."

Bryce switched off the set as his father exited the bathroom in a cloud of fresh steam. One look at his son's stricken face and Donnan knew something was amiss.

"What is it, Bryce?" the older man asked.

"We're leaving now, Dad. Get your things. Carissa's in trouble." He explained what he had just seen on the set as he gathered up his belongings and those of his father's.

Donnan shook his head in displeasure as he thought of what the young woman must have been going through. He found Bryce's sense of urgency contagious as he preceded his son and the large dog out the door of the hotel, heading for his car with keys in hand.

"Don't worry, Bryce," he called over his shoulder as he opened the trunk lid. "We'll get this whole mess straightened out, you'll see. Springfield is only a couple of hours away."

Chapter 20

"Where are we?" Donnan asked as he looked up from his road atlas.

"I think this is called Dirksen," Bryce responded as he surveyed the businesses on either side of the road. "I'm going to stop somewhere and find a phone book. See if I can locate her address."

"First thing we're going to do is find a hotel. You can't go see your lady looking like something the cat dragged in."

Bryce ran the tips of his long fingers down the raspy growth of whiskers that shadowed his face, feeling the rough patch of scar tissue that marred the left side. "I suppose you're right. Skoll could probably use a walk, too."

"Looks like a couple of places ahead. Grab one and let's see if they have anything available." Donnan closed up the atlas, folding it and stashing it in the glove box.

Neither man had spoken much after leaving Hannibal, both lost in thoughts of what the day would hold once they reached their destination. Bryce, with an expression as hard as flint, could think of little else but the distraught face of Carissa as he had seen her on the television set earlier. He was anxious to find her and he wanted to beat her ex-husband mercilessly for what he was putting her through. More than that, he was cursing himself for sending her home to face the man and his under-handed tricks, alone.

"Looks like a Holiday Inn Express ahead, Dad." Bryce informed him.

"We'll probably be there for a few days, so I'd rather be someplace with all the extras."

"The place next to it looks like that type," Bryce said as he pulled into the right lane. "You want me to stop there?"

"Yeah, let's check it out. It's a Crowne Plaza – not too bad, I guess," Donnan surmised. "It'll do as well as anything else."

"Skoll, old boy," Donnan said as they settled into the large suite that he had acquired. "I hope you're worth the extra cash I had to fork over to keep you here."

The dog wagged his tail, nudging the hand of the tall, older man as if to beg for a pat. Donnan obliged, smiling at the animal while offering him the sweet treat of a cookie from the courtesy basket on the table.

"You're going to spoil my vicious guard dog, Dad," Bryce stated bemusedly.

"He's starting to grow on me. He's not a bad dog, Bryce."

"Yeah, he's been good company all this time. Listen, I wish you would let me pay for the room. I feel bad enough dragging you out here."

"Nothing doing. Consider it my Christmas present to you and your future bride. The concierge is going to send someone up to take Skoll out for exercise. While they're gone why don't we see if we can find you a barber and a decent set of clothes? My stuff looks good on me," the elder Matheney said, flexing his shoulders in a comical pose. "But on you it just looks like old-man rags."

Bryce looked down at the dungarees and soft flannel shirt his father had loaned him for the trip. "I wish I had time. I have to try to find Cari. Besides I don't feel comfortable leaving some hapless stranger alone with Skoll. I'm not sure I trust him not to have the person for lunch."

"Okay, then we leave the dog in the car, but you are going to a barber. You look like a wild savage. Time to clean up your act, boy. You don't want that woman of yours to be scared off the minute she lays eyes on you, do you?"

"Hell, Pop," Bryce said with a grin. "If my ugly mug didn't scare the shit out of her up there in the woods, I doubt she'd notice if my hair's too long. To be honest, she cut my hair a few weeks back. I think she likes it long."

"Well, I don't. You look like crap. Now get your coat," Donnan ordered, good-naturedly. "And muzzle that beast. I don't want to get sued because he decided to take a bite out of one of the locals."

Bryce dropped his smile. "Dad, I need to find Carissa first." He picked up the phone book, flipping to the letter "J", searching for her name.

"You kept her waiting this long, fool. She can wait a couple more hours. Bring the book with you. You can look her up and use my cell phone while I drive." Donnan headed for the door, signaling that he would listen to no more arguments.

Bryce was given little choice. Snapping the leash back on Skoll's collar and grabbing the hotel room phone book, he followed his father out into the hallway. A quick glance at the clock on the desk told him that it was still early, only 9:22 AM.

Less than half a mile north of their hotel, the two men located a department store where Bryce found a limited selection of items that would fit his large frame. He chose a few simple articles – dark-colored slacks and cotton button-down shirts – to wear during his visit. He also purchased shorts, undershirts, socks and a pair of leather shoes. He had wanted to replace his worn parka but failed to find any coats that were large enough to fit the wide span of his shoulders.

Carrying the purchases to the vehicle, Bryce dumped them into the trunk, slamming the lid down firmly. He climbed back into the passenger seat to open the phone book and await his father, who was still in the store. He looked through the extensive listing of people with the name of "James" but found no one named Carissa. He found the name "C.A. James" but that person was listed with a Lincoln address and not Springfield.

Belatedly, he realized just how little he knew about the woman who had so drastically changed his life. He did not even know her middle name. How could he have not learned more about her in all the days they had spent in each other's arms? *Because,* he answered his own question with self-condemnation, *you were too busy rutting like a teenager with raging hormones.*

A well-pleased Donnan returned to the Cadillac, a large sack clutched in his grasp. He ducked quickly into the car against the chill of the rising December wind. "Weather changes fast around here," he stated as he carefully settled the large package between Bryce and himself. "What's up, son? You're looking mighty peevish."

"There's no Carissa James listed," he muttered in response.

"No 'C. James' either?"

"Not in Springfield," Bryce sighed. He ran a frustrated hand down his face. "What do I do now?"

"Well, hell," Donnan chuckled good-naturedly. "You didn't think it would be that easy, did you?" At his son's baleful expression, he laughed again and offered, "Don't worry. We'll think of something. This town can't be *that* big. Seems to me she has a fairly high-profile job. Could be she's at work right now."

"You're right," Bryce hissed as he grabbed up the phone book once again, flipping impatiently through the pages. "We'll go to that TV station and find her there."

* * * *

"Now just hold your horses. The clerk inside told me where to find a good barber and then you're going back to the room for a shower."

"Dammit, Dad..." Bryce started to yell at his father.

"Mind yourself, boy. You ain't so big your old pap can't whoop ya. You're going to get cleaned up before you start harassing that girl and that's final."

Since he was a youngster, Bryce knew when his father's voice took on that tone not to argue with him. It did not make sense to the younger Matheney. No matter how much grooming he did, he would still look as if someone had driven over his face, and in the meantime, he would not know how Carissa was doing or if she needed help.

The little sleep he had gotten the night before was immersed in dreams of unfathomable verdant eyes clouded with distress. It was all he could do not to put his foot down and insist that they spend every moment searching the central Illinois town until he found her.

"So," a resigned Bryce asked, "what's in the bag?"

Donnan grinned as he pulled the slightly dented Cadillac out of the parking lot and back onto Dirksen Parkway, heading south. "Gifts."

"Gifts?" Bryce blurted, incredulous. "We haven't even found her yet and already you're buying her gifts?"

"You may be an idiot, son, but it didn't come from my side. I have no intention of meeting my future daughter-in-law – this close to Christmas – empty-handed. And I got a few things for her kids, too. It's sure going to be fun having children in the family again."

"Dad," Bryce interrupted. "I wish you wouldn't get your hopes up. I'd hate to see you be disappointed. There's no guarantee that she'll even talk to me."

"That may be, but she's still carrying my grandchild. And *I* didn't abandon her. I'm sure she'll like me just fine."

Bryce was not at all sure that he liked the satisfied grin he saw on his father's face. The man was having entirely too much fun with all of this. "Would you like me to get a box of salt for you to rub into the wound, Pop? I'm sure you could milk just a little more guilt out of me, if you try."

Donnan guffawed loudly, recovering briefly to answer, "You did this to yourself, boy. Don't complain to me."

Twenty-five minutes later, the pair was sitting next to each other in barber chairs at the Laketown Barber Shop. Every time that Donnan chanced a glance at his son, he found himself snickering all over again at the impatient resignation on the younger man's face. Bryce, for his part, was not having nearly as much fun as a mascara-wearing young man pawed his head, telling him how "fabulous" his hair was, in a decidedly effeminate inflection.

"Just cut the stuff so I can get out of here," Bryce commanded.

The barber offered a mock shudder and exclaimed, "Ooh, so forceful!" before doing his job.

Donnan snorted out another laugh, watching as his son, who had only so recently returned to civilization, stare bullets at him in the wall mirror. The older man was enjoying immensely the indignation his son was experiencing at being clipped and curried; the sort of thing a father enforced upon his teenage son, not a man of thirty-three years.

Once his hair was cut, the back of Bryce's chair was lowered abruptly, causing his head to flop backwards, bouncing against the neck-rest. His irritated eyes fixed upon the smiling face of the man who called himself a barber, wishing it were legal to choke the life out of the imbecile.

"Just what the hell do you think you're doing?" he growled.

The prissy little man retreated, cowering as he stared into the glittering, dark eyes. "Only what I'm told," he squeaked, his nasal whine grating on Bryce's nerves. "That other man said I was to cut your hair and give you a shave."

A sudden vision of Carissa flashed into Bryce's mind; her eyes alight with merriment as she dangled the straight razor in front of him. He remembered how it felt, being so close to her, her hands touching him so softly, while her sweet voice filled the kitchen of his cabin with warmth. Her scent came to him, even now, from the recesses of his mind, and mingled with the desire to touch her rounded curves and kiss her succulent lips. He had never considered himself homophobic, but there was no way that he was going to allow this person to perform so intimate a task on him, not after his memories had stirred in him all the longing he had been trying to keep at bay.

Bryce tore the barber cape from around his neck, tossing it to the side while sitting up. "No, thank you," he grumbled as he stood. Then, turning to his father, he said, "You ready, Dad?" He tossed a few bills onto the counter by the door on the way out, not waiting to see if Donnan was following.

"Wait up, Bryce," Donnan called as he jogged outside after him. He was still laughing at the scene of fear and confusion that Bryce had left in his wake. "Just hang on, now. I'll drive."

"Get me back to the hotel. As soon as I'm showered I want to get over to that TV station and see what we can find out."

"All right, son," Donnan laughed. "Just take it easy. We'll find her, so set your mind at ease." He climbed behind the wheel, still grinning at his son, thinking how good it was to see that the boy cared about something – better still – someone again.

* * * *

"I don't understand. You can't seriously mean it!" Carissa yelled at the man sitting opposite her. How she hated him and the arrogant smirk he wore while pretending to show concern and sympathy. She wanted to slap that twisted smile off his face, to make him regret what he was doing to her.

"It's what's best for everyone, Carissa. I know that once you calm down you'll agree. Now," he simpered, holding a pen and a neatly-typed document in front of her, "all you need do is sign this and we can put all this unpleasantness behind us."

"You bastard," she hissed, her voice low and menacing. Standing to lean over the massive desk that separated them; she struggled to keep herself from screaming. "I won't sign anything. This is bullshit and you know it. You're just pissed because I won't let you use my family and my misfortune to boost your ratings. I told you off but good that day at the airport and it really sticks in your craw. You'll not get another damned thing out of me, including my signature."

"Carissa," Tom Mavis said, his own irritation rising. "I want you to calm down."

"I have a good idea, Mavis. Why don't you shit in one hand and *want* in the other and see which one fills up first." She whirled around, yanking the door open so hard that it crashed against the wall, the noise reverberating through the building. She stalked down the hall without a second glance, knowing Mavis stared after her in triumph.

It had been strangely nice to be back in the station again when she had first arrived after that mystifying phone call. When Betty, Tom's assistant, had called her, she had no way of knowing that *this* would be the outcome of the meeting.

She walked into what was now her former office and took a good look around. An overwhelming urge to scream nearly took possession of her as the reality of her situation was only just beginning to sink in. She had just lost her job.

No job meant an even worse outcome in family court. The thought hit her hard, causing her to feel as if her children were already slipping away. She looked at the crumpled document in her hand, her copy of the settlement agreement that the egotistical station manager had devised. The deal offered the equivalent of a half-day's pay for each month she had worked for the company, and nowhere near enough to cover the expenses of rearing two children while paying a mortgage and utilities. After seven years of employment, the tally worked out to just over two-month's pay.

She would have to find another job fast and who was going to hire a pregnant woman? Working in Human Resources for as long as she had, she knew that the law was supposed to protect women from such discrimination, but she also lived in the real world. In the real world, women were lucky if they got half the consideration afforded to men.

All of that aside, what really rankled was that Mavis had done this to her family at *Christmas time*. How did the man sleep at night, knowing he was capable of effecting the destruction of whole families?

Carissa fought against the sadness that was trying to form in her heart. She had made so many friends through the station; so many people worked there that she would miss. There had been too many changes in her life of late, with the ill-fated trip, falling for a man who had tossed her aside and the new life that grew in her womb. Now she had to contend with unemployment, leaving her feeling as if her life had been turned completely upside-down.

Reminding herself that she was a practical person, she shoved all those thoughts aside as she turned to go in search of boxes in which to stuff her belongings. In her rush to get the distasteful task of packing done, she ran straight into Christopher Davidson, who was just entering the room.

"Whoa," he said, a big smile on his face as he reached out a steadying hand. "You okay? How are you? I heard you were back. It's great to see you."

Carissa's initial feeling of shock after the impact turned to one of fury. She wrenched her shoulder free of his grasp, glaring at the tall man with glittering, accusing eyes.

"I see you're still mad at me. Carissa, you had to know that I didn't want to be at that airport anymore than you wanted me there. Tom was hell-bent that we get the exclusive on your story. I told him you wouldn't like it." When she continued to glare at him, her body quivering in rage, he realized that something else was at the root of her anger. "What is it? What's happened?"

"You knew, you bastard!" she ground out, her jaw clenched against the need to scream at the top of her lungs. "You knew and you didn't have the decency to pick up the phone. Some friend you are. Get the hell out of my way."

Chris refused to move, kicking his foot against the door, propelling it shut with a firm click of the latch. He leaned toward her, looking squarely into her eyes, trying to fathom what she was going on about. "Knew what? What're you talking about?"

"Don't you *dare* act innocent with me. You know everything that goes on around here. You and Mavis are always in cahoots."

The news director thought she looked as rigid and cold as ice, as if a single tap against her brittle body would cause her to shatter into a million pieces. "I honestly don't have a clue what you're talking about, Carissa. What happened?"

"*Bullshit*," she spat. Snatching the rumpled document off her former desk, she shoved it at him, slapping him squarely in the chest with it and her fist, not waiting for him to grab it before she withdrew her hand. "How do you people live with yourselves?"

The harsh silence that followed stretched into long moments as Chris scanned the pages, his face changing expressions in degrees. When he was confident that he understood the words, he glanced sharply at her, his grimace one of disbelief. "Fired? That son of a... He fired you?"

Her eyes narrowed, the anger like two daggers stabbing out at him. "Oh, don't give me that."

Chris' own anger was becoming evident, as he felt unjustly accused. "This is the first I've heard of it," he said, his voice cold and calm.

Carissa watched his face closely, noting the sincerity in his voice. "He didn't tell you?"

"No, goddammit!" he nearly yelled, tossing the termination agreement on the nearby table. "You know I would have told you straight out. We've been friends a long time, Carissa."

Her anger ebbed away from this man, funneling into an impotent hole at the center of her being. She felt her legs quaking and found it necessary to sit, taking the nearest chair and sinking unsteadily into it. Clasping her shaking hands in her lap, she wondered if she would lose control, something she hated to do.

"I'm sorry, Chris."

Chris sat opposite her, taking up the agreement again and studying the pages more closely. "He cites the morals clause in your contract. This is absolutely the lowest." He slammed the papers down with a thud on the surface of the table. "I can't believe he's doing this."

Carissa slowly looked up, drawing him into the glassy green depths of her eyes. "I'm fucked, Chris. He just destroyed what's left of my life," she murmured, her voice barely audible. "I'm going to lose my kids. I've lost so much already..." she let her quivering voice trail off as she fought to keep herself together.

"No. No. No!" he exclaimed. "No, you won't, CJ. They can't take your kids because you lost your job."

A tiny smile that did not reach her forlorn eyes played at the corners of her lips. "In case you haven't heard, news man, I'm about to be brought up on charges of homicide, and the whole world thinks I'm a whore. I'm pregnant by a man that doesn't want me, two men are dead and John is telling everyone that I went up to that mountain for a lover's tryst. I'm fucked and we both know it." Her chin began to tremble as she added, "I can't live without my babies, Chris. They're all I have left to go on."

He reached out, patting the icy fingers that lay in her lap. "No, Carissa. You went there on company business. We were all at the meeting that day when you were selected to go. I'll stand in court and say so. So will the others. John's just grasping at straws, and no one will take it seriously."

"They're taking it serious enough to put it out on the national news," she whispered harshly. "Claire-Smith is taking it seriously enough to let that shithead fire me under the morals clause. I was beaten and nearly raped by two men who as much as said they were going to kill me when they were done. I was left to die in the heart of a hostile wilderness, and nearly froze to death. I have the ugly scars to prove it. And then I nearly died from disease and injury. I was taken from my family for two months; my mother nearly worried herself into an early grave – all for this fucking company that just tossed me out." Her voice dropped even lower, the pain so thick she could barely speak. "Just like he did. When he was finished with me, he threw me away. Bryce, my job, and now I might just lose my sanity."

Chris stood, deep concern evident on his face as he reached a hand to her. "We need to get you out of here. You need to go home. Let me drive you. I'll get one of the guys to drive your car."

His words triggered something in the back of her mind: a need to be self-sufficient, to not rely on anyone. She pulled herself up a little taller and stood without assistance. "No. I'm going to pack my things. I don't want to have to come back here. I'll take everything out today."

Seeing the determination in her eyes, he jumped into action. "I'll go scrounge up some boxes. Be right back."

Carissa did not wait for him to leave before she began cleaning out drawers and cabinets, carelessly pulling down pictures and mementos of her family and friends and the happy times she had known with her fellow employees. She tossed everything into a large heap on the conference table, going to the computer and downloading contact information and anything of a personal nature onto a jump drive that she kept in the desk.

She was just tucking her downloaded files into her purse when Chris returned with several empty boxes. He helped her to pack everything, being careful with the items while she shoved and crammed without thought.

"Give me your keys," he said, extending an open palm. "I'll take a load to your car and come back for the rest. You wait here."

She tossed her car keys at him before taking time to do a final check for anything she might have missed. Satisfied that she had gotten everything, she put the remaining items into the last box, her hands shaking at the disaster that her life had become. Seven years was a long time in the process of accumulating things, and the boxes totaled four. It was a sad moment when she realized that the part of her life spent here would be held within those boxes.

Chris returned after depositing the first two in the back of her Saturn, eyeing her to assure himself that she was steady on her feet. "The hallway's empty. Now's a good time to leave," he offered, reaching for the boxes.

"I'll take this one," she returned, pulling the smaller box toward herself. "It's got the breakables in it." Stuffing the detestable termination papers into it, Carissa lifted the container. "Let's go."

The duo had only traveled partway down the long hallway when Darla, the traffic and sales assistant, waddled into their path. Planting her hands on her ample hips and tossing her over-bleached hair, she fixed them with a curious stare. "What's going on here? Where you going, Carissa? Did you quit?"

Carissa cringed inwardly; loathe to face the company gossip with the shock of her circumstances still turning her blood cold. Chris leaned close to his friend's ear and hissed, "*Go.*" He immediately turned to Darla, running interference while Carissa made good her escape.

Carissa, nearly running, made it to the lobby, headed for the front door and the relative safety of the parking lot. As she passed the front desk, the receptionist spoke to her, distracting her from her objective. Looking over her shoulder, she opened her mouth to say something to the woman without faltering a step. The non-committal farewell was lost in a sharp grunt as she was hurled backward, the box and its contents scattering across the floor while Carissa fought to stay on her feet.

A vicious growl of frustration erupted from her throat as she snatched the box from the floor near the enormous feet of the person she had crashed into. She did not look up or offer any apology when she crouched down to retrieve her possessions and stuff them back into the damaged container. Having the presence of mind not to cut herself on the broken glass of a picture frame, she didn't notice when the person bent down in front of her until his massive hand covered hers on the floor.

Carissa froze, her heart leaping into her throat as she stared at the huge, masculine paw that completely swallowed and lifted hers. The man was so near that she could feel his heat, detect his scent that was so familiar and haunted what little sleep she had been able to get. His other hand reached under her chin, prying her face gently upward, forcing her to look at his face.

That face – so handsome in its angular lines, those scars that crawled along the left side to make him only more appealing in her eyes – held an expression so tender that it made her heart stop. She felt herself drawn in by the heat of that secret fire that burned behind his eyes, smoldering in their mysterious, gray depths. Her mind went numb, robbing her of any logical thought as she lost herself in the touch of his hands and the intensity of his gaze.

"Bryce." The single word left her lips on the scant breath of air she had been holding. The world stopped for her, time and space standing still as he slowly pulled her to her feet. From somewhere unnamed, the realization that his hand cupped her cheek came to her as she instinctively pressed her face against its heat. She said it again, "Bryce."

Chapter 21

She was in the circle of his arms as the tempest of her life passed from her consciousness. It was as if she had just run through a door, out of the raging wind, taking shelter from the storm. His big hands cradled her head against his chest, stroking down her spine as she melted against him. His presence surrounded her, filling her senses with nothing but him, both oblivious that they blocked the doorway of the building or that people were staring.

Then his lips were at her temple, raining feathery kisses along her brow as she lifted her hands to touch his face. She ran the pads of her fingers over the coarse scars on his cheek and beyond, to slide through the silky black strands of his hair. His arms tightened around her frame, lifting her feet from the floor, crushing her against him. He lowered his head, watching her pale face as his lips hovered only a sigh away from hers. She could feel his breath on her skin as his large hand moved up, cupping the back of her head.

His mouth touched hers at long last, in a kiss that blazed a path through her. Blood roared in her ears, her heart pounding against her ribs in joyous crescendo. To be with him again, touching him and holding him pushed all the uncertainty of the past weeks away, leaving only this moment in this man's arms. She gave herself over to the spell that wove around them, returning his kiss with an eagerness born of deep need.

The spell was broken with the loud thump of a cardboard box against a hard surface, snapping Carissa out of her trance. "I'll be damned!" a voice boomed from behind her.

The kiss ended; Carissa slid down Bryce's body until she was on her own feet again. She turned to see Chris Davidson standing at the reception desk, that newsman's leer on his face. Her friend had disappeared again, replaced by the hard-nosed journalist that he was. He approached, his hand extended, a thousand questions written in his expression.

"You have to be Bryce Matheney. I'm Chris Davidson, the news director here. It's really great to meet you," Chris said, reaching for his hand. "I want to thank you for what you did. It was a remarkable thing you did, saving Carissa."

Carissa groaned, rolling her eyes upward, knowing what was going through Davidson's mind. She watched in irritation as Bryce shook the man's hand before introducing another man that appeared from behind. The man bore a striking resemblance to the scarred mountain man, standing just a fraction of an inch shorter with lighter hair and the signs of age only making a brief appearance on his face. His most striking feature was his eyes that seemed to study her with their shocking blue gaze.

"Cari," came Bryce's deep, masculine timbre as he slipped his palms down her arms to take her hands gently into his. "This is my father, Donnan."

Feeling as if she were trapped somewhere in the twilight zone, she looked from Bryce's handsome face to that of his father's. She reached out a hand, intending to shake his, only to have the man grab her in a bone-crushing hug.

"Finally," his voice roared. "I finally get to meet and thank the woman who pulled my son off that mountain. Thank you for giving him back to me."

When he finally released her, she felt as if she had been caught in a vise, causing her to gasp for wind. The man beamed at her and she knew she liked him immediately. He was warm, with a kind face that made her feel appreciated. She opened her mouth to speak only to be cut off by Chris's clipped, businesslike tones.

"Mr. Matheney," he said, specifying after both men looked his direction, "Bryce. I'd really like to talk to you if you have a few minutes. We have a lot of questions that you could answer for us."

"No!" Carissa fairly screeched. "Step back, Chris. You're not going to air my business like yesterday's dirty underwear. Just leave it alone."

Undaunted, the news director continued his pitch, "As you may know, Carissa's in a lot of trouble here. I think that you could help clear this whole mess up."

She could see a newsman's lust gleaming in Chris' eyes. He was all but drooling over what it would mean for his department if he could nail the exclusive interview of Bryce Matheney, the man at the heart of the scandal.

"I want to do whatever I can to help her, but I'm not sure about this," Bryce answered.

"I promise you that we would handle it with the utmost sensitivity," Davidson assured him. "You would get the chance to tell it like it is, and you won't be taken out of context."

Bryce ran a hand thoughtfully down his face, touching lightly on the hated scars. "Do you really think this would help?"

Looking incredulously from the face of one man to the other, Carissa was incensed, yelling in frustration, "*Am I not even here?* I won't be discussed like I'm not even in the room. I don't want any part of this on the evening news – local or otherwise. Is that clear?"

When Davidson started to speak again, Bryce held up his hand and turned to her. He put his hands gently on her arms, looking her in the eye. "Maybe you should tell your side of it, Cari. Your ex is really working you over in the media. You might have to take a stand."

She could not believe what he was saying. That Bryce, of all people, would want to go on television, speak to the media, was so far outside the realm of understanding that she laughed. "I can't believe what I'm hearing," she sneered. "It's my stand to take and I'll take it in court."

She watched as his face darkened; saw the irritation that sparked in his eyes. "Not," he said softly, "as long as you are carrying *my* kid. I want my son or daughter born safe, not caught up in some sordid mess."

Her eyebrows shot up, dropping again as her eyes narrowed. "Is that why you're here? Because you want *your* kid?" she scoffed.

His eyes darkening and his face growing rigid, he tightened his grip on her upper arms. "Of course. Did you think I would just let my kid grow up without a father? I thought that's what you wanted too. Isn't that why you left me that spiteful note?"

"Silly me, I almost thought you were here because you gave a damn about me. I've got news for you, the kid's not yours, it's *mine*. You threw me away, remember?" She paused for breath, inhaling deeply before rushing on. "Hey, I know. Why don't you just join John in court on Monday? That way the two of you can finish picking over my bones all at once. He can take Sheanna and Zane away from me, and you can take this one.

"Then the two of you can pat each other on the back and congratulate yourselves on what a fine job you did of killing me. Go ahead. And then Chris can have his department cover the whole debacle. If not, I'm sure the tabloids will pay you big money for the story. Probably enough money to keep you and the baby hidden up there on that mountain for a long time."

The telltale muscle in Bryce's scarred jaw began to twitch, signaling the fury that he was keeping at bay. "That's enough, Carissa," he said in that menacing tone that she remembered so well.

"You know what? You're absolutely right. It *is* enough," she ground out as she jerked her arms free of his grasp. Taking a step, she nearly tripped over the forgotten box on the floor. She gave it a vicious kick, sending the box and its contents slamming against the lobby wall before stalking out of the building to her waiting car.

The Matheneys followed her into the parking lot – Bryce calling her name – with Davidson hot on the men's heels. Carissa pulled the car keys, which Chris had returned to her earlier, from her jacket pocket as she reached the door. It only took a moment for her to gun the engine to life and leave the parking lot, screeching away from the men as they tried to stop her.

In her ten-minute drive home, she went through a whole range of emotions. The rage she was feeling ebbed, making room for the pain of realizing Bryce was only there for his child – *her* child – and did not really care about her. Her lips were still throbbing from the kiss he had given her, fueling the pure sexual desire he had inspired with that simple touch. Sadness followed, accompanied by the empty loneliness of heartbreak that threatened to swallow her whole. Then there was the sense of loss and impending doom, stemming from her new status as unemployed. Finally, anger flared again when she recognized there was nothing she could do to change it. By the time she reached her house, she was bordering on mental exhaustion.

Alice, a bright smile gracing her lips, greeted Carissa at the door. "Hi, Honey. How did the meeting go?" she asked cheerily.

Carissa's glassy eyes looked past the woman as if she were invisible. Without acknowledging the question, she walked by, her legs moving slowly, her posture, drooping. Her only objective was bed, to fling herself upon the mattress, close her eyes and never open them again. She felt broken and disconnected from life.

There was a vague awareness, somewhere near the corners of her consciousness, that someone was speaking, but she paid the words no mind. Jolting her from her stupor, a hand took hold of her arm, shaking her, as that far-away voice sharply snatched at her attention.

"Carissa Jane!"

She turned slowly, her blurry eyes coming into focus upon the face of her mother as the older woman eyed her with concern, seeming to expect something from her. Her own voice sounded from a distance, "Hmm? What, Mom?"

"I asked how your meeting went. Are you all right, dear? You look ill." Alice reached out a hand, as only a mother would do, to touch her face, checking her temperature.

"I'm all right," she answered softly. Then her face contorted into a painful frown. "I'm really tired."

Her mother eyed her skeptically but decided not to pursue the question of her daughter's health. "What happened with your boss?" she asked, the concern on her face turning to suspicion.

"Oh, that. Um, well, he fired me," Carissa stated softly before continuing her ambling gait down the hall. In her room at last, she crawled onto the bed, curling her numb body into a tight ball.

"Carissa?" Alice said uncertainly. Something was terribly wrong, and it was more than just the loss of her job. The girl was in shock, her skin so pale as to be almost translucent. "Carissa, what happened to you?" There was no answer from her daughter, no acknowledgement of any kind. "Carissa. *Answer me.*"

Carissa's glazed eyes slowly focused on Alice again as she turned her head only slightly. "I... I think..." she could not find the words to tell her mother what had just happened. Her body began to tremble as she tried to sit up, her mother rushing to her aid.

"You're freezing!" Alice exclaimed as she touched her daughter's face again. She pulled the bedspread around her child as she pushed her back down against the pillow. "We have to get you warmed up, and fast." She began to rub briskly at Carissa's arms and legs in an effort to stimulate her circulation.

"Mama," the stricken woman whispered. "Bryce found me."

Alice froze, her hands lying still against her daughter's calf. "What do you mean, he found you? Is he in Springfield? Where is he?"

Carissa shrugged slightly against the bedding, sorrow surfacing in her glassy eyes. "I don't know. I left him standing in the parking lot at the station."

"Why? What happened?"

Carissa's whisper became even softer. "He doesn't want me."

"Don't be silly. If he didn't want you, why would he be here?"

"The baby," was all the younger woman could manage before the tidal wave of emotions that had swamped her came to the surface. A broken sob forced its way out of her throat as her body began to shake in earnest. The horror of the past hour and a half – her confrontation with Mavis, the loss of her career, seeing Bryce, knowing the only reason he had come was not because he loved her or wanted her – came out in a torrent of anguished weeping. She would lose her children, her hope and everything that she had fought so hard to keep. She would lose it all, have no reason for going on, and John, the hyena, would be standing in the shadows, waiting for her downfall.

"We'll just see about that," her mother hissed with a venom that was uncharacteristic.

* * * *

"*God-damn-it!*" Bryce swore as he watched Carissa leave the parking lot. "Give me the keys, Dad," he demanded, holding his open hand out to his father.

Donnan folded his arms across his chest, a stern admonition narrowing his eyes. "Nothin' doin', son. You leave that girl be. She needs time to calm down."

Bryce pulled his gaze from the vehicle that was growing quickly smaller on the horizon to fix his father with a chilling glare. "I have to go after her. She thinks... I have to tell her, dammit."

"Seems to me that you missed that opportunity. Just calm down. We'll figure something out." When his son did not relax his stance, Donnan added, "Bryce, you go after her now and there's liable to be an accident. She's in a real snit and driving like a bat out of hell. If she sees you coming up behind her, she's likely to loose control of her car."

Those words took the wind out of Bryce's sails. Dropping his hand, he turned again to look in the direction down which her car had disappeared. He had found her, had held her in his arms, had kissed her lips and felt her kiss him back. She had looked at him with so much emotion in her green eyes that they fairly danced. If he had just kept his damned mouth shut, she would still be there, pressed against him.

"I can't take this, Pop," Bryce said, shaken by the ugly turn the situation had taken.

"I know, son. Just give it a little time."

"Carissa's had a very bad day, gentlemen," the voice of the forgotten news director interrupted. "She was already pretty upset when you got here. Why don't you come in and I'll tell you all about it. It concerns you, Bryce."

The giant turned, his steely eyes trained on Davidson's. "What do you mean by that? What happened?"

Chris held the door open, waiting for the two big men to enter. When they made no effort to move, he pasted on his most sincere smile. "There's a conference room around the corner. We can go in there and I'll tell you."

The Matheney men followed Davidson, Bryce feeling less than trusting toward the guy as they entered the room. Chris closed the door, motioning for them to take a seat each before pulling out a chair for himself. He folded his hands on the table and turned to face Bryce.

"Have you seen the national reports about Carissa and the new allegations and rumors surrounding her time in Wyoming?" He waited for Bryce's curt nod before continuing. "Carissa has been on short-term leave. When the story broke, our station manager took the opportunity to use her employment contract, the morals clause in her contract, to fire her. The two have never seen eye to eye, and well, this was the clincher."

Bryce felt his blood turn to ice in his veins. His eyes never left Davidson's face as the truth of her situation came to light. Now there were two men in this world that he wanted to beat to within an inch of their lives. "Does that son-of-a-bitch know what this means for her?" his voice growled, sounding like a savage animal.

"Yes, I'm sure he does," Chris answered, his gaze unflinching. "I'm not going to lie to you. I want your story. It would be a hell of a coupe for my news team, but I have another interest in this, as well. CJ is my friend. She's a good person who has come through a lot. I respect her and I'm genuinely fond of her. If I'd had a daughter, I would've wanted her to be Carissa.

"She's been dealt a rough hand here and I'm not sure she has enough left to play it. Only two people know what really happened on that mountain and she's not talking. That leaves you. If you're willing, Bryce, you could tell the story, let people know the truth."

Bryce leaned back in his chair, crossing an ankle over the opposite knee and affecting a posture of relaxed confidence. It amazed him how easy it was to fall back into the attitude of the self-assured advisor after so many years away from the business of high finance. "I appreciate your honesty, Mr. Davidson, so I'll return the favor. I don't like the media. I don't like reporters. You guys have fucked me before. What makes you think I'd trust you enough to sit in front of one of your cameras?"

"Because, as I told you, I have a vested interest. She's my friend and I hate to see this happen to her. She was fired because of the publicity she has gotten, or more to the point, the publicity surrounding her affair with you.

"The Teton County sheriff has reopened the investigation into the deaths of Kyle Pritchert and Bert Adams because of what John James has been accusing her of. I have to tell you, it doesn't look good for her. I know she didn't do anything wrong. She doesn't have it in her. You were there and you can clear it all up."

Bryce held his hands up, the palms pressed together, his elbows resting on the arms of the chair. He studied the man in front of him with an unwavering gaze, silently measuring his integrity. "If Carissa refuses to talk to you then I would be breaching her confidence by stepping forward," he stated plainly. "Why should I do that?"

Chris was beginning to betray a small amount of the frustration he was feeling. Bryce could see it on his face as he took a deep breath to steady his mind. He was not sure that he could trust the newsman completely, but he could easily see that Davidson was concerned for Carissa. That was enough for Bryce but he wanted to hear the man's answers.

"Because, as much as I care about her, CJ is the most stubborn and independent woman I have ever known. She refuses to accept help and she won't step forward to defend herself. Someone has to do something, dammit."

Bryce turned his head, looking at his father, the two locking eyes and exchanging silent signals. He looked at Chris again. "And what about James? Will you interview him, too?"

Chris met his gaze squarely. "Yes, if he'll do it. I think that once we get him in front of a camera, the whole world will see how crazy he is. You know about him, don't you, that he has a mental illness?"

Bryce nodded. "As I understand it, the illness is controlled with medication."

"He may think it is but the bastard's just plain nuts. He's unpredictable and full of strange ideas. He'll want to rebut as soon as he sees you. He's that type. How CJ put up with him all those years, I'll never know. She ought to be canonized."

Bryce exchanged another look with his father before sitting up and uncrossing his legs. "I'll do it," he said gravely. He held up his hand at the quick smile on Davidson's face. "Under one condition: you tell me how to find her when it's done."

Davidson scratched his head, grinning devilishly. "I shouldn't. It's wrong, but after seeing the way she looked when you... Okay, you have a deal." Chris stood as he thrust out his hand, offering it to the young man who might just be his friend's salvation.

* * * *

Carissa heard the phone ring, heard her mother run to catch it before it rang a third time. She was awake, had been for some time, staring at the ceiling without feeling anything. Her mother's voice, hushed and somber, floated down the hall and through the closed door of her room. There were other sounds, too, of children giggling, their conspiratorial whispers reaching her from the playroom at the other end of the house.

Thinking of all that had transpired, all the changes that had buffeted her life in the past months – even the past hours – had her shuddering on the bed. She could not really focus on any one point, could not get her mind around her situation as a whole. Nothing really made sense to her as she tried, and tried again, to formulate some plan of action, something that would help get her life back together.

Finally giving up, she hauled herself off the bed to stand upon wobbly legs. Carissa could not remember ever being so tired, but then, she could not remember ever having such a day. Her numb body did not want to cooperate, her muscles stiffly protesting each step she took. Opening the door, she shambled into the hallway, took a deep breath and walked the rest of the way to the kitchen.

She could not hear what her mother was saying, only the tone of voice she used. There was no doubt that the conversation was about her, something that Carissa detested. "Who are you talking to, Mother?" she groused when she drew near.

Alice nearly dropped the phone, startled by her daughter's sudden presence. "Oh, honey. I thought you were still sleeping. It's Melissa. Do you feel up to talking?"

Carissa reached for the phone, wondering just exactly what her mother had told her friend. "Hi," she muttered into the receiver.

"Carissa, how are you? Ashley called me from the station a little while ago and told me what happened,"

Melissa said, her voice low and concerned. "Are you all right?"

"Yeah, I'll live. Just seems to be par for the course for me lately. How're you doing?"

"I'm fine," Melissa stated quickly. "Listen, um, I don't know how to tell you this, but I think you should know. Ash said that your, uh, mountain man and you had..."

"A brutal confrontation," Carissa supplied. "A nasty argument. An ugly falling out."

"Yeah. Anyway, you should know what he's doing. He's going live on the six tonight..."

"He *what*?" Carissa hissed into the phone. "I told him to stay out of it, damn him! I... I'll call you later." She slammed the receiver onto the cradle and glanced at the clock. It was 6:03 and the evening news had already started. If she knew Chris Davidson, he would have Bryce live, in the studio for an in-depth interview. The news director would make it a special report, taking up the entire first segment of the half-hour show.

Stalking into the living room, she snatched up the remote and punched the buttons. It seemed to take forever, impatient as Carissa was, for the set to buzz to life, and when it did, Bryce's face filled the screen. The camera was angled just right to capture his handsome, unmarked right side and still offer glimpses of the damaged part of his face in close-up. His eyes were glittering in the studio lights, his expression, a grave mask of conviction.

Carissa raised the volume to better hear the deep timbre of his voice. "...buried in the snow. She was barely alive, badly injured and unconscious. She was wearing what looked like a business suit, no coat or protection from the elements. She had frostbite on her hands and feet and a little on her face and ears. She was pretty torn up, cuts and bruises. Someone had beaten her up pretty bad.

"She had a fever that lasted for days. She alternated from convulsions to hallucinations. There were many times when I didn't think she was going to make it."

The director switched cameras to a view of the anchor, Ashley Gaston, her pretty face a study of concern as she moved to the next question. "It sounds as if it was pretty serious. Why didn't you take her to a hospital?"

Carissa remained standing in the middle of the room, her eyes trained on the TV as the view switched back to Bryce's face. "There just wasn't any way to do that. My home is a cabin, set pretty far up along the mountain. There aren't any roads, and even if there were, there was a pretty fierce blizzard raging up there. I don't own a vehicle. I don't have a phone or transmitter to call for help." He smiled sheepishly at the anchor. "I don't even have electricity." His face sobered again. "I'd've had to pack her out on foot and she'd never have survived the trip. All I could do was try to get her fever down and dress the wounds."

The camera panned out, showing Bryce – Skoll at his side – and Ashley, sitting, facing each other at an angle on the sit-down set. Carissa knew Ashley well, knew that the expression on the anchor's face was real. She could understand the emotion behind that expression, since she had experienced it herself the day she had removed Bryce's beard. It was difficult to be a woman in his presence without feeling his intensity or the pure masculine sexuality that flowed from the man.

"And, after Ms. James had recovered, why did she not leave then?" Ashley asked, her eyes never leaving his face.

"She'd have never got out on her own. It takes about four days to walk out, and that's without the several feet of snow that covered the ground. Took me almost a week to walk out when I left after the park service came for her."

The view switched to a single shot of Ashley. "Why didn't *you* bring her out when she was recovered?"

The shot changed to Bryce, his face taking on a slightly wistful quality. "It took quite a while for her to recover. You have to remember – there wasn't any medical help. She had lost a lot of weight and was pretty weak."

Off camera, Ashley asked, "But once she was strong enough, why didn't you take her out then?"

The right corner of Bryce's mouth twitched, almost smiling. He cleared his throat. "Well, for one, she didn't have the right clothing for it. How she managed to survive out there in that blizzard without the proper gear, I'll never know."

"Didn't you have something she could borrow?"

The smile that had been tugging at his lips finally formed, a crooked, endearing smile that played mysteriously on screen. "Well, you know Carissa. She's a very small person and well..." his voice trailed off as he waved a hand indicating his own long frame.

The camera view switched to a blushing Ashley who was trying to stifle a nervous titter. "Yes, well, I can see where that would be a problem. So, what you're saying is that she was trapped and there was no way out."

Off camera, he answered, "Yes. It was too dangerous to leave."

"How did she finally get out of the wilderness? We know that the park service came for her, but how did they know where to find her?"

The shot switched back to Bryce, his face somber again. "I hiked for a couple of days to a neighboring cabin. I knew the owner of the place had a radio and could call for help."

Skoll whimpered softly and Bryce turned his attention to the dog, his big hand resting on the animal's massive cranium, with the camera panning out to show his actions.

"Why did you wait nearly two months to get help? Surely you could have made that trip sooner than you did," Ashley asked, her voice coolly professional.

The camera zoomed in on Bryce. He face betrayed his surprise at the question only briefly. There was a moment of hesitation before he answered. "Quite honestly, the thought had never occurred to me before that time. I've lived on that mountain for several years with almost no human contact. Trekking through the snow-covered mountains to visit my neighbors is just not something I normally do. You become pretty self-sufficient up there, and tend to forget that there are other people around.

"It's not like the guy lived a couple of miles down the way. His cabin is over on the next peak. It's a hard trip down and back up again. The mountains can be treacherous, especially in winter. One step in the wrong direction and you can crash through the snow and end up at the bottom of a gorge with your neck broken. If you get injured or stuck you can freeze to death, be food for the scavengers."

When he fell silent again, the shot moved back to the anchor who had become caught up in his story. "You took a pretty big chance, then. Why? Why risk your life for this stranger?"

Bryce's face was on the screen again; his eyes cast downward, hiding the sadness that Carissa could feel watching him. "She wanted to go home," he said softly. He raised his vision to the camera, the force of his gaze reaching into her living room through her TV screen. "She needed to get home. No mother should ever be forced to live without her children, and Carissa was suffering the hell of the damned, without hers. She worried every minute of the day if they were safe. I think she was concerned that their father would get his hands on them. That was something that really scared her. I had to find a way to get her out. So that's what I did."

Carissa felt her knees grow weak, needed to sit down. She never took her eyes off the TV as she felt around behind her, finding the coffee table and sinking onto it. There was a message in his eyes that went beyond the words he spoke, something he was trying to tell her.

"What did Ms. James tell you about her injuries? How had she been hurt?" Ashley continued the questioning.

"She told me that she was on a company trip – for you people, as I understand it. She was working for you, until... Well, anyway, she said that her rental car had broken down when the blizzard started. Basically, she was kidnapped by one of the two men that died up there. He picked up his partner and tried to carry her off to... cause her harm. She fought them and managed to escape, but not before she took a fairly nasty beating."

"How long had she been wandering in the wilderness before you found her?"

Bryce hesitated, looking thoughtful as the camera panned back to him. "I'm not really sure. I don't think even she knows. She was pretty much done-in by the time she'd made it as far as the hollow below my cabin. But it was Skoll here that really found her." He turned to pat the dog again, the big animal looking up and licking his face. "He's the real hero. If he hadn't kept at me until I went outside to investigate, she'd've frozen to death out there. All I did was follow his lead."

Ashley smiled at the dog. "He seems like a pretty good animal to have around."

"Yep, he's been good company."

"I guess we should warn the viewers, though. If you see the dog out anywhere, you might want to resist the urge to run up and pet him," Ashley said. She let a malicious little giggle slip. "He nearly took the arm off our station manager when they met in the hall."

Her words gave Carissa a satisfied smirk. She had loved that dog the moment she saw him in that cabin and now she knew why. He was a good judge of character.

The shot panned back to Bryce, his face held an almost cruel light at the anchor's words. He looked as if he wished the dog had finished the job. "Yeah, but he can sense a person's disposition. He knows when someone isn't worthy of trust."

Carissa and Alice both snorted.

Ashley cleared her throat, fighting back the urge to laugh. "When Ms. James was returned to civilization, so to speak, it came to light that she spent two months trapped in a cabin with someone who was – I hope you'll forgive me – accused of murdering his wife. Though the charges were dropped, you were accused of killing her so that you might get control of her trust fund. Would you like to speak to those allegations?"

The view immediately switched back to camera one, showing Bryce's face, capturing his initial response to her question. His face darkened ominously, his gray eyes burning with the fire of rage long kept at bay. That muscle under the scar tissue of his left jaw constricted, ticking dangerously. He took a breath in the next instant, and his expression changed to one of pain before he wrested control of his emotions, looking directly at Ashley.

"I loved Anna. She was a wonderful woman. You can't imagine the kind of love a man can have for such a person... There was an accident while we were on vacation in Yellowstone..." He stopped, his voice faltering as the camera zoomed a little tighter, catching every nuance of expression that crossed his face. Taking a pained breath, he continued haltingly, as if each word wracked him with pain. "I... I never spoke of this to anyone except Carissa. It's a little hard..." he cleared his throat. "I... the truck that hit us plowed over the top of our car. When I came to she was pinned under the truck, her seat was crushed under her and pushed to the back of the car."

Bryce fidgeted in his seat, obviously fighting the memories that flooded his mind. Carissa felt a pang near her heart, knowing how painful this very public disclosure was for him. She suddenly wished she could reach her arms around him, hold him close and make the hurt go away.

Clearing his throat again, Bryce continued, lost in the trauma of the memories. "She was... hurt bad. She was awake... in more pain than she could stand. She begged... there was no way she was going to survive. Everything below her ribs was just... gone... She wanted me to help her, needed me to. I did what I needed," his expression began to change, his voice growing stronger as if he were having some great revelation. "I did what was necessary to ease her pain and give her peace. Her face relaxed and she smiled at me. Some see what I did as horrible – and I do too – but she... she seemed so grateful. I know that now. She was no longer in pain."

There was a tense pause, the camera panning to catch both subjects. Ashley was mesmerized by the intensity of Bryce's confession. Snapping out of her stupor, she raised a document in front of her. "According to the coroner's report that we were able to get a copy of, Anna Matheney died from her injuries. Her spine, and in truth, nearly her entire torso, was severed below the third thoracic vertebra, with massive internal trauma. It lists as secondary cause-of-death, asphyxiation due to the blood in her lungs. But the ranger's report on the incident has you... smothering her. The ranger claims to have witnessed your blocking her air passage. Was that what happened."

Without flinching, Bryce answered, "Yes."

"That's an amazing admission. It was your father-in-law, Sam Cannon that prompted the charges against you; saying that you had killed her for financial gain. What have you to say about that?"

"Sam's a good man," Bryce said, an air of wistful sadness in his expression. "I can't really blame him. He needed someone to blame and it was my fault. I was driving that night. I should've taken better care of his daughter.

"Her trust fund is still intact. Every dime of it is still sitting in the bank, untouched. I'll probably give it to charity or return it to Sam so he can do something with it. I don't want the money. We had no need for it when Anna was alive. We wanted to give it to our children..." he let his voice trailed away, lost in what might have been.

Ashley sighed as her face appeared again on the screen. It was apparent that he had easily won her over. "You, yourself, were injured quite badly. You told me that the scars on your face were caused by that accident. It says here that you nearly died of your own injuries. Is that true?"

"Yes. I think I wanted to die. It took nearly two years to recover."

"And then you retired, so to speak, to your mountain home."

"Yes, I just couldn't face the world anymore." Bryce's expression changed again, the view zooming closer, capturing the essence of what was going through his mind, what was written in his heart. His face softened, his eyes heating with that hidden fire, smoldering hotly as he looked into the lens. "I would have stayed up there forever, alone, if I hadn't found a beautiful woman buried in the snow. She has a gift for bringing joy to a person's life. She gave me something that I haven't had in a long time: hope. That's why I'm here. I want to spend the rest of my life making her smile." He paused for just a moment, as if in thought. "You know, Ashley," Bryce said, turning to the anchor as the camera panned out to capture them both.

"Yes?"

"You can't imagine how disgusted I was to come to this station and find that she had been fired because of her association with me. You should know, she's beyond reproach. She's a fine person and never did anything to warrant the judgment that your station manager dropped on her. I hope she takes his backside to the cleaners."

There was a weighty pause as the camera captured the pure malevolence in Bryce's eyes and the icy smile on his lips. Shock registered briefly on the anchor's face, followed by a touch of malicious glee before she cloaked her emotions with a cool smile.

Clearing her throat, Ashley looked at her note cards before raising her head to ask another question. "It seems as if you both went through a lot. Ms. James went through a harrowing experience and barely survived, and you worked to save her, to nurse her back to health, then risked your life to get her out. I'm sure there's one more question that our viewers would like answered: Why did you leave your mountain after being up there for so many years? If you had no communication with the outside world, you couldn't possibly know of the allegations that were made against her. Why are you here now?"

The shot switched back to Bryce, zooming slowly in on his face. The smoky glow of his eyes looked straight into the lens and out of Carissa's television screen, seeming to look straight into her soul. "After she was gone, nothing was the same... I missed her."

"So your presence here is of a personal nature."

"Yes. Very personal, if she'll have me."

"Dear God," Alice cried. "Did he just propose to you on the six o'clock news?"

The view switched again to Ashley, a soft, dreamy expression on her pretty face. "That's really..." Ashley cleared her throat again, pasted on her professional anchor smile. Her gaze darted off-set, then returned to Bryce's face. "I can see Mike, our floor director, signaling that our time is almost up. Is there anything else you'd like to add?"

The camera zoomed once more, tightening on his face. Carissa could feel the heat of his gaze as if he were in the room with her. "Yes. I'd like to say that I'm sorry I wasn't here sooner. It took me a long time to find my way, but I'm here to stay now."

Bryce disappeared from the screen, replaced by Ashley as she read from the script on the prompter. Carissa sat frozen as the news show cut away to commercial, her heart fluttering in her breast as she tried to get her mind to translate the meaning behind his words and the messages in his eyes.

"Bryce," she whispered in bewilderment. She turned to look at the amazed face of her mother. "Mama, what am I going to do?"

Chapter 22

Carissa asked again, "Mom, what am I going to do?" She was still feeling the passionate heat she had seen in Bryce's eyes as they gazed at her from the television set.

The kids, fed and tucked in for the night, the dishes done, both women sat on the couch facing each other and discussing the day's events. Even though Bryce had been on television more than two hours before, Carissa hadn't heard from him. She kept reminding herself that she was unlisted, and it would be difficult for him to locate her.

After the way she had acted earlier at the station, she did not know if he would go to the trouble of trying to find her – but that was not what he had said on the news. With no way of knowing where he was staying, she had little hope of finding him.

"You could call Chris, see if he knows where Bryce is staying," Alice suggested.

"I tried," Carissa answered dourly. "He didn't pick up. Left him a message. I just know he's avoiding me. I'll bet he's afraid I'm going to chew his ass."

"I'm sure," returned Alice, one finely arched eyebrow lifting. "Just keep trying to get hold of him. I think this might be where you reap what you sow."

"Thanks, Mom," Carissa muttered. She flipped her hair out of her eyes and sighed, "I know I blew up at him, but I hate being used like this. Why did this mess have to be my fifteen minutes of fame?"

Alice was just about to respond when the phone rang – again – causing both women to jump skittishly at the sound. Checking the caller ID, she saw that it was a Baltimore number. She groaned, "Jesus, it's Mike Claire." Carissa grabbed at the receiver before taking a deep breath, forcing herself to be calm. "Hello," she snapped.

"Carissa James?" the demanding, masculine voice at the other end asked.

She felt her heart sinking with bitter disappointment, wishing it had been Bryce. "Yeah?"

She had become suspicious about answering the phone since her return from the mountains. Her unlisted number had somehow gotten into the hands of some members of the national media, their calls coming at the most unexpected moments. They used countless tricks to get her to answer, and she wasn't unsure if this might be one of them. It had been especially bad this evening, since Bryce had gone on TV. She was certain that the national media had the full story by now.

"Mike Claire, here. I'd like to talk to you about Tom Mavis," the terse voice returned.

Carissa flopped back on the couch, irritation showing itself in the frown on her face. "I hope you'll forgive me, Mr. Claire, but I really don't want to talk to you or anyone else from Claire-Smith. In case you weren't informed, you people approved my dismissal. I don't work for you anymore."

"No, we didn't, Carissa," he snapped. "That's what I wish to discuss with you."

Carissa's brows shot up, surprise registering in her expression a moment before a wicked smile danced across her lips. She caught Alice's eye with her sudden movement as she bolted upright. "Is that so? You mean he acted without authority? Why doesn't that surprise me?" She signaled to her mother to pick up the extension.

"Yes, well, I'd like to hear your side. What transpired today? What was the conversation you had with Mavis?" the man asked, his voice tightly controlled.

"Basically, he told me that I'm a whore and he didn't want me working in *his* station anymore."

"Did he actually use that word?"

Carissa let out a harsh laugh. "Oh, hell no. He danced around it, just as he always does about everything. I believe he said something to the effect of my being a distraction to my fellow employees in light of my recent 'escapades' with 'a man of questionable morals'. I don't mind telling you, Mr. Claire, it really pissed me off, considering that those 'escapades' were the result of a trip that *your* company sent me on, and that the whole business nearly cost me my life." She paused only long enough to catch her breath before rushing onward. "You people sent me up there, unprepared, without protection, with no one to meet me at the airport – just sent me off on a wild goose chase. I was beaten, almost raped, left to freeze to death in a mountain blizzard, separated from my family for two months – and then I come back to a firing squad."

"Carissa," Claire fairly snapped. "We didn't send you off at all. It was Mavis. I shouldn't be telling you this, but he was supposed to take that trip. Instead, he pushed it off on you. The man was already in trouble before you were found. I want you to know that this will be the last straw with him. We intend to take him to task for this."

"Oh really," Carissa sneered. "I'll believe *that* when I see it. In the meantime, you should know that

I'm considering legal action for the discrimination, and for putting my life in jeopardy."

"That is certainly your right, Carissa, and to be honest, I don't blame you. I only ask that you wait for the outcome of our actions. You will be taken care of, and so will Mavis. I want you to consider yourself to still be employed with the company, with all pay and benefits. Please, just enjoy the holiday with your family, and let us handle this mess."

"I want to ask you something. If you were in the dark about this, how did you find out about it now? It's not like anyone is in their offices at this hour."

There was a momentary pause before the CEO of the Claire-Smith Broadcasting Group answered. "The interview your young man gave tonight was broadcast live to all sixty-four CS stations, as well as CNN."

Carissa moaned, the sound ending on a frustrated growl. "That's just grand. I just love having my life slapped out there for the entire world to scrutinize."

"Well, we *do* appreciate it, Carissa. It's a truly amazing story – your survival against absolutely astronomical odds. Most would have given up, let alone, had the intelligence and tenacity to survive everything you did. There will be many, many people talking about your exploits. And again, I want you to know how sorry I am that you were put through all that."

"I'd thank you but I'm still pissed off at you," Carissa retorted. She knew that she should watch her mouth since he had just handed her career back to her, but what she wanted was to tell him where to go.

Mike Claire guffawed loudly, the sound nearly puncturing Carissa's eardrum as she pulled the phone away from her head. "I can understand that," he said, chuckling. "I spoke with your Mr. Matheney tonight. He's a good man, and I think the two of you have a bright future together." He gave her no chance to respond as he added, "I want you to take a couple more weeks off, as well, to give us time to sort all this out. Don't speak to anyone about this conversation, and whatever you do, don't speak to Mavis. You let us take care of him."

"Trust me, talking to *him* is the last thing I want."

"Good. We might just borrow that dog of Matheney's to finish the job on Mavis. Were you really trapped with that beast?"

Carissa, laughing, responded, "Yes, and he's a sweet puppy. I agree with Bryce about his ability to judge character, though. He doesn't think too highly of your station manager."

"I may have to put the animal on the payroll in Human Resources. We might have better luck with our hires. You rest and take care of your family. I'll call you in a few weeks."

"All right, Mr. Claire, thanks for calling."

"Call me Mike," he chirped. "Talk to you later."

The phone went dead, leaving Carissa to contemplate what had just transpired. Unless she missed her guess, Mavis was about to be handed his hat, and shown the door. She allowed herself a moment as a mental image of the arrogant ass being told his services were no longer needed conjured itself in her head.

"Well, that was certainly interesting," Alice said, standing in the kitchen doorway, her hands resting on her hips. "Seems your old station manager over-stepped his bounds."

Carissa grinned at her mother, reveling in the moment of triumph. If only all her problems could be so easily solved, she could relax and finally get some sleep. With a sigh, she sobered, thinking of all the hurdles yet ahead.

Where was Bryce? How was she going to be able to find him? Standing, she walked to the kitchen and pulled the phone book from a drawer.

"Who are you calling?" Alice asked, her curiosity evident as she poured herself a glass of water.

"Every hotel and motel in town. I have to find him, Mom."

"Why don't you try Chris again? If he still doesn't answer, call his wife."

"Good idea," Carissa answered, pulling the phone off the wall hook.

Alice returned to the front room, settling on the couch, switching the stereo on to listen to the soft tones of jazzy Christmas tunes as her daughter dialed, disconnected and dialed again. After a few moments, she heard a frustrated growl from the kitchen, guessing that there was still no answer.

"*Karen's not even picking up.* I'm telling you, there's a conspiracy. He's punishing me, they all are, that's what it is," Carissa muttered as she joined her mother on the couch, cordless phone and directory in hand. She opened the book, flipping through until she found the listing for hotels in the yellow pages.

"Would you like me to help you with that?" her mother asked sweetly. "I'll get my cell phone." She left the room in search of her purse, returning with it in hand and pulling out her little phone.

"Thanks, Mom. I'll start with the 'A's' you take 'B'." They each dialed their respective phones, going down the listings in the book, and getting little cooperation from the hotels' switchboards. The staff at all of them had refused to confirm or deny if the man was staying there, stating that she needed a room number in order to be privy to that information. She had finally started plainly asking to speak with a guest named Bryce Matheney by the time she had gotten to the letter 'C'.

It wasn't until Carissa had gotten to the number for the Crowne Plaza that she found any measure of success. As she asked to speak with Bryce, the slightly nasal voice at the other end fairly squealed at her.

"Carissa, baby, is that you?" he asked.

"Yes, who... Rodney?"

"*Yes*. Honey, I'm so glad you're all right. We all missed you at the station. When are you coming back? Hey, I saw that man of yours on the TV tonight. Man, is he in love with *you*. Did you know he's staying here? Damn, girl, he's hot."

Carissa laughed at her friend. In the years that he had worked mornings at the television station as a part time studio camera operator, she had never been able to get a word in edgewise. He worked four jobs, doing various tasks, and still had the energy of ten people. "Rodney, slow down. I need to talk to Bryce Matheney, can you connect me to his room?"

"Oh, fine. You disappear without a word for two months and worry us all sick, and then when you get back you don't have time to speak to me. Well, that's just grand, sunshine. Merry Christmas to you too."

Carissa rolled her eyes. "Rodney, sweetie, you know I love you, but this is an emergency. I really need to talk to him."

"You know I'm just playing with you. I'll put you through. Just hang on. You're so impatient." There was silence on the line before he came back. "CJ, bad news. He's not answering. He must be out. You want to leave a message?"

Sighing, she shook her head, "No, Rod. Thanks. I'll give you a call tomorrow or something, and we can catch up."

"Well, I won't hold my breath," he huffed. "If I had a man like that to keep me busy, I sure as hell wouldn't be calling anyone. Talk to ya later, CJ."

Carissa, disappointed and discouraged, turned back to her mother. "Well, I found out where he's staying, but he's not in. It's after 10:00 now, Mom. Where can he be?"

"I don't know, honey, but I'm going to bed. Tomorrow is Christmas Eve and the kids will be heathens. I suggest you get some rest, too."

* * * *

"Not at this hour, son," Donnan intoned, adamantly. "You can't go barging into a woman's house in the middle of the night. I raised you better than that."

"Pop," Bryce sighed with a patience he did not feel. "I need to see her. I have to know... if she's going to... Look, I have to see her."

"Bryce, you're not thinking. She's got a family. Her friend, Chris says that her mother is staying with her. You can't mean to go in there and wake up an old woman and two small children. It's not right, and you know it."

Bryce let out another exasperated sigh, his breath curling out before him in a cloud of frozen vapor while he dragged his fingers harshly through his hair. His eyes trailed longingly down the road that led away from the parking lot to the highway that he was told would take him to Carissa's house. He was so close, he knew how to find her, and yet, she was still so far away.

"Let's just go up to the room, try to get some sleep and see her tomorrow. Tomorrow's Christmas Eve. It's a day for visiting and a day for fixing things-gone-wrong. C'mon," Donnan urged, his arm out to lead his son.

Casting a last glance down the long, darkened street, Bryce turned away reluctantly, following his father to the building. Inside all was quiet, with few people milling about, and the shops closed as a testament to the hour.

"It's not really that late, Dad. Carissa may still be up. It's only 11:15." He stopped in his tracks, swearing under his breath, "*Dammit.* Why didn't I think to get her number from Davidson."

He heard his father's amused chuckle. "Because your big head isn't doing the thinking. Your little head is," the man tossed at him, pushing the button on the wall.

The two men waited, hearing the elevator ding, indicating it had landed on the bottom level of the hotel. It carried them twelve flights to their floor without stopping. Bryce heard his big shoes as they stomped down the silent hall that led to their rooms, wishing he could turn and run to her. It was going to be a long, restless night waiting for the sun to come up.

Bryce had been correct, the night was long and sleep was a fleeting thought held at bay. By the time he finally gave up, pacing his room around the disheveled bed, the urge to go to her was nearly overpowering. It was all he could do to keep himself from throwing caution to the wind, snatching his father's keys, or calling a cab and heading out.

He stared through the window as a fine, powdery snow began to fall in the darkened world outside. He had to fight down the dread of being snow-bound, reminding himself he was no longer in the mountains, but in the Midwest where snow seldom proved to be so confining. Even so, he continually checked the weather's progress as he resumed his pacing. When the first streaks of dawn climbed reluctantly over the horizon, the flakes that drifted down from the sky had changed to large, feathery clumps, and the ground had been covered by at least two inches.

He did not wait for his father to wake, but jumped in the shower and rushed through his shave, nicking the scar tissue on his jaw and cursing. The elder Matheney was just tossing the blankets aside when Bryce stepped out of his room, fully dressed and ready to face the day, whatever it held.

Donnan grinned widely as he took in his son's appearance. "Are you going to a funeral?"

Bryce had dressed in a black, cotton/silk blend shirt, black jeans and black leather shoes. His face held a grave expression, as if he were about to face a firing squad. "Funny, Dad," he snapped. "Why don't you stay here until I get this over with? No sense in both of us dealing with this shit. I'll come back for you after the fireworks are over."

Donnan stood, the amused grin replaced with a stern frown. "No way, boy. I got a right to watch that little, bitsy woman tear you a new one, and that's what I'm going to do."

A grumble near his leg told Bryce that Skoll was in complete agreement with Donnan; both would accompany him and witness his folly. "If you're going with me, you better hurry. I want to get going," he snarled as he returned to his own room.

"Just slow down," his father called after him. "That Davidson fellow and his wife are supposed to join us for breakfast downstairs. They won't be here until 8:00. It's only 6:30 now."

Standing in his room, rubbing viciously at his forehead, Bryce felt as if he would go mad. "Does the whole world have to witness this?" he grumbled under his breath.

"Yep," his father answered, hearing him even though he had been speaking to himself.

Bryce thought of Carissa, could think of little else but the little, spellbinding elf of a woman that had so changed his life. He could still feel the way her heart beat against his, and the touch of her warm breath on his skin when she sighed out his name. The craving for her silken skin pressed under his body was so strong as to cause him physical pain. Her eyes, brightly burning with passion, flashed into his mind, causing him to stifle a groan of frustration.

"You look like you could use a drink," his father laughed. He had come out of his room after dressing to find his son in the sitting room, on a chair, clutching his head in his hands. Donnan was reminded of himself in the waiting room of the maternity ward the day Bryce was born. He shook his head in begrudging sympathy for what the man was going through. "Hell, Bryce, if this is how you are just waiting to see if the woman will have you, how bad are you going to be the day she gives you a baby?"

Bryce raised his head, giving his father a withering glare before standing. "Let's go, Pop," he muttered as he grabbed his coat and headed for the door. Skoll danced at his feet nervously, indicating his need to leave the rooms. "Shit. I have to walk Skoll first," he said as he reached for the leash.

"Nope, took care of that," Donnan said, taking the leash from his son. "Got one of those dog walkers to come in. S'posed to be waiting in the lobby."

Hooking the leash on the collar of the large dog, Donnan waited for Bryce to open the door, snapping the leash sharply when Skoll tried to take control. The animal recognized the older man's authority and fell into step along side him.

"Why, this dog is gentle as a kitten, Bryce. Don't know why you can't control him on a leash."

"Cute, Dad. Don't push me today, okay?" Bryce grumbled as they reached the elevator. Once they had boarded, it swiftly moved downward, stopping at the fifth floor. The doors opened to an older couple who took one look at Skoll's snarling muzzle and declined to enter. Bryce punched brutally at the buttons, willing the doors to close again.

When they finally reached the bottom and the doors opened, a shy young woman wearing a T-shirt that said, "Playtime Pals Pet Sitting" stood uncertainly near the exit. Bryce thought that she did not appear big enough to walk herself, let alone a dog that outweighed her by at least forty pounds.

Donnan stepped up to the woman and offered a warm handshake, making certain that she was there for Skoll. She smiled, a faint blush creeping along her neck as she put her coat on and turned to the dog. Immediately, she started cooing and the dog's tail was set to wagging. It was no problem for the animal to reach up and lick her face without raising his front legs off the floor.

Bryce took the leash from his father, pulling Skoll back from the diminutive woman. "I don't know about this. Skoll doesn't really like too many people. He could end up taking after someone and dragging you down the road."

The woman smiled again, "Sir, I've been doing this for ten years and I haven't lost a dog – or a body part – yet. Don't worry, I'm a professional."

She took hold of the leash, pulling it from Bryce's reluctant fingers and heading for the exit. When Skoll tried to bolt in his excitement, she gave the leash a gentle tug. Bryce watched in amazement as the dog fell obediently into step beside her, taking from her hand the treat she offered.

"See there? No problems. Even Skoll meets his match with a woman," Donnan laughed, guffawing at his own joke, clapping his son on the back. "Let's get upstairs and get ourselves a table. We can wait in the restaurant for that news guy to get here."

Sitting his chair near the window of the restaurant, looking at that street that would lead him to Carissa, Bryce could do little more than stir impatiently as they awaited the arrival of the Davidson's. "Remind me why you decided to take up Davidson's offer of breakfast. I just want to get going."

Donnan sighed, becoming frustrated with his son's impatience. "Because he will take us to your Carissa's house, that's why. Just settle down. It won't be long now."

"Hello, gentlemen," a voice said from behind. "Merry Christmas. I trust you slept well?"

"Yeah, just great," Bryce grumbled, grudgingly standing to shake Chris Davidson's hand.

"Don't mind my son," Donnan offered as he greeted Chris. "He seems to have a nasty case of the humbugs this morning."

"That's all right," Davidson answered. "Let me introduce my wife, Karen. Karen, this is Donnan Matheney, and *this* is the famous Bryce Matheney."

Bryce tried to stifle his irritation as he shook hands with the tall woman and offered her a chair. Within moments, he was ushering the little party to the plentiful buffet, ladling food onto his plate and rushing the others along. He wolfed down his meal, not bothering to taste it, and encouraging his companions to do the same.

Donnan exchanged amused glances with Davidson, watching as the younger Matheney called for the check before the others were finished with their coffee. He pushed his chair back and tossed some cash on the table, pulling his coat off the back of the chair. Karen Davidson joined her husband and Bryce's father in laughter as the young man headed for the exit, not waiting to see if they followed.

They waited in the lobby for the pet sitter to return Skoll, the dog shaking off the melting flakes of ice as soon as he was indoors. Bryce fairly tossed twice the money she required into the woman's face as he snatched the dog's leash away and headed for the door. He was irritable, waiting next to the blanketed Cadillac before the others had crossed the parking lot.

The group took separate cars, the Davidsons in the lead, as they drove to Carissa's house. Bryce felt nervous as a schoolboy ready for his first date, and he wasn't enjoying it a bit. The snow on the road forced the two cars to move at a much slower pace than he could stand, though the snowplows had already been through. Chris had assured him that it would not be a long drive, but it certainly seemed that way to him.

Finally, Chris Davidson turned off the highway and into a pretty subdivision. The houses were well spaced, alight with merry, twinkling decorations, casting a mystical quality upon the snow in the gray morning. A few children darted about the neighborhood, enjoying the holiday snow, as only kids can do.

All of this was lost on Bryce whose only objective was to find Carissa, see that light in her eyes that he had once seen before he sent her away. Bryce let out a miserable groan as the cars slowly wound their way through the twisting streets to the back of the quarters over the pristine layer of sparkling white.

"Am I doing the right thing here, Dad?"

Donnan patted his son's knee, a small gesture intended to reassure. "We'll soon see, Bryce. Just take it one step at a time, and for God's sake, think before you speak."

Bryce offered his father a shaky, wry smile. "Thanks, Pop."

* * * *

The wooden spoon moved in slow, lazy orbits through the thick soup, a delectable fragrance wafting on the puffs of steam that curled upward from the simmering pot. A memory flooded her mind on the heels of that aroma, a memory that shook her with its intensity.

As she stood at the stove in her kitchen, Carissa thought of that night, when Bryce had come up behind her as she stirred a similar brew, his hands slipping into the folds of the soft blanket that had covered her against the chill of a winter-locked cabin. The touch of his callused hands on her skin was still fresh in her mind, his heat still warming her flesh. A flush crept up her neck, staining her cheeks with color, when she remembered what happened on the table that night, after they had abandoned the soup for more intimate pursuits.

Sighing, she lifted the spoon from the soup, settling the lid on the pot and laying the utensil on a plate beside the stove. With a peek in the oven to assure herself that the bread was not baking too fast, she turned to pick up her cup of tea. *Where is Bryce?*

Her large cat, Blondie, wove between her ankles, purring sweetly and begging for a morsel to delight his palate. Carissa had to scoot the cat aside to keep from tripping over him. She soothed his ruffled dignity with a scratch behind the ear before turning to set her cup down again.

She had called the hotel several times, only to be told that there was no answer in Bryce's room. After a restless night spent alternating between tossing on her bed and pacing throughout the house, Carissa had become almost maudlin about the situation.

"Cari, why don't you go sit with the children," her mother coaxed. "You look completely worn out. Did you sleep at all last night?"

Fighting back tears, the younger woman only shook her head, casting her eyes downward to gaze sadly at the floor.

"Aw, Honey, it'll be all right. I know it will."

"I hope so, Mama," Carissa murmured, wishing she believed her mother.

A keening sound, much like the howl of a wolf, caught her attention, snapping her head up. Within moments, the younger of her two children ran into the kitchen, crying pitiably, reaching for her mother.

"Zane says Santa won't bring me presents. He says Santa hates me," she wailed as Carissa lifted her tiny body.

She cuddled her daughter close, shushing the child and stroking her back to soothe her heartache. "What a terrible thing to say. Why don't I just go have a talk with him?"

"You have to spank him, Mommy. He's bad," the little girl wailed enthusiastically.

Chapter 23

Carissa had her hands full, refereeing the dueling siblings, when the doorbell rang. Alice walked to the foyer, answering the door and allowing her daughter time to work with the kids. Carissa heard the muted greeting and the sounds of feet entering the house.

"Stay here, kids, and *behave*," Carissa said before moving to find out what was happening. "Who is it, Mom?" she asked as she rounded the corner. "Chris, Karen – how nice to see you. Merry Christmas," she said upon seeing her visitors.

As Carissa neared the open door, she saw something very large and black dance past. She lost all interest in what the Davidsons were saying as she excused herself to investigate further. Condensation from the warm air of the house was collecting on the windows of the screen door, prompting her to push it open so that she might better see.

All at once, a huge, drooling pile of fur bounded through the door, nearly swamping her with his massive tongue. "*Skoll!*" she screeched, bending to hug the wiggling dog. She still had her arms about the beast when she saw Bryce's father pull the door open again, stepping through with a grin on his face. Releasing her grip on Skoll's neck, she reached a shaky hand out to the man, a question in her eyes.

Donnan, still grinning, inclined his head toward the driveway. "He's getting the gifts."

Carissa glanced at the smiling faces collected in front of her, then turned her head to glance through the foggy panes. "Mom, this is Donnan Matheney,

Bryce's father," she murmured absently, before stepping through the door.

The snow was still descending from the sky, its sticky flakes adhering to her hair and clothing. The world, cloaked in a muting, white blanket, added to the surrealism of the moment when Bryce stepped from behind the open trunk lid of the silver Cadillac in the drive. Her eyes locked with his as the two stood still with a few feet of ground and the whole world between them.

Carissa took the first halting steps, her eyes never leaving his, wanting to rush into his arms but feeling suddenly shy. She watched as he took another step, approaching her slowly. Everything, even the sounds of a cat screeching and a dog barking, amid the crashing of glass and furniture within the house, went unnoticed as their silent glances spoke immeasurably.

At long last they were within touching distance, neither of them reaching, both of them longing. There was so much that Carissa wanted to say, but had no words. Bryce was beautiful to her eyes, his tall frame towering over her, his dark gaze imprisoning her heart.

With her face turned up to see his, the feathery snow fell on her bare skin, adhering to her lashes, causing her to blink against the icy wetness. Bryce raised one large hand to brush the flakes from her eyes, causing Carissa to whimper softly, almost imperceptibly at his warm touch.

Like the snow, she melted into him as his arms wrapped around her shivering frame, dragging her against his hard body. His head dipped low, his lips descending slowly, his movements fluid and almost predatory. She sensed, more than heard, the low growl that rumbled in his chest, his hand sliding up her back, his fingers digging into her hair and pinning her head. His mouth crushed hers in a brutal kiss born of savage desperation, while his arms gripped her tightly against his muscular frame.

She was trapped against him, her hands caught between them with her fingers digging through the front of his open coat, into the fabric of his shirt. She felt his tongue stab into her mouth, seeking and finding all the hidden treasures within. The hardness of his need pressed against her belly, pushing deeply into her soft flesh through the knit of her sweater, melding against her with the fire that swept through them.

"*Jesus*," he hissed against her lips when the kiss finally ended, both gasping for precious oxygen. His mouth captured hers again, this time more tenderly. Carissa gave herself to him as she had in the cabin in the high wilderness, without hesitation, feeling only the pleasure of his touch.

Bryce released her mouth again, tugging at her hair, pulling her head back to better see her face. From some distance away, Carissa heard the front door of her house closing and the resounding click of the latch as the noises from inside faded. The man who held her, who held her heart in his hands, lifted her against him, dragging her feet from the snow, and carrying her to the open trunk of the car. He set her upon its contents, amid the crinkle of plastic bags and the rustle of paper and cardboard.

He bent low over her, to slide his lips over hers and along the line of her jaw, finding the petal-soft skin of her throat and tasting it with his tongue. One hand, hot despite the chill of the morning air and the falling snow, wound under her sweater, cupping her breast as she moaned his name.

Carissa could feel the tips of his fingers as they slid under the elastic of her bra, causing her to whimper as he worked his way inside the cup to find her nipple. Somewhere in the back of her mind, a tiny voice whispered a warning, told her to stop him. With all her might, she tried to squelch that voice, wanting to ignore it and let the moment continue, but that warning grew louder, refusing to be denied.

"Bryce," she rasped, pushing her hands weakly at his chest.

His head rose above her, his smoldering eyes wary as they met hers. "Carissa..." his husky voice trailed away into the muting snow.

"We can't do this," she breathed, wanting so much for his hands and mouth to continue their pleasurable exploration. She watched as the passion in his eyes ebbed away into lonely disappointment. Reaching out to touch the scars on his face, she smiled brightly, a hint of amusement dancing in her eyes. "We're not on a mountaintop here, big man. This isn't the open wilderness. I have neighbors."

Her words startled him, had him looking around at the busy neighborhood and the children that played in the snowy yards. He laughed aloud, grabbing her in a bone-crushing hug. "I guess I forgot where I was for a minute. One look at you and I lose all control."

"That's encouraging," she said, giggling against the front of his shirt. Shifting her position, she felt something sharp nudge her bottom. "What am I sitting on?"

Bryce refused to loosen his grip on her body as she tried to turn. "Gifts. Pop and I wanted to get the kids a few things, and your mom, too." He raised his head to smile at her.

Carissa saw his grin, so boyish and charming that it made her giggle. "You're a sweetheart. The kids are going to love you – and Mom, too, as soon as she gets over being mad at you."

"What's she mad at me for?" he asked, frowning in his confusion and worry.

She laughed again, nuzzling into his chest, speaking in muted tones into the soft fabric of his shirt. "You made her little girl cry, silly. Why do you think?"

"I can see I'm going to have to pull all the stops out to win that one over. I'll show her my most charming side."

"Do you have one of those?" Carissa's joke earned her a slap on her bottom, making her wiggle against the gifts in the trunk. "I better get up before I break something." She tried to pull herself off the packages but Bryce was not moving. "Hey," she said, pulling her head back and giving him a pouting glance. "You said gifts for them. You didn't get anything for me?"

He kissed her again, softly pulling her lower lip into his mouth and suckling on it. He released her mouth and pressed his forehead against hers. "I got you something," he whispered hoarsely. "I just wasn't sure you would want it."

Bryce kept one arm wrapped tightly about her ribs while he reached into his coat pocket with his other hand. He pulled a small velvet box out and held it up for her to see. "I... I didn't... *Jesus*, this is hard," he hissed.

Her heart lurched in her chest when she saw the black velvet box, knowing what it was and knowing what it meant. She tilted her head back to see his face, and the uncertainty his eyes held. Her body began to shake, matching the tremor in his as she reached for his face again.

"After you left," he said softly, his voice husky. "I... I was a mess. I didn't know if I was going to survive without you, and to be honest, I didn't want to try. Days went by before I could bring myself to dare to look at the cabin with you gone. I just sat there. I couldn't eat or sleep. I think I wanted to die.

"Then I found your note. Damn, I was pissed when I read it. I was mad at you for what you wrote – and I was mad at me for letting go of you. I left as soon as it was daylight. I was determined to find you and make you pay. But, then, when I was driving with my dad, I realized something. It took a long time for it to sink in, but when it did, it hit home hard.

"You said what you did – or wrote, anyway – because you knew it was the only way to light a fire under my ass." He stopped, laughing at himself and taking a deep breath before plunging onward. "I suppose you know me better than I know myself.

"Something happened up on that mountain. When I found you and brought you in out of the weather, I thought I was helping someone who was in trouble. I thought I was saving a life to make up for the one I took.

"That's not what happened, though. It was *you* who saved *me*. You gave *me* shelter, not the other way around. I didn't think there was anything left within me to give or to feel, but you showed me that I was wrong. You gave me back my life and I don't ever want to live without you again. I never want to let you go again.

"I didn't come here for the baby, Carissa. I came here for you. I love you."

Bryce released Carissa only long enough to open the box in his hand, revealing the glittering diamond that caught in the gray light of the wintry day. Raising a shaking hand to her face, he laid his palm against her cheek, looking at her with eyes full of uncertain hope. "Carissa, marry me. Marry me and I will spend the rest of my life making you happy."

She pushed aside the hand that held the small jewelry case, reaching up to take his face in her hands. "I don't need expensive diamonds, Bryce. I only needed to hear you say the words. I'll marry you," she said, watching his smoldering eyes, as that secret fire burned ever brighter. "*God, yes*, I'll marry you," she squeaked as she threw her arms around his neck.

His kiss nearly drowned her, robbing her of breath as he wound his arms around her body, pulling her up close. She felt the rumble of laughter, heard it erupt from his throat as he pulled his head up. "You better want this damned diamond. It cost almost all my life's savings."

He set her back down again, pulling the ring from the box and sliding it onto her finger before kissing her hand. It fit her hand perfectly, she realized, something that had her amazed. She cocked her head to the side, shooting him a playful glance. "You mean you're not rich? Deal's off."

He grabbed her around the waist, lifting her against him and swatting her backside. "No way, you already said yes." He kissed her again, then lifting his head, feeling her shiver against him. "I better get you inside before you catch cold. I won't have you endangering my child this way."

"*Your* child? I don't see you getting swollen ankles or tossing your cookies every morning," she retorted with mock severity.

"Yes," he said softly. "My child, my wife, my love."

He swung her up in his arms as if she weighed nothing, carrying her to the door and inside where he found the faces of those assembled staring at them in silence, waiting to find out what had happened. Walking past the Davidsons and Alice to where his father sat on the couch, Bryce set her down next to him, looking at his father and grinning. "She said yes."

"Wonderful!" Donnan yelled, hugging Carissa tightly, as the others joined in with a cacophony of celebration while two small children squealed, wanting to know what was going on. "I have a new daughter."

"Well, I'm glad *that's* finally settled," Alice voiced. She walked straight to her future son-in-law and sized him up with her appraising gaze. "You must be Bryce. Welcome to our little family."

When Bryce eyed her cautiously, both she and Carissa laughed before Alice wrapped herself around him in an affectionate hug. He returned the warmth of her action, hugging her fiercely in return.

Donnan pried them apart, telling his son to go get the gifts from the car, before following Alice as she left the room. Zane and Sheanna ran to their mother, asking questions too fast to be answered, and quieting only when Bryce entered again, his arms laden with bags and boxes. He set the offerings at Carissa's feet, going back to the car to retrieve the rest. Once all the presents were in the house, the children began pawing through them, wondering if Bryce were really Santa Clause in disguise.

"Come here, kids," Carissa called, saying it a second time before she got their attention. "I want you to meet someone," she said, putting an arm around each of her precious children. "This is Bryce. He and I are going to get married."

Zane spoke first, turning to his mother with sharp eyes. "Does that mean he's gonna be our new daddy?"

"If you let me," Bryce answered softly, dropping to one knee in front of both kids. "I always wanted a little boy like you. Will it be all right? Do you think you would like another dad?"

The little boy thought for a moment before a smile crossed his face. "Okay, but you gotta play ball with me."

"It's a deal," Bryce said, grinning at the child and sticking out his hand. "Shake on it."

Sheanna immediately began crying, wrapping her arms about her mother's neck, wailing pitifully against her snow-dampened sweater. "I want a new daddy too," she sobbed. "No fair."

Bryce crouched down and laid a hand on the child's shoulder, turning her toward him gently. In this child he could see the eyes of her mother, and a resemblance to the woman he loved that was so uncanny as to cause his heart to lurch. He knew it would be hard not to pick her as his favorite. "Can I be your new dad? I promise to hug you and tuck you in every night, and I'll always be there whenever you need me."

Placated, the little girl nodded, giving him a teary smile and sniffling her acceptance. She drew back shyly against her mother, staring at the giant man who was holding out his hand to her.

"How about a hug, then, baby girl," he said, still smiling.

He was rewarded when the child wrapped her tiny arms around his neck. She drew back, running her little fingers over his left cheek. "You gots a bumpy face," she said, giggling in childish glee.

It was the first time that Bryce ever laughed at his own scars and it felt strange. He lifted Sheanna up as he stood when his father and Alice returned to the room, bearing trays of eggnog and hot chocolate, passing the mugs out to all who were gathered.

"To the happy couple," Donnan said, raising his mug.

"Hear, hear," bellowed Chris.

Chris and Karen had just taken their leave when Donnan cleared his throat, catching the attention of the remaining gathering. "Alice and I are going to take the kids to the park for some sledding and give you two a little time to yourselves."

"Aw, I wanted to open presents," Zane muttered.

"Zane." Alice chided. "You can't do that until later, young man. You know the rules."

Undaunted, he lifted and shook a package, gracing his grandmother with a charming grin. "That's okay. Sledding's fun." He dropped the gift and ran for his coat, his little sister tagging along behind him.

"You'll need these," Bryce said, grinning as the children stopped in their tracks. He pulled two large boxes from the huge pile of gifts and laughed as the children tore into them. Each child sang out in delight at the little sleds they had unwrapped.

"Thank you, Bryce," Carissa whispered as she stood beside him. "They love you already."

"They're incredible," he said as he turned to give her a tender kiss.

"That's enough, you two," Alice interrupted with a knowing smile. "At least let us get these kids out of here."

After much cajoling, they were able to get the kids dressed in warm coats, hats and mittens before herding them out the door, with Skoll bounding happily after them. The dog had taken right to the children, allowing them to climb on him and pull his ears.

Donnan appeared to be falling into his new role as grandfather with zeal. He escorted the little troupe out the door with his hand resting on the small of Alice's back. He shot his son a wink as they disappeared, closing the door behind them. Carissa was left to stare after them, her eyebrows arching high in surprise at the man's actions, and at how Alice did not seem to mind.

"Alone at last," Bryce said, turning, dragging Carissa against him and running his hands down over her posterior. "I thought they'd never leave."

He ducked his head, pressing her lips in a gentle, passionate kiss, slipping his tongue into her mouth. His arms came up, sliding under her sweater to the warm flesh beneath. A moan escaped her throat as she dissolved against him with her arms reaching for his neck.

"Show me to your bedroom," he said, his breath coming in short pants, his hands slithering between them to skim along the lacy edge of her bra.

She pulled away, taking his hand as it slid from beneath her sweater, making promises with her smile. Leading him into the hallway, she stifled a protest when the doorbell rang, followed by raucous pounding on the inside door. "Be right back, lover," she cooed as she walked away from him.

Opening the door, she was expecting to find one of her family members had forgotten something and had locked themselves out. What she found on the other side of the threshold, propping the outside door open with his body, gave her a mixture of shock and disgust. "What do *you* want?" she hissed at the intruder.

"Get off your high horse, sugar-tits," the man said, looking her up and down with over-bright eyes. He pushed his way into the house, glancing around the area before turning his attention back to Carissa. "I want my kids."

"John, I did not invite you in my house and the kids aren't here. Besides, you don't get to see them until tomorrow, remember?" She felt her anger rising, wanted to shove him back through the open door.

"Tomorrow's not good for me. I'll take them now and Santa can visit them at my house tonight. Get their little duds together. *Zane. Sheanna.* Get your asses out here."

"Get out of my house, *now*. The kids aren't here," Carissa said, hearing Bryce walk up behind her. "Even if they were I wouldn't let you have them. Your day is tomorrow and not before noon."

John James looked from Carissa's livid face to the big man that had placed his hands on her shoulders. "So you're the guy that shacked up with my wife, eh? Fancy finding you here," John said, his words coming out in an uncontrolled rush. He turned back to Carissa. "I want my kids. Where are they?"

"No," Carissa said, feeling Bryce move away from her. "You don't get them. Now leave."

Bryce had stepped into the living room, coming back with his coat on, taking a large, folded manila envelope out of the inside pocket. "James," he commanded. "You and I need to go outside for some words."

"Bryce, leave it be. John's leaving." Carissa was suddenly filled with dread over what her new fiancé was planning, whatever it was.

"Yeah, mind your own business, fuckwad," John snapped.

With a heavy sigh, Bryce looked at the man in front of him. He was a big man, at least six feet in height and more than a few pounds overweight, but no match for himself. He grabbed the man by the scruff of the neck with his free hand.

"You're the man who beat Carissa, put those scars on her back. Were I you, I'd be very careful how I choose my words."

He shoved the smaller man out the door and onto the stoop. Bryce turned back around at the sound of Carissa's protest, placing a kiss on her forehead and saying, "Don't worry, he'll live." Then he dragged John around the side of the garage, disappearing from sight.

For several anxious minutes, Carissa paced, stopping to glance out the front windows from time to time. She had visions of her wedding taking place in a prison chapel, with her groom shackled at the ankles and wrists. *What is he doing?* she asked herself.

Finally, just as she was going to go investigate, both men appeared from behind the garage, John looking terrified and Bryce looking triumphant. Her ex-husband hurriedly climbed into his car without a glance while Bryce walked in the front door. Carissa faced Bryce, her hands on her hips, a question in her eyes.

"Don't worry. He won't be bothering us anymore," he said with a grin on his lips.

"What did you do?" she asked, fearing the answer.

"Just talked to him," he said, tossing his coat aside. "Now, where were we before we were so rudely interrupted."

"*Bryce*," she demanded, stomping her foot. "What did you say to him?"

Bryce smiled, a charming mix of amusement and sweetness. "I told him that you didn't need him causing you anymore trouble, that I thought he should leave you alone and drop the suit for the kids."

"And what else? I know he didn't run away like a scared rabbit because of that."

Pulling the folded packet out of his hip pocket with a sigh, he handed it to her, saying, "I told him I would hand this over to the authorities, if he wasn't a good boy. I told him to stay away from you and leave the kids alone. I informed him that he is no longer welcome in their life. He took one look and agreed. He says you'll never see him again."

Carissa opened the envelope, wondering what could be so bad that he would consent to such a mandate. She was horrified at what she found – pictures with notes explaining the significance of each. Looking at him, her eyes huge with disbelief, she questioned him again. "Where did you get these?"

"I was a little busy last night," he said softly, his face sober. "One of those reporters gave me a tidbit of information about the asshole. I bought a camera and did a little reconnaissance. Your ex-husband's been paying his legal fees with dirty money. He's got quite a little business going, from what I could tell." He took one of the photos from her hand, pointing at one of the subjects. "I'm told this is his attorney, the one with the straw up his nose."

Carissa looked again, seeing the man that had represented John in their earlier court appearances. All the pictures contained what appeared to be illegal drugs, in one form or another. Baggies and cash were everywhere, and in one picture, an unsavory-looking woman had her head in his lap, looking to be performing a sex act. She stuffed the pictures back in the envelope – repulsed by what she saw – and handed it back to him.

"I won't give these to the police just yet. Apparently, they're already investigating him, from what I heard last night. If I still have these then we have some control over him. I'll turn them over when they make an arrest. They can use them for evidence. Until then, we'll have to keep them in a safe place."

"I have a safe deposit box at the bank. That would be a good place. I can't believe this. He's turned into a real dirt-bag. I'm glad he never had a chance to expose my children to that. I mean *our* children," she corrected herself, looking into Bryce's eyes. She glanced at the envelope in his hand, a smile dancing at the corners of her mouth. "So this is what you were up to last night, eh? No wonder I couldn't find you."

"Well, that, and a little shopping," he laughed, indicating the pile of gifts behind her and touching the ring on her finger. Like I said, I was busy." He kissed her mouth, savoring the taste of her before asking, "You were looking for me?"

She nodded, her head moving against his chest. "Yes, I thought I'd go crazy when I couldn't find you. I found your hotel but you weren't there, dammit."

Bryce pulled her back from him, lifting her face with a curled finger under chin. "I wish I'd known that. I worried myself half-daffy wondering if you would even see me."

"I wanted to tell you I was sorry. I wanted to tell you I love you," she whispered.

Bryce smiled at her, his hand sliding up to her cheek, caressing her warm skin with his thumb. "Those are words a man can live on the rest of his life."

His touch on her face and the heat of his body, so near her own, had her feeling giddy. His dark eyes fairly sparkled with the love she saw there, that she was sure was mirrored in her own eyes. "Take me to bed, Bryce," she rasped. "I missed more than just your smile."

He chuckled softly, glancing lustfully at her sensuous lips. "As you wish. I live to serve." This time his kiss was not so tender, more passionate, and left her dizzy when he stopped. "Point the way, my love," he said, his voice husky with emotion. "I'm at your command."

"I like that in a man," she returned, a wicked giggle bubbling up from her throat, as she took his hand in hers.

Once in the bedroom, Bryce closed the door, locking it against any intrusion. He tossed the envelope onto the dresser and turned to her. "I've dreamt of this moment," he growled as he pulled her close. "I don't think I'll ever get enough of you."

His mouth engulfed hers, his hands pulling at her sweater, his lips leaving hers only long enough to drag the garment over her head. Grasping her hips in his hands, he hauled her close again, kissing her and trailing his lips along the delicate line of her jaw. He pushed his hands against the small of her back, pressing her belly into the hardness behind his zipper.

Carissa moaned, her fingers making short work of the buttons on his black shirt before pulling it out of his waistband and skimming the lean muscles of his abdomen with her fingertips. "I missed you, Bryce. Thank you for coming for me," she whispered against his chest.

He raised his head, the fire behind his smoldering eyes igniting into an inferno. "If you don't mind your hands, I'll be coming for you right here where I stand," he growled, his voice thick with emotion and lust.

As if answering a challenge, she reached for the zipper on his fly, a wickedly innocent smile on her full lips. "Oh? So you wouldn't want me reaching in here, would you?" she asked as she opened his fly, reaching in to wiggle her fingers through the opening of his shorts.

Bryce lifted Carissa, tossing her on the bed before snagging the waistband of her slacks. "I'll teach you to tease me, woman," he huffed as he stripped her naked with less-than-gentle motions, hearing Carissa's impassioned laughter.

He fell upon her, his lips devouring hers before moving lower to nip at the skin of her neck. Carissa felt the heat rising in her belly as he caressed her skin, his mouth forging a lane of fire over her flesh, scorching everywhere that he touched. She moaned out his name as she arched against him, trying to get closer to his mouth, his body.

Impulsively, he jumped off the bed, throwing off his clothes before flipping her onto her belly and pulling her up onto her hands and knees. She felt his movements behind her, knew he was positioning himself. With a mighty lunge, he buried himself in her slick flesh, a feral snarl falling from his lips.

Carissa bucked against him, crying out in sheer delight at being filled by him once again. She loved the way he felt inside her body, the way his hands held her hips as he drove into her repeatedly. The way her body responded to him amazed her, as she matched his rhythm.

"*Bryce*," she cried. "You feel incredible."

"Tell me, baby," he growled in return. "Tell me what you feel."

She crooned his name again as he reached under her, finding the hard knot of nerves hidden in the folds of her sex. "I... I'm feeling..." she stammered, panting against the rising waves that threatened to take her. "I'm going to come," she rasped.

"I want you to come for me. Let me feel you come," he groaned.

She lifted herself back against him, circling one arm around his neck, pressing the fingers of her other hand against his fingers between her thighs. She threw her head back, a soft, keening wail emitting from her throat as she surrendered to the intense swells of sublime orgasm. Her muscles clamped around his shaft, holding him tightly in her body's embrace. Her frame shook against him, convulsing in pleasure as she was nearly swallowed by darkness. With one last immense drive, he shot his hot seed into her, bending his head to nip at her shoulder and holding himself deep within her.

His body shaking in the aftermath, he gently laid her down on the bed before falling next to her, both panting. "So much for sweet, tender love-making," Bryce laughed.

Carissa rolled to her side, reaching out to touch the beads of sweat that had formed over the scars on his face. "We have time yet."

"Yeah," he grinned. "We have the rest of our lives."

Epilogue

It had been a long time since he had made this climb, a lifetime it seemed, since Bryce had left these mountains in search of a woman who had managed to break through the ice that had surrounded his heart. Now, as he folded the lightweight nylon shell of his tent, he thought back on that winter and the hope – and the anger – that had kept him going through the worst of the blizzard that had raged during most of his descent. That had been the last time he had seen the cabin where he had hidden himself from the world.

The squeals of two small children brought him out of his memories. Sheanna and Zane chased after the Northern Crescent and Tiger Swallowtail butterflies that scattered in giant clouds of gold, yellow and black. Bryce watched them for a minute, smiling at the pride he felt for his new family and the way that the big black dog bounded after them.

He glanced around until he found his wife, his Cari, sitting on a boulder, playing patty-cake with their tiny daughter. They had named the child Morna, after his grandmother, to honor his grandfather – the man who had built the cabin where they fell in love. Not yet, a year old, the baby had a gift for joy.

She had her mother's delicate, heart-shaped face and lovely smile. Her hair was the color of his – raven black – with the curls that graced Carissa's head. Morna's infant-blue eyes were changing quickly, but not to the olive-green shade he had hoped for. They were darkening to gray, as his own, and from time to time, they glittered with anger when she was out of sorts. This one was going to have his temper, he feared. Carissa only laughed when he voiced his concern, saying that the temper only showed the child to be strong of will and would never be given to weakness.

He thought back to that Christmas, as he finished packing the tent, to the time when he had finally found Carissa. When he had seen that light in her eyes again – the light that burned brighter than the sun – his heart had skipped a beat. The world around them had disappeared as he had taken her in his arms, feeling as if he had finally come home. Then he thought of how he had almost made love to her, right there in the trunk of his father's car, and he grinned at the memory. It was a good thing she had still had some presence of mind that day, else he would have had her stripped naked and bent over the bumper right there in the snow, for the whole world to see.

That afternoon, after Donnan and Alice had returned with the children, he and Carissa had been a disheveled mess, barely dressed, before the family had entered the house. Carissa had blushed profusely at the knowing glances of their parents as Bryce had helped her clean up the toppled Christmas tree and demolished ornaments from the earlier go-around Skoll had had with the cat, Blondi. It must have been a terrible fight, one that Bryce wished he had seen. After that, Skoll, the fearless mastiff, had kept a healthy distance from the hissing furball.

Alice and Carissa had insisted that he and Donnan stay with them. Alice had spoken the loudest at the time, stating there was no way she would let them wake up in a hotel on Christmas morning. If he had known then what he knew now about their parents, he would have been suspicious about Alice's motives that night. She had bunked with Sheanna, giving the guestroom to Donnan, while Bryce slept next to Cari.

Another grin lifted the scars on his left cheek as he thought of how he and Cari had sneaked out that night, to his room at the hotel, losing themselves in each other's bodies. They had returned home before 5:00 AM, exhausted and sated, and had cuddled on the couch, awaiting the moment when two excited little imps awoke, screaming about Santa's latest visit. The warmth he had felt that first Christmas morning, watching the excited children as they pawed through the copious mounds of gifts, was more than any man could hope for – and more than he ever thought to have.

"What are you grinning at?" Cari asked as she handed his daughter to him, bringing him back to the present.

He tickled the cooing baby held in the crook of his arm, leaning over to kiss his sweet wife's mouth. "Just thinking of how lucky I am. Thank you for marrying me and giving me a family."

Carissa smiled back, her heart swelling. "I love you, too," she whispered before spreading a sleeping bag on the ground. She took Morna from him and laid her on the bedroll, then turned to help him finish breaking camp. "I'm so glad we decided to do this. It's great to get away."

Bryce raised an eyebrow at her. "That's funny, I seem to remember someone saying that she couldn't afford to be away from the station right now."

Cari popped him on the arm, playfully sticking her tongue out at him. "You know I'll follow you anywhere," she purred as he pulled her up under his arm to deposit a burning kiss on her lips.

Bryce, chuckling at her heated sigh, returned to the task at hand – packing up the camp. By nightfall, they would reach the cabin for a much needed vacation from the civilized world that they had been occupying. His mind wandered again to the happy days that had followed their reunion. They had married exactly one week after that day, on New Year's Eve, with their parents and their children in attendance. Their honeymoon had been a two-day stay in that same hotel suite that Bryce had occupied upon his arrival in Springfield. Carissa had not wanted to go far, or be separated for long from her children after the amount of time she had been away in Wyoming.

Donnan had gone back to Wyoming after the holidays, placed his home on the market and returned to start a life in Illinois, where he could be close to his son and his new family. Thinking back, Bryce wondered exactly what his father's motives had actually been. The man had immediately begun a courtship with Alice, spending a great deal of time at the home of Carissa's mother, until he had finally proposed to her after Morna was born. Alice had accepted immediately, though the two had yet to take the final step.

It was not too long after Bryce and Cari had settled into the bliss of their new life when the CEO of her company, Mike Claire, had called her. He had asked that she and Bryce meet him at the television station, in the front parking lot. When they had arrived at the appointed time, it was to witness the former station manager, Tom Mavis, escorted from the building after being fired. She was offered the station manager position with a substantial pay raise.

Bryce had to hand it to his wife. She had made Mike Claire wait for nearly a week while she mulled over the decision. Of course, in the end, she had taken the job and had created a much more relaxed atmosphere for the employees, while still managing to nearly double the performance of the sales department. She had given Christopher Davidson his head in the News Department, and the ratings had gone through the roof. It had been a very advantageous arrangement for all concerned.

Bryce, on the other hand, had declined a job offer with a local investment firm, opting, instead, to choose a career that allowed for a much more flexible schedule, and one that would allow him the freedom of the outdoors. He and his father had started a business outfitting what they called, dudes – persons with urban backgrounds – for hunting and other excursions that would take them into the wilderness and game reserves. He had plans to buy up some forested land and wetlands in central Illinois that he would use for conservation purposes. Deer hunting was the big money maker for his new business, and autumn had become his busiest season.

As Cari strapped Morna into the carrier that Cari would shoulder across her back, and rolled up the bedroll where the child had been happily playing, Bryce thought again how lucky he had been that night when he and Skoll had found her. She was a force to be reckoned with, and one of the strongest people he had ever met. Even when her ex-husband had been arrested and jailed for his numerous crimes, she had not faltered a step. She had immediately visited the man in prison, handing him papers to sign away his parental rights to Zane and Sheanna. John James had signed the documents without blinking, knowing that he could no longer use the kids to hurt her, given his present circumstances.

Bryce had adopted Carissa's children as soon as the paperwork could be completed. Now her family was truly his family too, and the children had the security of knowing that they had a real father, one who would be devoted to them and their mother. It was becoming more and more difficult for him to remember what the world had been like without the people he now loved in his life. His former life seemed so long ago and this life was all he wanted to remember.

Whenever thoughts of Anna, and what he had done that terrible night, came to mind, he only had to see Carissa's smiling face to know that he was redeemed, that his soul was saved by her. The few single nights he had spent away from her, taking care of his hunting and fishing tours, had been miserable without her warm body beside him, and her sweet sighs to lull him to sleep.

Only once had he spent more than one night away from her. That had been when he had traveled to Washington State. Anna's father, Sam Cannon, had died, succumbing to a heart attack and dying alone, a broken man with no one left to see to him. Hatred and bitterness had consumed him since the loss of his daughter. In the end, everyone, including his wife, had been driven away by the festering anger that he had refused to let go.

When Bryce had received word that the man had passed, he had gone to see to the arrangements, paying for the funeral himself and laying him to rest next to his beloved daughter. Carissa had been supportive, knowing that Bryce had needed to do this thing, to lay to rest his own guilt, along with the man who had so persecuted him. It had saddened Bryce to see that the once-vibrant man had died without a friend, with no one showing for the simple graveside service except his former son-in-law.

The money Anna had left, her trust fund, had gone to charity, as Bryce had promised. He had divided it among several groups that worked to help educate underprivileged children, a cause that had been close to Anna's heart. It felt good to help those children, and he had the strangest sensation that she had been smiling down at him as he had signed the last of the money away.

"Daddy," Sheanna moaned, "I'm tired. How much longer?"

Her grumbling voice brought Bryce out of his thoughts of the past and into the present. The child looked so like her mother he could not help but pamper her. He grinned, taking the small pack from her shoulders and slinging it over his arm, adding it effortlessly to the weight of his own load. He stopped to look at the position of the sun in the sky and the terrain that surrounded them. Before long the sun would be setting, he realized, and wondered where the day had gone.

"We'll be coming out of the trees soon, Sprite," he said with a wink. "Then we cross a meadow and the cabin will be just over the rise from there."

"Zane, don't get too far ahead," Cari called out as she had done countless times in the days the trip had taken. "Let the rest of us catch up."

"I see it!" the boy called back. "I see the clearing."

Sheanna, despite her statement about being tired, ran to catch up to her older brother. Both children waited at the edge of the woods for their parents to reach them. Once there, Carissa lowered the baby, in the pack, to the ground, her lower jaw dropping in awe at the sight laid out before her. Bryce knew in an instant what she was seeing, even without looking.

The meadow before them was ablaze with every color imaginable. The summer mountain grasses held all the shades of green, broken only by a myriad of brightly hued wildflowers. Butterflies, birds and small mammals scattered as the children ran into the open field, dancing in the colorful scene.

"Oh, Bryce," Cari's reverent voice whispered. "It's so beautiful. I never imagined…"

He slipped an arm over his wife's shoulders, dropping a kiss on her head, taking in the view with her. "Welcome to my home, darlin'," he said softly.

"Mama, look!" Sheanna sang out, her finger stabbing the air excitedly.

Bryce turned to see what the little girl was pointing at, and was struck silent. He glanced at his wife, knowing that she saw it too.

There, on the other side of the meadow at the top of the rise was a wolf, its pale form silhouetted by the low set of the sun. The animal danced across the ridge playfully, seemingly delighted in having caught their attention. With a flash of white fur, the wolf loped over the edge, disappearing from sight. Bryce looked down to see his wife gazing up at him, the wonder he felt reflected in her eyes. He knew that their union was blessed and all the years they faced together would be well worth living.

The End

ABOUT MOLLY WENS

Known as SweetWitch by many readers, Molly Wens weaves spells of passion and romance in her writing. Her characters leap off the page and become a part of your world as they explore the forces at work in their lives. Sometimes gritty, often sensuous and always riveting, her stories are born of her fertile imagination and remarkable life experiences.

Molly has been writing for much of her life, starting at the tender age of eleven when she won her first national award in a school-sponsored essay contest. Her love of the written word has never wavered, and she has continued to win prizes and accolades for the many short stories she has in print.

Now living in the Midwest with her family, Molly can often be found reading, working, playing with her child and even jumping from the occasional airplane. Shelter from the Storm is the first of what we hope to be many commercially published novels by Molly Wens.

Web Site: www.mollywens.com

If you enjoyed **SHELTER IN THE STORM**, you might also enjoy:

LEADER OF THE PACK
By Leighann Phoenix

Running for her life, hiding as a waitress in a sleazy bar, Aislinn never dreamed she would meet her soul mate. Compelled to save her, Cullen finds himself inexorably drawn to this mysterious woman. Aislinn believed her life couldn't get any stranger than it already was, until she happened across Cullen. As Aislinn discovers her lost past and Cullen works to protect his pack, they find themselves stronger together then they ever were apart. Now they just have to convince the pack elders that the alpha werewolf in the pack should be mated to a supposedly human girl.

Warning: This title contains graphic language, nonconsensual, f/f and group sex.

Review by Breia Brickey from Paranormal Romance Reviews

This is...wonderfully written and descriptive... I enjoyed every minute of it... Most of the characters are lovable and the ones that aren't, you love to hate... I look forward to hearing more from Leighann Phoenix... and this pack.

Review by Chris from Night Owl Reviews

This is a highly intricate, imaginative story, peppered throughout with spicy interludes. This is a love story full of violence, anguish, betrayal and secrets. Not a walk through the park to read at an estimated 8-12 hours for the average reader, this book is well worth the time and effort. And I definitely detect a sequel in the future.

Review by Sandy Potterton, Dark Angel Reviews, 5/5 Angels

...A monster of a story with multiple plot lines, mystery, romance, danger and magic! I loved the richness of her characters, the unrelenting action and the heartwarming romance...an intriguing world of danger, betrayal, love and friendship I would certainly love to visit again.

Review by Dawn D, Manic Readers Reviews, 4/5 stars

Leighann Phoenix has created a fascinating world of werewolves and magic, with enough action, sex and danger to keep you on the edge of your seat. The complex internal politics of the pack were well crafted, and the glimpses of day-to-day life (werewolves running casinos) were fun to read as well. Following along as Aislinn comes into her true power, and Cullen protects his pack from external enemies proves to be a thrilling ride. Does true love prevail? You bet and getting there is well worth the trip.

Excerpt From LEADER OF THE PACK:

Aislinn approached the new guy who sat down at the bar near the wall. He was impressive. His presence caused most of the other patrons to make more than enough room for him, resulting in an unnatural amount of space at that end of the bar. Aislinn was perfectly happy to have a short lull in the number of people she had to deal with.

The man was pretty big, even sitting on the stool. He had black hair, brown-black eyes, and tanned skin. He looked hard muscled even under the black leather duster he was wearing. But the strangest thing was this ageless appearance to him. At first look she might have said he was in his late twenties/early thirties. Then, at second glance, he looked almost 100. Whether that was normal for him or due to the fact that he just had the worst day of his life was up for grabs. "What can I get you?"

The guy looked up at her as if he only just realized that he was in a bar. Aislinn waited and when he didn't respond she asked again. "What can I get you?"

Cullen stared appraisingly at the girl speaking to him. She had an odd scent. It was hard to make out between the rancid smell of the bar, the smoke from the people around him soaking into everything, and some awful perfume she seemed to have bathed in. But there was something to it that caught his attention. She was attractive, but she wasn't remarkable in any way. She had brown hair, blue eyes, pale skin, and medium build. She wasn't his type. I would probably break her, he thought and grinned at himself. Besides she wasn't what he was here for. The last thing he wanted was a woman tonight. No matter how intriguing her scent was…

BUY THIS AND MORE TITLES AT
www.eXcessica.com

welcome to eXcessica

sweet hot forbidden

eXcessica's BLOG
www.excessica.com/blog

eXcessica's YAHOO GROUP
groups.yahoo.com/group/eXcessica/

Check out both for updates about eXcessica books, as well as chances to win free E-Books!

Made in the USA